P9-DHG-460

The critics raise a glass to
DAUGHTERS OF THE BRIDE!
~An *Amazon* Best Book of the Month~

"Funny, tender, moving, and shot through with enough emotional drama to resonate with anyone who's survived a family wedding, Mallery's hardcover debut is pure delight and a rewarding read for romance and women's fiction fans alike."
—*Library Journal*, starred review

"Mallery enthralls readers as she follows the lives of a bride's three daughters… [She] thoroughly involves readers in the lives of her characters as they face realistic, believable problems and search for their own happy endings."
—*Publishers Weekly*

"Susan Mallery never disappoints and with *Daughters of the Bride* she is at her storytelling best."
—Debbie Macomber, #1 *New York Times* bestselling author

"Heartfelt, funny, and utterly charming all the way through!"
—Susan Elizabeth Phillips, *New York Times* bestselling author

"Four women find true love in Mallery's heartwarming sisters' tale. [Her] strong talent for revealing the dynamics of the different relationships in a woman's life makes for a resonant story."
—*Booklist*

"If you love your romance with plenty of family dynamics and drama, you're going to adore this book!"
—*RT Book Reviews*, Top Pick!

"Readers looking for sister relationships, wedding details, and steamy scenes will enjoy Mallery's latest."
—*Kirkus Reviews*

Also by Susan Mallery

Secrets of the Tulip Sisters
Daughters of the Bride

Happily Inc.

Second Chance Girl
You Say It First

Fool's Gold

Best of My Love
Marry Me at Christmas
Thrill Me
Kiss Me
Hold Me
Until We Touch
Before We Kiss
When We Met
Christmas on 4th Street
Three Little Words
Two of a Kind
Just One Kiss
A Fool's Gold Christmas
All Summer Long
Summer Nights
Summer Days
Only His
Only Yours
Only Mine
Finding Perfect
Almost Perfect
Chasing Perfect

Mischief Bay

A Million Little Things
The Friends We Keep
The Girls of Mischief Bay

For a complete list of titles available from
Susan Mallery, please visit www.SusanMallery.com.

SUSAN MALLERY

Daughters
of the
Bride

If you purchased this book without a cover you should be aware
that this book is stolen property. It was reported as "unsold and
destroyed" to the publisher, and neither the author nor the
publisher has received any payment for this "stripped book."

HQN™

Recycling programs
for this product may
not exist in your area.

ISBN-13: 978-1-335-00856-5

Daughters of the Bride

Copyright © 2016 by Susan Mallery Inc.

Promotional consideration provided by Middle Sister Wines, Santa Rosa, CA

All rights reserved. Except for use in any review, the reproduction or utilization
of this work in whole or in part in any form by any electronic, mechanical or other
means, now known or hereinafter invented, including xerography, photocopying
and recording, or in any information storage or retrieval system, is forbidden
without the written permission of the publisher, HQN Books, 225 Duncan Mill Road,
Don Mills, Ontario M3B 3K9, Canada.

This is a work of fiction. Names, characters, places and incidents are either the
product of the author's imagination or are used fictitiously, and any resemblance
to actual persons, living or dead, business establishments, events or locales is
entirely coincidental.

This edition published by arrangement with Harlequin Books S.A.

For questions and comments about the quality of this book, please contact us
at CustomerService@Harlequin.com.

® and TM are trademarks of Harlequin Enterprises Limited or its corporate affiliates.
Trademarks indicated with ® are registered in the United States Patent and
Trademark Office, the Canadian Intellectual Property Office and in other countries.

www.HQNBooks.com

Printed in U.S.A.

To Kaycee. Thank you so much for everything.
This one is for you.

* * *

Being the "mom" of an adorable, spoiled little dog,
I know the joy that pets can bring to our lives.
Animal welfare is a cause I have long supported. For me that means
giving to Seattle Humane. At their 2015 Tuxes and Tails fund-raiser,
I offered "Your pet in a romance novel" as a prize.

In this book you will meet two wonderful dogs—Sarge and Pearl. One
of the things that makes writing special is interacting in different ways
with people. Some I talk to for research. Some are readers who want to
talk characters and story lines, and some are fabulous pet parents. I had
a wonderful time learning about Sarge and Pearl. They are well loved
and a little spoiled…as all pets should be. I enjoyed the opportunity to
work them into my story and I hope you enjoy their charming antics.

My thanks to Sarge and Pearl, to their fabulous pet parents and to
the wonderful people at Seattle Humane (www.SeattleHumane.org).
Because every pet deserves a loving family.

1

ONE OF THE advantages of being freakishly tall was easy access to those upper kitchen cabinets. The disadvantages... well, those were probably summed up by the word *freakishly.*

Courtney Watson folded her too-long legs under her as she tried to get comfortable in a chair incredibly low to the ground. Adjusting the height wasn't possible. She was filling in at the concierge desk only while Ramona hurried off for yet another bathroom break. Apparently, the baby had shifted and was now reclining right on her bladder. From what Courtney could tell, pregnancy was a whole lot of work with an impressive dash of discomfort. The last thing she was going to do was change anything about the chair where Ramona spent a good part of her day. Courtney could pretend to be a pretzel for five minutes.

Late on a Tuesday evening, the lobby of the Los Lobos Hotel was quiet. Only a few guests milled around. Most were already up in their rooms, which was where Courtney liked the guests to spend their time at night. She wasn't a fan of those who roamed. They got into trouble.

The elevator doors opened and a small, well-dressed man stepped out. He glanced around the lobby before heading directly to her. Well, not to *her*, she would guess. The concierge desk at which she sat.

Her practiced smile faltered a bit when she recognized Milton Ford, the current president of the California Organization of Organic Soap Manufacturing, aka COOOSM. Mr. Ford had arranged for the annual meeting to be held in town, and everyone was staying at the Los Lobos Hotel. Courtney knew that for sure—she'd taken the reservation herself. But the meetings, the meals and all the income that flowed from them were taking place at the Anderson House.

"Hello." He looked at the nameplate on the desk. "Ah, Ramona. I'm Milton Ford."

Courtney thought about correcting him on her name but figured there wasn't much point. Despite his giving all that pretty catering money to one of their competitors, she would still do her job—or in this case, Ramona's—to the best of her abilities.

"Yes, Mr. Ford. How may I help you this evening?" She smiled as she spoke, determined to be pleasant.

Even if Mr. Ford had decided to hold his stupid awards luncheon at the Anderson House instead of in the hotel's very beautiful and spacious ballroom, Courtney would do her best to make sure his stay and the stays of his colleagues were perfect.

Her boss would tell her not to be bitter, so Courtney returned her smile to full wattage and promised herself that when she was done with Mr. Ford, she would head to the kitchen for a late-night snack of ice cream. It would be an excellent reward for good behavior.

"I have a problem," he told her. "Not with the rooms. They're excellent as always. It's the, ah, *other* facility we've booked."

"The Anderson House." She did her best not to spit the words.

"Yes." He cleared his throat. "I'm afraid there are...bees."

Now the problem wasn't a lack of smiling but the issue of too much of it. Joyce, her boss, would want her to be professional, she reminded herself. Glee, while definitely called for, wasn't polite. At least not to Mr. Ford's face. Bees! How glorious.

"I hadn't heard they were back," she said sympathetically.

"They've had bees before?"

"Every few years. They usually stay outside of town, but when they come into the city limits, they like the Anderson House best."

Mr. Ford dabbed his forehead with a very white handkerchief, then tucked it back into his pocket. "There are hundreds of them. Thousands. Entire hives sprang up, practically overnight. There are bees everywhere."

"They're not particularly dangerous," Courtney offered. "The Drunken Red-nosed Honeybee is known to be calm and industrious. Oh, and they're endangered. As a maker of organic soap, you must be aware of the issues we're having keeping our honeybee numbers where they should be. Having them return to Los Lobos is always good news. It means the population is healthy."

"Yes. Of course. But we can't have our awards luncheon in the same house. With the bees. I was hoping you'd have room for us here."

Here? As in the place I offered and you refused, telling me the Anderson House was so much better suited? But those thoughts were for her, not for a guest.

"Let me check," she told him. "I think I might be able to make room."

She braced herself to stand. Not physically, but mentally.

Because the well-dressed Mr. Ford, for all his dapperness, was maybe five foot six. And Courtney wasn't. And when she stood…well, she knew what would happen.

She untangled her long legs and rose. Mr. Ford's gaze followed, then his mouth dropped open a second before he closed it. Courtney towered over Mr. Ford by a good six inches. Possibly more, but who was counting?

"My goodness," he murmured as he followed her. "You're very tall."

There were a thousand responses, none of them polite and all inappropriate for the work setting. So she gritted her teeth, thought briefly of England, then murmured as unironically as she could, "Really? I hadn't noticed."

Courtney waited while her boss stirred two sugars into her coffee, then fed half a strip of bacon to each of her dogs. Pearl—a beautiful blonde standard poodle—waited patiently for her treat, while Sarge, aka Sargent Pepper—a bichon-miniature poodle mix—whined at the back of his throat.

The dining room at the Los Lobos Hotel was mostly empty at ten in the morning. The breakfast crowd was gone and the lunch folks had yet to arrive. Courtney got the paradox of enjoying the hotel best when guests were absent. Without the customers, there would be no hotel, no job and no paycheck. While a crazy wedding on top of every room booked had its own particular charm, she did enjoy the echoing silence of empty spaces.

Joyce Yates looked at Courtney and smiled. "I'm ready."

"The new linen company is working out well. The towels are very clean and the sheets aren't scratchy at all. Ramona thinks she's going to last until right before she gives birth, but honestly it hurts just to look at her. That could just be me, though. She's so tiny and the baby is so big. What on earth was God thinking? Last night I met with Mr. Ford of the California Organization of Organic Soap Manufacturing. Bees have invaded the Anderson House, and he wants to book everything here. I didn't mock him, although he deserved it. So now we're hosting all their events, along with meals. I talked him into crab salad."

Courtney paused for breath. "I think that's everything."

Joyce sipped her coffee. "A full night."

"Nothing out of the ordinary."

"Did you get *any* sleep?"

"Sure."

At least six hours, Courtney thought, doing the math in her head. She'd stayed in the lobby area until Ramona's shift had ended at ten, done a quick circuit of the hotel grounds until ten thirty, studied until one and then been up at six thirty to start it all again.

Okay, make that five hours.

"I'll sleep in my forties," she said.

"I doubt that." Joyce's voice was friendly enough, but her gaze was sharp. "You do too much."

Not words most bosses bothered to utter, Courtney thought, but Joyce wasn't like other bosses.

Joyce Yates had started working at the Los Lobos Hotel in 1958. She'd been seventeen and hired as a maid. Within two weeks, the owner of the hotel, a handsome, thirtysomething confirmed bachelor, had fallen head over heels for his new employee. They'd married three weeks later and lived blissfully together for five years, until he'd unexpectedly died of a heart attack.

Joyce, then all of twenty-two and with a toddler to raise, had taken over the hotel. Everyone was certain she would fail, but under her management the business had thrived. Decades later she still saw to every detail and knew the life story of everyone who worked for her. She was both boss and mentor for most of her staff and had always been a second mother to Courtney.

Joyce's kindness was as legendary as her white hair and classic pantsuits. She was fair, determined and just eccentric enough to be interesting.

Courtney had known her all her life. When Courtney had been a baby, her father had also died unexpectedly. Maggie, Courtney's mother, had been left with three daughters and a business. Joyce had morphed from client to friend in a matter of weeks. Probably because she'd once been a young widow with a child herself.

"How's your marketing project coming along?" Joyce asked.

"Good. I got the notes back from my instructor, so I'm ready to move on to the final presentation." Once she finished her marketing class, she was only two semesters away from graduation with her bachelor's degree. Hallelujah.

Joyce refilled her coffee cup from the carafe left at the table. "Quinn's arriving next week."

Courtney grinned. "Really? Because you've only mentioned it every morning for the past two weeks. I wasn't completely sure when he was getting here. You're sure it's next week? Because I couldn't remember."

"I'm old. I get to be excited about my grandson's arrival if I want to."

"Yes, you do. We're all quivering."

Joyce's mouth twitched. "You have a little attitude this morning, young lady."

"I know. It's the Drunken Red-nosed Honeybees. I always get attitude when they take over the Anderson House. Gratitude attitude."

"Quinn's still single."

Courtney didn't know if she should laugh or snort. "That's

subtle. I appreciate the vote of confidence, Joyce, but let's be honest. We both know I'd have a better shot at marrying Prince Harry than getting Quinn Yates to notice me." She held up a hand. "Not that I'm interested in him. Yes, he's gorgeous. But the man is way too sophisticated for the likes of me. I'm a small-town girl. Besides, I'm focused on college and my work. I have no free boy time." She wanted her degree within the next year, then a great job and then men. Or a man. Definitely just one. *The* one. But that was for later.

"You'll date when you're forty?" Joyce asked humorously.

"I'm hoping it won't take that long, but you get the idea."

"I do. It's too bad. Quinn needs to be married."

"Then you should find him someone who isn't me."

Not that Quinn wasn't impressive, but jeez. Her? Not happening.

She'd met him a handful of times when he'd come to visit his grandmother. The man was wildly successful. He was in the music business—a producer, maybe. She'd never paid attention. On his visits, he hung out with Joyce and her dogs, otherwise kept to himself, then left without making a fuss. Of course, the fuss happened without his doing a single thing other than show up.

The man was good-looking. No, that wasn't right. Words like *good-looking* or *handsome* should be used on ordinary people with extraordinary looks. Quinn was on a whole other plane of existence. She'd seen happily married middle-aged women actually simper in his presence. And to her mind, simpering had gone out of style decades ago.

"You really think he's moving to Los Lobos?" she asked, more than a little doubtful.

"That's what he tells me. Until he finds a place of his own, I've reserved the groundskeeper's bungalow for him."

"Nice digs," Courtney murmured. "He'll never want to leave."

Although to be honest, she couldn't imagine the famous, Malibu-living music executive finding happiness in their sleepy little Central California town, but stranger things had happened.

"I'll check his arrival date and make sure I'm assigned to clean it," she told her boss.

"Thank you, dear. I appreciate the gesture."

"It's not exactly a gesture. It's kind of my job."

While she was considered a jack-of-all-trades at the hotel, her actual title was maid. The work wasn't glamorous, but it paid the bills, and right now that was what mattered to her.

"It wouldn't be if you'd—"

Courtney held up her hand. "I know. Accept a different job. Tell my family about my big secret. Marry Prince Harry. I'm sorry, Joyce. There are only so many hours in a day. I need to have priorities."

"You're picking the wrong ones. Prince Harry would love you."

Courtney smiled. "You are sweet and I love you."

"I love you, too. Now, about the wedding."

Courtney groaned. "Do we have to?"

"Yes. Your mother is getting married in a few months. I know you're taking care of the engagement party, but there's also the wedding."

"Uh-huh."

Joyce raised her eyebrows. "Is that a problem?"

"No, ma'am."

It wasn't that Courtney minded her mother remarrying. Maggie had been a widow for literally decades. It was long past time for her mom to find a great guy and settle down.

Nope, it wasn't the marriage that was the problem—it was the wedding. Or rather the wedding *planning.*

"You're trying to get me into trouble," she murmured.

"Who, me?" Joyce's attempt to look innocent failed miserably.

Courtney rose. "All right, you crafty lady. I will do my best with both the party and the wedding."

"I knew you would."

Courtney bent down and kissed Joyce's cheek, then straightened, turned and ran smack into Kelly Carzo—waitress and, until this second, a friend.

Kelly, a pretty, green-eyed redhead, tried to keep hold of the tray of coffee mugs she'd been carrying, but the force was too great. Mugs went flying, hot liquid rained down, and in less than three seconds, Courtney, Joyce and Kelly were drenched, and the shattered remains of six mugs lay scattered on the floor.

The restaurant had been relatively quiet before. Now it went silent as everyone turned to stare. At least there were only a couple of other customers and a handful of staff. Not that word of her latest mishap wouldn't spread.

Joyce stood and scooped Sarge out of harm's way, then ordered Pearl to move back. "What is it your sister says in times like this?"

Courtney pulled her wet shirt away from her body and smiled apologetically at Kelly. "That I'm 'pulling a Courtney.' You okay?"

Kelly brushed at her black pants. "Never better, but you are so paying for my dry cleaning."

"I swear. Right after I help you with this mess."

"I'm going to get changed," Joyce told them. "The prerogative of being the owner."

"I'm really sorry," Courtney called after her.

"I know, dear. It's fine."

No, Courtney thought as she went to get a broom and a mop. It wasn't fine. But it sure was her life.

"I want to match my dress. Just one streak. Mo-om, what could it hurt?"

Rachel Halcomb pressed her fingers against her temple as she felt the beginnings of a headache coming on. The Saturday of Los Lobos High's spring formal was always a crazy one for the salon where she worked. Teenage girls came in to be coiffed and teased into a variety of dance-appropriate styles. They traveled in packs, which she didn't mind. But the high-pitched shrieks and giggles were starting to get to her.

Her client—Lily—desperately wanted a bright purple streak to go with her floor-length dress. Her hair was long, wavy and a beautiful shade of auburn. Rachel had clients who would fork out hundreds to get that exact color, while Lily had simply hit the hair lottery.

Lily's mom bit her bottom lip. "I don't know," she said, sounding doubtful. "Your father will have a fit."

"It's not his hair. And it'll look great in the pictures. Come on, Mom. Aaron asked me. You know what that means. I have to look amazing. We've only been living here three months. I have to make a good impression. Please?"

Ah, *the most amazing boy ever asked me out* combined with the powerful *I'm new in school* argument. A one-two punch. Lily knew her stuff. Rachel had never been on the receiving end of that particular tactic but knew how persuasive kids could be. Her son was only eleven but already an expert at pushing her buttons. She doubted she'd had the same level of skill when she'd been his age.

Lily swung toward Rachel. "You can use the kind that washes out, right? So it's temporary?"

"It will take a couple of shampoos, but yes, you can wash it out."

"See!" Lily's voice was triumphant.

"Well, you *are* going with Aaron," her mother murmured.

Lily shrieked and hugged her mother. Rachel promised herself that as soon as she could escape to the break room, she would have not one but two ibuprofens. And the world's biggest iced tea chaser. She smiled to herself. That was her—dreaming big.

Lily ran off to change into a smock. Her mother shrugged. "I probably shouldn't have given in. Sometimes it's hard to tell her no."

"Especially today." Rachel nodded at the gaggle of teenage girls at every station. They stood in various stages of dress… or undress. Some had on jeans and T-shirts. Others were in robes or smocks. And still others modeled their gowns for the dance that night. "And she *is* going to the dance with Aaron."

The other woman laughed. "When I was her age, his name was Rusty." She sighed. "He was gorgeous. I wonder what happened to him."

"In my class, he was Greg."

The mom laughed. "Let me guess. The football captain?"

"Of course."

"And now?"

"He's with the Los Lobos Fire Department."

"You kept in touch?"

"I married him."

Before Lily's mom could ask any more questions, Lily returned and threw herself into the chair. "I'm ready," she said eagerly. "This is going to be so awesome." She smiled at Rachel. "You're going to do the smoky eye thing on me, right?"

"As requested. I have deep purple and violet-gray shadows just for you."

Lily raised her hand for a high five. "You're the best, Rachel. Thank you."

"That's what I'm here for."

Two hours later Lily had a dark violet streak in her hair, a sleek updo and enough smoky eye makeup to rival a Victoria's Secret model. The fresh-faced teenager now looked like a twentysomething It Girl.

Lily's mom snapped several pictures with her phone before pressing a handful of bills into Rachel's hand. "She's beautiful. Thank you so much."

"My pleasure. Lily, bring me pictures of you with Aaron next time I see you."

"I will. I promise!"

Rachel waited until mother and daughter had left to count out the tip. It was generous, which always made her happy. She wanted her clients—and their mothers—to be pleased with her work. Now, if only one of those eccentric trillionaires would saunter in, love her work and tip her a few thousand, that would be fantastic. She could get ahead on her mortgage, not sweat her lack of an emergency fund. In the meantime, Josh needed a new glove for his baseball league, and her car was making a weird chirping noise that sounded more than a little expensive.

If she'd mentioned either of those things to Lily's mom, she would guess the other woman would have told her to talk to Greg. That was what husbands were for.

There was only one flaw with that plan—she and Greg weren't married anymore. The most amazing boy in school slash football captain slash homecoming king had indeed married her. A few weeks before their tenth anniversary he'd cheated and she'd divorced him. Now at thirty-three, she found herself living as one of the most pitied creatures ever—a divorced woman with a child about to hit puberty. And there wasn't enough smoky eye or hair color to make that situation look the least bit pretty.

She finished cleaning up and retreated to the break room for a few minutes before her last client—a double appointment of sixteen-year-old twins who wanted their hair to be "the same but different" for the dance. Rachel reached for the bottle of ibuprofen she kept in her locker and shook out two pills.

As she swallowed them with a gulp of water, her cell phone beeped. She glanced at the screen.

Hey you. Toby's up for keeping both boys Thursday night. Let's you and me go do something fun. A girls' night out. Say yes.

Rachel considered the invitation. The rational voice in her head said she should do as her friend requested and say yes. Break out of her rut. Put on something pretty and spend some time with Lena. She honestly couldn't remember the last time she'd done anything like that.

The rest of her, however, pointed out that not only hadn't she done laundry in days, but she was also behind on every other chore it took to keep her nonworking life running semismoothly. Plus, what was the point? They would go to a bar by the pier and then what? Lena was happily married. She wasn't interested in meeting men. And although Rachel was single and should be out there flashing her smile, she honest to God didn't have the energy. She was *busy* every second of every day. Her idea of a good time was to sleep late and have someone else make breakfast. But there wasn't anyone else. Her son needed her, and she made sure she was always there. Taking care of business.

She'd been nine when her father had died suddenly. Nine and the oldest of three girls. She still remembered her mother crouched in front of her, her eyes filled with tears. "Please,

Rachel. I need you to be Mommy's best girl. I need you to help take care of Sienna and Courtney. Can you do that for me? Can you hold it all together?"

She'd been so scared. So unsure of what was going to happen next. What she'd wanted to say was that she was still a kid and, no, holding it together wasn't an option. But she hadn't. She'd done her best to be all things to everyone. Twenty-four years later, that hadn't changed.

She glanced back at her phone.

Want to come over for a glass of wine and PB&J sandwiches instead?

I'll come over for wine and cheese. And I'll bring the cheese.

Perfect. What time should I drop off Josh?

Let's say 7. Does that work?

Rachel sent the thumbs-up icon and set her phone back in her locker, then closed the door. Something to look forward to, she told herself. Plans on a Thursday night. Look at her— she was practically normal.

2

"MRS. TROWBRIDGE IS DEAD."

Sienna Watson looked up from her desk. "Are you sure?" She bit her lower lip. "What I meant is, how awful. Her family must be devastated." She drew in a breath. "Are you sure?"

Seth, the thirtysomething managing director of The Helping Store, leaned against the door frame. "I have word directly from her lawyer. She passed two weeks ago and was buried this past Saturday."

Sienna frowned. "Why didn't anyone tell us? I would have gone to the funeral."

"You're taking your job too seriously. It's not as if she would have known you were there."

Sienna supposed that was true. What with Mrs. Trowbridge being dead and all. Still… Anita Trowbridge had been a faithful donor to The Helping Store for years—contributing goods for the thrift shop and money for various causes. Upon her death, the thrift shop was to inherit all her clothes and kitchen items, along with ten thousand dollars.

Unfortunately, nearly six months before, Sienna had received word of Mrs. Trowbridge's passing. After the lawyer had given his okay, she'd sent a van and two guys to the house to collect their bequest…only to be confronted by Mrs. Trowbridge's great-granddaughter. Erika Trowbridge had informed the men that her great-grandmother was still alive and they could take their vulture selves away until informed otherwise.

"It wasn't your fault," Seth said now as he pushed up his glasses. "The lawyer gave you the key to the house."

"Something he shouldn't have done. You know, it wouldn't have happened if they'd hired a local lawyer. But no. They had to bring one up from Los Angeles."

Sienna had apologized to Mrs. Trowbridge personally. The old lady—small and frail in her assisted-living bed—had laughed and told Sienna she understood. Great-granddaughter Erika had not. Of course, Erika was still bitter about the fact that Sienna had not only snagged the role of Sandy in their high school production of *Grease* but also—perhaps more important—won the heart of Jimmy Dawson in twelfth grade.

"She was a nice old lady," she murmured, thinking she would have liked to have sent flowers. Instead, she would donate that amount to The Helping Store in Mrs. Trowbridge's name. "I wonder if there's anything left in her kitchen."

"You think the granddaughter took things?"

"Great-granddaughter, and I wouldn't put it past her. If she had her way, Erika would clean the place out. At least we'll get the cash donation."

"I'm meeting with the lawyer in the morning."

Sienna was the donation coordinator for The Helping Store, one of a handful of paid staff. The large and bustling thrift store was manned by volunteers. All the proceeds from the store, along with any cash raised by donations, went to a shelter for women escaping domestic violence. Getting away from the abuser was half the battle. Over the years, The Helping Store had managed to buy several small duplexes on the edge of town. They were plain but clean and, most important to women on the run, far from their abusers.

Her boss nodded toward the front of the building. "Ready to tap-dance?"

Sienna smiled as she rose. "It's not like that. I enjoy my work."

"You put on a good show." He held up a hand. "Believe me. I'm not complaining. You're the best. My biggest fear is that some giant nonprofit in the big city will make you an offer you can't refuse and I'll be left Sienna-less. I can't think of a sadder fate."

"I'm not going anywhere," she promised. Oh, sure, every now and then she thought about what it would be like to live in LA or San Francisco, but those feelings passed. This small coastal town was all she knew. Her family was here.

"Isn't David from somewhere back East?" Seth asked.

She pulled open her desk drawer and collected her handbag, then walked out into the hallway. "St. Louis. His whole family's there."

Seth groaned. "Tell me he's not interested in moving back."

There were a lot of implications in that sentence. That she and David were involved enough to be having that conversation. That one day they would be married and, should he want to return to his hometown, she would go with him.

She patted her boss's arm. "Cart, meet horse. You're getting way ahead of yourself. We've only been dating a few months. Things aren't that serious. He's a nice guy and all, but..."

"No sparks." Seth's tone was sympathetic. "Bummer."

"We can't all have your one true great love."

"You're right. Gary is amazing. Okay, then, let's get you to the Anderson House so you can dazzle the good people who make— Who are you talking to?"

"The California Organization of Organic Soap Manufacturing, and they're at the Los Lobos Hotel. The Anderson House has bees."

Seth's expression brightened. "The Drunken Red-nosed Honeybees? I love those guys. Did you know their raw honey has thirty percent more antioxidants than any other raw honey in California?"

"I didn't and I could have gone all day without that factoid."

"You're jealous because I'm smart."

"No, you're jealous because I'm pretty and our world is shallow so that counts more."

Seth laughed. "Fine. Go be pretty with the soap people and bring us back some money."

"Will do."

Sienna drove to the hotel. She knew the way. Not only because her hometown was on the small side—but also because nearly every significant event was celebrated there.

The Los Lobos Hotel sat on a low bluff overlooking the Pacific. The main building was midcentury modern meets California Spanish, four stories high with blinding white walls and a red tile roof. The rear wing had been added in the 1980s, and luxury bungalows dotted the grounds.

Given the pleasant Central California weather, most large-scale events were held outside on the massive lawn in front of the pool. A grand pavilion stood on the lawn between the pool and the ocean, and a petite pavilion by the paddleboat pond.

Sienna parked the car and collected her material. As she walked toward the rear entrance of the hotel, she saw that the windows sparkled and the hedges were perfectly trimmed. Joyce did an excellent job managing the hotel, she thought. She was also a generous contributor to The Helping Store. And not just with money. More than once Sienna had called to find out if there was a spare room for a displaced family or a woman on the run. A year ago Joyce had offered a small room kept on reserve for their permanent use.

Helping women in need was something Joyce had been

doing forever. Nearly twenty-four years before, when Sienna and her sisters had lost their father, and Maggie, their mother, had been widowed, the family had been thrown into chaos. A lack of life insurance, Maggie's limited income and three little girls to support had left the young mother struggling. In a matter of months, she'd lost her house.

Joyce had taken them all in to live at the Los Lobos Hotel. Now Sienna smiled at the memory. She'd been only six at the time. Missing her father, of course, but also discovering the joy of reading. The day the Watson family had taken up residence in one of the hotel's bungalows, Joyce had given Sienna a copy of *Eloise*. Sienna had immediately seen herself as the charming heroine from the book and had made herself at home in the hotel. While it wasn't the same as living at The Plaza, it was close enough to help her through her grief.

Sienna remembered how she'd called for room service and told the person answering the phone to "charge it." Most likely those bills had gone directly to Joyce rather than to Maggie. And when she'd begged her mother for a turtle, because Eloise had one, a guest had stepped in to buy her one.

While there was pain in some of the memories, she had to admit living at the hotel had been fun. At least for her. It was probably a different story for her mother.

She entered through the rear door and started down the hall toward the meeting rooms. At the far end, she saw a familiar figure wrestling with a vacuum. As she watched, Courtney tripped over the cord and nearly plowed face-first into the wall. A combination of love and frustration swelled up inside her. There was a reason the phrase was "pulling a Courtney." Because if someone was going to stumble, fall, drop, break or slip, it was her baby sister.

"Hey, you," Sienna called as she got closer.

Courtney turned and smiled.

Sienna did her best not to wince at Courtney's uniform—not that the khaki pants and polo shirt were so horrible, but on her sister, they just looked wrong. While most people considered being tall an advantage, on Courtney the height was simply awkward. Like now—her pants were too short and, even though she was relatively thin, they bunched around her hips and thighs. The shirt looked two sizes too small and there was a stain on the front. She wasn't wearing makeup and her long blond hair—about her best feature—was pulled back in a ponytail. She was, to put it honestly, a mess. Something she'd been for as long as Sienna could remember.

Courtney had had some kind of learning disability. Sienna had never been clear on the details, but it had made school difficult for her sister. Despite their mother's attempts to interest Courtney in some kind of trade school, the youngest of the three seemed happy just being a maid. Baffling.

"You here to talk to Mr. Ford's group?" Courtney asked as Sienna approached.

"Yes. I'm going to guilt those California Organization of Organic Soap manufacturers into coughing up some serious money."

"I have no doubt. The A/V equipment is all set up. I tested it earlier."

"Thanks." Sienna patted her large tote bag. "I have my material right here." She glanced toward the meeting room, then back at her sister. "How's Mom's engagement party coming? Do you need any help?"

"Everything is fine. The menu's almost finalized. I've taken care of decorations and flowers. It will be lovely."

Sienna hoped that was true. When Maggie and Neil had announced their engagement, the three sisters had wanted to throw Mom a big party. The hotel was the obvious venue, which was fine, but then Courtney had said she would handle the details. And where Courtney went, disaster was sure to follow.

"If you need anything, let me know," Sienna told her. "I'm happy to help." She would also stop and talk to Joyce on the way out. Just to make sure everything was handled.

Emotion flashed through Courtney's blue eyes, but before Sienna could figure out what she was thinking, her sister smiled. "Sure. No problem. Thanks for the offer." She stepped back, bumped into the wall, then righted herself. "You should, um, get going to your meeting."

"You're right. I'll see you later."

Courtney nodded. "Good luck."

Sienna laughed. "While I appreciate the sentiment, I'm not going to need it."

She waved and headed for the Stewart Salon. The meeting room was set up with glasses of wine and plenty of hot and cold appetizers. At one end was a large screen, a podium and a microphone. Sienna removed her laptop from her tote and turned it on. While it booted, she plugged it into the room's A/V system. She started the video and was pleased to see the pictures on the screen and hear the music through the speakers.

"Perfection through planning," she murmured as she set the video back to the beginning.

Ten minutes later the good members of COOOSM bustled into the salon and collected glasses of wine and appetizers. Sienna circulated through the room, chatting with as many people as she could. She knew the drill—introduce herself, ask lots of friendly questions and generally be both approachable and charming, so that by the time she made her pitch, she was already considered someone they knew and liked.

She made as much effort with the women as the men. While studies were divided on which gender gave more to charity,

Sienna had always found that generosity came in unexpected ways, and she wasn't about to lose an opportunity based on stereotypes. Every dollar she brought in was a dollar the organization could use to help.

Milton Ford, the president of COOOSM, approached her. The little man barely came up to her shoulder. So adorable. She smiled.

"I'm ready whenever you are, Mr. Ford."

"Thank you, my dear." He shook his head. "This town does have its share of very tall women. There's a young lady who works here at the hotel. Ramona, I believe."

Sienna happened to know that Ramona was about five-two, but she didn't correct him. No doubt Courtney had done something to confuse Mr. Ford, but this wasn't the time to set him straight. Not with donations on the line.

"Shall we?" he asked, gesturing to the podium.

Sienna walked over to the microphone and turned it on, then she smiled at the crowd. "Good afternoon, everyone. Thank you so much for taking time out of your schedule to meet with me today." She winked at a bearded older man wearing overalls. "Jack, did you ever decide on that second glass of wine? Because I think it will help you make the right decision."

Everyone laughed. Jack toasted her. She smiled at him, then pushed the play button on her computer. Music flowed from the speakers. Carefully, slowly, she allowed her smile to fade. A picture of a large American flag appeared on the screen.

"Between 2001 and 2012, nearly sixty-five hundred American soldiers were killed in Iraq and Afghanistan. During that same period of time—" the screen shifted to the face of a battered woman clutching two small children "—almost twelve thousand women were murdered by their husbands, boyfriends or a former partner. Even now, three women are murdered every single day by the man who claims to love them."

She paused to let the information sink in. "Through the money we raise at The Helping Store, we provide a safe haven for women and their families in their time of need. They are referred to us from all over the state. When they arrive here, we offer everything from shelter to legal advice to medical care to relocation services. We take care of their bodies, their hearts, their spirits and their children. One woman in four will experience some kind of domestic violence in her life. We can't stop that from happening across the globe, but we can keep our corner of the world safe. I hope you'll join me in making that happen."

She paused as the voice-over on the video started. She'd planted the seed. The material she'd brought should do the rest.

Two hours later the last of the guests left. Sienna carefully put away the pledge forms. Not only had the group been generous, they also wanted to challenge other chapters of their organization to match their donations.

"How's the most beautiful girl in the world?"

The voice came from the doorway. Sienna hesitated just a second before turning. "Hi, David."

"How did it go?" her boyfriend asked as he moved toward her. "Why am I asking? You impressed them. I know it."

He pulled her close and kissed her. Sienna allowed his lips to linger for a second before stepping back.

"I'm working," she said with a laugh.

"No one's here." He moved his hands to her butt and pulled her close again. "We could lock the door."

If the words weren't clear enough, the erection he rubbed against her belly got the message through. How romantic—

going at it on a serving table while surrounded by dirty plates and half-full glasses of wine.

Sienna chided herself for not accepting the gesture in the spirit in which David meant it. Successful and smart. He loved his family, puppies, and as far as she could tell, he was an all-around nice guy.

"Remember you telling me about the time you took a girl home to meet your parents and realized you couldn't do it in their house?" she asked, her voice teasing.

He chuckled. "I do. Humiliating."

"Joyce, the owner of the hotel, is a little bit like my grandmother."

"Ouch." He drew back. "Grandma is even worse than Mom." He nibbled on her neck. "Rain check."

"Absolutely. Thanks."

He released her and pushed up his glasses. "You heading back to the office?"

She'd kind of wanted to head home after her presentation. She could deliver the pledge forms to her boss in the morning. But if she said that, David would want to make plans. Wow. She would rather go back to work than spend the evening with her boyfriend? What was up with that?

She looked at him. He was about her height, with dark brown hair and dark eyes. A nice build. He wasn't handsome, but she'd never cared much about that. Once a guy crossed the "not a troll" threshold, she was fine.

David Van Horn should have been the man of her dreams. Lord knew she'd been looking. He was the thirty-five-year-old senior vice president at the recently transplanted aerospace design firm in town. She was pushing thirty and had no idea why she hadn't been able to find "the one." Maybe there was something wrong with her.

Not a conversation she wanted to have with herself right now, she thought. Or ever.

"I don't have to go back to work," she told him.

"Great. Let's have dinner here."

"I'd love that."

A statement stretching the truth more than a little, but who was going to know?

3

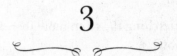

"WANT ME TO put vodka in yours?" Kelly asked as she handed Courtney a tray of glasses filled with lemonade.

"I wish," Courtney told her. "Alas, no. I have a meeting."

"Uh-huh. With your mom. Just give me the high sign and I'll start screaming. That will give you a good excuse to come running." Kelly wrinkled her nose. "I'll have to think of a reason. Maybe a broken ankle."

"You'd look adorable in a cast. Tiny and broken. Men would be flocking."

Kelly grinned. "I could use a good flocking."

Courtney was still laughing as she walked out of the bar and around to the pool area, where Joyce sat with Courtney's mother, Maggie, at one of the tables on the far side. A large umbrella protected them from the mid-May afternoon sun. Sarge and Pearl lay on the grass a few feet away.

Joyce wore her usual St. John separates—today she had on black knit pants and a three-quarter sleeve black knit shirt. A blue, black and gray scarf pulled the look together. Maggie had come from her office. Her tailored dark green dress brought out the color of her eyes and complemented her blond hair.

As Courtney approached, her mother caught sight of her and quickly scrambled to her feet. Her haste to get to Courtney and rescue the tray would have been comical if it wasn't a metaphor for their entire relationship. *Assume, no matter the circumstances, that Courtney can't handle it.* Although given her somewhat predictable ability to create a disaster out of thin air, she supposed she shouldn't be surprised.

"I'll just take that," her mother said with a smile. She carried the tray back to the table.

Courtney hesitated only a second before joining them. Too bad Neil hadn't come along. He was always a calming presence. Courtney and her sisters enjoyed spending time with him. He was sweet, with a quirky sense of humor. But there was no Neil-buffer today, and as Joyce considered herself as much Maggie's friend as Courtney's, there would be no help from that quarter, either.

Courtney sat next to Joyce and reached for a glass of lemonade. As she took a sip, she thought that maybe she should have taken Kelly up on her offer of vodka. That would have taken the edge off the meeting.

"As we discussed before," Joyce began, "the party is going to be out here." She motioned to the grassy area in front of the pool. "We'll have an open tent for dinner, but I'm hoping the weather cooperates and we can have drinks and appetizers out under the stars."

"Sunset's about eight ten," Courtney said, putting her drink back on the table and opening her tablet cover. "We'll be having drinks and appetizers with the sunset."

"That will be so beautiful." Maggie smiled at her daughter, then leaned toward Joyce. "What about the food?"

Joyce turned to Courtney and raised her eyebrows. "What are we having?"

Courtney found the menu in her file. "We've talked about a buffet. That gives us the most options. You and Neil both like spicy food, so I suggest you serve barbecue jerk chicken and grilled sweet-and-spicy shrimp as the main entrées."

She listed the side dishes offered and the appetizers, along with the idea of having watermelon mojitos as the signature drink.

"They're pink," she told her mother. "We could do cosmopolitans, too." The latter was much easier and would make her popular with the bar staff. In theory, the catering department didn't ever want anything labor-intensive like a mojito as a signature drink at an event, but she'd called in a few favors to get it approved.

"I do love pink," Maggie murmured, glancing between the two of them. "And Neil would say whatever makes me happy. Oh, let's do cosmos. They'll remind me of *Sex and the City*."

Courtney could practically hear a collective sigh of relief from the bar staff. She made notes on her tablet.

When her mother had first started dating Neil Cizmic, none of her daughters had thought much about it. A widow for nearly twenty-four years, Maggie had dated on and off, sometimes getting involved with a man for a few months at a time. But the relationships had never gotten serious. Then Neil had come along.

On the surface, they couldn't be more different. Maggie was tall and thin. Neil was at least two inches shorter and much more round. But he'd won her over with his kind heart and honest love. Now they were getting married. Every now and then Courtney poked at her heart to see if she minded that her late father was being replaced, but there had been no reaction. More than enough time had passed. If marrying Neil made her mom happy, then Maggie should go for it.

As for the "until death do us part" section of the vows, well, Courtney wasn't the one getting married. She was willing to admit she'd never been in love, but from what she'd seen, most romantic relationships ended badly. As for the nonromantic kind of love, well, that hurt, too.

"The cosmos will be so pretty," Joyce said. "And there's an open bar for anyone who wants something different."

Maggie leaned back in her chair. "I'm so excited. I always wanted an engagement party, but my mother said we couldn't have one." She looked at Joyce. "I was only eighteen when Phil and I got engaged, and nineteen when we got married. My mother made *all* the decisions. It was awful. We argued every day for a year. I wanted different dresses for the brides-maids, a different cake. I hated the flowers she picked. So I swear, this time, I'm going to do everything the way *I* want. Convention be damned."

"You have good taste, Mom. No one's worried," Court-ney assured her. Something she'd passed on to her other two daughters. Sienna could make a paper bag look like high fash-ion, and Rachel made her living by doing hair and makeup. Courtney knew she was the only one missing the style gene in their family.

Her mother grinned. "You should be a little worried. I started planning my wedding when I was fourteen. I have a lot of pent-up ideas." She eyed the pool. "Is that treated with chlorine?"

Joyce looked a little startled by the question. "Of course. Why?"

"Oh, I was just thinking swans would be nice. But they can't swim in chlorinated water, can they?"

Courtney felt her eyes widen. "No, and swans poop a lot, Mom. Cleaning the pool after the fact would be a nightmare."

Her mother sighed. "Too bad. Because I've always wanted swans."

Joyce shot Courtney a look of concern. Courtney quickly

flipped through the files on her tablet, then turned it so her mother could see the photo on the screen.

"I've been playing around with some ideas based on pictures I've seen on Pinterest. For example, a champagne fountain before the toast. Kelly, one of the waitresses here, knows how to stack the glasses and is going to help me with it. Won't that be great?"

She figured it was the adult equivalent of shaking keys at a fussy baby, and her odds were about the same.

Maggie leaned forward and nodded slowly. "That's lovely. Neil and I would like that very much."

"Good." Courtney flipped to another picture. "This will be the table runner for the head table."

Her mother stared for a second, then her eyes widened before filling with tears. "How did you do that?" she asked softly.

"It was easy. I uploaded the pictures to the website, then arranged them. The company prints out the runner and ships it."

The custom table runner was made up of a collage of photographs. Most of the photographs were of the sisters as they grew up. A few pictures showed Maggie with her daughters. Interspersed were pictures of Maggie and Neil on their various trips.

"Where did you get these?" her mother asked. "They're wonderful."

"Rachel had a lot of them on her computer. I borrowed a couple of photo albums the last time you had us over for dinner. I got the ones of you and Neil from him."

"It's lovely. Thank you. What a wonderful idea."

Courtney was surprised by the praise. Pleased, of course, but surprised. This was good. They were making progress. And no swans would be forced to swim in chlorinated water.

"It sounds like we have everything under control," Joyce said as she got to her feet. "Excellent. I need to go check on some arriving guests. They're new and, to be honest, sounded a little shady on the phone."

Courtney groaned. "Did you take reservations? We've talked about this. You need to stay off the phone."

Joyce, while a lovely person, could be overly chatty with new guests. Most people simply wanted to know availability and price. Joyce wanted them to share their life story, and if they weren't forthcoming with the information, they were labeled "shady."

"It's my hotel. I can do what I want."

Courtney grinned. "That would be true." She turned to Pearl and Sarge. "Be gentle with the new people. I'm sure they're perfectly nice."

"My dogs are excellent judges of character. Don't try to influence them."

"I'm trying to keep you from scaring the guests away."

Joyce grinned. "Where else are they going to stay? The Anderson House has bees."

"You're impossible."

"I know. It's part of my charm."

Joyce waved and walked toward the hotel. Courtney turned back to her mother and found Maggie studying her.

"What?"

"I'm glad you and Joyce get along so well and that she looks out for you."

Courtney carefully pulled the cover over her tablet and braced herself. In some ways, Maggie was harder to deal with than Sienna. Her middle sister thought she was inept and borderline dull-normal. Her mother feared she was…broken.

"She's a good friend and a great boss," Courtney said lightly. "I'm lucky."

Maggie pressed her lips together. "I know. I just wish you

had a little more ambition. I worry about you. Is it that you think you can't do better or you don't want to?"

Breathe, Courtney told herself. *Just breathe.* There was no win here. She simply had to endure the conversation, then she could get back to her life.

"The fact that you're helping out with my engagement party got me to thinking you might be interested in doing something more than being a maid." Her mother reached into her handbag and pulled out a brochure. "I know you said you weren't interested in being a dental assistant, but what about a massage therapist? You like people, you're very nurturing and you're physically strong."

Courtney took the brochure and studied the first page. She honest to God didn't know what to say. Joyce would point out this was her own fault. She was the one who let her family believe she was working as a maid at the hotel. Well, technically she *was* working as a maid, but only part-time as she continued her education. That was the part they didn't know.

She supposed she could simply come clean—but she didn't want to. She wanted to wait until she could slap down her diploma and watch them all stare in disbelief. That was a moment worth waiting for.

"Thanks, Mom," she said with a smile. "I'll think about it."

"Really? That would be wonderful. I'd be happy to help pay for it. I think you'd do well." Maggie hesitated. "There are so many wonderful opportunities out there. I hate to see you wasting your life."

"I know and I appreciate it."

Her mother nodded. "I love you, Courtney. I want the best for you."

All the right words. All warm, affectionate sentiments. On her good days, Courtney could believe them. On her bad

days, well, sometimes it was hard to let go of the past enough
to forgive.

"Thanks, Mom. I love you, too."

"A glove's important, Mom."

"I know it is."

"I really need a new one."

Rachel didn't doubt that. Josh was basically a good kid. He
didn't whine, he didn't ask for a lot. His passions were simple—anything sports-related and the occasional computer
game. That was it. Christmas and birthday presents revolved
around whatever sport most had his interest. As they had for
the past three years, spring and summer meant baseball.

Los Lobos didn't have a Little League team, but there was
a county league. Josh insisted they sign him up the first hour
they could, something she was happy to do. He was eleven—
she figured she had all of two, maybe three years before he
became a raging male hormone and then all bets were off.

"Dad said he would buy it for me but I had to check with
you first."

At least she was driving and had an excuse not to look at
Josh. Because she couldn't—not without him seeing the rage
in her eyes. Damn Greg, she thought bitterly. Of course he
could afford to buy his son a new glove. Greg had only himself to worry about.

Her ex-husband made a good living as a Los Lobos county
firefighter. He also had excellent medical benefits—something she'd lost after the divorce. Even more annoying, his
schedule was a ridiculous twenty-four hours on, twenty-four
hours off for six days, followed by four days off. Which gave
him plenty of time to play, and play he did. Add in the fact
that he'd moved back home with his folks, so he basically

had no living expenses, and the man was swimming in both cash and time.

Don't think about it, she instructed herself. Dwelling on how good Greg had it only made her angrier. She had to remember that the man paid his child support on time. That was something. But as for the rest of it—she couldn't help resenting how easy he had it.

Yes, she did well at the salon. She was able to support herself and her son. The child support covered the mortgage, and she paid for everything else. But it wasn't as if there was a bunch of extra cash at the end of the month. She was doing her best to build up an emergency fund and keep current on household repairs. There wasn't anything left over for things like baseball gloves.

When she was sure she could speak in a happy, excited tone, she said, "Go for it, Josh. You need a new glove. It's great that your dad can afford to get it. Do you already know what you want, or do you need to do some research?"

"I know exactly what I need." And he was off, describing the glove down to the kind of stitching.

Oh, to be that young and innocent, she thought with regret. To trust that everything was going to turn out the way it was supposed to. To believe in happily-ever-after.

She'd been that way, once. She'd had hopes and dreams—mostly of finding her handsome prince. And when she'd laid eyes on Greg, she'd known, just known, he was the one. Back then *everyone* had believed he was the one. Greg had been the guy every girl wanted.

And she'd been the one to get him—right up until he'd cheated on her.

She turned the corner, then pulled into Lena's driveway. Josh was out of the car before she'd come to a full stop.

"Bye, Mom. See you later."

He ran into the house without bothering to knock. She was still shaking her head when her friend Lena appeared on the porch. Lena turned back to kiss her husband, then hurried to the car. She got inside and waved the bag she held.

"Great cheese *and* dark chocolate. Am I good to you or what?"

They hugged.

"You're the best," Rachel told her. "Thanks for coming over tonight. I could use some girl time."

"Me, too. Tell me the wine is red."

"It's red and there are two bottles."

"Perfect."

She and Lena had been friends since elementary school. They were physical opposites—Lena was petite and curvy, with brown hair and dark eyes. Rachel was taller and blonde.

They'd played together, dreamed together, and when they'd grown up, they'd been each other's maids of honor. They'd married young and then had sons within a few months of each other. But things were different now. Lena and Toby were still happily together.

"What?" her friend asked. "You're looking fierce."

"Nothing. I'm fine. Just the usual crap."

"Greg?"

Rachel sighed. "Yes. Josh needs a new glove and his dad is going to buy it for him."

Her friend didn't say anything.

Rachel turned onto her street. "I know what you're think-ing. I should be grateful he's an involved father. That the extra money he has could be spent on women and drinking, but he spends it on his kid."

"You're doing all the talking."

Rachel pulled into her driveway. "I just wish…"

"That a really big rock would fall on him?"

She smiled. "Maybe not that, but something close."

Because it was Greg's fault their marriage had failed. He'd chosen to have a one-night stand with a tourist. She'd known the second she'd seen him—had guessed what he'd done. He hadn't tried to deny it, and that had been that. Her marriage had ended.

When they got back to Rachel's, they poured wine. Rachel eyed the beautiful wedge of Brie and knew there had to be maybe five thousand calories in that chunk of soft goodness, and she honestly couldn't care. Had she put on weight lately? Probably, but so what? Her clothes still fit, at least the loose ones did. She worked hard and deserved to reward herself. It wasn't as if she had anyone to look good for.

She sipped her wine and knew that the right response was that she needed to look good for herself. That she was worth it and all those other stupid platitudes. That if she wanted to feel better, she had to take better care of herself. All of which didn't get the laundry washed or the bathrooms cleaned.

"You need to get over him."

Lena's comment was so at odds with what Rachel had been thinking that it took her a second to figure out what her friend was saying.

"Greg? I am. We've been divorced nearly two years."

"You might be legally divorced, but emotionally you're still enmeshed."

Rachel rolled her eyes. "Did you have too much waiting time in a doctor's office? Did you read some women's magazine? *Enmeshed?* No one actually uses that word."

"You just did."

Rachel made a strangled noise in her throat. "I don't want to think about him," she admitted. "I want to move on with my life."

"Find a man? Fall in love?"

"Sure."

A lie, she thought, but one her friend would want to hear. Fall in love? She couldn't imagine going out with someone who wasn't Greg. He'd been her first date, her first time, her first everything. The world still divided itself neatly into Greg and not Greg. How was she supposed to get over that?

"You're so lying," Lena said cheerfully. "But I appreciate that you're making the effort to humor me."

"I want to move on," Rachel admitted. "I just don't know how. Maybe if I could get away from him. But with us having Josh together, there's no escape."

"You could move."

The suggestion was spoken in a soft voice, as if Lena knew what Rachel would think. Rachel did her best to remain calm when on the inside she wanted to start shrieking.

Move? Move! No way. She couldn't. She loved her house. She needed her house and all it represented. It was proof that she was okay. She would take a second job to pay for the house, if she had to.

None of which made sense. She understood that. She also knew she was reacting to a traumatic event in her childhood— the death of her father and the fact that her family had been forced out of their house a few months later.

Rachel remembered hating everything about living at the Los Lobos Hotel. Looking back, she knew she should be grateful that they'd been taken in, that they hadn't had to live in a shelter. But she couldn't get over the shock and pain the day she'd come home from school to find her mother sobbing that they'd lost everything and it was her father's fault. She'd been so scared. Daddy was dead—how could he continue to be in trouble?

When she'd been older, she'd realized their father hadn't

been a bad man—just financially careless. There hadn't been any life insurance, no savings.

When she and Greg had married, she'd been focused on buying a house. They'd been young and it had been a financial struggle, especially with a baby, but they'd made it. This was her home—she was never leaving.

But the price of that was living with the ghosts of her lost marriage. Greg's memory still lingered in every room.

"Maybe I could get someone to do a spiritual cleansing of the house. With sage. And salt. Do you need salt?"

Lena briefly closed her eyes. "I love you like my best friend."

"I am your best friend."

"I know, so please understand why I'm saying this. The problem isn't the house, Rachel. It's you. And there isn't enough sage or salt in the world to get you over Greg. You're going to have to decide once and for all to emotionally move on. Until you do, you're trapped. Forever."

The truth, however lovingly delivered, could still hurt like a son of a bitch.

Rachel blinked a couple of times, then reached for the wine. "We're so going to need another bottle."

4

"YOU LIKE THIS, BABY? I picked the leather to match your beautiful curly hair."

Quinn Yates waited for his companion to say something, but Pearl only stared at the car as if expecting him to open the passenger door. Which he did. The large standard poodle jumped gracefully inside, then returned her attention to him as if ready for a compliment.

"You look good," he told her. "Where do you want to go? For a burger?"

"She prefers ice cream."

He turned to see his grandmother walking down the stairs by the side of the hotel. She was dressed as always in her beloved St. John tailored knits and Chanel flats. She wore her white hair in that poufy old lady bubble style he would always associate with her. He knew she would smell of L'air du Temps and vanilla. He crossed the driveway to meet her and pulled her into a hug. The tension that had been with him on the drive north faded.

"You made it," she said, wrapping her arms around him as if she would never let go.

He'd always liked that about her. Joyce gave good hugs. When he'd been a kid, she'd been his anchor. When he'd gotten older, she'd always been there, ready to offer advice or a kick in the ass—depending on what she thought he needed. Now she was simply home.

He held on a few more seconds, pleased that she didn't seem any frailer than she had when she'd visited him six months before. She was well into her seventies, but as vital and sharp as ever. Still, lately he'd found himself worrying.

"Ice cream, huh," he said, glancing at the dog sitting in the passenger seat of his Bentley. "Then that's what we'll go get."

Joyce stepped back. She barely came to his shoulder and had to look up to meet his gaze. "You're not taking the dog for ice cream. I don't know what ridiculousness you get up to in Los Angeles, but here in the real world, dogs don't eat ice cream."

He raised his eyebrows. "I've been back thirty seconds and you're already lying to me."

She smiled. "All right. They do, but at home. We don't take them out. Besides, if you take Pearl, you need to take Sarge, too. He'll get jealous otherwise."

As if he heard his name, a small white fluffball barreled through the open doorway and down the path. Pearl jumped out of the Bentley and ran to greet her companion.

They were an odd pair. The tall, stately blonde poodle and the small, white bichon-poodle mix. Pearl was nearly four times Sarge's size, yet he clearly ran the show. Now they circled Quinn, sniffing and yipping. He crouched down to greet them both. After letting them sniff his fingers, he offered pats and rubs.

"Your man arrived yesterday," his grandmother told him.

"He's my assistant, Joyce, not my man. We're not living in a 1950 Cary Grant movie."

"But wouldn't it be fun if we were? I tried to check him into the hotel, but he said he was staying somewhere else."

Quinn straightened and closed the passenger door of the

Bentley. "He is. Wayne and I work best when there's some separation between us."

"You're not moving back because you think I'm getting old, are you?"

She always did like to cut to the heart of the matter. He leaned over and kissed her cheek. "I've thought you were old for a long time now, and not everything is about you."

She touched his face. "You are so full of crap."

"That is true." He held out his arm. She tucked her hand into the crook of his elbow and he led her back into the hotel.

Quinn's mother had been Joyce's only child. He'd spent as much of his childhood with Joyce as with his mom. By the time he'd turned fourteen, his mother had abandoned him and he'd moved into the hotel permanently.

Now as they entered the lobby, he took in the high ceilings, the crystal light fixtures and the big, curving reception desk. The furniture was comfortable, the food delicious and the bartenders generous with their pours. Add in the beach-front location in quiet Central California, and the Los Lobos Hotel had nearly everything going for it.

At seventeen, he couldn't wait to be anywhere but here. Now some twenty years later, he was grateful to be back.

The dogs led the way into the bar. He and Joyce took seats at a corner table. The dogs settled at their feet.

He was sure having a couple of canines in an establishment that served food had to violate several state ordinances, but as far as he could tell, no one complained. If they did, they were told the dogs were excellent judges of character. That tended to quiet all but the most offensive of guests. And the ones who weren't quieted were asked to leave.

A pretty redhead appeared at their table. "Hello, Joyce. Quinn."

He recognized her face from his previous visits, if not her name. Fortunately, her name tag was easy to read.

"Nice to see you again, Kelly."

She smiled. "What can I get you two?"

"I'll have a glass of Smarty Pants chardonnay."

Quinn laughed at his grandmother. "I can't believe you're still bitter about what happened."

"I haven't forgotten because I have an excellent memory. Besides, I love my new wines. I'm serving them as the exclusive house wine in the hotel."

A few years back, the local winery Joyce had sourced from decided to change winemakers and therefore the style and taste of their wines. Joyce had complained, the winemaker had done his own thing and, in protest, she'd gone looking for wines she liked better. Middle Sister Wines, based in Northern California, had won both her taste buds and her business.

The chardonnay was very popular with the ladies who lunched at the hotel, with a fresh, California bouquet that had hints of citrus and pear. Another of their whites, Drama Queen pinot grigio, had been racking up awards from wine competitions around the country.

"They've become a tradition," Joyce added.

He squeezed her hand. "You're my favorite tradition. I adore everything about you."

How could he not? She was delightful, and even if she wasn't, she was the only family he had left.

Kelly turned her attention to him. "And for you?"

"I'll have the same."

White wine wasn't his favorite, but when with Joyce...

"And a cheese plate," his grandmother added. "Quinn is hungry."

He wasn't, but there was no point in arguing.

"Right away," Kelly told them.

"I've reserved the groundskeeper's bungalow," Joyce said when Kelly had left. "You should be very comfortable there."

He knew the cottage—it was at the south end of the property, private and large. "It's one of your most expensive suites," he protested. "I just need a regular room for a couple of weeks while I figure out what I'm doing."

"No. I want you to have it. You'll be more comfortable there."

He knew she didn't need the money renting it would provide, but still. "Thank you."

"I've blocked it for the summer," she added.

He raised his eyebrows. "I'm forty-one. Don't you think it's time I moved away from home?"

"No. You're just back and you'll find your own place soon enough. This way you can settle in and find what's exactly right. Assuming you really are staying."

"You doubt me."

"Of course. You live in Malibu, Quinn. You have a business there. Whatever will you do in sleepy Los Lobos?"

A good question and one he was looking forward to answering.

"I can run my business from here. Once I get a recording studio set up, my artists will come to me."

"You're really that important?"

Her voice was teasing, her smile impish. He winked.

"I am all that and more."

She laughed. "I hope it's true and you do stay. And I don't even care if you're moving because you're worried about me. What kind of place do you need for your studio?"

"Almost anywhere would do. We'll be remodeling regardless. So a house or a warehouse. I'd prefer a stand-alone building with good parking." And privacy. Where people could come and go without being seen or photographed.

"Is that nice mute man going to be joining you?"

Quinn sighed. "Zealand isn't mute. He just doesn't talk much."

"I've never heard him speak at all. Are you sure he can?"

"Yes. He's said words at least twice."

Zealand might not have much to say, but he was the best soundman in the business. He would be the one deciding if the space Quinn was interested in could be converted into a killer studio. One where they could work and turn sound into magic.

Movement caught his attention. He looked up and saw a tall blonde walk to the bar. She had long hair pulled back into a ponytail and wore black pants and a long-sleeved black shirt.

It wasn't her face that caused him to keep looking, although she was pretty enough. It was more the way she walked—partially hunched, with her shoulders rounded—as if she didn't want to be noticed.

When she reached the bar, she and Kelly spoke. They both laughed. The blonde said something else, then turned to leave. As she took a step, she somehow got tangled in a bar stool and stumbled. She righted herself, glanced around to see if anyone had noticed, then hurried away.

"That was Courtney," Joyce told him. "You've met her before."

Quinn knew his grandmother well enough to say, "No," in a firm voice.

"I'm only—"

"No. Whatever you have in mind, no."

"There's more to her than meets the eye."

Kelly delivered their wine and the cheese plate. Pearl and Sarge immediately sat up. Quinn saw there were two dog biscuits on the tray. Kelly handed one to each dog, then smiled and left.

"You're not too old for her," his grandmother added, dashing his hope that the arrival of their drinks had been a distraction. On the bright side, there was obviously nothing wrong with her mind. On the not-so-bright side...damn.

"She's what? Twenty-five?"

"Twenty-seven. That's only a fourteen-year difference."

"It's not the years, it's the miles."

"You're still a handsome man."

He paused in the act of raising his glass. "Okay, that's creepy."

She laughed. "You know what I mean."

They touched glasses. Quinn sipped the crisp, buttery chardonnay. "Nice."

"I like it. Now, about Courtney—"

He held up his free hand. "Not happening. I love you like my grandmother, but I'm not going there."

"You have to at some point. Don't you want to fall in love?"

A familiar question. The answer to which had always been *hell, no.* But lately...he'd started to wonder. A year ago there'd been someone in his life who had made him think there were possibilities. Before he could figure out what, she'd fallen in love with someone else. While he'd gotten over her, the fact that he'd been considering more than his usual no-strings we're-in-it-for-the-sex had surprised him. And gotten him to thinking. Did he want more?

He hadn't reached the point of defining the question as *did he want to fall in love?* He wasn't sure there was a guy on the planet who thought that way. But having someone around on a permanent basis—that might work.

"I need to figure it out," he admitted.

"Figure fast. You're not getting any younger."

He laughed. "What happened to I'm a good-looking man?"

"Beauty fades."

He raised his glass to her. "Not yours."

Joyce rolled her eyes. "Your charm is lost on me. I'm old."

"You are perfection."

She didn't smile back. Instead, she looked at him intently. "I mean it, Quinn. I want you to find someone. Settle down. Have children. I worry about you."

"I can take care of myself."

"Yes, dear, but sometimes it's nice if you don't have to."

Actually *writing* a marketing plan wasn't that big a deal. It was getting to the point where it could be written that was the tough part. Courtney decided to reward her three hours of tedious research and number crunching with some ice cream and maybe a cookie chaser.

She stood and stretched as she weighed the sugar high against having to leave her room. In truth, the trip from the fourth floor to the kitchen was no big deal. Still, it was late and she should probably just go to bed.

But the thought of ice cream could not be denied. She saved her work on her laptop, then walked to the door.

Her room in the hotel was at the end of the hall, by the stairs. It was tucked next to the linen closet and right by one of the HVAC units, not to mention several water pipes. There was also a large tree that had grown tall enough to completely block any hope of a view beyond leaves. In short, a complete disaster to rent to guests.

Joyce had tried remodeling it several times and even offering it at a discount, but there were always complaints. A couple of years back, she'd come to Courtney with a trade. Free room and board in exchange for a certain number of hours of maid labor. For the time Courtney worked beyond that, she got a paycheck.

The deal gave them both what they wanted. Courtney had

taken possession of an old twin bed Joyce had been ready to toss, along with a battered desk and a dresser. She was a sound enough sleeper not to care about the HVAC or pipe noise and the lack of view was totally fine with her. Free rent, meals and utilities meant she only had to work enough to pay for her car, cell phone and books. The money she'd saved for college wasn't quite enough to cover tuition, but she'd been lucky enough to land a few scholarships and grants. Every semester she managed to squeak by. Now she was only a year away from graduating, and with luck she would do so without a loan.

"Yet another reason to celebrate with ice cream," she told herself.

She took the stairs to the main floor and crossed the quiet lobby. Her sneakers were silent on the hardwood floor. While her threadbare jeans and secondhand USC sweatshirt weren't exactly haute couture, she knew the odds of running into a guest at this hour were slim.

She didn't bother with overhead lights in the kitchen. She knew her way in the twilight produced by the soft glow from under-the-counter illumination and exit signs. She collected a bowl and a spoon, then crossed to the walk-in freezer to pick her flavor.

She walked out with a three-gallon container of vanilla chocolate chip and found herself in the brightly lit kitchen, facing a tall, broad-shouldered man.

She shrieked and jumped. The ice cream slipped from her hands. She grabbed, he grabbed and they both ended up with their arms wrapped around a very cold, very large container.

They were close enough for her to see the various shades of blue in his irises and inhale the scent of clean fabric and man. His jaw was strong, his beard about two days old and his gaze piercing. Her heart thundered in her chest, but it had very little to do with shock and everything to do with attraction.

"One of us should let go," he said.

"What?" Oh, right. She immediately released the container and straightened. "Um, sorry. You startled me."

"I got that." He put the ice cream on the counter. "Late-night snack?"

"Something like that."

They continued to watch each other. One corner of his mouth turned up in a smile.

"I'm Quinn."

Seriously? "We all know who you are. There are all kinds of pictures of you in Joyce's bungalow. Plus, she talks about you all the time."

He groaned. "I don't want to know what she says."

"Most of it is good."

His brows rose. "Most?"

Courtney grinned. "You said you didn't want to know. I'm Courtney, by the way. We've met a few times before."

"I remember."

She doubted that. A man like Quinn would remember meeting Rihanna and Taylor Swift, but not someone like her. She would have been nothing but staff, and who remembered the woman who cleaned his room?

She pointed at the container. "It's vanilla chocolate chip— our flavor of the month. You want some?"

"Sure."

She grabbed a second bowl and spoon, then scooped out ice cream for both of them. She returned the container to the freezer. When she walked back into the kitchen, she half expected to find Quinn had gone. But he'd pulled up one of the stools by the counter as if he planned to stay. She did the same, careful to leave a polite amount of space between them.

"Oh, there are cookies, too," she said. "If you want some."

"No, thanks. This is enough."

Not a philosophy she could get behind, but now she wasn't comfortable adding a couple of crushed cookies to her bowl. Later, she promised herself. She would take them up to her room.

"You're up late," he commented.

"I like the hotel at night. It's quiet. All the guests are asleep. Or at least not wandering around, making trouble."

"Is that how you see them?"

"You've never cleaned up a hotel room after a rowdy party."

"That's true."

They ate in silence for a few seconds. Courtney found the moment surreal. Quinn might not be an actual rock star, but he was famous for discovering musical talent of all kinds and taking those talents to the top of the charts.

"A fan?" he asked, nodding toward her.

It took her a second to realize he meant her sweatshirt. She glanced down at the USC college logo. "Not really. One of the guests left it behind and it was way too nice to throw out."

She remembered the pretty but tearful coed who'd tossed the sweatshirt at her, demanding it be burned.

"It had been her fiancé's, and it turned out he'd slept with one of the strippers hired for his bachelor party." She licked her spoon. "I'll never understand the whole concept of inviting trouble a few days before you commit yourself to someone for the rest of your life. But weddings are all about drama." She eyed him. "Are you really moving back to Los Lobos?"

He nodded.

"But you live in LA."

"That's not necessarily a good thing."

"Isn't your business there?"

"It's mobile. I'm ready for a change."

She wondered if any part of his decision was about his

grandmother. "She's doing fine, you know. Mentally and physically."

"Thanks for the update. She's not the only reason, but she's one of them." He paused.

Courtney took a bite of ice cream. As if he'd been waiting for her to be in that delicate act of swallowing, he then said, "She's trying to fix us up."

Courtney began to choke.

He waited until she'd regained control to add, "Or have me take you on as a project. Which makes me wonder why you need fixing."

The door was so far away, Courtney thought longingly as she glanced toward the exit. She ignored the heat burning her cheeks. There was no pretending that wasn't happening, not with the overhead lights blaring down. In a matter of seconds, she knew her face was as brightly colored as her sweatshirt.

"You're imagining things, I'm sure," she managed, thinking that as much as she loved her boss, she was going to have to kill her. There was no other response that was appropriate.

He waited.

She sucked in a breath. "I don't need fixing. I'm doing great. I'm only two semesters from graduating with my bachelor's in hotel management. I have a good job and lots of friends."

"You're twenty-seven."

She was torn between wondering how he knew that and the relevancy of the statement.

"So?"

"You waited a while to go to college."

A statement, not a question. Yet she was somehow compelled to explain. Maybe it was the way his dark blue gaze settled on her face. Maybe it was the fact that it was nearly one in the morning. Maybe it was a latent babbling gene choosing this inopportune moment to surface. Regardless, she started speaking and then couldn't seem to stop.

"Not everyone makes it to college out of high school," she began. "Did you know that returning female students are the most successful demographic in college?"

"I did not."

"It's true. My theory is they've tasted fear. They know what it's like to try to survive without a good education and it's not easy."

"Because you've done it?"

"Uh-huh. I left high school when I turned eighteen. I was only in eleventh grade because I got held back a couple of times. I didn't wait for the semester to end or anything. I legally became an adult and I was gone." She licked her spoon. "It wasn't so much about everything happening at home, although that was a part of it. Mostly I couldn't stand being two years older and labeled as dumb." She glanced at him, then back at her ice cream. "I had a learning disability that didn't get diagnosed until I was nearly ten."

She didn't bother with the whys of that. No reason to go over that material.

"After I left high school, I got a job at Happy Burger."

"I love Happy Burger," he told her.

"Everyone does. I rented a room in a house on the edge of town and supported myself." Which was mostly true. She'd been forced into a series of second jobs to make ends meet, had cut off ties with her family for nearly a year because she was eighteen and angry and needed to grow up, and had taken up with a series of really bad-for-her guys.

"I was going nowhere. Around the time I turned twenty, two things happened. I got a job here as a maid, and the manager of Happy Burger told me that if I earned my GED, he would recommend me for a management position. He told me that I had a real future at Happy Burger."

"Was that good news or bad news?"

"It was the worst. I didn't want to spend my life at Happy Burger. But it was the wake-up call I needed. I got my GED and started at community college. Along the way, I quit the burger job."

"And now you're two semesters away from your bachelor's."

She waved her spoon. "You know it."

"Impressive."

"The info dump?"

He flashed her a sexy smile. She was sure he didn't mean it to be sexy, but he probably couldn't help it. Quinn was just that kind of guy. It wasn't in the way he moved, because right now he was sitting still. But whatever it was still existed. Maybe it was a confidence thing, or a pheromone thing. Either way, she found herself wanting to lean closer and sigh.

"You're impressive," he clarified. "Look at where you started and where you ended up. I respect that. I work with a lot of talented people. Most of them don't follow traditional paths to success. Good for you for doing the work." He smiled again. "You're right. You don't need fixing."

His words made her beam as a warm glow filled her. A glow that lasted all of eight seconds, right until ice cream dripped off her spoon and onto her sweatshirt. She held in a groan and wiped at it with her finger.

Couldn't she just once be sophisticated and elegant? Or even casual and coordinated? Did she always have to be spilling, bumping and dropping?

This was what her sister Sienna would call "pulling a Courtney"—a phrase Courtney had always hated but had to admit existed for a reason. And speaking of her family—

"You can't tell anyone what I told you," she said quickly. "About the college stuff."

Quinn frowned. His eyebrows drew together and little lines formed. It was even sexier than the smile had been.

"What do you mean?"

"Joyce knows, but no one in my family does. About me going to college. I don't think they know I have a GED. If you run into them, it would be great if you didn't, you know, say anything."

"Okay. Interesting. Why?"

She raised a shoulder. "It's a long story."

"Right. And you're not one to overshare." He stood. "Don't worry. Your secret is safe with me."

"Thank you."

He studied her for a second. She had no idea what he was thinking but figured that was probably for the best.

"Good night, Courtney."

"'Night, Quinn."

He put his bowl in the dishwasher, then walked out of the kitchen. She watched him go, allowing herself the pleasure of admiring his butt and the way he moved. The man had grace and style. He was sophisticated and unexpectedly nice. If she were someone other than herself, she would so want to start something with him. But she wasn't. Besides, she was focused on school and working and getting through her last year of college. *Then* she would land her dream job and find someone to date. A smart, kind man who thought she was exactly what he was looking for. Assuming that man existed.

She put her bowl next to Quinn's before hunting down the cookies and grabbing a handful. As she walked back to her room, she imagined what would have happened if Quinn had reached across the table and pulled her close. No doubt she would have dropped her spoon and spilled all over him. Or burped during their kiss. Because that was how her life went. Even in her dreams.

5

RACHEL WAS CONFIDENT that laundry multiplied in the night. What had been a single load a couple of days ago was now four. Five if she did Josh's sheets. He would tell her it wasn't necessary, but she thought differently.

She glanced at the clock and held in a groan. It was five on Sunday afternoon. She'd worked late the previous day with the idea that on a weekend when Josh was with his dad, she could earn a little extra money. Which was great, but by the end of her workweek, she was always exhausted. That had turned into sleeping late, which she probably needed, but it didn't get any of her chores done.

She'd done grocery shopping, paid some bills and spent the past two hours weeding in the yard. In between, she'd baked cookies, put a stew in the Crock-Pot and made her son's lunch for the following day. Now she faced laundry and cleaning the kitchen. Once Josh got home—which should be any second now—they would go over his homework, assuming his father had remembered to make him do it, review his schedule for the week and then watch a show for an hour before bed. And starting tomorrow, she would do it all over again.

She put the whites in the washer, added detergent and bleach, then hit the start button. She already had the baseball uniforms in the sink in the laundry room. Between the grass stains and the ground-in dirt, those had to be pretreated or they would never get clean. Honestly, she didn't know how professional sports organizations kept their uniforms so nice. Maybe they didn't bother. Maybe every player wore new ones for each game.

She heard footsteps in the front of the house followed by a familiar "Mom! I'm home!"

There were a million things to do and she was still tired and maybe a little cranky, but none of that mattered. Josh's voice was the best sound in the world, and knowing he was back made everything a little easier.

She walked toward the living room and smiled when she saw her son.

He was tall for his age. All gangling with too-long arms and legs. At eleven, he was on the verge of adolescence. His voice hadn't changed yet and he'd yet to get a single chin hair, but she knew that was coming.

He'd inherited his father's dark hair and eyes, but her smile. He was a good kid. Smart, caring, generous. Easygoing. Now he dropped his duffel on the floor and hurried to greet her.

"Dad bought me a new glove," he said, holding it out in one hand while he reached for her with the other. He gave her a quick hug, then he stepped back and offered the glove.

"It's exactly what I wanted. Dad and I played catch yesterday, to break it in, then he hit balls and I caught them. Try it on."

She slid her hand into the glove and was surprised when it wasn't too small for her.

"Is this an adult size?" she asked.

Josh grinned. His too-long hair fell into his eyes and he swept it back with a gesture that reminded her too much of his father. "Uh-huh. The guy at the store said I was in between, so we decided it made sense to get the bigger one."

She held up her right hand and he held up his left. They both spread their fingers. Rachel was stunned to discover her eleven-year-old son's hand was nearly as big as hers.

"When did that happen?" she asked.

Josh laughed. "I'm going to be as tall as you soon, Mom. Then taller."

"I can't decide if that's good or bad," she admitted.

"Me, either."

The voice came from behind her. She took a second to brace herself against the inevitable reaction to seeing her ex-husband, then turned.

"Hello, Greg."

"Rachel."

He looked good, but wasn't that always the way? Every time she saw him, she looked for some sign that he was aging. Decaying would be better. But there was only the ever-present handsome face, perfect hair and sex-god-like body.

"I thought I'd go get pizza for dinner," he told her. "The usual for you?"

She wanted to say no. That she wasn't interested in eating with him. That pizza was the last thing she needed. That her constant exhaustion, and the feeling that no matter how hard she worked the best she could hope for was to not lose ground, had led to a horrible snacking habit that was taking its toll on her body. That or elves were shrinking her clothes while she slept.

She felt fat and old and tired, while he got to be handsome and toned and in his prime. Of course, if she had every other day off, she would have time to do things like eat right and exercise. If she lived with someone who cooked the meals and cleaned the house and took care of every other chore, she wouldn't be so rushed or exhausted. If she wasn't the custodial parent, then...

She drew in a breath. The mental litany wasn't new, nor was her frustration. But there was much she couldn't change and more she didn't want to. Being Josh's mother, having him most of the time, was important to her. The price of that was one she was willing to pay. The same with the house. She needed to be here. The rest of it would take care of itself.

"Pizza would be fine," she said, thinking the Crock-Pot dinner would keep for tomorrow.

"You okay?"

"Fine. Doing laundry, getting meals ready for the week. The usual."

"How can I help?"

The unexpected question stumped her. Help? Greg didn't help. He played. He surfed with his best friend, Jimmy. He hung out with the other firefighters. He tinkered with his truck.

"I'm fine," she told him. "Did Josh do his homework?"

"Uh-huh, and I checked it. The essay needed some work, but he did great on the math."

"Good. Only another month until summer vacation. I'm going to have to look into the park camp for him."

An expense that would eat into her budget. Greg would pay for half of it, but she would have to cough up the rest.

"I'll get you my work schedule for the next two months this week," Greg told her. "Once I have it, let's sit down and plan out the summer as best we can. I can be responsible for him on my days off. If he's in camp, I can take him and pick him up so it's one less thing for you to deal with."

She told herself not to be surprised. While Greg hadn't been that great a husband, he'd always cared about Josh. Although he wasn't into the details, no one could doubt his love for his son.

"It would be nice if he could spend more time with you," she said cautiously.

"Then it's a plan."

She nodded.

He flashed her a smile. "I'm going to get the pizza. You didn't say if you wanted your usual."

"Yes, please."

"Then we'll be right back."

Josh returned from taking his things to his room. "Can I have soda, Mom?" he asked.

"No."

He laughed. "One day you're going to say yes."

"One day you're not going to ask."

"Never gonna happen."

"I did make cookies."

He gave her a quick hug. "You're the best."

"Put that in writing."

"I could paint it on the garage door."

"That would be nice."

Greg held open the front door. "You say that now, but if he really did it, you'd be pissed."

"Don't get any ideas," she told him. Because helping Josh paint phrases on the garage door was exactly something Greg would do. He would think it was funny.

Rachel set the table. She got a beer for Greg, a glass of wine for herself and juice for Josh. In the distance, the washer chugged away. She checked the Crock-Pot, then went to change the sheets on Josh's bed.

Her son's room was big and bright, with a large window and an oversize closet. Sports equipment was strewn everywhere, along with clothes and sports magazines. About once a quarter she got on him to clean up the space, but most of the time she simply let him be or picked up herself.

Now she put away the clothes he'd taken to his dad's, putting still-clean shirts on hangers and throwing the dirty clothes into the hamper in his closet. She pulled back the comforter and blanket before tugging off the sheets.

She retreated to the hallway linen closet to collect clean bedding. The smooth cotton fabric was a solid color now. Gone were the cars and trucks Josh had once loved. He was growing up so fast.

She remembered when he'd been born—so small and helpless. She and Greg had been overwhelmed. They were the first of their friends to get married, get pregnant and have a baby. Lena had followed six months later and by then Rachel had considered herself an expert. But those first few weeks had been terrifying.

It wasn't supposed to have happened that way, she thought as she pulled the fitted sheet over the corners of the mattress. She and Greg had wanted to travel for the first five years of their marriage, *then* start a family. But she'd forgotten her birth control pills at home on their honeymoon and he hadn't wanted to wear a condom. One thing had led to another.

It had always been that way with them. Too much, too fast. Back in high school, he'd been the most popular guy around. Two years older, he'd been a senior while she'd been a lowly sophomore. She hadn't realized he'd known her name until he stopped her in the hall outside her English class. He'd smiled at her and asked her out. Just like that. In front of God and everyone.

She'd said yes because he was Greg, and even then she'd been unable to resist him. As she smoothed the top sheet into place, she recalled how nervous she'd been. About everything. She'd never been on a date before. She hadn't even been sure her mother would let her go. But Maggie had had a meeting with one of her accounting clients and hadn't made it home until late. By then, Rachel was out with Greg and nothing would ever be the same again.

She finished making the bed and carried the dirty sheets to the laundry room. By the time she'd transferred the clean clothes to the dryer and put in a second load, Greg and Josh were back.

"The Dodgers are tied," her son informed her when she walked into the kitchen. His tone was pleading. "It's a really important game."

Which should have impressed her. Only, in Josh's opinion, they were all important.

"Are you saying you'd rather watch TV than eat dinner with your parents?" she asked, pretending to be shocked at the notion.

"Please, Mom."

How much longer would he ask rather than simply do? How many more years until the hormones kicked in and she became nothing but an irritation in his life?

When it was just the two of them, she generally agreed. Often she joined him in the living room to watch whatever game was on TV. But if she said yes tonight, she would be dining alone with Greg. Did either of them want that?

She risked a glance at her ex. Greg shrugged. "He loves the Dodgers. It's fine with me."

Josh whooped, as if all was now decided, then hurried into the living room to set up a TV tray. Seconds later the sounds of the baseball game were audible. He returned to the kitchen, put two giant slices on a plate, grabbed his glass of juice and disappeared again.

"We'll miss you," Greg called after him.

A mumbled response came in reply.

"Kids," he said with a grin as he took the seat across from hers. "What are you gonna do?"

He held open the smaller of the two boxes of pizza. She saw the veggie with extra cheese she liked but rarely got. Because when it was just her and Josh, it didn't make sense to pay for an extra pizza or toppings.

"Thank you," she murmured as she took a slice.

He set a couple of the all-meat slices on his plate.

"What did you two—"

"How was your—"

They spoke at the same time. Rachel looked away, then back at him. "What did you and Josh do this weekend?"

"We spent a lot of yesterday shopping for his glove. We went to three different stores before finding the right one."

Which meant they'd gone way out of Los Lobos. Something that would make her crazy—mostly because of the time. But Greg wouldn't mind. He'd always been more adventurous than her. There was a reason he'd chosen a job that put his life on the line.

As he talked about the different gloves they'd looked at, she remembered what he'd been like that first night they'd gone out. She'd been beyond scared. Barely sixteen and she'd been kissed only one other time.

After dinner, they'd gone to the park. The night had been warm—too warm. The unseasonable temperature had meant lying in the grass was comfortable. They'd found a secluded spot and settled down. He'd kissed her. She still recalled how magical his mouth had felt on hers. He hadn't pushed her, hadn't taken too much, and they'd kissed for what felt like hours. Then he'd touched her breasts.

No one had ever done that, and she'd been unprepared for the tingles that had swept through her. Her head had warned her to stop him, but her heart had whispered that this was

Greg, and anything he wanted to do had to be right. Her body had loved the heat and excitement his touch had generated. She hadn't known she could feel such things. One thing had led to another, and before she'd realized what was happening, she was naked and he was inside her.

The feeling of being swept away had ended the second he'd taken her virginity. Pain was a quick road to reality. She'd thought about telling him to stop, but it was really too late. So she'd waited the three or four seconds until he'd finished, then had gotten dressed.

Neither of them had spoken on the drive home. She'd jumped out of his car and raced inside—not sure what to think. She'd done something wrong, she knew that much. A slut. If her mother ever found out...

The next morning Rachel had thought about faking being sick. Only, she didn't want anyone asking about her. Speculation was death. Better to simply pretend to be fine and get through the day.

She'd been shocked to find Greg waiting for her as she left the house. He'd told her they had to talk. Reluctantly, she'd gotten into his car, even though she had no idea what they were going to say. They'd done *it*. Now they had to deal with having done *it*. What was there to say?

Apparently, a lot.

"Are you okay?"

Not the question she'd expected. She'd nodded.

"I'm sorry," he told her earnestly, his dark gaze locked on her face. "Not that we had sex, but because it happened so fast. It should have been after we'd been going out for like six months, and been a lot more romantic." His concern turned sheepish. "I kept waiting for you to tell me no, and when you didn't—" He shrugged. "I couldn't believe you were going to let me do that."

"Why wouldn't I? You're you. Everybody loves you."

"Do you?"

Love him? Did she? "I don't really know you. I know of you, but that's different."

"So you're saying you used me for sex."

After that time in the park, she would have sworn she would never laugh again, never smile, never feel good about herself. But right then, she couldn't stop her lips from curving up.

"I wish I was brave enough to do that," she admitted. "But I'm not."

"You're the most confusing girl I've ever known. And the prettiest. Can I drive you to school?"

She'd said yes and that had been the beginning of their relationship. They'd dated exclusively until she'd graduated from high school and then they'd gotten married.

"What are you thinking?" he asked, drawing her back to the present. "And don't say nothing. It's obvious you didn't find my glove descriptions riveting."

"Sorry. I was just going over what I have to get done this week." A flat-out lie, but there was no way she was going to admit to reminiscing. While their marriage had been her whole world, Greg hadn't felt the same way. He'd cheated on her.

"Josh's game's Wednesday afternoon, right?" he asked. "I want to make sure I'm there."

"Yes. It's at four." She picked up her pizza slice and took another bite.

"I know you're one of the team moms. Anything I can do to help with that?"

As a team mom, she was expected to collect money from the other parents to pay for drinks and snacks. She was also in charge of making sure the equipment was collected at the end of the game. If any was left behind, she brought it home with her until the next practice. There were usually two team moms. Heather was the other one, but she was turning out to be a flake.

"I'm good," she told him.

"You sure? Josh mentioned that Heather hadn't remembered to bring snacks last time. I could take care of that."

"I'm handling it. Besides, you have to miss some of his games for work."

"Yeah, but I could help when I'm not working. You wouldn't have to do it all yourself."

"I don't mind."

"At least that way you know it will be done right?" he asked. The tone was light, but there was something in his words.

"What do you mean?"

"You don't trust easily."

She put down her pizza and glanced toward the living room. When she returned her attention to Greg, she made sure her voice was low.

"If you're asking if I trust you, I would say it depends. You're a good father and I appreciate that. Josh needs his dad in his life. As for the rest of it, we're divorced, Greg. What does it matter what I think of you?"

He pushed his plate away. "You're never going to get over what happened, are you? It doesn't matter how many times I tell you I'm sorry. That I want to make things right. You don't care. I screwed up and you can never forgive me."

Her stomach started to hurt. "You don't care about my forgiveness. You just don't like being the bad guy. It cuts into your self-image. Get over it. Like I said, you're a good father. I never say anything bad about you to Josh. We work well with him. That's more than most divorced couples have."

"Don't you ever wish we could be friends again? There

were rough times while we were married, Rachel, but there was a lot of good, too."

There had been, she thought to herself. Lots of laughter and love. At least at first. But then things had changed. She'd grown up and he hadn't. While she'd taken care of their child and their house, Greg had gone out with his friends. He might have cheated only after ten years of marriage, but he'd let her down a long time before that.

"I like things how they are now," she told him. "Separate. You have your life and I have mine."

For a second she thought he was going to protest. To say he wanted something else. Something more.

Her chest tightened and her heart pounded. Hope, anticipation and fear blended into a churning mess that didn't sit well with her pizza. Because no matter what face she showed to the rest of the world, she knew the truth. That despite what she said and how she acted, she'd never gotten over Greg. It wasn't that she couldn't forgive him, it was that she couldn't forget him. He'd obviously moved on and she was stuck still in love with him.

"That's what I thought," he told her, his voice resigned. "What's done is done and there's no going back."

The hope shriveled and died, much like her heart had done that day two years ago when she'd taken one look into his eyes and had known the truth.

"I should be going," he told her. "Have a good week."

"You, too."

He called out a goodbye to Josh, then let himself out the back door. Rachel wrapped up the rest of her small pizza. She couldn't eat any more tonight. And while Josh would protest the lack of meat, he would still snack on it tomorrow when he got home from school.

Later, after her son was in bed, Rachel sat alone in the living room. The house was quiet, the only sounds coming from outside when a car drove by. She told herself that everything was fine, that she was doing okay, but she knew she was lying about all of it.

Quinn stared at the house. It was three stories and about forty-two hundred square feet. Big windows, a nice yard, on a quiet street.

"Never gonna work," Wayne announced.

"You haven't seen the inside," Quinn pointed out. "What if it's perfect?"

Wayne—a sixtysomething former marine—sighed the sigh of those cursed with too much intelligence who were forced to deal with ordinary mortals.

"I'll explain it to you Barney-style," he said, speaking slowly.

Quinn held in a grin. Explaining something Barney-style meant speaking slowly and simply, as if to a child. Wayne was nothing if not colorful.

The older man had been with him about seven years. Before that he'd been a dispatcher for a trucking company and before that a marine. They'd met under unusual circumstances. When Wayne's son had died, he'd tried to drink himself to death. Quinn had been the one to take him in and sober him up. Then he'd offered him a job as his assistant. He'd been shocked as hell when Wayne had accepted.

"You Barney-style all you want," he said. It was Monday morning. He hadn't slept well the night before, and he needed more coffee. Having Wayne walk him through the details just might be entertaining enough to make him forget his lack of caffeine.

"It's not a verb," Wayne grumbled. "You're getting the phrase all wrong. Damned civilians."

Quinn held out his hand. Zealand groaned, then handed over five bucks. Because whoever got Wayne to complain about the world not being "marine enough" first won five dollars.

Quinn pocketed it, then nodded at Wayne. "Tell me why this isn't a good idea."

Wayne swore under his breath. "There's not enough parking," his assistant began. "We could pave over the grass, but you know the neighbors are going to complain. All those windows—" He pointed to the front of the house. "Every one of those is a place for noise to get in from the street and out from the studio."

"I produce music, not noise," Quinn protested.

"That's what you call it. The folks who live in the neighborhood won't agree. What are you going to do? Cover the windows and put up soundproofing?"

Quinn looked at Zealand, who shrugged.

"Then why have windows?" Wayne asked. "You're running a business that goes late into the night. You can't have bands coming and going at two in the morning. This is a small town, boss. They have their ways."

"What do you know about small towns?" Quinn asked.

"Enough."

"I take it you're not a fan."

"Not really. But you said you wanted to move here, so here I am."

"Poor Wayne."

"Yeah, I'm suffering."

Zealand chuckled.

Quinn thought about what his assistant had said. "You're right. A house doesn't make sense. Why don't the two of you go check out some industrial spaces? But they have to be relatively quiet. We can't be next to some factory that bangs all day and night."

"Right. Because only the bands can do that."

Quinn looked at him. "Which kind of banging do you mean?"

Wayne frowned. "Both, I guess."

"You've learned our ways well, young Obi-Wan."

Wayne sighed again. "You're really moving here."

"I am. You'll learn to love it. There's a boardwalk and a pier. It's over a hundred years old."

"Piers do not get better with time."

"Lots of families with kids. Teenagers during spring break. What could be more perfect?"

Wayne started for the car. "Are you talking? Because all I hear is a buzzing sound."

"Speaking of buzzing, there's a very famous honeybee that summers here sometimes."

"You say one more word about the bees and I'm going back to LA. I mean it. I'll quit."

Zealand chuckled as he slid into the backseat.

Quinn started the engine of the Bentley. "The Drunken Red-nosed Honeybee is known to be industrious and gentle."

Wayne rested his head in his hands. "Kill. Me. Now. That's all I ask."

"Sorry, my friend. You're the only one with that kind of training. You're going to have to suck it up and suffer. Like you always do."

Wayne straightened. "Tell me about it. My life is pain."

6

SIENNA HANDED OVER a wrench to the man stretched out under her kitchen sink. "You could just call a plumber."

"I know how to replace a garbage disposal."

"So you say. But if it explodes, it will take me with it."

"That would be a loss for all of us."

Jimmy, her landlord, friend since grade school and ex-fiancé, turned so he could see her. "I mean that. The loss part."

"You'd better. I don't want to be sliced into little pieces by an exploding garbage disposal."

"No one does."

She sat cross-legged on the kitchen floor of her rented duplex. The small, two-bedroom place suited her. It was clean, pretty, and had a yard. Jimmy was the best kind of landlord— he mowed the lawn, did repairs quickly and had the carpets cleaned at least twice a year. In return, she paid her rent on time and did her best to be a good tenant.

Theirs was a relationship that worked.

"How's business?" she asked.

"Good. I have a couple new listings. Three houses closing this month."

"Who would have thought?"

Jimmy chuckled. "That I would turn out respectable? Stranger things have happened."

"I'm not so sure."

Back in high school, Jimmy had been more interested in surfing than studies. He'd drifted through school. Still, he'd been funny and kind, with a sexy attitude that had captured her schoolgirl heart. They'd dated all through senior year. When she'd left to go to UC Santa Barbara, he'd followed. While she'd attended classes, he'd surfed and worked odd jobs. Sometime during her freshman year, they'd gotten engaged. That had lasted nearly a year. Their breakup hadn't been dramatic, just the realization that they were too young and they wanted different things. He'd gone home and she'd stayed in college. But they'd remained friends. She liked knowing that Jimmy was in her life.

She glanced at the clock on the wall. It was nearly five thirty. She still had time.

"Hot date?" Jimmy asked.

"A date."

"Ouch. Does he know about your lack of enthusiasm?"

"I'm enthused."

"Not really. It's that David guy, right?"

"Uh-huh."

"I take it he's not *the one.*"

"No. He's very nice and we have fun."

"But?"

She wrinkled her nose. "I don't know. We have a lot in common. He's smart, well-educated. We vote the same."

Jimmy snorted. "You vote the same? Seriously? That's your criteria now?"

"Of course not. It's just…"

Jimmy slid out from under the sink. "Stand back. I'm about to test this thing." He pointed to the far side of the kitchen.

"Go stand there. I'll put my body between you and the explosion."

"Talk about a gentleman," she teased. "There are so few of you left these days."

"Most of us have died in garbage disposal accidents."

She scrambled to her feet and walked to the other end of the kitchen. Jimmy turned on the water and flipped the switch. The steady hum of the garbage disposal filled the room.

"Impressive," she told him when he turned it off. "Very impressive."

"I've got game, I'll admit it." He washed his hands, then dried them with a towel. "So why do you see him? It's not like you need a boyfriend."

Ugh. They were back to David. She leaned against the counter. "I don't know. I like him, I guess."

He raised his dark eyebrows. "You guess?"

"He's very solid and stable. That's nice."

"Unlike your surfing ex-fiancé?"

"You're plenty stable now."

"I'm practically staid."

She took in the dark, shaggy hair, the three days' worth of beard, the earrings and the tattoos on his arm. "Jimmy, people will call you many things, but staid isn't one of them."

"You say the sweetest things. So what's up with David? Why don't you dump him?"

"I don't know. Maybe I should." She frowned. "It's so strange. I love my job. Seriously—it's the best. And I like living in Los Lobos. I have a really good life."

"But?"

"But there's something I can't put my finger on." A restlessness, she thought. The sense of missing something important.

"Are you upset about your mom?" he asked. "About her getting married?"

"God no. She's been a widow twenty-four years. If anyone deserves to move on, it's her. Neil's a great guy. We all like him."

"Just checking. Weddings do funny things to people."

"I promise, there will be no drama with my mother's wedding. She's a mature, responsible woman marrying a great guy."

"I got an invitation to the engagement party."

The thought of Jimmy being there made her smile. "Good. Are you going?"

"I thought it would be fun. You and David will be there, right?"

"We will." She found herself wanting to ask if he was bringing a date but then realized she didn't want to know. Which wasn't fair. Of course she wanted Jimmy to be happy. He was a great guy.

"Why aren't you engaged or married?" she asked.

He pressed a hand to his chest. "You spoiled me for other women."

That made her laugh. "Right. You were so broken after our engagement ended that you took up with the one person I dislike more than anyone."

"You are referring to the fair Erika?"

"You know I am."

"But she's lovely."

"She's mean, and if I recall correctly, she dumped you."

Jimmy's expression of amusement never wavered. "That she did. I suspect she was only trying to prove she could get me, not that she could keep me."

"If I had an ego, I would say she went after you because I stole you from her in the first place."

"You do have an ego and it's well deserved. And you did

steal me." He glanced at the clock. "You have a date and I have to clean up my mess here."

"What?" She followed his gaze. "You're right. Thanks for reminding me."

She walked down the tiny hall to the master bedroom. It wasn't big, but her queen-size bed fit fine, along with the dresser she'd had since she was twelve when her mom bought all three girls new furniture. The piece wasn't anything she would have chosen now—it was too ornate, with carving on the corners and drawer pulls in the shape of birds. But somehow it connected her to her past.

She walked into the en suite bathroom and used a headband to hold back her short hair. After washing her face, she applied moisturizer and sunscreen, then put on makeup.

David was taking her out for Mexican food, which meant casual rather than fancy. She slipped on a white tank top and short denim skirt, then chose black suede peep-toe wedges with a little fringe at the ankle. Drop earrings and several bangles completed the outfit. She fluffed her short hair back into the spiky style she wore, then grabbed a cropped black faux leather jacket for later—when it got cool—before returning to her kitchen.

Jimmy had mopped up from his work and put everything back under the sink. He looked up from loading his toolbox and whistled. "You clean up good. I prefer you messy, but clean works."

She laughed. "Thank you. You're very kind."

"Nope. Just observant. David doesn't stand a chance. But none of us ever did."

Sweet words. Not true, but sweet.

Her second engagement had been to a guy named Hugh. They'd met her senior year of college. He'd been from a prominent banking family in Chicago and had been in Santa Barbara for his post–graduate school first job. Apparently, he was required to work his way up in another bank before joining the family empire.

Hugh had been charming, successful and easy to be with. They'd fallen in love almost immediately. She'd met his family over winter break at a ski resort in Vail, then had brought him home over spring break. He'd proposed at sunset on the beach.

After graduation she'd taken a job at a nonprofit in Santa Barbara and had started organizing their wedding. The plan had been to stay there for three or four years before moving to Chicago when he entered the family business.

Everything had changed when his father had had a heart attack and Hugh had gone back to take care of the company. She'd quit her job and joined him a few weeks later.

What she told everyone was that once she got to Chicago, she'd realized they weren't as in love as she'd thought. That she didn't like the city or being so close to his family. But the truth was different.

The truth was that his family hadn't liked *her*. Apparently, they never had, especially his mother. She hadn't fit in with their friends or their lifestyle. She wasn't classy enough. All of which Hugh had explained within a week of her arrival. He hadn't ended things, exactly. Instead, he'd asked for more time. And for her to change.

"You're beautiful," he'd told her, his voice and expression equally sincere. "That helps. But you simply don't have the right background. With some coaching and time, you could really be the right package. I can't make any promises, Sienna, but I want us to try to make this work."

Not exactly the words a fiancée longs to hear. Assuming she was still his fiancée. Which he'd clarified with a slight shrug and "Oh, and Mom thinks you should return the ring until we're sure."

She'd handed him the two-carat diamond ring he'd placed on her finger only three months before and had walked out. When she'd flown back to Los Lobos, she'd told everyone that Chicago and Hugh weren't for her. She'd never once admitted the truth. That she hadn't been good enough. At least not on the inside. While her outsides had passed muster, the rest of her had been lacking.

She shook her head to chase away the memories. Right then, the doorbell rang.

"Your handsome prince," Jimmy said with a grin.

"Be nice," she told him. "I mean it."

"Will you spank me if I'm not?"

"Stop it!"

She opened the door. "Hi," she said brightly.

David stepped inside, then bent down to kiss her. In the nanosecond before his mouth touched hers, she heard a loud "Hey, David. How's it hanging?"

David straightened. "Jimmy. What are you doing here?"

Jimmy held up his toolbox. "Changing out the garbage disposal. I'm handy that way. You two run along. I'll lock up."

She shook her head. "You're done. Get out of here."

Jimmy walked to the door and squeezed past her and David. "You're welcome."

David carefully closed the door behind him. "A new garbage disposal?"

"Yes. Want to check it out?" She drew in a breath. "Or are you asking if there was something else going on? David, I've known Jimmy my whole life. We're friends and he's my landlord. I have a lot of flaws, but being unfaithful isn't one of them. If you can't trust me, this isn't going to work between us."

For a second she found herself wishing he would push back. Would make a fuss. Because then...well, she wasn't sure what.

She would break up with him? Did she want that? She honestly wasn't sure.

He put his hands on her waist and drew her close. "You're right. I'm sorry. There's something about Jimmy that gets to me, but that's my problem, not yours. Of course I trust you. Sometimes I can't believe my luck, but I trust you."

"Thank you."

He kissed her. A soft, sweet kiss that should have stirred her heart, but didn't. What was wrong with her?

"Ready for dinner?" she asked, drawing back just enough that he couldn't kiss her again.

"I am." He took her hand in his and smiled at her. "Come on. There's a margarita with your name on it just a few short blocks away."

"I can't wait."

A margarita sounded good. And an evening with David, well, that would be fun, too. He was a great guy. She needed to remember that. David would never tell her she wasn't good enough. He thought she was a prize. Compared to the alternative, being a prize sounded really good to her.

Rachel spent the Wednesday afternoon baseball game fuming. Heather not only hadn't shown up, but she hadn't even bothered to call. Which meant Rachel arrived with snacks but no drinks. She'd been forced to run to the store and buy water and juice packs for twenty boys. When she'd returned, there hadn't been any close parking, so she'd had to lug everything nearly two blocks, which had taken her two trips. By the time she was set up, the game had already started and her lower back was throbbing.

Ice, she promised herself. She would spend the whole evening icing her screaming muscles. She knew the price of ignoring the spasms. If she didn't take care of the problem early, it would get worse, and she couldn't afford to miss any work.

She sat down by the team bench and handed out drinks as the boys requested them. When Ryan Owens scraped up his arm sliding into home plate, she was the one who brought out the first-aid kit and cleaned his wound.

"Did you see?" the twelve-year-old asked excitedly. "I got a run."

"You did. It was fantastic." She used first-aid wipes on the scrape, then applied a nonstinging disinfectant and a couple of bandages.

"This will hold you until the game is over," she told him. "Have your mom look at it when you get home."

Ryan nodded and returned to the bench, where he was congratulated for his run. Rachel shifted on her seat, wishing the game would end so she could go lie on an ice pack. But there were several innings to go. She dug in her purse for some ibuprofen and took two pills, then waited and endured. She saw her friend Lena up in the stands and waved. Greg was there, too, but didn't seem to notice her.

Nearly two hours later, Josh's team had won. The boys cheered, then lined up to shake hands, like they'd been taught. Lena walked over.

"We're taking Kyle out for a celebration pizza. You and Josh want to come?"

"My back's acting up. I'm going to pass."

Lena's mouth twisted. "I'm sorry. Why don't we take Josh with us and bring him back afterward? That will give you some time to just relax."

"Would you? Thanks. That would be great."

"Need any help with the drinks or equipment?"

"I'm good."

Her friend waved and returned to the boys. Fifteen minutes later nearly everyone had left the field. Rachel had three bags of trash, leftover snacks and water, along with five bats, three mitts and all the bases. Because Heather hadn't shown up, and whichever parent was supposed to be responsible for the equipment had forgotten.

Greg came up to her. "No Heather?"

"No. She didn't call or anything. I had to go get the drinks she was supposed to bring." She stood up and did her best not to groan as pain shot through her back. "I'm going to always bring extra in the car from now on, just in case."

Greg frowned. "You're hurting. Your back?"

"I'm fine."

He ignored that. "Where's your car? I don't see it in the lot."

"I had to go shopping for the drinks," she snapped. "When I got back, there weren't any spots."

He held out his hand. "Give me your car keys. I'll get it and move it closer for you, then help you carry everything. You need to get home and on ice."

She wasn't sure why, but his offer annoyed her. Or maybe it was that he knew what was wrong. Or the whole situation with Heather.

"I said I'm fine."

"You're not. Let me help, Rachel."

"I can do it myself. I should just leave the equipment out here. Someone will steal it, but maybe the parent responsible will learn a lesson. Only, they won't and I'll be the bad guy for letting it happen. I have to do everything."

"Do you know who the parent is?"

"There's a list. I have it at home."

"Are you going to call them?"

"What? No. That's not my job."

"And you're not going to say anything to Heather, are you?"

"What's the point? She doesn't take this seriously. She

knows I'll pick up the slack and she takes advantage of me. I'm not even surprised."

Greg stared at her. "You're not going to give me your car keys, are you?"

"I told you, I'm fine."

"Yeah, that's what I thought."

He shocked her by picking up her handbag and digging through it until he found her keys.

"Hey! You can't do that."

"I just did."

He walked toward the street. She watched him for a second, then walked slowly to collect the bases.

Every step was agony. Pain shot down her right leg, and she was terrified that the muscles were about to seize up. She had muscle relaxers at home, along with the healing ice. But first there was this mess to clean up.

By the time Greg got back, she'd stacked the bases and collected the forgotten equipment. He shook his head.

"You couldn't wait, could you? What the hell, Rachel? Why do you always have to be the martyr? It's like you're the only one who gets to be right and everyone else has to be—"

He stopped talking.

"I don't think everyone is wrong," she told him. "But sometimes they are. Like Heather is today."

"Yet you won't confront her. You'll simply stew about it. You'll be snippy with her the next time you see her and she won't know why. She'll think you're a total bitch, but you get to have righteous indignation on your side. Then at some parent meeting someone will mention the team mother thing and you'll get to be the one who always showed up."

She didn't like the sound of that. "You're saying I'm wrong to be here on time, doing her job and mine?"

"No. I'm saying you're wrong for not calling Heather and telling her to get her butt down to the game."

"That's not my style."

"You're right. It's not." He turned and walked a couple of steps, then faced her again. "It's never been your style. You are the queen of passive-aggressive."

"What?"

He put his hands on his hips. "I always knew it, but I didn't get what it meant. I never realized how it affected everything."

She sank onto the bench and stared at him. "You're acting crazy."

"I'm not. I'm right, aren't I?" He moved closer, then sat a few feet away and faced her. "I've been thinking about this for a while. Us and what went wrong."

"You cheated."

"Yeah, but it's more than that. You've been mad at me for years. Because of how I acted. Because you had to be the grown-up in the relationship. I loved you, Rach, but I wasn't ready to be a husband or a father. But there I was—playing at both."

"Leaving me with all the work," she grumbled.

"You're right. I did leave you with everything. You couldn't depend on me to support you the way you needed. And you sure wouldn't ask for help. That's the part that gets me. Why didn't you ask?"

He paused, as if waiting for an answer. Not that she had one. She'd liked the conversation much better when they'd been talking about his flaws rather than hers.

"Do you think it's about your dad dying?"

"What?" she yelped. "Leave my father out of this."

"I know it was hard for you when that happened. You missed him, and your mom depended on you to take care of things. There was so much responsibility for you. So much more than you were equipped to handle. But you couldn't ask for help."

How had he figured this out? She searched for an escape, but there was only her car and he still had her keys. It wasn't as if she could simply limp away.

"I don't want to talk about this," she told him.

"You had to do everything," he continued, as if she hadn't spoken. "There's a part of me that thinks you really *like* doing everything. I'm not sure if it's a control thing or being the one who's right or something else. But like today. You could have asked a dozen people to go get the drinks, but you didn't. You had to do it all yourself, even with your back hurting."

Tears threatened, but she blinked them away. She wouldn't give him the satisfaction of seeing her cry. Humiliation burned, but so did determination. And the latter was going to win.

"Or with us," he continued. "You should have reamed me a new one, but you didn't. You simply endured my bad behavior. I played and you were the faithful, long-suffering wife. You got to be right, though, and you enjoyed that."

"You're wrong," she whispered, wrapping her arms around her midsection. "About everything."

"I'm not. It's taken me nearly two years to put together the pieces, but I think I have them now. I was wrong to cheat on you, Rachel. I knew the second I did it, I would regret it for the rest of my life. And I do. I was wrong and I'm sorry. I broke your trust and you were right to throw me out. I needed that and you deserved your pound of flesh. But you were wrong about a lot of other things."

He leaned toward her. "Here's where it gets fuzzy for me. The asking for help thing. Is it that you really need to do it all yourself, or do you think you're the only one who can do it right? Because I think that's the key. Getting the answer to that question."

"Why are you doing this? Why are you treating me this way?"

"Not to hurt you. I hope you can believe that. The thing is, I don't think we're finished. I'm not sure what that means, exactly, but I haven't moved on, and I don't think you have, either. We're both in limbo. I keep thinking that if I can finally understand you, I'll know what to do."

He stood and smiled. "Thanks for talking to me. This was really good. I understand a lot more now."

How nice for him. He'd laid her bare, talked about how awful she was, and now he felt better? Lucky him. She felt sick to her stomach. She wanted to crawl into a hole until the entire world went away.

"I'm not going to ask if you need help," he told her. "I know you'll say no. I'm just going to do it. You sit here while I load the car. Then I'm going to follow you home and unload it. You just worry about yourself. I'll take care of everything else."

She felt as if he'd slapped her. Of all the awful, mean, cruel things to say—that was the worst. Because he wanted her to believe in him. To trust him. To hand over control and let him run things.

She'd tried that before. With him, with her mother, even with her friends. And she knew how it ended. With the other person letting her down and her all alone. It had always been that way and it always would be.

He looked at her, then shook his head. "I can see you don't believe me. It's okay, Rachel. Now that I know what's wrong, I can fix it. Maybe that makes me a fool, but I've got to try. You'll see. Everything is going to be fine."

Famous last words, she thought grimly. A little bit like "I'll love you forever." She'd fallen for that one, too. And look where it had gotten her.

7

COURTNEY WHEELED HER cart down the path to the final room on her list. Unless a guest requested a special time for housekeeping, she had the option of cleaning the rooms in any order she liked. At the risk of being just a little weird, she'd saved Quinn's bungalow for last.

It was nearly one in the afternoon. She was tired, but happy. She'd stayed up until three to finish her marketing report and had sent everything to her professor. She had one more paper to write, then she was done for the summer.

The thought of not studying for nearly twelve weeks was strange. She'd been going year-round since she'd started at community college. With all her general education requirements filled, she only had classes in her major left. And the last few she had to take weren't offered in the summer.

Not that she was going to be overwhelmed by free time. Her mother was getting married at the hotel in August. August 20, to be exact. Joyce had already made it clear she was putting Courtney in charge of the wedding. On the one hand, Courtney appreciated the fact that her boss had faith in her. Plus, handling an event that large would look good on her résumé. On the other, she suspected Joyce had an ulterior motive—to bring mother and daughter back together. Not that they were actually *apart*. They were more, um, casually involved in each other's lives.

She supposed that had always been the case. After her father died, her mother had been frantic to hold her family together and restart her husband's accounting business. Then the bills had piled up and they'd lost their house. Maggie had been scrambling.

Courtney got that. She respected all her mother had done. As an adult, she could look back and see how hard things had been. But as the youngest kid in the family, the one who was frequently overlooked and ignored, she couldn't help still being resentful.

For those reasons, and maybe some others, she and her mother had never been close. She could live with that. But, according to Joyce, she should make more of an effort. Something that wasn't going to happen in the middle of her shift.

She stopped her cart in front of the door to the bungalow and knocked. "Housekeeping," she called loudly.

She hadn't checked the parking lot to see if Quinn's car was there. Not that she usually kept track of guests' vehicles. Except in his case, it was pretty easy to tell. There was only one Bentley parked there.

She was about to knock again when the door opened. Quinn stood in front of her, all tall and sexy in jeans and a— she blinked—Taylor Swift T-shirt.

"I wouldn't have taken you for a Swifty," she admitted. "This changes things."

"I like the irony of the T-shirt."

"No one believes that." She rubbed her temples. "Oh, God. Now I can see you dancing to 'Shake It Off.' My eyes! My eyes!"

Quinn chuckled. The low, rumbly sound did odd things

to her stomach. She, um, shook it off and reminded herself she was here to work.

"Okay, time for me to clean your room. Move aside."

Quinn didn't budge from the doorway. One brow rose. "Do you talk to all your guests that way?"

"No, but you're different."

"I have no doubt of that."

"I meant like family. Joyce and I go way back and you're her grandson. So that makes you…" She wasn't sure what.

"An uncle?" he asked drily.

"No. That seems a little creepy. We could be cousins."

"I don't think so."

"Whatever our relationship, I need to clean your room."

"I'm good."

A voice in her head unexpectedly whispered that she was sure that was true. No doubt Quinn was very good. All that experience, not to mention rhythmic ability.

"It's my job to clean the rooms. It's what I do here." She smiled brightly. "You don't want to keep me from my work, do you?"

He studied her. "Not your destiny?"

"No way. I have a plan."

"The college degree."

"Exactly. But to pay for that, I must work."

"Why a maid?" he asked.

"As opposed to a train engineer—assuming I had the appropriate skill set?"

"Something like that."

She thought for a second. "I like working for Joyce. The work is physically tiring, but I don't have to interact with a lot of people, so I'm free to think about stuff." She tapped the phone in her shirt pocket. "Or listen to lectures I've downloaded from the internet. The money is fair, sometimes people tip and it gets me closer to my master plan. Oh." She smiled. "It also makes my mother crazy. Not the most mature reason, but one of them nonetheless."

"You're honest."

"I don't have a great memory, so being honest helps me keep my life straight."

His gaze settled on her face. "No great moral compass you live by?"

"Sure, but everybody says that and no one believes it."

One corner of his mouth twitched. "You're unexpected."

Was that the same as being sexy? Probably not, but a girl could dream. Quinn was a really interesting man. He drove a Bentley and wore Taylor Swift T-shirts. He'd been in tabloids, but he adored Joyce's two dogs. Not that people who appeared in tabloids *didn't* like pets.

She drew in a breath. "Wow—you're really good. I'm totally confused and it's been five minutes. Are you going to let me clean your room or not?"

"Not."

"You don't want to think about that? You have a cleaning service back in LA. How is this different?"

"It just is."

Because I want you desperately. She smiled to herself. Right. Because that was exactly what Quinn was thinking.

"Inside joke?" he asked.

"Oh, yeah."

She heard a cart coming down the path and turned to see one of the room service guys pushing it toward the bungalow.

"Hey, Courtney."

"Hi, Dan." She looked at Quinn. "Lunch?"

"Uh-huh. Want to join me?"

Dan winked at her as she pulled her cleaning cart out of the way. She smiled back.

Quinn stepped outside to let him in. "On the dining room table," he said, then turned to Courtney. "I got sweet potato fries."

"How can I resist an offer like that?"

"You can't."

She positioned her cart to the left of the front door, then walked inside. The layout for all the bungalows was the same—a living room–dining room on one side, the bedroom-bathroom-closet on the other. There was a private patio with a couple of chairs and a small table. In Quinn's case, the patio faced the pond with the paddleboats.

Dan set down the lunch on the table, then left. Courtney crossed to the half bath by the door and washed her hands. By the time she returned, Quinn had cut the burger in half and split the fries. He stood by the minibar.

"What do you want to drink?"

"I'll take the glass of water, if that's okay," she told him.

"It is."

He removed a beer from the fridge. They sat across from each other.

For a second Courtney felt strange. A guest had never invited her to lunch before—not that Quinn was actually a guest. Which probably made it okay.

"Joyce said you live on the property."

"I do. I have a room on the fourth floor. It's one of those badly placed spaces with too much noise and a tree blocking the view, so I don't have to feel guilty when the hotel is full."

"Why would you feel guilty? The room is part of your pay."

"Oh, sure. Use logic. My mind doesn't work that way."

She took a bite of her burger. Quinn had ordered the California special with avocado, bacon and jalapeños. Delicious.

"I used to live here, too," he told her.

"With Joyce," she said when she'd chewed and swallowed.

"I remember hearing about that. What happened to your parents?" She reached for her water. "Am I allowed to ask that?"

"You can ask me anything you want."

She told herself not to read too much into that statement. "Okay, where are your parents?"

"I never knew my dad. My mom got pregnant young and he took off." One broad shoulder rose and lowered, while his expression remained neutral. "She wasn't into having a kid around and used to leave me here all the time. Joyce was great, but I didn't take well to being ignored by my mother, so I acted out. When I was fourteen, I got caught shoplifting. My mother told the judge she couldn't handle me and that I should be locked up. I spent a month in juvie. When I got out, she was gone. She'd taken off without telling anyone where she was going."

Courtney stared at him. "That's so awful. I'm sorry. You must have been devastated."

The shoulder rose again. "Some, but it wasn't a total surprise. She blamed me for pretty much everything that went wrong in her life. Joyce moved into the two-bedroom bungalow and dragged me along with her. It was tough for a while, but we made it work."

There was no emotion in his voice—it was as if he was talking about getting his car serviced. But she knew there had to be a lot of feelings. No one could go through what he had without feeling scarred.

"Joyce loves you. You had to know that, even as a kid."

"I did." He smiled. "She blames herself for my mom. She says she was too busy with the hotel to be there for her daughter."

Courtney reached for a fry. "My mom was too busy for us after my dad died. I guess a lot of parents have to wrestle with balancing work and family, especially if they're a single parent."

"But?"

"I didn't say but."

"It was there in the subtext. But she should have done a better job?"

Courtney leaned forward and rested her elbows on the table. "I know, I know. I should get over it. But jeez, I was held back twice in school and she barely noticed. Do you have any idea how hard that was? How the kids tormented me? And then I got very, very tall. That didn't help."

"I like that you're tall."

She felt herself smile. "Really?"

"Tall women are sexy."

Could she extrapolate from that? Probably not while dressed as a hotel maid, but maybe there was hope.

"Joyce always said that I was her redemption," he said. "I think of myself more as a do-over."

"No. Go with being her redemption. That's way cooler. Who gets to say that about themselves? Of course, there is a lot of responsibility that goes with it, but it would be worth it."

"You're an idealist."

"Mostly. You're a cynic."

"You can't know that."

"I can guess."

"Because I'm older and wiser?"

"And you've seen the world."

He laughed. "While you've been trapped here in Los Lobos. Life happens everywhere."

"Yes, but it's not exciting here."

"It's not exciting anywhere. Don't buy into the press reports. They're lying."

She felt as if there was a hidden meaning in his words, but she had no idea what it was.

"How old were you when your father died?" he asked.

Talk about an unexpected shift in conversation. "Three. I don't remember him at all. I don't remember much about that time. I'm sure it was horrible, but it's all blurry to me. I know it was tough for my mom. She worked as a secretary at my dad's office, but she wasn't an accountant like he was. When my dad died, a lot of people in the company quit and most of the clients left. There wasn't any life insurance and my mom lost the house."

"What happened?"

"Joyce took us in. Funny how she took you in, and then when you left for college, she took us in."

"I doubt the events are related."

"Probably not. Anyway, we lived in one of the bungalows. My mom studied accounting at night, hung on to the employees and clients she could and slowly built her way back. Over time, she became a CPA, bought a house, then a bigger house, put Sienna through college."

His gaze was steady. "You must be proud."

"I am." The words were automatic.

"But?"

"There's no but. I'm very proud of my mother. She went through something really horrible and came out the other side. Her three daughters are productive members of society."

"But?"

"I love my mom."

"No one is saying you don't."

He had a nice voice, she thought absently. Low and kind of seductive. Compelling. She found herself wanting to answer the unspoken question. Not because she felt the need to share, but because he was drawing it out of her.

"I'm still angry."

"For not noticing you got left behind?"

"That and other things. I had a learning disability. That's why I didn't do well in school. It wasn't diagnosed until I was ten. Nothing that dramatic, just a slightly different wiring in my brain. With the right tools, I started doing better. Plus, it was the kind of thing I would eventually outgrow."

She reached for another fry. "Once I could read and understand, I worked really hard to catch up with everyone else. I started doing well. I was transferred out of the remedial classes and into mainstream ones. I got As and Bs. My mom never noticed. I tried to tell her, but she never had time."

Courtney rolled her eyes. "I know, I know. I'm still the baby."

"Why would you say that? You went through something difficult. You feel how you feel. You're not wrong."

"Are you secretly a woman?"

He leaned his head back and laughed. "I work with artists. I've learned how to be sensitive. But thank you for affirming my masculinity."

"Anytime."

"How did you let your mother know you were angry?" he asked.

"What makes you think I did?"

"You wouldn't have suffered in silence. Not your style." He smiled. "I know because you're not afraid of me. A lot of people are."

"Maybe I hide my fear with humor."

"You hide a lot of things with humor, but not fear."

Yikes. This was not a topic she wanted to deal with. The *how did you let your mother know you were angry?* now seemed so much easier by comparison.

"I left high school when I was eighteen. Just walked out. There was nothing the state could do. She didn't like that."

"I remember. You had a promising career at Happy Burger and you threw it all away."

"I had the chance to do more, so I did. Not everyone has that chance."

"Point taken. What else?"

"I didn't speak to her for a year. Or my sister Sienna." She wrinkled her nose. "Not that Sienna and I have ever been close."

"Why not?"

"I don't know. Have you met her? She's so perfect. I mean physically beautiful. Which I guess I don't technically care about, but things come easily to her. She was good in school without really trying, and the guys were all over her. She's been engaged twice and broke it off both times. No one's ever wanted to marry me."

"Have you wanted to marry anyone?"

"No, but that's not the point. I want to be asked. I never was. Not to a school dance or anything."

"You've had boyfriends."

Not a question, but close enough that she felt compelled to answer. "I've had guys in my life. When I turned eighteen, I didn't just leave high school, I left home. I was on my own. I got involved with some real jerks. They were a little older and I thought they were so cool." She picked up the last fry. "I was wrong."

"You figured it out."

"After a while, yes."

"Some people never do."

"That's sad. Anyway, I didn't speak to my mom or Sienna. I stayed in touch with Rachel. She and I are close. Eventually, she talked me into meeting with Mom and we reconnected."

Sort of. They were a family, but they weren't all that involved in each other's lives. Or to be completely honest, she didn't let anyone know what was happening with hers.

"Oh," she said brightly, "I got a tattoo. The day I turned eighteen. It was supposed to be a symbol of my freedom."

"Is it?"

"No. It was silly. And because I was so young, it's on the small of my back." She held up a hand. "Don't judge."

"I would never." He leaned back in his chair. "What is it? The tattoo?"

"I am so not going to tell you." His steady gaze made her squirm. "Stop it."

"What?"

"Trying to influence me."

"I haven't said a word."

"You don't have to. I'm susceptible." Okay, that came out wrong. "I mean you're so much older and..." She sighed. "You know what I'm trying to say."

"I haven't a clue. Although it's clear you think I'm old. That's very flattering."

"Not old, old...just, you know, experienced."

"Are you calling me a man whore?"

"Do you deserve the title?"

He laughed. "Some days." He finished his beer. "Tell me about the other tattoo."

She felt her mouth drop open. She consciously closed it. No way he'd guessed. "What are you talking about?"

"If you got one as a symbol of your freedom and realized it was more about being trapped by a bad choice, you probably got another one when you figured out what to do with your life."

"You're good."

"Like I said. I work with a lot of artists. Some days it's an entire ocean of deep emotion. Very little surprises me."

Did that mean he knew she thought he was sexy? Probably, she decided. And if that was the case, his complete lack of response meant he wasn't interested. No surprise, but still disappointing.

"Between the shoulders?" he asked.

She sighed. "I hate being a cliché."

"Only if it's wings."

She glared at him. "That's not fair."

"Sorry," he said, not looking the least bit contrite. "For what it's worth, I'm sure they look good on you."

"Now you're just placating me." She narrowed her gaze. "If you're so smart, what's the one on the small of my back?"

"A butterfly or dragonfly."

"Not even close. So there!" She stood. "I win."

He chuckled. "Yes, you do." He rose and walked around the table until he was a few inches from her. He was only a couple of inches taller, so she barely had to raise her head to look into his eyes.

"You don't want to get involved with me," he told her quietly.

She told herself not to blush even though she was pretty sure it was too late.

"It's not going to go the way you think," he added.

"ED?" she asked, before she could stop herself.

Quinn stared at her for a second, then he started to laugh. The happy sound made her smile. Something warm and just a little smug filled her chest. She might be out of his league, but at least she'd survived the encounter. That had to count.

He touched her face. "There are flashes of power. The trick will be whether or not you can channel them into something that can be used. It's all there, inside of you. Have a little faith."

She wanted to tell him he didn't know what he was talking about. She wanted to ask him to explain what he meant. She wanted him to shut up and kiss her. In the end, she chose escape.

"Are you sure you don't need more towels?" she asked.

"Get out."

"I was just going. Thanks for lunch."

"Anytime."

8

"THREE COATS," RACHEL said firmly as she handed over the volumizing mascara. "There are going to be pictures. You'll want to look beautiful."

"As long as it doesn't look like spiders are resting on my eyelids." Her mother took the offered tube. "No scary old lady pictures for me."

"You'd have to be an old lady for that to happen."

Maggie Watson smiled. "You're very sweet, Rachel girl. I appreciate it."

The familiar endearment, one she hadn't heard in years, made Rachel smile.

She watched her mother lean toward the big mirror and begin to apply mascara. Maggie was in her midfifties. She worked out regularly, dressed well and looked at least ten years younger than she was. All of which made Rachel equally proud and depressed. The former because her mother was the poster woman for getting ahead on sheer determination. The latter because Maggie made it look easy and Rachel happened to know it wasn't.

While her mother dressed in upscale suits and dresses, her own wardrobe consisted of black pants and black shirts, all in manmade fabrics that washed easily. There were days when she wished she wasn't in the beauty industry, so she wouldn't always be expected to have perfect hair and makeup herself. Both were time consuming. But no one wanted to go to a stylist who looked frumpy. She was battling an extra twenty pounds and the constant fear that she was the "before" picture, while everyone around her was an "after."

Like now. Maggie looked amazing in a fitted sleeveless white shift dress with a pale pink lace overlay. Age appropriate, beautiful and sophisticated. Rachel had on black pants she used for work and a gauzy green shirt she'd owned, oh, six years.

Maggie straightened. "Enough?" she asked, waving the mascara.

Rachel studied her. "One more coat."

"I knew you were going to say that."

"Then you didn't have to ask, did you?"

Maggie smiled, then returned to the task.

Rachel had already done her mother's makeup. Now she would do her hair. Sienna and Courtney had gotten themselves ready earlier and were double-checking the party prep.

"We're going to need a schedule for the wedding," she said absently, thinking that one bride and two attendants was nothing. She'd done hair and makeup for much bigger wedding parties, sometimes starting at six in the morning for a midday wedding. "After we figure out how you want us made up and styled."

Her mother smiled. "That will be fun. Maybe all three of you could have Princess Leia hair?"

"Sienna will need extensions. Or hair pieces, if you mean the little ear buns."

"You're not going to shriek that I'm crazy and you're not wearing Princess Leia hair?"

"I know better than to argue with a bride."

"That's right. I'm going to be the bride and everyone has to do what I say. Enough?" She blinked dramatically.

Rachel looked at her. "You're perfect. Now have a seat and I'll do your hair."

They were in the bride's room on the ground floor of the Los Lobos Hotel. The space had once been a regular guest room, but years ago had been converted for the wedding business. Floor-to-ceiling mirrors covered an entire wall. Opposite was a ten-foot counter with plenty of electrical plugs and mirrors with good lighting. The closet had an extra high rail to keep long wedding gowns off the floor.

In the bathroom, the tub had been pulled out to make room for open shelves and a double sink along with a cabinet stocked with everything from bandages to hair spray to needles and thread. Spot-cleaning kits sat next to airplane-size bottles of vodka and bourbon. Joyce had thought of everything.

If you booked a wedding—or engagement party—at the hotel, access to the bride's room came with it. The space was great for pre-wedding prep and post-wedding clothing changes. She'd heard rumors that more than one bride and groom had chosen not to wait to consummate their marriage and that the bride's room had seen more than its share of action.

Rachel blew out her mother's layered hair. She worked quickly and easily, familiar with what had to be done. An unfortunate state of affairs, because it gave her time to think. Mostly about Greg.

She hadn't seen him since he'd attacked her on the baseball field. Well, not attacked, exactly. But he'd said some things and she still didn't know what to think. She knew that Maggie had invited him to her engagement party, which meant she was going to have to figure out what she was going to say soon enough. Or maybe not. Maybe he would just ignore her.

She drew in a breath. No, that wouldn't happen. Greg would be friendly. He always was. Even when they'd been getting a divorce, he hadn't been a jerk.

She smoothed her mother's bangs in place, then used a curling iron to fluff a few pieces. Then she got out her jumbo can of hair spray. When she finished, she put her hands on her mother's shoulders.

"You're so beautiful. Neil's a lucky guy."

Their eyes met in the mirror. Rachel could see the similarities. Hazel eyes. The same shaped mouth and chin. She would look more and more like her mother as she aged. Not a bad thing to have happen, she decided.

Their hair color was different. Rachel didn't bother coloring hers, so it was a dark blond. Maggie used an all-over color to hide the gray, along with highlights. Sienna had chosen to go platinum, while Courtney was more like Rachel. No color for her honey-blond hair.

Variations on a theme, Rachel thought. Maggie with the green-hazel eyes, Rachel's just plain hazel, while Sienna and Courtney had blue eyes. All blondes, all tall. They were the classic California family. Practically a cliché.

"Thank you," her mother said. "I can't believe this is happening."

"That I did such a good job with your hair?"

Maggie laughed. "That, of course." She sniffed. "The engagement. He really is wonderful to me. I never thought I'd fall in love again." She reached up and touched her daughter's hand. "I wish you would…"

Rachel stepped back. "Thanks, Mom. I'm fine."

"I want more for you than that. How are things with Greg?"

"You're not very subtle, are you?"

"I'm your mother. I don't have to be. I know he screwed up, but he was so sorry."

"Sorry doesn't change what he did."

Maggie pressed her lips together. Rachel knew what she was thinking. That Rachel should consider forgiving her husband. It had only been a one-night stand, so she should give him another chance. But what if she did? What if she believed in him again and he hurt her a second time? She would never survive.

"Ready for your party?" she asked. "I'm sure Neil is anxious to see you."

Her mother rose and faced her. "At least tell me that you're happy."

"Of course I am. I have Josh and my family. And I'm about to get a stepfather." She leaned close and hugged her mom. "You know I'm going to ask him for a pony."

Maggie laughed. "I wouldn't joke about that, if I were you. Neil's a giver and he just might buy you one."

They were still laughing when they walked out of the room and toward the lobby.

The late-May weather was perfect. Warm without being hot and plenty of sun. They were still about an hour from the party starting, and the west lawn was filled with activity. Large open tents had been installed. Servers were setting the tables where dinner would be served. The pre-and post-mingling area had two bars and a dance floor. Flowers sat on tables and by tent poles.

Rachel spotted Sienna and waved her over. Her sister walked toward them, all long and lean in a stunning ankle-length black dress made entirely of one-inch open-crocheted squares. The dress was lined from the bust to midthigh, but her skin peeked through the rest of it. Even knowing her sister had probably bought it at The Helping Store didn't take away from the look.

She had accessorized it with classic hoops, strappy flats and simple makeup. Her short hair was spiky.

"Killer look," Rachel said, knowing she couldn't in a million years pull that off.

"Thanks." Sienna smiled at them both. "Mom, you look great."

"I'm so nervous," Maggie admitted. "Have you seen Neil? He's not going to stand me up, is he?"

"I don't think you can be stood up at an engagement party," Rachel said.

"She's right." Sienna pointed. "He's over there, telling the staff how amazing you are."

Maggie saw her fiancé and waved. "I'll see you girls later."

"Have fun," Rachel told her, then looked at her sister. "Where's David?"

"He's meeting me here. I wanted to come early to see if anyone needed help. Oh, no."

Rachel followed her sister's gaze and saw Courtney carrying a large bowl filled with oranges, lemons and limes. As they watched, Courtney caught her foot on an extension cord, stumbled forward and dropped the bowl.

"It's been five minutes and she's already pulled a Courtney," Sienna complained. "What is with her?"

"Just stop it," Rachel said, starting forward to help her baby sister.

"What? Don't snap at me. She's a disaster. Admit it, Rachel. She never even graduated from high school. It's been nearly ten years and she's a maid here at the hotel."

Rachel ignored Sienna and went to help Courtney with the fruit. Her baby sister smiled as she approached.

"I thought I'd get my awkward moment out of the way early. So I can enjoy the party."

"Don't beat yourself up. Nothing bad happened."

"Oh, but the night is young."

They collected all the fruit and then stood. As Courtney delivered the bowl to one of the bars, Rachel studied her sister.

The shapeless dress couldn't have been less flattering on her. The navy-and-cream print was okay, but the length was an awkward two inches above the knee, which just looked bad on Courtney. The elbow-length sleeves were matronly, and the top kept slipping around on her shoulders. As always, her sister had pulled her hair back in a ponytail, which could have looked stylish, but didn't.

"Come with me," Rachel said, grabbing her hand. "Give me fifteen minutes."

"What? No. I'm fine."

"You're a mess. Come on, Courtney. You could be gorgeous. Why do you always try to blend in with the drapes?"

"I'm not attractive. I'm tall and gawky."

"Maybe at fourteen, but not anymore. Fifteen minutes," she repeated. "You don't have a choice."

"Fine."

Courtney clumped along behind her as they returned to the hotel. Rachel went directly to the bride's room and started opening cupboards. She found straight pins and fabric tape. A lost-and-found bin yielded a hot-pink scarf that would have to do.

"Get out the ironing board and iron," she instructed. "We want heat but no steam, so make sure it's empty."

She found navy thread and threaded a needle, then had Courtney stand in front of the wall-size mirror while she folded up both sleeves and pinned them in place. Now instead of a baggy elbow-length sleeve, the dress had little cap sleeves.

She walked around her sister and studied the dress. "You get this at the thrift store?"

"Of course."

"Good." Rachel pinned both sides of it back, from mid–

shoulder blade to the fullest part of Courtney's butt. "Go put on a robe. I need the dress."

Her sister pulled it off and handed it over. Rachel used the fabric tape to secure the sleeves, then the pleats she'd created on the back. Once the fabric cooled, she would tack the material down to make sure the tape stayed.

Courtney came out of the bathroom in a white terry-cloth robe.

"Sit," Rachel said, pointing to the chair. "And take out your ponytail."

"You don't have to do this."

"I want to. My baby sister is a stunner. It's time the world knew."

She combed out Courtney's long, thick hair. Quickly, before her sister could protest, she combed the front part forward and grabbed her scissors.

"You are so not giving me… What did you do?" The second part of the sentence came out as a shriek. "I don't want bangs."

"I know and I don't care. I've started now. There's no putting them back."

"I thought Sienna was the bitch in the family," Courtney grumbled. "You tricked me."

"Yes, I did. Now be still."

Rachel combed more hair forward and began to cut across Courtney's forehead. She moved carefully, keeping the line straight. She combed everything again and trimmed a few stray hairs, then pinned the hair back and went to work on her sister's makeup.

Courtney's clear skin and big blue eyes didn't need much enhancement. Rachel brushed on shadow, then mascara, used a brow pencil, then added a light touch of blush. A pretty, dark pink lip stain finished the look.

She unclipped the bangs and moved behind her sister. After spraying her hair with a shine spray, she brushed the long strands into a ponytail before pulling out one piece to wrap around the band holding it in place. She secured it with a couple of pins and sprayed her hair again, then smoothed her bangs.

"That," she said firmly, "is how you do a ponytail."

"What if I don't like it?"

"Suffer."

Rachel went back to the dress. She used the needle and thread to secure a few key points, then had Courtney pull it on over her head. The once shapeless dress now followed the curves of Courtney's body. Rachel twisted the hot-pink scarf into a long belt and tied it around her sister's waist. She tucked in the ends.

The faux belt helped define Courtney's figure even more and raised the hem a couple of inches. Just enough to go from awkward to sexy. Rachel turned her to face the mirror.

"See?"

Gone was the gawky, plain woman, and in her place was a stylish, well-groomed beauty. The bangs softened the strong lines of her face and made her eyes seem huge.

"All it took was fifteen minutes. You could do this if you tried. I'm happy to show you how."

Courtney smoothed her dress, then touched the belt. "It was twenty-five minutes, but I get your point. I look nice."

"Better than nice. You look stunning. I should hate you. The fact that I don't is a testament to my excellent character."

"I guess." Courtney hugged her. "Thank you. This is really amazing."

"I'm glad you think so. Now walk proud. You've earned it."

Quinn couldn't remember the last party he'd been to as just one of the guests. He was always feted or, at the very least, *that*

music guy. He found he liked being able to circulate and indulge in small talk without having to wonder what the other
person wanted from him.

He grabbed a glass of champagne from a passing tray and
took a sip. Joyce was chatting with a group of friends. The
engaged couple held court by the dance floor, and the three
Watson sisters were talking together.

Quinn watched as they interacted. The body language was
clear. Rachel and Courtney were comfortable with each other,
but Courtney didn't do well with Sienna. Every time the
platinum-blonde spoke, Courtney's shoulders tightened.

Quinn figured there was a lot of history in that tension.
A lifetime of experiences. He'd read an article a year or so
ago about how in a group, someone was always the goat. The
one who was less valued than the others. He would guess that
Courtney had been her family's goat for most of her life.

He studied the sisters. There were similarities and interesting differences. Rachel was the oldest. She was heavier and
trying to hide the fact with too-baggy clothes. She looked
tired. Or maybe resigned. Sienna was the obvious beauty of
the three, but he'd never been into what was obvious. Instead,
his gaze lingered on Courtney.

She looked different tonight. Sexier. Still not comfortable
in her own skin, but appealing as always. She kept smoothing
the front of her dress as if not sure of how it looked. Rachel
slapped her hands away, making him think Courtney's sister
had something to do with the transformation.

He walked over to the bar and ordered a shot of tequila and
a wedge of lime, then crossed to the sisters.

Courtney smiled when she saw him. "You remember
Quinn, don't you? Joyce's grandson."

"Nice to meet you," Rachel said, shaking hands with him.
"Watch out for Sienna. She'll hit you up for money."

"For an excellent cause," Sienna protested with a smile. "And if you write me a check, I swear I'll leave you alone."

"Not today," he said firmly as he handed Courtney the shot.

"We haven't had dinner yet," she protested. "It's early to try to get me drunk."

He chuckled. "This is medicinal. It's going to be a long night."

She looked from the shot to him, then shrugged. "Okay." After swallowing, she sucked on the lime wedge. "No salt?"

"Hard to transport."

Although he could have put it on his hand and she could have licked it off. He gave himself a full three seconds to think about how great that would have been, then firmly dismissed the visual and the imagined feel of her mouth against his skin. Courtney was not for him. She was young and impressionable and not anyone he should get involved with. He *liked* her, therefore he would protect her from himself.

"Nice party," he said. "I like the votive candles."

The small glass containers at every place setting had been painted with the phrase "She said yes!"

"A bit of whimsy," Courtney told him.

"Courtney's also responsible for the champagne tower," Rachel pointed out.

"As long as she doesn't touch it," Sienna murmured. "Because that would go badly."

"Sienna," Rachel hissed.

Courtney flinched and took a step back. "Have you tried the appetizers? The chefs really outdid themselves today. We're experimenting with some new finger foods, using locally sourced ingredients."

Rachel lightly touched Courtney's back before turning to Sienna. "Oh, look. There's David. You should go talk to him."

"You're both too sensitive," Sienna snapped before stalking off.

Quinn watched her go. Family dynamics, he thought grimly. They often sucked—although he was lucky when it came to Joyce. He turned back to Courtney.

"Did you do the table runner with the pictures? It's a clever idea."

She flashed him a grateful smile. "Um, yes. It's easy to do online. You could use it at one of your company parties. All your album covers."

"That's a great idea," Rachel told her. "I'm going to steal it for the end of baseball season. We always have a big party with the whole team. I'll email the parents and ask them to send me their favorite pictures of their kids from the season. Excuse me. I'm going to send myself a note so I don't forget."

She walked away. Quinn looked at Courtney.

"You okay?"

She smiled brightly. "Of course. I had tequila. Where's the bad?"

In her sister, for starters, he thought grimly. Worse, the encounter had made him feel protective, which, when combined with the fact that he already liked her, spelled nothing but trouble.

"You're the superstar," he told Courtney.

"I'm a maid. Sienna's raising money to help battered women start a new life. I think she would win on anyone's scale."

"Plus, she's always been the pretty one."

Courtney bit her lower lip. "There is that."

"What you have is better than pretty."

She raised her eyebrows. "Oh, please. We all know that's not true."

"Tell me about the tattoo on the small of your back and I'll tell you why you're wrong."

Courtney laughed. The sweet sound came from her belly, assuring him that her equilibrium had been restored.

"Not even for money," she told him. "That is going to be my secret and I will taunt you with it every chance I get."

"That's my girl," he said, taking her hand. "Now I want to look at the table runner again. You can point out all the pictures of you when you were little."

"Sienna really is the pretty one. You should look at her."

"I'm not interested in her."

Courtney stared at him. "Are you interested in me?"

The lie would be easy, and was probably the right thing to say, but as always, Quinn headed directly for the dark side.

"I am."

Her gaze locked with his. "Are you going to do anything about it?"

"I haven't decided."

"Why do you get to decide?"

"Because you won't."

"Oh. That's actually true. Will you let me know when the decision is made?"

"You'll be the first."

9

SIENNA GLARED AT her sisters down the length of the table. Sadly, neither of them seemed to notice. She and David were seated on one side of the engaged couple, while Rachel and Courtney sat on the other.

"Are you all right?" David asked.

"I'm fine. Just dealing with my family." She smiled at him. "Sorry. Have I been distracted? I won't be anymore."

He lightly kissed her. "Thank you. This is a really nice party."

"It is. Joyce did a good job."

The dinner had been excellent, and the decorations were just right. A small version of a wedding cake with a topper that spelled out "Maggie & Neil" had been dessert. The table runner was a beautiful touch. Apparently, Courtney had come up with that, which was hard to believe, but sure.

Thinking about her sister made her mood sink again. Rachel was always taking Courtney's side, which had made sense when they were kids. If anyone was going to be picked on, it was their baby sister. Not only had Courtney been a total fail at school, she'd been incredibly tall. Something that wouldn't have mattered as much if she hadn't also been two years older than all her classmates.

"What are you thinking?" David asked as he pushed up his glasses. "You look intense."

"Just Courtney. I worry about her. She's twenty-seven and still working as a maid in this hotel. I know she'll never be a rocket scientist, but she could at least make an effort. Mom is forever trying to get her into trade school, but she won't do it. I wonder if she's afraid."

David smiled at her. "You have such a sweet, giving spirit."

Ugh. That wasn't true—especially when it came to Courtney. Sienna mostly felt frustration and maybe some embarrassment.

"You'll be a great mom," he continued.

"I hope so." Sienna smiled at him. "I look at the women we help and most of them have children. Those kids are so scared. I know some of it is because they don't know what's going to happen. I want to hold them close and promise everything is going to be okay. Only, they wouldn't believe me and I'd just terrify them more."

"You like your work."

"I love it. Asking people for money isn't that hard and it's for a good cause. You talk about being excited to get to the office every day. I feel the same way. I want to get things done. I want to know that I've made a difference."

She wondered if any of her passion for her work came from the fact that she'd always—in her heart—felt ashamed of Courtney. She didn't like that part of herself, but there it was. In a town as small as Los Lobos, being Courtney's sister had been inescapable. Other students had teased her, accusing her of being stupid, too. Rachel had been old enough to escape it all, but Sienna had been in the thick of it.

She looked out at the large crowd in the tent. Nearly three hundred people had come to the party. She'd known most of them all her life. Rachel's ex-husband was there, as was Jimmy. Clients of Maggie's, old neighbors, longtime friends.

"I didn't want to move here," David told her. "I almost didn't take the job. I mean who's heard of Los Lobos?"

She smiled. "And now?"

"The best thing that ever happened to me." He stared into her eyes. "I love you, Sienna."

David had used the L-word a couple of times before. She'd always kind of dodged the issue, because she didn't know what to say. But now, feeling bruised about her family and knowing David saw only the best in her, she found herself leaning forward to kiss him.

"I love you, too."

He smiled. "Later, I'm going to make you say that about a hundred times."

She laughed.

The servers began to clear the dinner plates. Maggie stood and picked up a microphone on the head table.

"I know it's not technically our wedding," she began. "But Neil and I are still going to cut that beautiful cake over there. After, there will be dancing." She looked at Neil, then glanced down the table toward Sienna and David. "But before that, I've been asked to request a special song. I think something wonderful is going to happen—I'm just not sure what."

"Do you have—"

Sienna stopped talking when David stood. The music shifted to Lionel Richie's "Hello," an odd choice for an engagement party. What on earth? Was he going to give a toast? Was that appropriate? They'd been dating for nearly six months, but he didn't know her mother and Neil that well.

David took the microphone from Maggie and then faced Sienna. Overhead lights came on, illuminating both of them. Sienna felt herself get cold as she wondered if escape was possible. Whatever was going to happen, it was going to be bad. She could feel it.

"Sienna, you're amazing."

Her heart stopped. She felt it stop right there in her chest. No. *No!* He couldn't be going where she thought he was going.

She forced herself to smile. "Thank you. You are, too. I'm so happy you could be here, at my mom's engagement party."

A desperate attempt to remind him of where they were and why. It was her mom's moment. Oh, please, oh, please, let her be wrong. Just this once, wrong would be great. Perfect. Her wildest dream.

"I've talked to both your mom and Neil. They're wonderful people. I wish them every happiness. But I'll admit to a little envy. Because they know they're going to be together for the rest of their lives." He smiled at her. "I want that, too. The promise of forever, with the most amazing woman in the world."

Her sense of horror grew as he dropped to one knee. All around them, everyone gasped. Someone whispered, "How romantic." She wanted to find the woman and slap her. This wasn't romantic. This was a living, breathing nightmare. Why was he doing this? Oh, God, oh, God, oh, God.

David drew a ring out of his jacket pocket and held it out to her. "This belonged to my grandmother. She and my grandfather were together for sixty years. When I called and told her about you, about how I felt, she sent it to me. Sienna, I love you. I want to spend my life with you. Marry me."

No! No! She couldn't. She didn't want to marry David. At least she didn't think she did. They barely knew each other. It was too soon—too fast.

She was aware of the ticking of the seconds. Of everyone staring. This was the wrong time and wrong place and possibly the wrong man. It was also her mother's engagement party. How would it be remembered? As a stunningly romantic event, or that time when Maggie's daughter dumped her boyfriend?

Sienna forced herself to smile and stand. "Oh, David. Of course I'll marry you."

"That was lovely," Maggie said as she poured more champagne.

Rachel held out her glass. Lena and her husband were giving her a ride home, and she was going to get as drunk as she wanted. Right now a little drunk was called for.

"Did you see the terror in her eyes?" Rachel asked. "What was David thinking?"

"He was very sweet when he came to ask me for my permission." Maggie leaned back in her chair and sighed. "If I was a better mother, I would have told him no. Unless you think Sienna's really in love with him?"

"Do you?" Rachel asked.

"Not really, but I've been wrong before. I always thought she and Jimmy were the perfect couple. Too young at the time, but right for each other." Maggie looked out on the dance floor, where Neil danced with Sienna. "I'm a lucky woman."

"You are."

Maggie turned to her. "Are you sure? You remember your father the most. I don't want you thinking—"

Rachel cut her off with a shake of her head. "Mom, it's been twenty-four years. It's long past time for you to find someone else. Neil adores you and you adore him. That's what matters."

"Thank you." Maggie picked up her glass, then put it down again. "Did you know that David actually mentioned a double wedding? I told him I'd been planning my wedding since I was fourteen years old. My mother wouldn't let me make any of the decisions when I married your father, so this time I'm doing everything I want."

A somewhat scary thought. "Mom, you know your tastes have changed since you were fourteen. You might want to rethink the plan."

"No," her mother said firmly. "I know my colors are going to be every shade of pink and that there will be swans."

"Do the swans have to be pink, too?"

Her mother brightened. "Do you think you could dye them to match the decorations?"

"No. I only do human hair. Not feathers. Plus, the other swans would mock them."

"Or be jealous." Maggie picked up her champagne. "I know. We'll have flamingos instead."

"Very creative." Rachel stood. "I'm going to use the restroom, then have another piece of cake." She bent down and kissed her mother's cheek. "You are going to be a beautiful bride."

"Thank you, darling."

Rachel scanned the crowd as she headed inside. So far she'd managed to avoid Greg, which meant her plan was working. She still hadn't figured out what she was going to say when they were next together. "Hey, thanks for the emotional dump on my head the other day. It was great."

She made it to the women's restroom without spotting him and ducked inside. The bathroom was empty and she went into the last stall. She'd barely sat down when she heard two other women come in.

"Talk about a party," one of them said. "Sienna's in shock. I can't figure out if it's good shock or bad shock. This is what, her fourth engagement?"

"Her third, I think. I'm not sure."

Rachel froze, not sure how to say she was in the last stall.

She realized there was nothing to be done but wait for them to finish.

"Courtney looks good," the second woman said. "Rachel must have taken her in hand. Talk about the sister I don't understand. Rachel has all that ability. Why doesn't she make over herself? Did you see what she's wearing?"

"I know. Awful. It's the extra weight she's carrying. She looks so tired."

They went into their stalls but kept talking.

"It's not tired, it's depressed. Wouldn't you be sad if you lost Greg?"

"Tell me about it. He's so hunky. So what if he cheated? I heard it was only one time, so get over it. I mean, come on. She's totally let herself go. If you were married to her, wouldn't you cheat, too?"

They both laughed.

Humiliation burned through Rachel. She couldn't think, couldn't breathe. Was this really what people said about her? What everyone thought? That she was a fat loser who should take back her cheating husband?

"Maggie looks happy," the first one said. "Neil's an odd little duck, but totally in love with her. He looks at her as if she's his princess. I envy that."

"Me, too."

They flushed their toilets and exited the stalls.

"The food is delicious," one of the women said. "Joyce hires the best people."

"I know. That soup!"

"Maybe we can sneak some home."

They both laughed and left. Rachel finally flushed and stepped out into the empty bathroom. She told herself to keep moving. That what they said didn't matter. That she was fine.

She crossed to the sink and washed her hands, then reached

for a towel. As she did, she caught sight of herself in the mirror. The dark circles under her eyes seemed more pronounced
today. Her shapeless shirt hung on her body. Her hair needed
a trim and maybe a few highlights. Those other women were
right—she had let herself go.

But it wasn't her fault, she thought. She was running all the
time. She was the single mother of an active eleven-year-old.
She worked full-time. She was doing her best to hold it together when there was no one to help. Greg had cheated on
her. That wasn't her fault. No matter what, it wasn't her fault.

She blinked away tears before leaving the bathroom. She
took two steps, only to find herself standing in front of her
ex. He smiled at her.

"Rachel. Hi. I've been looking for you. Want to dance?"

His dark hair was too long. He wore a dark green shirt
tucked into black jeans. He was tall and lean and handsome
enough to make Angelina Jolie swoon. And once, he'd been
her husband.

Rachel had believed down to her bones that as long as she
could love Greg and be loved by him in return, nothing bad
would ever happen. She'd spent the night before her wedding equally excited at the thought of the upcoming day and
afraid that Greg would wake up and realize he could do so
much better. She'd loved him with everything she had, and
he'd betrayed her.

"I can't," she whispered.

"Aren't you feeling well? Do you want me to take you
home?"

"It's my back," she lied, thinking she had to get out of
there. She had to get away from what everyone was thinking and saying.

"Sure. Did you bring your tote with your supplies to do
your mom's hair? Where is it?"

"I'll get it. I can do that. If you could tell my mom why I had to leave, please."

"Of course. We'll meet back right here."

"Thank you," she murmured, stepping past him. She had to hold on for only a little while longer. Josh was staying at a friend's for the night, so once she got home, she would be alone. She could give in to the pain then. Where no one could see.

Maggie held up her champagne glass. It was close to midnight and everyone was feeling the effects of food and liquor. She swayed slightly. Neil kept his arm around her.

"Thank you all for coming," she said with a laugh. "I love you all."

"We love you, too," someone called.

Quinn sat at a table in the back, watching everyone else. He'd had a surprisingly good time. Maggie and Neil weren't an obvious choice to be a couple. At least not physically. Maggie was leggy and lean, while Neil edged more toward short and round. But they were happy together. Even he could see that, and he prided himself on seeing all things through a cynical lens.

Like the proposal. Sienna had been caught completely off guard. That had been easy to read. So had her reluctance to say yes. But what choice had she had? Refusing David would have been all anyone remembered. And now she was engaged. Quinn wondered how long until she broke things off.

"I never thought I'd fall in love again," Maggie continued. "But I did. With the most wonderful man in the world. I'm so lucky to have found you, Neil."

They smiled at each other, then shared a brief kiss. Maggie straightened and turned her attention to the crowd. "I also want to thank my daughters. I love you girls. I'm so proud of my daughters…and Courtney." She waved her glass. "Now everyone has to dance!"

Quinn stood and searched the room. He found Courtney on the opposite side of the open tent. She stood with her arms crossed, her shoulders hunched forward. As if trying to be small again.

He wished Courtney could accept that she would never be like everyone else. That she was so much more than she realized. But it was hard to be more when those who were supposed to love you most insisted on seeing you as less.

She caught sight of him as he made his way over. Her mouth twisted as if she wasn't sure what to do. Then her chin came up and her shoulders went back.

Good, he thought. She was still tough, still strong inside. He liked that.

He stopped in front of her and looked at her. She stared back.

"Are you not telling them about your degree because you're punishing them or yourself?" he asked.

"Most people start a conversation with 'how's it going?' or a comment about the weather."

"It's dark and clear. What about my question?"

"It's very to the point."

He waited.

"I don't know," she admitted. "Both, maybe. I have something to prove." She tilted her head. "For the record, I'm not happy about your insights. It makes it hard to keep up. I don't have any about you, which isn't fair. You should tell me something really intimate so we can level the playing field."

"You already have all the power, Courtney."

She laughed. "Yeah, right. This is me, filled with power."

"You just don't know how to use it yet."

"You're very good with one-liners."

"I write a lot of songs. It's great training for being cryptic."

"You use it well. What power? How do I find it?"

"By being brave."

"Are you brave?"

"Not as often as I'd like."

She pressed her index finger into his chest. "Be specific."

He took her hand in his and pulled her close. "There was a woman I was seeing."

"Seeing as in dating?"

"Seeing as in sleeping with."

"Without dating? Just sex?"

"It's easier."

"I guess, but lonely."

Funny how she'd guessed the truth so quickly.

"I wanted more from her, but I didn't say anything. I wasn't brave."

"She left?"

He nodded. "Married someone else. She's happy and that's a good thing."

"Is she why you moved here?"

He smiled. "No. I wasn't heartbroken. Just disappointed by the missed opportunity."

"So your advice to me is more of a do-as-I-say-not-as-I-do thing?"

He laughed. "Yes. Very much so."

"Okay. I'll think about it."

"Just like that?"

She looked surprised at the question. "Sure. You have a whole lot more experience than I do. Not only because you're, well, old, but you've lived a lot more, too."

He tugged her a little closer. They were almost touching. She had on flats, so barely had to tilt her head to meet his gaze.

"Old?"

"You keep telling me you are, so I've decided to believe you. In fact, now that I'm thinking about it, you've been standing a really long time. Do you need to sit down?"

He tugged on her hand again and she took that last half step. The one that brought her body in direct contact with his. They touched from chest to thigh…or in her case, from breast to thigh. While her figure was boyish, there were just enough curves to satisfy him.

"You sass me."

She smiled up at him. "I do. I should be afraid of you. But I'm not. Why is that?"

"Because you want me."

The statement was more about testing the waters than stating a fact, but Courtney didn't know that. She flushed, started to move back, opened her mouth to speak, then pressed her lips together. Which told him everything he needed to know.

"I want you back," he told her, right before he touched his lips to hers.

He released her hand as he kissed her. He'd never been the type who had to hold on to a woman to keep her. While he had always enjoyed women in his bed, he wanted them there willingly, even eagerly. The chase he enjoyed was intellectual, not physical. When it came to sex, he expected his partner to be his equal.

Courtney wasn't intimidated by him, but they were still at different places in their lives. So he wanted her to be sure.

For a single heartbeat, she didn't move. Then she eased into him and put her hands on his shoulders. He moved his to her waist.

She was warm and felt good against him. He liked how she kissed him back, tentatively at first, but then with more confidence. When she parted her lips, he allowed himself a brief foray into her sweet mouth. The feel of her tongue against his was enough to get him hard, but this was neither the time nor the place. He drew back and kissed her forehead.

"It's late," he told her. "I'm going to thank your mother for inviting me and call it a night."

"That sounded a lot like a statement and not an invitation," she said.

"You're right."

"What happened to wanting me back?"

"I still do."

She glared at him. "You're the most confusing man I know."

"Part of my charm."

"Is that what we're calling it these days?"

"Good night, Courtney." He turned and started walking away.

"Did I mention you were annoying? Because you are. Seriously annoying. And if you think you're going to see my tattoo anytime soon, you're sadly mistaken."

He was still chuckling when he got to his room.

10

RACHEL WANTED TO spend the rest of her life curled up in a small, dark corner. Unfortunately, circumstances weren't going to cooperate. She'd had a long night of alternating between shame and fury. She'd wanted to figure out who had said those mean things and confront them. She'd wanted to pack everything she owned and slink away in the night. Those hard overheard words mingled with all the things Greg had said. By dawn, she was exhausted and confused, but also clear on the fact that she had to do something. Because she'd been stuck in limbo for too long, going through the motions without a plan.

She supposed that was just how life went. However awful she might be feeling, she still had to clean the house and plan meals for the week and do laundry and put gas in her car. She also had to meet her sister for brunch. Part one of her new still-unformed plan—show up at the restaurant looking good so no one had any reason to talk. After that...well, she would figure it out as she went.

She forced herself out of bed and showered. Rather than pull on black knit pants yet again, she dug through her closet for a pair of jeans that fit, then pulled on a cheerful red blouse.

After spending extra time on her makeup, she vowed she really would get one of her work friends to cut her hair that week.

Those women in the bathroom had been mean and bitchy, but they'd been right about one thing. She *had* let herself go. Some of it was the divorce—she'd felt so awful, she just hadn't wanted to bother. Some of it was Greg—without him in her life, what was the point? Although that last thought was going to get her kicked out of any feminist group she might want to join. Because, jeez, talk about defining herself by a man.

She wanted to be stronger than that. She wanted to be one of those cool women who was busy and self-actualized without being married. The kind of person who would go on an African photo safari by herself. Not that she ever would. She'd yet to figure out how to eat in a restaurant alone.

She slipped into a pair of heels she hadn't worn in years, then held on to the doorjamb of the closet while she tried to get her balance. Flats or tennis shoes would be easier, but she would be damned if she was going to let those two get her down. Yes, she'd had a few crappy days, maybe a bad year or two, but she refused to let anyone pity her. Maybe Greg had been right, too. Maybe she did have to do it all herself. But so what? She would do it better and bolder. Or at least try more than she had been.

Courtney was already at a table when she got to the hotel restaurant. She waved Rachel over. Rachel took a second to admire how good the bangs looked before crossing the room. Courtney stood and hugged her gently.

"How are you feeling? Is your back better?"

It took Rachel a second to figure out what her sister was talking about. Then she remembered the lie she'd told so she could leave the engagement party early.

"It's fine," she said. "I must have tweaked something, but it's all better now."

"Good."

Rachel ordered black coffee and an egg white omelet with vegetables. She figured she might as well take advantage of her resolve while she could. Maybe she would lose a few pounds in the process.

"Did I miss anything exciting?" she asked when the server had left.

"No. David's proposal was the highlight." Courtney wrinkled her nose. "Or lowlight, depending on your point of view."

"I know. What was up with that?" Rachel leaned toward her sister. "Do you think anyone else noticed Sienna's panic? It was bad. She so didn't want to say yes."

"Oh, God. It was horrible. I mean he's a nice guy and all, but I never thought they had chemistry."

"He must assume they do. This is engagement number three."

Courtney eyed her. "You're kind of liking her pain, aren't you?"

"What? No. Of course I want my sister to be happy. Maybe David's the one."

"You really think that's possible?"

"I honestly have no idea. Sienna's hard to read."

Rachel supposed that in most families, siblings connected on different levels. She and Courtney had been the close ones. Maybe because they were so far apart in age. With their mom gone a lot—working and going to school—Rachel had stepped in where she could. It had made sense that she would help with the baby in the family.

She'd done her best, Rachel told herself. She'd worked hard to teach Courtney all that she could. But she'd never been able to help her with her schoolwork. For a long time, Rachel had assumed the fault was hers—that she wasn't doing it right. When Courtney had been held back, Rachel had been devastated, knowing she was the reason. Finding out her sister had a learning disability had been a relief. And on the heels of relief had been guilt for being glad it hadn't been her fault.

No wonder she liked to control everything, she thought grimly. If she messed up, there was no one to blame but herself. Not that she was admitting Greg might have been right about a few things.

Courtney's phone chirped. She glanced at the screen and groaned. "She remembered."

"Who?"

"Mom. Last night at the party, she said she'd been thinking a lot about the wedding. She didn't want to keep bothering Joyce, so she was going to run everything through me." Courtney held out her phone so Rachel could read the text.

I want swans not flamingos. And a pink cotton candy machine.

"When did she want flamingos?" Courtney asked.

"Last night she talked about wanting swans, but the color was wrong." She held up her hands. "I told her I wouldn't color their feathers, so we discussed flamingos."

"Oh, joy."

The server returned with their coffee. Courtney grabbed on to hers with both hands. "Does she mean the cotton candy machine itself is pink or just the cotton candy?"

"You're going to have to ask her." Rachel took a sip of the hot coffee and sighed. "Did you know that she didn't get to plan her wedding to Dad?"

"What do you mean?"

"Grandma Helen said she was too young to make those kinds of decisions and did everything her way. At least that's what Mom told me. She had all these ideas that have been stored up inside of her. Waiting. Now some forty years later, she's determined to have the wedding of her dreams. I tried to explain that her tastes may have changed just a little, but she doesn't want to listen."

"Did I say 'oh, joy' before, because I was thinking it." Courtney looked at her. "I'm handling the wedding."

"What do you mean? I thought Mom was talking to Joyce."

"Oh, she has her meetings with Joyce, but I'm the one doing it. I did the engagement party. All of it. From the tents to the placement of the bar to hiring the DJ."

"I thought you worked as a maid," Rachel blurted before she could stop herself.

"I do, but I fill in when I'm needed. I've served in the restaurant, been a bartender, worked the front desk. A year ago, our wedding planner got food poisoning the night before a huge wedding. I stepped in and handled the day. Since then I've been planning some events when needed. Because this is a family thing, Joyce thought it would be easier if I did it. I'm not sure who it's supposed to be easier for, though."

"Not you," Rachel said, studying her sister. Little Courtney was all grown-up. When had that happened? "Does Mom know?"

Courtney shrugged. "I don't know. I've been at all the meetings. I'm her point of contact."

"So, no."

"She'll be upset. She won't trust me to handle things. She'll worry."

All of which was true.

"I'll tell her after the wedding," Courtney said. "When everything turns out fine."

"And if it doesn't, you can blame Joyce."

They laughed.

Their breakfasts came. Rachel took a couple of bites, but she wasn't that hungry. An aftereffect of the previous night?

She could still hear those women in her head, talking about how she'd been a fool to let Greg go.

"Do you think I was wrong to divorce Greg for cheating on me?"

Her sister blinked. "I don't know. You were so angry and hurt. He was a jackass for what he did."

"But you don't hate him."

"He's Josh's dad and kind of in our lives. Hating him would make things difficult for everyone. I was mad at him for a long time, for what he did to you." She cut a piece of her Belgian waffle. "To be honest, I never understood what went wrong. You two were so crazy about each other. I couldn't figure out why he would do that. You were everything to him."

Rachel thought about how much they'd been fighting all the time. With his twenty-four hours on, twenty-four hours off schedule, he'd had way too much free time. Rather than put it to good use, he'd wanted to go hang out with his friends. She would have been okay with that if he hadn't left her with everything around the house and with Josh.

But while she wanted to say it was all his fault, she kept remembering what he'd said after the baseball game. That she wanted to be the only one looking after things. That she needed to be right. That she would rather be a martyr than ask for help.

"We married young," she said slowly. "I'm not saying it was a mistake so much as it was an added pressure. We were hoping to wait to have kids, but then Josh came along. We had to grow up fast and Greg wasn't ready. He wanted to be a young guy in his twenties—not a married man with a baby."

"Sounds like you've forgiven him."

"Forgive is a little strong. I don't still hate him. You're right—he's not going anywhere. We have a son together. I have to keep seeing him."

"Are you sorry about the divorce?"

Was she? Did she want things back the way they'd been before? "I don't miss what we were like right before the end. That was ugly. We were both so angry at each other. But when it was better, I miss that."

"Do you think about getting back together with him?"

A ridiculous idea! "That's not an option."

"Why? Greg's single. You're single."

"We barely speak, and when we are together, it's all about Josh."

"Does it have to be?"

Rachel didn't have an answer for that. Greg's emotional dump the other day hadn't been about Josh, and she could go the whole rest of her life without having that conversation again. She and Greg were done. Finished.

"I've totally moved on."

Courtney smiled. "Um, not really. You haven't been on a single date that I know about."

"I'm not looking to have a man in my life."

"Why not? You must miss the sex."

Rachel stared at her. "We're not talking about that."

Her sister laughed. "I don't want to upset you, but I'm twenty-seven. I know about *the sex*. I've even done it a few times."

"As have I, but we're still not talking about me having sex with other men."

"Or Greg?"

"Him, either."

"Okay." Courtney took a bite of her waffle and chewed. "But I'll bet he was pretty good in bed. Am I right?"

"Yes, and that's all I'm going to say on the topic."

Mostly because talking about it would mean she had to remember. Whatever other things she and Greg had had going on, they'd always found plenty of time for lovemaking. Whether it was a five-minute quickie before Josh got home from school, or two hours on a Saturday night. They'd known how to arouse each other, please each other. Sex had never been their problem...until he'd done it with someone else.

"What about you?" she asked to distract herself. "Anyone interesting in your life?"

If Rachel hadn't been watching her sister, she wouldn't have noticed the slight hesitation. She was intrigued by the possibility of news and relieved to deflect the attention away from herself.

"Who?"

"No one."

Rachel simply waited. Courtney had never been able to hold out long. Back when they'd been younger and Courtney had done something wrong, Rachel had simply asked the question, then stayed quiet. After a few seconds, the truth would come rushing out.

"Fine," her sister grumbled. "It's not anything. I mean there's nothing going on, except maybe..." She cleared her throat. "Quinn is interesting."

"Quinn? Joyce's Quinn? Are you insane?"

Courtney pushed away her waffles. "This is you being supportive?"

"What? Sorry. No. You're adorable and he would be lucky to have you. As for him being attracted to you, of course he would be. You're pretty and sweet and innocent. My concern isn't that you're not his type, it's that you totally are and he's going to chew you up and spit you out."

"That was a visual I could have lived without. You think he's dangerous?"

"Not like a psychopath, but he's very experienced. There have been actresses and models and who knows who else. I would worry that he would have all the power and that's not right. You need to be the one in charge."

Rachel was afraid she was saying it all wrong. "Courtney, I love you. You're my sister. I don't want him hurting you."

"I don't think I'm at risk. Honestly, I'm not going to fall for him. That would be ridiculous. I was thinking more along the lines of using him for sex."

Her baby sister *was* all grown-up, Rachel thought. "I'm impressed. I wouldn't have the guts. If that's how you feel, you should go for it. You deserve a hot guy in your life, and Quinn is surely all that. Go for it, then."

Courtney laughed. "I just might have to."

Monday morning Sienna found herself just as unsettled and disbelieving as she had been Saturday night. She couldn't really be engaged, could she? Maybe it had never happened. Maybe the whole night had been a nightmare. Maybe David had been drunk and would forget.

They'd stayed to the very end of the party, then David had taken her home. Of course, he'd wanted to stay the night. She'd been forced to fake both her excitement at his company and later her orgasm. He'd fallen asleep after, murmuring he would love her forever.

Sunday morning God had shown a little mercy by causing a crisis with some airplane part. David had rushed off to the office and not been able to get away until hours and hours later. By then he was exhausted and wanted only to sleep. Of course, she'd understood.

Now she sat at her desk and wondered what she was going to do. Everything had happened so fast. She felt confused and trapped. Not a happy combination.

It wasn't that she didn't *like* David. Of course she did. He was smart and kind and he was crazy about her. On paper, they made a great couple. She knew he would never decide she wasn't good enough, the way Hugh had. But married? She couldn't see it happening.

They would talk, she decided. Calmly, over dinner at her place. He'd probably let the romance of the engagement party sweep him away. Maybe he was having second thoughts, too. They could wait a few weeks, then quietly end things. It would be best for everyone.

Kailie, one of the volunteer staff members, walked in with a huge bouquet of flowers.

"These were just delivered for you," she said eagerly. "They're beautiful." The teen grinned. "Someone's trying to get on your good side."

A rock dropped into Sienna's stomach. A big, heavy rock. She reached for the card.

We are so excited to welcome you to the family. I've always wanted a daughter and now we'll have you. Much love, Linda and David Sr.

Sienna was grateful she was sitting down. Otherwise, she would have fallen. Of course, hitting her head might not be so bad. Maybe she could get amnesia.

"They're from David's parents," she whispered. "He told them."

"About the engagement? That is so cool." Kailie dropped her gaze to Sienna's hand. "Why aren't you wearing the ring?"

Sienna thought about the old-fashioned setting and did her best not to shudder. It wasn't that she didn't treasure old things. Nearly everything she owned had been purchased at the thrift store. It was that his grandmother's ring had been hideous. A heavy, badly made design that only emphasized the tininess of the diamond. It had also been about two sizes too small.

"It was his grandmother's ring," she said, hoping she sounded more cheerful than she felt. "It didn't fit. He's taking it to a jeweler."

"A family heirloom. That's so special. You'll be connected with his past forever."

There was a thought.

Kailie flashed her a smile. "You're so lucky, Sienna. David's the greatest guy. I know you'll be happy with him."

"Thanks."

Sienna moved the flowers to the table behind her desk. That way she wouldn't have to look at them. Although she could still smell them, and the rock in her stomach remained.

Just when she thought her day couldn't get any worse, a short, curvy redhead stalked into her office and slapped a piece of paper down on her desk.

"Here. It's all you're getting, so don't ask for more. I have no idea why my great-grandmother liked you, but she did."

"Hello, Erika," Sienna said as graciously as she could. "Would you like to take a seat?"

"No."

"Coffee?"

Erika rolled her green eyes. "Hardly."

Sienna picked up the check. It was made out for ten thousand dollars, as promised by Mrs. Trowbridge.

"Thank you for this," she said. "It will help. Would you like to know how the money is used?"

Erika sank into the seat across from Sienna. Her mouth formed a pout.

"No. I don't care. You're not getting anything from the kitchen, just so you know. There's nothing left."

"Why are you so mad at me?"

"You stole my boyfriend."

"That was thirteen years ago. Then you stole him back and dumped him."

"I didn't steal him back," Erika pointed out. "You were already done with him. For the record, I only stopped dating him. You broke up with him after you were engaged. That's a lot worse."

Sienna thought about saying she and Jimmy had been young and foolish, and neither of them had been particularly heartbroken about parting ways. But that wouldn't play into Erika's self-talk.

"Thank you again for the check," she said quietly. "Your great-grandmother was always a generous supporter and we will miss her."

"Whatever," Erika snapped. She rose and left.

Sienna completed the paperwork to record the gift and printed out the tax letter to be mailed to the estate. When she was done, she walked into Seth's office.

"We have Mrs. Trowbridge's donation," she said. "Ten thousand dollars."

"Excellent. There's another duplex coming on the market. I'm hoping we can buy it." He grinned. "I heard about the engagement."

She did her best not to wince. "Did you?"

"You could ask the groom-to-be to buy us a house. That would be a great wedding gift."

"For you."

"And you. You support the cause."

"Maybe I'd like some china instead."

"That's what a gift registry is for. Besides, you're not the china type."

"I'm not asking David to buy the duplex, so you can forget it."

Seth sighed. "I hate it when you're not a team player."

"Ha-ha."

She retreated to her office. She had plenty of work waiting for her. Work she enjoyed. Only, she couldn't seem to focus. After about fifteen minutes, she realized part of the problem was that she could smell the flowers, even if she couldn't see them.

She carried the bouquet to the lunch room, then walked back to her office and cracked the small window. With the first breath of fresh air, she felt herself relax. Everything was going to be fine, she promised herself. She didn't know how, but it would be.

11

COURTNEY PULLED THE bag of limes out of the back of her sister's car. Rachel already had the chips and salsa, along with a quart of guacamole they'd picked up at Bill's Mexican Food on the way over. Sienna's car was in the driveway of their mom's house, next to Neil's gleaming white Mercedes.

"I thought it was girls only," Courtney said as they walked up the path to the front door.

"I'm sure Neil will be leaving. No way he wants to hang around for one of our evenings."

Every couple of months the grown daughters were summoned to Maggie's house for an evening of margaritas and fun. The tradition had been going on since Rachel had left home to marry Greg. Courtney remembered waiting anxiously to turn twenty-one so she could have real margaritas instead of the virgin ones her mother had made her drink until then.

Now she both enjoyed and dreaded the family nights. Sometimes they were a lot of fun. But other evenings were more of a challenge. Especially when her mother and sisters decided to tell her exactly how to improve her life.

What they didn't know, mostly because she wouldn't tell them, was that she was doing really well. She'd gotten a note from her professor telling her he was very impressed by her marketing project and suggesting she take his advanced by-invitation-only seminar next fall. Talk about a coup.

The front door opened before they reached it. Sienna beckoned them inside.

"Help me," she whispered. "I'm so very afraid."

She was hard to hear over the loud music pouring out of the built-in speakers Maggie had had installed a few years before. It took Courtney a second to recognize the song. "Love Runs Out" by OneRepublic.

Courtney followed her sisters into the house. The three of them came to a stop as they stared at Maggie and Neil dancing to the upbeat song. Arms flailed, hips swayed, feet shuffled back and forth. Neil grabbed for Maggie's hand and spun her in a move that was part something from the 1950s and part Grapevine.

Their mother caught sight of them and waved them in. "Join us," she called over the music. "I love this song. Neil and I were talking about having it played after the ceremony. We'd dance down the aisle to it. What do you think?"

Rachel smiled. "That's great, Mom. I, ah, just have to get the guacamole into the refrigerator."

She escaped to the kitchen. Courtney went after her, with Sienna trailing behind.

"I don't know if I should be impressed or appalled," Rachel admitted. "Good for her for being so happy and in love."

"I was here *alone* with them," Sienna complained. "You have no idea how that scarred me."

"We should be grateful that when we get old, we'll be like that," Courtney pointed out. "Better too full of life than not full enough."

"Weird expression, but I get what you mean." Rachel pointed to the blender Maggie had left out on the island. "I believe it's your turn to make the margaritas."

"It's always my turn." But Courtney wasn't complaining. She liked knowing what was expected when she came home to visit. It made things easier.

She added ice, then began juicing limes. By the time she'd pulled the tequila out of the freezer, the built-in speakers were playing "It's Five O'Clock Somewhere."

Maggie walked into the kitchen. "Neil's off for a night with the guys," she said, holding open her arms. "How are my three favorite daughters?"

They hugged their mom in turn. Courtney hung on for a second, hoping tonight was going to be one of the good ones. She inhaled the familiar scent of Arpège. It had always been her mother's favorite perfume.

"Just to be clear," Maggie said as Courtney handed out the margaritas, "I plan to talk about the wedding. A lot."

Sienna raised her glass. "That's exactly what we want to hear, Mom."

Someone nicer than Courtney would assume that Sienna was being a good daughter rather than trying to make sure they didn't discuss her recent engagement. Oh, to have been a fly on the wall after David and Sienna had gotten back to her place.

"Let's get dinner together," her mother said. "Then we can talk."

The meal was usually more about assembling than actually cooking. This time Maggie had picked up a rotisserie chicken from the grocery store, along with corn tortillas, shredded cheese and tomatoes. There was a bag of coleslaw and ingredients for Maggie's famous jalapeño salad dressing.

Rachel took the chicken apart and cut the meat into small pieces. Maggie assembled the dressing, while Courtney made another batch of margaritas and Sienna put out the fixings for tacos, along with the chips, salsa and guacamole. The food was served family style, with the pitcher of margaritas front and center on the dining room table.

Maggie raised her glass. "To my girls. I love you all very much."

Courtney thought about the toast from the party and silently said, "And Courtney." Then she told herself not to be bitchy. Her mother meant well. Mostly.

"I want to go first," Maggie said. "So oldest to youngest."

Sienna sighed. "I hate being the middle child."

"You get to be the beautiful one," Rachel pointed out.

Sienna brightened. "That's true."

Maggie reached for a tortilla. "My good thing is the engagement party. It was wonderful. Courtney, I know you did a lot of the work. Joyce told me. Thank you for that. I loved the runner for the table best of all."

Sienna stared at her sister. "I still can't believe you did that all by yourself."

Courtney leaned toward Sienna. "I didn't. Little cartoon woodland creatures came and helped me while I sang. Of course by myself. It's not that hard, and despite what you think, I am capable."

"I didn't say you weren't," her sister snapped. "I'm surprised you know how to work a computer that well. You're a maid. There's not much call for being tech savvy when you're cleaning toilets."

"Hey," Rachel said, raising her voice a little. "We're having a nice dinner."

"I was only stating the obvious."

"If it's obvious, why state it?" Rachel asked. "Go on, Mom. What's the bad thing?"

"I was going to say I don't have one, but I suppose it's that my girls don't always get along."

"Mom," Courtney began.

Maggie held up a hand. "No. We're doing our one-good, one-bad. We can talk later."

Rachel scooped chicken, salsa and tomatoes onto her plate. "My bad thing is I got on the scale the morning after the party and realized I've gained thirty pounds." She grimaced. "Josh is eleven. I can't call it baby weight anymore. So I joined an online diet group. The program's pretty easy to follow."

She held up her glass. "I saved all my extra calories for the week so I could have a margarita tonight. That's my good thing."

"We could go walking, if you want," Courtney told her. "Do laps at the high school."

"I'd like that."

"I'll join you," Maggie told them. "I want to be in shape for the wedding."

They all looked at Sienna, who was busy dipping her chip into guacamole.

"What?" she asked. "No, I don't want to do laps at the high school." She took a bite and chewed. When she'd swallowed, she said, "My bad thing is I'm not a joiner, which you all know already. So stop glaring at me."

She turned to Rachel. "I'm glad you're losing weight. You'll feel better about yourself."

Courtney winced. Really? That was Sienna's way of being encouraging?

"What's your good thing?" Maggie asked.

"Seth has found another duplex that's coming on the market. It's in bad shape and the price will reflect that, so we have a chance of buying it."

Rachel leaned toward Courtney. "So not the engagement, then," she said in a low voice.

"Are you surprised?"

"Stop whispering," Maggie instructed. "That's excellent,

Sienna. I'll talk to Neil and see how much we'd like to contribute."

"Thanks, Mom. I'll get you the information on the building."

"Is Jimmy the listing agent?" Courtney asked.

"He is. He knows the family that wants to sell. They're being transferred and the tenant living in the other unit is moving out, so the timing is perfect."

Sienna's ex-fiancé had become a successful real estate agent in town. All Courtney's former flames had been of the loser variety. She wouldn't have wanted to stay in touch with any of them. But Sienna had better taste, so it made sense she and Jimmy had stayed friends.

The three of them turned to Courtney. Rachel raised her eyebrows. "And you, young lady?"

Courtney thought about the praise from her instructor and how she was only two semesters away from graduation. She thought about the different responsibilities she'd taken on at the hotel.

"My good thing is that the party went well," she said at last. "I wanted it to be everything you'd dreamed of." She smiled at her mom. "If you're happy, then I'm happy."

"Thank you, sweetie."

"You're welcome. My bad thing is one of the toilets backed up at the hotel and I had to clean the mess."

Everyone groaned.

"That *is* a bad thing," Rachel said. "Poor you."

"Thank you all for sharing," Maggie told them. "Now let's talk about the wedding, shall we? We barely have three months to get everything planned, and there's so much to do."

She looked at Courtney. "You got my text about the swans?"

"Yes, and we already had this conversation. Remember? The poop? The chlorine?"

"Fine. I'll come up with something else." Maggie refilled her glass. "I've decided on my colors."

Courtney braced herself. "Not just shades of pink?"

"No. The entire spectrum between vanilla and pink. With an emphasis on pink. I don't know what I want to do about my dress. I'm leaning toward something traditional. I thought we could all go shopping together. But I don't know if I want it more vanilla-colored or pink."

Courtney exhaled. While it wasn't exactly a broad palette, it was one she could work with. There would be a lot of options.

"We could have fun with the colors," she said. "You could serve pink champagne. Decorating will be easy. There are lots of flower options and the foliage will be a beautiful contrast. Oh, we want to make sure the bouquets aren't the same color as the dresses. If they are, the flowers disappear into the dress and the pictures aren't wonderful."

Her sisters and mother were staring at her. She carefully pressed her lips together, then cleared her throat. "What?"

"You sound like you know what you're talking about," Sienna said flatly. "When did that happen?"

"Hey," Rachel started.

Courtney stopped her. "I'm sure Sienna meant that as just a maid, I shouldn't know any of this."

"What she said," Sienna told Rachel. "You always assume the worst about me."

"You usually deserve it."

"Courtney's a grown-up. Stop babying her."

"Girls," Maggie said mildly. "Let's focus our attention on me and my wedding."

Courtney laughed. "How long have you been waiting to say that?"

"Awhile now. I get to be the bride. Perhaps even a bridezilla.

This time around, I'm going to have exactly what I want. Neil and I are determined to have the wedding of our dreams."

Sienna made another taco. "Mom, what did Neil do? I know he's retired now, but before? He never talks about it."

"Oh, he owned a few of those gaming places."

Gaming? "Like a casino?" Courtney asked.

"No, those places where you play video games and eat pizza. There was a chain."

"Like a franchise?" Rachel asked.

Maggie busied herself pouring more drinks. "Yes. Like that. So back to the wedding. I can't decide on the dresses for you three. We can do the same style in different colors or different styles in the same color. What would you prefer?"

"Different styles."

"Different colors."

Rachel and Sienna spoke at the same time. They looked at Courtney. She held up both hands. "I am so not breaking that tie. Mom?"

Maggie picked up her glass. "I say we all get a little drunk, then decide."

Quinn sat in the lobby of the hotel, reading. It was late—close to eleven. The French doors were open and despite it being nearly the first of June, there was a cool breeze blowing in off the ocean.

Sarge lay on the carpet, chewing on a stolen sock. Every couple of months someone on the staff went through the lost and found, rescuing any socks. They were then left in strategic spots around the hotel for Sarge to find and destroy.

Pearl lay next to him. As Quinn watched, she stood and stretched. After shaking, she gracefully jumped onto the sofa and pushed her head under his arm in a not-very-subtle bid for attention.

"Missing your mom?" Quinn asked as he rubbed the side of Pearl's face. "Joyce will be back in tomorrow."

His grandmother had driven to San Francisco to have dinner with a friend. Rather than make the return trip late at night, she would stay over and drive back in the morning.

He continued to stroke the dog. Eventually, she stretched out next to him, her head on his lap. He could see the white spot on her chest—the one that gave the beautiful blonde poodle her name.

They were an odd pair, he thought with a smile. Sarge—fourteen pounds of bichon-mix terror—and Pearl, a lean, elegant poodle princess. But their relationship wasn't about appearances. It was about being a family. They were a bonded pair. Years ago he'd promised Joyce that if something ever happened to her, he would take her beloved dogs and make sure they were always together.

"Not to worry," he told the two. "Joyce will outlive us all."

Sarge growled in agreement as he continued to show the sock who was in charge. Quinn turned his attention back to his book. Sometime later, close to midnight, when he was thinking he would take the dogs for a last quick walk before turning in, the main lobby door opened and Courtney walked inside.

He hadn't seen much of her since her mother's engagement party. He'd been busy looking for a place for his business and she'd been doing her thing here at the hotel.

He watched her careful and controlled stride as she walked across the hardwood floor and realized she was completely drunk.

He held in a grin. "Have a good time?"

She jumped and shrieked. Sarge came to his feet as if ready to take on danger, while Pearl simply appeared anxious.

Courtney put a hand on her chest. "You scared me. What are you doing, lurking like that?"

"I'm reading with my peeps." He stroked Pearl. "Joyce is visiting a friend in San Francisco."

Courtney dropped her arm to her side. "So you're pet sitting? That's nice."

Her gaze was slightly unfocused and her cheeks flushed. She looked about seventeen—all bangs and long legs. She wasn't wearing anything special. Just a plain yellow T-shirt and jeans. No makeup. But there was something appealing about her. Something that spoke to that dark, empty place inside him.

"I was at my mom's," she continued. "We get together every few months. Girls only. Girls and margaritas." She paused. "Rachel drove me home. I wouldn't drive like this."

"Good to know."

"I'm responsible."

"I see that." He studied her for a second. "Did you eat?"

"A taco. It was good, but then Sienna made some crack about me being a maid and it wasn't as fun after that." She put her hands on her hips. "There's nothing wrong with being a maid. Someone has to do it. It's a necessary service. I take pride in my work and so does everyone else who works here. Maids are good people, but sometimes the way she says it..." Courtney shook her head. "We should respect honest work and the people who do it."

"You are drunk."

She stomped her foot. "I mean it, Quinn."

"I know you do. And you're right. Honest work should be respected. Let's go in the kitchen and get you a big glass of water and some aspirin. Maybe a snack. Otherwise, you're going to have a really bad morning."

She wrinkled her nose. "I probably should have stopped at three margaritas."

He rose. Pearl jumped off the sofa and joined him. He went over to Courtney's side and put a hand on the small of her back. "Three is a good limit."

"Too late now." She giggled.

He gave her a little push in the direction of the kitchen. The dogs came along with them, Sarge carrying his sock. As Pearl and Sarge settled in the giant dog bed set up for them in a corner of the kitchen, Quinn had a brief thought about health inspectors, then told himself Joyce had it all under control.

He got a glass from the cupboard and ice from the ice machine, then filled the glass with water. Courtney perched on one of the bar stools by the massive island.

"I think you're right," she told him. "About me punishing my family. By not telling them the truth, I mean. They don't know any of it. Not that I have my GED or my AA or that I'm getting my bachelor's."

"Drink," he told her, pointing at the glass.

She took several gulps. "My marketing professor has asked me to be in a special class he teaches. You have to be *invited*. It's very exciting."

"Congratulations."

"Thanks. We're supposed to say a good thing and a bad thing and I didn't tell."

Quinn leaned against the counter. "For those of us who haven't had margaritas, what does that mean?"

She laughed. "At dinner. We have to say one good thing and one bad thing." Her eyes widened. "Sienna's good thing wasn't her engagement."

"Are you surprised?"

"No. She wasn't happy at all. But jeez, if you're going to

fake it, go all the way." Her smile faded. "Did that sound dirty? I didn't mean it to."

"It didn't."

"Good. Hey, you took me off your room."

He repeated the words in his head, searching for either context or meaning, and found neither.

"Your room," she repeated. "I'm not your maid."

"My honest, hardworking maid. Yes, I know. I did ask for someone different."

She glared at him. "I do a good job."

"I'm sure you do. My request wasn't about your work, it was about the fact that I know you. It was too strange—you picking up after me."

"Then pick up after yourself." She giggled. "Okay, I get what you're saying, but it's not like I was going to snoop in your underwear drawer."

"What makes you think I wear underwear?"

Her eyes widened.

He chuckled. "Drink your water."

She took a few more swallows, then asked, "Am I a project?"

"Do you want to be?"

"I'm not sure. I think it would be interesting. You know stuff I can't even imagine. You've been successful in business. That would be interesting to talk about. But the whole project thing—that makes me feel like you'll never take me seriously."

"Do you need me to?"

"Sure. I'm not a little girl. I'm a woman."

"I'm very clear on your status in the girl versus woman arena. For what it's worth, you're not a project. I don't do that anymore."

"Why not?"

"My last project died." Quinn swore silently. Where had that come from? He hadn't meant to tell her the truth.

Her mouth dropped open. "For real?"

"Yes."

"I'm sorry."

"Me, too."

"It wasn't your fault."

"You can't know that," he told her.

"Not for sure, but I can guess. You want the world to think you're really cynical and disconnected, but you're not."

"How do you know that?"

She smiled. "You love your grandmother."

"Even serial killers love their grandmothers."

"I don't think so. From my very limited understanding on the subject, family members are often the first to go." She slid off the stool. "I should probably eat something."

"Good idea."

"I know where the secret stash is."

He was a little afraid to ask "of what?" Knowing Courtney as he did, it could be anything.

She crossed to one of the cupboards and reached up to a high shelf. As she stretched, her T-shirt rose, and he saw the small of her back and the tattoo there.

"Well, hell," he muttered.

She pulled down a bag of Oreo cookies, then faced him. "What?"

"Your tattoo."

"Ha-ha. Not what you expected at all. Admit it. I surprised you."

"Very much so."

She opened the package and pulled out a cookie. "Do you know the song?"

He nodded.

"I'm not sure I believe you. What's the whole line?"

"'You can walk me to the river,'" he quoted, "'but you can't make me drown.'" She'd tattooed lyrics onto her skin.

"That's right. Hey, the artist—Zinnia. She died a few years ago." Her mouth parted. "Is she the one? The project? Did you have something to do with that song?"

"Yes."

She put down the package of cookies and rubbed her temple. "Was that yes to all the questions?"

"Yes, I worked with her, and yes, we were involved. She killed herself a few months after we broke up." He held up one hand. "The events were not related." As far as he knew.

"And the song?"

"I wrote it."

Her expression of surprise was almost comical. "But you're a music producer. I thought you sat in a booth and pushed buttons or moved levers or something."

"How flattering."

She rolled her eyes. "And discovered talent and all that, but you write songs?"

"I do nearly everything that needs to be done."

Courtney collected her bag of cookies and returned to the counter. He refilled her glass while she ate a couple of Oreos.

"What was she like?" Courtney asked when he set the glass in front of her. "Zinnia?"

He thought of her slight build, her long red hair, her energy. "She was fire."

"That sounds so great, but in real life, it has to be a pain. The drama." She clamped her hand over her mouth. "I'm sorry. You're not supposed to speak ill of the dead and I just did. Plus, I don't know her. I really hate it when people are critical of someone they don't know. Like we all have this great insight. I apologize. I'm weak and spineless. Do you want a cookie?"

She pushed the bag toward him.

He honest to God had no idea what to do with her. Zinnia had been pure flame and Courtney was right—sometimes it had been a pain in the ass. But art came at a price. Courtney was different—quicksilver, maybe. Light and bright and impossible to hold. He decided he liked that about her best.

"You should finish your water," he told her. "Then take a couple of aspirin and go to bed."

"Want to join me?" She grinned. "You've seen my tattoo, so I can't offer you that unveiling, but still."

"You're drunk."

"Well, duh. I just asked you to have sex with me. You don't think I'd be brave enough to do that sober, do you?"

He stepped toward her. After taking her face in both his hands, he lightly kissed her lips, then her forehead.

She exhaled. "Well, crap. There's never sex after a man kisses your forehead."

He stepped back. "You're so worldly."

"Don't mock me. I'm humiliated and in pain."

She was smiling as she spoke and still eating cookies. So not either of the things she claimed.

"I suspect you'll recover. Can you get back to your room on your own?"

"Of course. I made it here."

"Your sister drove you."

She brightened. "That's right. I was at my mom's tonight. Did I tell you that?"

"You did. You are going to have one nasty hangover."

"I'll be fine. You sure you don't want a cookie?"

"Yes, but thanks for asking."

"Anytime. Were you at least a little tempted?"

He'd learned enough about how her mind worked to figure out what she was asking.

"More than a little. But drunk is not my style."

She beamed. "It's so nice that you have standards."

He was sure there was a compliment buried in there somewhere. "Thanks. Good night, Courtney."

"'Night."

12

SIENNA STARED AT the ring David held out. "You got it sized so quickly," she said, hoping he couldn't hear the disappointment in her voice. "I'm surprised."

"I paid extra for a rush job. Put it on. I want to take a picture to text my folks."

Sienna took the small ring with the ugly setting and slid it on her finger. It fit perfectly and looked even worse on than off.

She'd never thought of her hands as oversize, but the petite setting seemed lost on her finger. The diamond was nonexistent. David, who sat next to her on her sofa, beamed.

"It's perfect."

She glanced down. "It's unique." And oddly heavy, for something so tiny. Or maybe it was just guilt and unhappiness that made it feel as if it weighed fifty pounds.

He took several pictures of her holding out her hand, then put away his phone and faced her.

"We have a lot to talk about," he said.

"We do."

He took her hands in his and stared into her eyes. "I know you were surprised by the proposal."

She squirmed. "We hadn't discussed marriage at all."

He nodded. "I should have said something. It's just you're the one, Sienna. You're beautiful and caring, and every time I'm with you, I know in my gut that we're meant to be together."

He moved his thumbs against the backs of her hands. "I know you're scared. Of us, of the future. I know you've been engaged before. I get that you're having second thoughts."

She hoped she didn't look as shocked as she felt. "You do?"

"Of course. You lost your dad when you were what, six? Then your mom had a tough time. You're scarred by that. You're afraid to believe in a happy future. This has to terrify you."

She managed a slight smile. "Maybe a little."

"I'm here for you. I believe in you and I believe in us. I want to make you happy. I want you to realize you can trust me with every part of you. The good and the bad. I'm all in. Can you give us a chance? Can you take a leap of faith?"

He really did understand, she thought, both shocked by his insight and shamed by her own doubts. He got her. Okay, sure, there wasn't a lot of the superhot chemistry between them, but weren't steadiness and acceptance more important than a few fleeting chemicals?

David believed in her, believed in them. He was a really good guy with roots and a desire for them to have a future together. He was right—she'd had a tough childhood, and that had influenced her all her life.

"I think I'm really lucky to have you in my life," she told him, then leaned in to kiss him.

He released her hands. "I'm glad. Because like I said before, we have a lot to talk about."

She leaned against him and studied the ring. Maybe it wasn't so very awful. "Like what?"

"My mom's been calling every day. She's going to want to talk to you as soon as possible."

She straightened. "About what?"

"The wedding. She wants it to be in St. Louis, but I told her I thought you'd prefer to have it here. Do you agree?"

She'd barely accepted the fact that they were engaged and he wanted to talk weddings?

"Um, I don't know."

"If you don't have a preference, then St. Louis would be better for me." His voice was eager. "Although I have to warn you, between friends and family, my half of the guest list will be about four hundred."

"People?" she asked faintly. "That's huge."

"I know, but it's a big deal for me and my family." He put his arm around her and pulled her close. "Now, Mom had a crazy idea this morning. I told her it wasn't possible, but I have to admit, part of me is thinking maybe it would actually work out."

"W-what?" she asked, genuinely afraid to hear the answer.

"A Christmas wedding."

She sat up and stared at him. "Christmas *this* year?"

He nodded.

"That's only seven months away. I couldn't possibly pull a wedding together in that short a period of time."

"Your mom's doing it in three months and my mom would help." He leaned toward her. "Or we could skip the big event and have a destination wedding. The Caribbean or Hawaii. Then have a giant celebration party in the spring. That way we could invite everybody."

Because the four hundred he'd mentioned before wasn't everybody?

"My head is spinning," she admitted. "I need to think about this."

"Take all the time you need," he told her as he kissed her. "Or at least a week. This is going to be great. You'll see. The third time's the charm, Sienna. I just know it."

"I've ordered the shoes already," Maggie said. "So the dress is going to have to work with them."

Betty Grable—no relation to the 1940s movie star—stared at Maggie. "You bought your shoes before your wedding gown?"

Courtney wanted to tell the transplanted thirtysomething that there was no point in trying to understand Maggie-logic. Easier to simply go with it.

"Wedding dresses always need alterations," she said, stepping between her mother and the brunette salesperson. "At least that's what I've picked up from my *Say Yes to the Dress* marathons." She smiled at Betty. "You'd know a lot more about that than we would. Wouldn't any pair of shoes work as long as the dress isn't too short to begin with? If it's going to have to be hemmed anyway, what's the problem?"

"I suppose that's true," Betty admitted, still sounding doubtful.

"Mom, didn't you bring a pair of shoes that are the same height?" Courtney asked. "Be sure you wear those when you're trying on the dresses so we can all have an idea of the end look."

Rachel leaned close. "Nicely done. You defused that potential powder keg beautifully."

"Thanks. I've worked with a lot of fussy people at the hotel."

They were at For the Bride, the only wedding gown shop for a hundred miles. Despite being in the middle of a small town, the store had a very upscale clientele. Betty was known for getting in beautiful samples and having tons of contacts in New York and San Francisco. Whether your budget was three hundred or thirty thousand, Betty provided a one-stop go-to bridal gown experience.

Maggie had made her appointment right after Neil had popped the question and several weeks before the engagement party. She'd informed her three daughters they were expected to be there for the full five hours. Yes, an initial consultation really could take that long, she shared. At least Betty would provide lunch, Courtney thought. And the hangover from the previous weekend's margarita-fest was long over.

While the morning after—one spent with a massive headache and roiling stomach—was firmly etched in her brain, the evening that had caused it was a little fuzzier. She remembered the dinner at her mom's, how Sienna had annoyed her and the unfortunate consumption of too many margaritas. It was the part after that had her confused.

She knew Rachel had driven her back to the hotel and that she'd met up with Quinn. The bits that followed were more of a blur. There had been water and Oreo cookies, and she was pretty sure Quinn had told her he'd written the lyrics she'd had tattooed on her back. But the rest of it… Not so much with the details.

She was hoping that her asking Quinn for sex had happened in her head rather than in life. Either way, she'd ended up in her bed. Alone. Which meant either she hadn't asked the question or he'd been a gentleman. While she believed that he was a nice guy who didn't take advantage of drunk women, she was really hoping that the topic had never actually come up. Only, she was kind of afraid it had.

"Based on our phone conversation and the Pinterest pictures you sent me, I've pulled several samples for you to try on," Betty told Maggie. "You're not expected to find your dress today. In fact, if you fall in love with one, I'm not going to let you buy it. This is the most important decision you're going to make about your wedding. You have to be sure. You have to love it."

"Now look who's defusing the situation," Courtney said in a low voice.

Rachel grinned. "Maybe this will be fun."

"Don't tempt fate with that kind of talk."

They laughed.

"Let's get started," Betty said. "Maggie, you're in this dressing room here."

She led their mother through wide double doors. The three sisters settled into comfortable chairs in the waiting area. Sienna pulled out her tablet, opened the cover and then frowned. "There's no Wi-Fi."

Rachel pointed to a small sign on the wall.

There is no Wi-Fi available. Today is about the bride.

"I'm not sure if that makes me like Betty more or less," Courtney admitted. "Either way, you have to respect her style."

"I just wanted to check work emails," Sienna grumbled. "Seth is contacting donors about the new property we want to buy. I have to be able to give him input."

"You could call him," Rachel offered.

"She probably has cell service blocked," Sienna grumbled.

Rachel grinned. "I would have to agree with you."

Sienna looked at Courtney. "Do you know Joyce's grandson? The rich music guy?"

"Quinn?" Courtney hoped she asked the question with the right amount of polite disinterest. "He's staying at the hotel, so I've seen him around."

Not a lie, she told herself. She had seen him around. She might have asked him to have sex with her, but no one needed to know that.

"I wonder if he'd be open to hearing a presentation about what we're doing," Sienna said. "Getting another duplex would be huge for us. That's at least two more families who'll be safe. Or if we use one of the properties for women without kids, then three victims could stay there at a time."

Courtney felt the familiar tendrils of guilt coil through her. While she wasn't sure how to define her relationship with Quinn, she supposed she did know him well enough to introduce him to her sister. And it was for a good cause.

"Talk to Joyce," Rachel interjected. "Get her on board, then let her go after Quinn. He adores his grandmother and I suspect he would do anything for her."

"What makes you say that?" Sienna asked.

"The way she talks about him when I see her. They're close."

"She's right," Courtney said quickly, mentally apologizing for throwing her boss under the bus. "She could really go to work on him."

The double doors to the dressing room opened and Betty came out.

"Your mother requested dresses that weren't white. So cream, ecru and ivory are our main choices. We can do a special order in blush, if that's what she prefers. Time is tight, but there are a couple of designers who can be pushed a little. For a fee, of course."

Betty stepped aside and Maggie walked into the main part of the salon.

Courtney hadn't known what to expect. She'd seen pictures of her mother's first marriage to Courtney's dad. Maggie had worn a long-sleeved gown with a full A-line skirt. There'd been a bit of lace, but for the most part the dress had been plain. This dress was anything but.

The strapless champagne-colored dress clung from bust to

knees. It was completely covered with a beautiful lace that had a slight sparkle. From the knees to the floor was a huge pouf of rippling champagne-colored fabric. Courtney didn't know enough about wedding dresses to know if it was satin or something else that was shiny. The pouf formed a bit of a train.

The sisters stared as Maggie walked to the dais and stepped up in front of the huge mirror. As Maggie studied herself, Courtney saw that the dress dipped low in back.

"That's got to be one amazing bra," Rachel murmured.

"It's doing the job," Maggie said, turning to the left, then the right. "But it's not comfortable. I don't know. What do you three think?"

"You're stunning," Courtney said, telling herself that she came from a really good gene pool. She might be freakishly tall, but at least she would most likely age well.

Sienna walked closer. "It's pretty, Mom, but the color is wrong. Champagne isn't in your palette. I doubt this dress can be special ordered in time. There's a lot of custom work in it."

"She's right," Betty informed them. "You would have to take it in this color. You could, of course, adjust your wedding palette."

"No," Maggie said firmly. "I won't do that. I like this, but I worry it's too young for me."

"You have the body," Rachel told her. "I'm seriously bitter. You're in great shape, Mom."

Courtney took in the amount of bare skin and had to admit her mother was right. While she could physically carry it off, it didn't seem...appropriate somehow. Not that she was going to walk through that minefield. Still, it was her mother's wedding and she should be happy.

"Let me try on something else," Maggie said and stepped down.

Two hours and several more gowns later, Maggie came

out in a simple lace gown that had thin shoulder straps and a
U-shaped neckline. The heavily beaded fabric followed the
lines of her body until the hips, where it fell to the floor in a
gentle flare. Beadwork and lace covered every inch, and the
beads had a distinct pink cast.

The bodice wasn't particularly low, and in the back it more
than covered a regular bra strap.

"That works," Sienna said. "It's really nice, Mom."

Courtney nodded in agreement. "I like the way the skirt
forms a train. It's not too long, but it makes a statement."

"The color's right, too," Rachel added. "Well within the
palette."

"One to consider." Maggie turned in a slow circle, then
stopped and pointed out the window. "Oh, my."

They all looked. Courtney moved to get a better view, then
felt her mouth drop open when she saw a familiar blue Bentley pull up at a red light by the store.

She wasn't sure what was more eye-catching—the con-
vertible with the top down, the handsome man driving it or
the blonde poodle sitting next to him in the passenger seat.

As if sensing their attention, Quinn glanced in their direction, then waved. Pearl turned as well, showing off her pink,
sparkly Doggles.

"You know," Maggie said slowly, "it takes a very secure
man to pull that off, but damn if he doesn't do it."

Courtney had to agree. Only Quinn, she thought with a
smile as the light turned green and he drove away.

Maggie walked over to the mirror, where they all studied
the gown.

"It's a contender," she said after they'd discussed various
ways to bustle the train for the reception. "Would I be able
to buy the sample?"

"Of course. We'd have it cleaned, then fitted to you. I'll

put it aside for you, but you can't buy it. Not on the first day."
She smiled. "Now, you must all be exhausted. Let's break for
lunch. I have a few more gowns for you to try on after you
rest for a bit."

The store had a small patio, where a table was set up. There
were box lunches offering different salads, along with some
cut-up fruit and cheese. Maggie put on a white terry-cloth
robe Betty provided and joined them.

"That last dress was the best," Rachel said as she passed out
the lunches. "What did you think, Mom?"

"It's beautiful, but I'm not sure it's the one."

"On the shows I watch, all the brides say they know when
they're trying on the right dress," Courtney said. "If they're
right, you have to wait for the feeling."

"I don't know. Maybe I'm too old for that kind of thing
to happen."

"Mom, you're not old," Rachel said. "You look amazing
and you're in love. You'll know the dress when you find it."

"You're right. It's too early to be discouraged." Maggie
picked up a fork. "Courtney, I have a few more ideas for the
wedding."

"Of course you do. Go ahead, frighten me. I can take it."

"Nothing that should be scary." Maggie paused, then
grinned. "All right, that might not be true. I was thinking
we could get a hot air balloon to take people over the ocean."

"Like parasailing?" Sienna asked. "What if people are afraid
of heights or get motion sickness?"

"Then they don't have to go."

Courtney met Sienna's gaze and nodded. "I'm with you.
I think that might be a bit much. But if you're looking for a
way to make the day special, what about a different kind of
guest book? Instead of having people simply sign a book, we
have cards made."

She held up her hands so her index fingers and thumbs formed a circle about six inches across. "They're about this big. We'd use a good quality card stock that we have cut into a jigsaw puzzle. People write their messages on the puzzle, break it up into pieces and put them in an envelope for you and Neil to assemble later. It's fun for them and fun for you."

Maggie clapped her hands together. "I love that. Yes. I want that for sure. What else? Oh, did I tell you I want to use that photo table runner at the wedding?"

"Actually, the place where I got it can also make it as your runner, so you could use it down the center aisle for the wedding."

"Perfect," Maggie said. "Now, what about a video confessional booth? People could share their deepest, darkest secrets."

The sisters exchanged looks.

"Maybe not," Rachel told her. "There's a little too much drinking at events like this."

"I know," Maggie said with a grin. "That's the best part."

Lunch passed quickly. Sienna listened more than she spoke as the others made plans for the wedding. It wasn't that she wasn't interested so much as she was terrified of having the conversation shift to her engagement. She still hadn't come to terms with what had happened and she sure didn't want to talk about it.

Maggie sighed. "Neil's a good one. I got lucky when I met him." Her expression was thoughtful. "I'll admit I almost didn't go out with him because he's shorter than me. Isn't that silly?"

She reached for a strawberry. "Your father was just so handsome. I was totally smitten from the first moment I saw him. Neil took a while to grow on me."

"Were you always happy with Dad?" Rachel asked. "I don't remember much, but I feel like you fought a lot."

Maggie looked startled. "We had our issues, of course, but…" She paused. "I never know what to say," she admitted. "About your father. He's been gone so long. He was a good man, and he loved you, but he wasn't all that concerned about taking care of us. The lack of life insurance for one. I still can't believe we lost our house."

"You took care of us," Rachel said quickly. "Look where you are now."

"I know, but it was so hard. I was terrified every second of every day. I was just a secretary at the company. He was the accountant. When he died, nearly every client left. The bills piled up. If Joyce hadn't taken us in, I don't know what we would have done. It was horrible."

Courtney reached for Maggie's hand. "For what it's worth, I don't remember much about that time. So I wasn't traumatized."

"I loved the hotel," Sienna added. "It was so much fun. Everyone looked out for us. You didn't fail, Mom. It wasn't your fault."

It had been their father's fault, Sienna thought. Although she'd heard bits and pieces of the story all her life, she'd never much thought about how hard everything must have been for Maggie.

David wouldn't do that, she told herself. He wouldn't leave her destitute with three children. He would take care of her.

Maybe she should learn from her mother's story. The fact that Neil hadn't blown her away at the beginning of their relationship. That love at first sight had turned out to be, if not a mistake, then problematic.

She glanced down at her engagement ring. The ugly setting was growing on her…at least a little. Maybe she would learn to love it.

Courtney looked at her phone. "We should get back to the dresses, Mom. You want to have as big a selection to choose from as possible."

"You're right, darling. Let's head back to the salt mines."

Maggie stood and motioned for Courtney to lead the way. Sienna thought about how Courtney had had so many ideas for the wedding itself. As if she was handling everything. It wasn't bluster, either. Courtney seemed to know exactly what she was doing. How strange.

"Sienna?" Betty put a hand on her arm. "Your fiancé called this morning and talked to me about dresses."

Sienna honest to God didn't know what to say. "David?" she asked weakly. "I told him what I was doing, but…" She swallowed. "I'm sorry. What did he say?"

"We talked ideas." Betty looked pleased. "He's very interested in your wedding plans. That's so unusual. Most grooms simply want to show up. You're a very lucky bride."

Was that what they were calling it? "Ah, thank you."

"There's one dress in particular he would like you to try on. I happen to have it, so if you're game…"

"This is my mom's day," she said quickly. "I don't want to take away from that."

"I'm sure your mother will enjoy sharing the fun. I've put the gown in the other dressing room. If you'll follow me."

She didn't know what to do. Saying no was the obvious solution, but then when David asked, what was she going to tell him? Knowing her mother, she knew that Maggie would be delighted to have company. As for what her sisters would think, well, she had no idea.

She walked into the dressing room area. Rachel and Courtney were already sitting together on one of the love seats. For a second Sienna felt a familiar stab of envy. They'd always been the closest two. Despite their age difference, or maybe because of it, they were the ones who looked out for each other. She was the odd sister out.

Now she paused and shifted her weight. "There's a, ah, dress I'm going to try on."

Her sisters exchanged a look.

"That will be fun," Rachel said. "Is this a dress you picked out?"

"David did."

Courtney pressed her lips together as if trying not to laugh. Rachel covered her mouth with a failed cough. For one unexpected second, Sienna felt her eyes start to burn as anger blended with a sense of betrayal. Damn them both, she thought grimly and raised her chin.

But before she could say anything, Courtney stood and hugged her. "Invite everyone you hate to the wedding, because you will cause them physical pain with how beautiful you'll be. A wedding may not be a traditional time for revenge, but you should so go for it."

The unexpected compliment left her speechless. Her anger faded as if it had never been and she hugged her sister back.

"Let's not get ahead of ourselves," she said with a smile. "This will be a dress picked out by a man. God knows what it will be."

"I'll bet it has that lace back we saw in Mom's magazines," Rachel said. "The see-through kind that shows your butt."

"I am not showing my butt on my wedding day."

Courtney raised a shoulder. "I don't know. If not then, when?"

Sienna was still laughing when she walked into the dressing room.

Fifteen minutes later she stared at herself in the mirror and didn't know what to think. The gown David had chosen was couture—exquisitely made and nothing she would have chosen herself.

It was strapless, with the V of the sweetheart neckline dipping low between her breasts. There was about an inch of beading around the top of the neckline. The dress was fitted down to midthigh, and the smooth silk was covered with strings of tiny pearls that went from the front of the dress to the back. The ropes of pearls moved with her, creating a shimmering effect. From midthigh to the floor was a cascade of tulle.

Between the beading and the pearls, the dress had to weigh twenty pounds. It was snug to the point of making it hard to breathe. Sienna couldn't tell if she liked it or not. *Shocked* didn't begin to describe how she felt. It wasn't that David had picked out a wedding gown—it was what picking out the wedding gown meant in the first place.

He genuinely thought they were getting married.

"Come on," Rachel said, banging on the closed door. "We want to see."

Sienna turned and opened the door. Her sisters and mom stood there. Maggie was still in her robe. They all stared—wide-eyed.

"I was right," Courtney breathed. "You are stunning."

Sienna looked back at the mirror. She had no sense of herself in the gown. She could see her body and her face and the dress, but she couldn't voice an opinion. Did she look good or bad? Pretty or ugly? Those were just words with no meaning. She felt nothing.

Betty appeared and sighed. "I knew you would be dazzling and I'm right. Come see in the big mirror."

Sienna found herself walking through the store to the dais. She climbed up, then, once again, faced her reflection. Her sisters and mother were talking. Betty made a few adjustments to the dress. Sienna simply watched and wondered why no one else saw the walls forming around her heart.

13

"ARE YOU ENJOYING your stay in Los Lobos?" Joyce asked pointedly.

Zealand nodded.

Joyce pressed her lips together. "I have to stop asking yes or no questions, don't I?"

Zealand shrugged.

Quinn chuckled. "Leave him alone. It's not nice to badger people."

Joyce didn't look convinced. She glanced back at Quinn's best sound guy and sighed. "Am I badgering you?"

Zealand held up his left hand, his thumb and index finger less than an inch apart.

"Well, that was very clear," Joyce grumbled. "I'll point out that if I could hear you talk, I would leave you alone."

Quinn nudged his friend. "Don't give in. You're driving her crazy and not many people can do that."

They were seated on the patio of the hotel's main restaurant. There were plenty of guests and tourists taking advantage of the warm, sunny weather to enjoy a leisurely lunch.

Wayne sat next to Zealand. Quinn's assistant had paperwork spread out in front of him as he looked over the various industrial spaces they'd toured the past couple of weeks. The older man looked focused, but Quinn saw him reach down to rub the side of Pearl's face. The standard poodle sat next to the table, while Sarge had claimed one of the two empty chairs.

"It's good you own this place," Quinn observed. "Otherwise, you'd have to leave your dogs at home."

"That would never happen," Joyce assured him. "They're a part of my family. Speaking of my family, are you going to leave me when you decide on which location to buy?"

"Yes, but I'm not in a hurry if you're not."

"Stay forever."

"We'd both get tired of that."

His grandmother shook her head. "I wouldn't, but a young man needs his privacy."

As he was over forty, Quinn wasn't sure about being a young man anymore, but he would take the title at least, for now.

"Two of these work," Wayne said. "None of them will be perfect, but we'll embrace the suck and move on."

"Embrace the suck?" Joyce asked.

"Military term," Quinn told her. "You can take the man out of the marines..."

"Of course."

He spotted Courtney on the patio. Joyce had mentioned she was filling in as a server today. He wasn't sure who had called in sick or had a personal crisis—not that it mattered. She was always ready to help where needed.

"She is pretty, isn't she?" his grandmother said.

Wayne and Zealand followed her gaze. Zealand raised an eyebrow. Quinn ignored him and the question.

"She should be doing more than cleaning rooms and picking up odd shifts everywhere else," Quinn said. "She could be a real asset around here."

"I agree, but she's stubborn. I've offered her several opportunities. She says she's waiting until she has her degree. Ridiculous, if you ask me, but she's not asking anyone but herself. I have to respect her decision."

He wasn't surprised by the information. Courtney was playing the same kind of game with her family—not telling them what she was doing until she had her degree in hand. He knew it was about more than the piece of paper. It was about what it represented. He wondered what would happen when she figured out that validation couldn't come from outside herself. That it had to be something she felt. He supposed that lesson, like many others, was a matter of having to live through the experience.

She looked up from where she was setting a table and caught his gaze. He winked. She laughed, then went back to work.

Wanting stirred. She appealed to him on every level and she'd made her interest in him clear. He planned to take her up on her invitation, just not yet. Long ago he'd learned that anticipation could be its own kind of pleasure.

"You were just as stubborn," Joyce said.

It took Quinn a second to remember what they'd been talking about. "Me? Never."

Joyce looked at his friends. "It's true. Quinn wanted what he wanted. But he was never any trouble. We never had a cross word between us."

He laughed. "You're lying and we all know it. I was a pain in the ass teenager—just like every other kid is. I stayed out too late, I talked back."

Her gaze was loving. "Maybe, but you were kind and so sweet to me. I appreciated having the chance to make up for my past."

She sighed. "I'm sure Quinn hasn't told you, but I was a terrible mother." She held up a hand before anyone could protest. "It's true. I was very young when my husband died and he left me this hotel. I wanted to make it a success, so I did everything I could to make that happen. That included ignoring my only child—Quinn's mother. I paid for it later. We were never close. She left and we didn't speak for years. She died before we could reconcile. A lesson to you all. Hold on to those you love."

He thought about what Courtney had told him about her past. "Is that why you helped Maggie Watson and her girls?"

Joyce nodded. "I could see she was going through a lot of the same kind of thing, although Phil didn't leave her nearly as well-off. I did what I could for them and she found her way. Now she's getting married again to a wonderful man and she has three lovely daughters. Everything turned out perfectly."

Quinn wasn't so sure about that. From what he'd seen, Sienna was engaged to a man she didn't want to marry, and Courtney hadn't told her family she'd gotten her GED and was nearly done with a four-year degree. He didn't know what secrets Rachel was keeping, but he suspected she had plenty. On the surface, all was well, but there was trouble brewing just below. He wondered how it was all going to come out.

"I have the power to create peace and happiness within myself," Rachel said aloud as she walked along the sidewalk in her neighborhood. She kept her voice low but spoke clearly. Although she felt foolish, doing something was better than doing nothing.

Those horrible few minutes when she'd been trapped in the bathroom at her mother's engagement party had been a turning point for her. She'd been angry and humiliated and hurt. Once she'd crawled into bed, she'd cried herself to sleep. But sometime before dawn, she'd awakened with the realization that she could either spend the rest of her life standing passively on the sidelines or do something to show those bitches they were wrong.

Righteous indignation had carried her through her first walk. She'd been breathing hard at the end of a single block, but she'd kept going. Then she'd joined an online weight-loss group.

Over the next few days, she'd battled sugar withdrawals, hunger and general crabbiness. Now, nearly three weeks later, she was actually starting to feel better. Last night she'd succumbed to a cookie, but for once she hadn't let the single slip derail her. Here she was, at seven in the morning, getting her walk out of the way.

Of all the things those two women had said, what had hurt the most was the comment about letting herself go. Sure, Sienna had been born with natural beauty, but Rachel had always prided herself with knowing how to work with what she had. She'd starting playing with hair—hers and her girlfriends'—when she'd been about ten. She'd begun experimenting with makeup as soon as her mother would let her. She'd read books and pored over magazines and she'd always known she wanted to be a hairstylist. Beauty school hadn't been work, it had been one giant revelation.

But ever since the divorce, she hadn't cared as much about her appearance. She'd been stunned to discover nearly everything she owned was torn, stained or both. Yes, the salon had a dress code that was pretty much all black, all the time, but that didn't mean she had to look frumpy. Black could be interesting and trendy.

She'd gone through her closet and tossed everything that was beyond repair. Then she'd spent an afternoon at the local thrift shop, searching for bargains. She'd found a cool burgundy leather obi belt for the unbelievable price of fifteen dollars and a pair of gently used knee-high boots. She'd also picked up a set of hand weights.

Change was hard, she thought as she turned the last corner and headed for home. Change was uncomfortable and she doubted herself every second. But what she knew for sure was that feeling like crap wasn't the solution. Nor was eating badly and hating her life. She had a great son and a home she loved and family and friends. If she was miserable, wasn't it her own fault?

"I have the power to create peace and happiness within myself," she repeated. It was the affirmation of the day from the free app she'd downloaded onto her phone. Hokey, maybe, but it was working and that was all that mattered.

She called to Josh as she opened the front door to make sure he was up and getting ready for school. She heard the sound of the shower, along with his off-key singing, so she went into the kitchen and loaded the disgusting ingredients into the blender for her smoothie.

The combination of protein powder, coconut milk and flaxseed was enough to make anyone gag. The only thing that made the drink possible was the peanut butter powder she added. At least the flavor was tolerable.

When the drink was ready, she poured it into a tall glass, then retreated to her bathroom. She emerged forty minutes later, showered, coiffed and dressed. She'd taken extra time with her makeup that morning. A smoky eye flattered her, but she hadn't bothered in forever. Because the extra four minutes were really that challenging? She supposed the actual problem was a downward spiral was difficult to stop. Momentum in any direction had power.

She pulled on black pants and a black tunic top, then wrapped the obi belt around her waist and tied it tight, then she looked at herself in the mirror.

She'd taken to sleeping with her hair in a braid to give it waves, then curling a few strands. The extra makeup looked good, and while she still had to lose about twenty-five more pounds, she appeared polished rather than pathetic. An improvement, she told herself.

She returned to the kitchen to find Josh at the table, eating, and his father sitting across from him. The sight of Greg brought her to a stop. For a second she felt flustered and nervous. As if she didn't know what to say to him.

Ridiculous, she told herself. He was just her ex-husband. They dealt with each other because of Josh and that was all. He showed up in her house on a regular basis, and she had never much cared before. Whatever he'd been going on about after the baseball game a few weeks before didn't matter.

"Good morning," she said crisply as she carried her empty glass to the sink and rinsed it out. She crossed to Josh and kissed the top of his head. He briefly leaned against her. Then she looked at Greg.

"Were we expecting you?"

"Nope. I just got off work and came by on my own."

He looked good in his uniform. A little tired, as if he'd had a couple of calls in the night, but still appealing. She remembered when they'd still been married and Josh had been sleeping late. How Greg would come home from his shift, crawl into bed with her and wake her up in the best way possible.

He held up a mug. "I started coffee. I hope you don't mind."

"Of course not." She got herself a mug and poured from the pot. "Did you, um, want something to eat?"

"I'm good, but you go ahead."

She scooped some cottage cheese into a bowl and added blueberries. Combined with the protein shake, it would last her all morning. On the days she worked, she tried not to snack between meals. As long as she kept busy, she wasn't thinking about food so much. She already had her lunch—she'd made that the night before. An effort to not have any excuses.

She sat at the table.

Greg smiled at his son. "Excited about the summer?" he asked.

"You know it. Three more weeks until we're done. I can't wait."

Greg looked at Rachel. "Don't forget we need to talk about his schedule. So I can help."

She started to tell him she was fine on her own, then pressed her lips together. One of her recent silly affirmations on her phone app had been about accepting help from others.

"That would be nice," she said. "Let's get together and talk about how we're going to handle the summer."

"You could start by getting me an Xbox," Josh offered with a grin. "That would be cool."

"Not gonna happen," Greg told him with a laugh. "Besides, you'd rather be outside."

"I would." Josh carried his bowl over to the sink, then reached for his backpack. "I'm ready."

Rachel took her own bowl to the sink and rinsed it out. "You're taking him to school?"

"Him to school and you to work," Greg told her. "Your car is due for an oil change. I'll take care of that this morning and leave it parked at the salon when I'm done."

She swung to face him. "How do you know it's time?"

"I wrote down when you had it last. You drive about the same every month, so it's not hard to figure out when it's about due. You're busy and I don't have much going on today."

He spoke easily, but she read the tension in his body. His shoulders were stiff, as if he were braced for a fight. Because she would usually tell him no, that she would handle it herself. She would rather not owe anyone anything. She wanted to be the giver, the one doing.

Accepting help is an act of graciousness.

Stupid affirmation app, she thought glumly. Now the phrases were getting stuck in her head.

"How will you get back to your folks'?"

He flashed her a smile. "I can walk. It's barely two miles."

He looked hopeful and eager, like the teenage boy she'd fallen in love with. His too-long hair fell into his eyes. He brushed it back with a careless gesture.

"Why don't you come by the salon about eleven thirty?" she told him. "I have an hour break. I'll cut your hair, then drive you back home."

He winked. "It's a date."

Silly words. Meaningless words. Yet they caused a distinct flutter. One she knew better than to believe.

14

IT WAS NEARLY ten o'clock, and the night staff was busy with their evening routine. It was as if everyone had somewhere to be but her. Courtney had already circled through the grounds and now, as she walked the length of the lobby, she realized she was running out of places to go.

She knew what she was really doing—she was looking for Quinn. Her aching restlessness had everything to do with how she felt when she was around him. Just watching him have lunch with Joyce and his friends the other day had affected her. He confused her and excited her and challenged her. Basically, he was catnip and she just wanted to purr and rub all over him.

"That's a really gross analogy," she muttered as she reached the stairwell. She was out of excuses and out of ideas. Short of simply knocking on his bungalow door and taking off her clothes—which seemed rude without an invitation—there was nothing else she could do. She might as well head to her room and have an early night.

She took the stairs two at a time and was out of breath when she reached the fourth floor. She walked into her room and saw a gift bag sitting on her bed. A gift bag that hadn't been there two hours ago when she'd gone looking for Quinn.

She looked inside. There was a bottle of expensive tequila, a room key and a card that said only: *Join me.*

Her stomach flopped over at least three times and her mouth went dry. While she knew who the gift and invitation were from, she didn't know who had put them in her room…or when.

She turned in a slow circle, as if looking for a clue, then realized she was wasting time. Okay, what to do? Should she change her clothes? Put on perfume? Grab a quick shower? Indecision held her in its grip for a second, then she glanced down at the jeans and T-shirt she had on. They were fine, she decided. She rolled her eyes at the thought of perfume—mostly because she knew she didn't own any—then grabbed the gift bag and headed back for the stairs.

She knocked rather than use the room key. That seemed just too…forward, maybe. He opened the door and smiled when he saw her.

"I was hoping you'd say yes."

"You're not wordy when you leave notes."

"I get my point across."

She supposed that was true.

She followed him into the bungalow. He took the tequila from her and crossed to the wet bar. He already had limes on a small cutting board and what looked like a lime-based mixture in a measuring cup. Now he added ice to a shaker, then poured in tequila and the juice.

As he worked, she prowled the edges of the small living room. He'd added a few personal effects—a book, a cell phone, a notepad with writing scrawled across it.

He shook the drinks, then poured. She watched him. Like her, he was in jeans. But instead of a T-shirt, he had on a white men's shirt, untucked and with the sleeves rolled up. His feet were bare. She wasn't sure why that last fact was sexy, but it was. Really sexy.

He handed her a drink, then motioned to the sofa. She took a seat and saw he had set a plate of appetizers on the coffee table.

"Are you seducing me?" she asked before she could stop herself.

He sat in one of the chairs perpendicular to the sofa and toasted her with his glass. "Do you want to be seduced?"

"I believe part of the process is not to be asked that question."

"I hadn't heard that."

She took a sip of her drink. "Of course it is. Otherwise, it's not a seduction. It's a meeting. Seduction is about being swayed."

His dark blue gaze was unreadable as he smiled at her. "You're so determined in everything else. You want to do things your way."

"You're annoying. Has anyone ever mentioned that?"

He chuckled. "Once or twice." He nodded at the plate of food. "Help yourself. You'll want to keep up your strength."

Her toes curled ever so slightly. She reached for a crab puff. "Have you and your posse found a building yet?"

"My posse?"

"What do you call them? Your bros? The gang?"

"How about my team?"

"Posse is better, but sure, we can go with team."

"We have a couple of prospects. Zealand is concerned with sound. Wayne worries about money."

"What do you worry about?" she asked.

"As little as possible." He leaned back in the chair. "I saw you in the restaurant the other day."

"I know. You winked at me."

"You fill in a lot."

"I go where I'm needed. They never let me cook, though. Probably for the best."

"My grandmother says you won't take a different job until you have your degree."

The delightful sense of anticipation faded just a little. "You were talking about me?"

"You're an intriguing subject."

"Not if your grandmother is part of the conversation." She waited, but he didn't say anything. She shifted slightly. "I just want to have my degree in hand."

"Like a talisman?"

"More like a badge of honor. It will be proof of all that I've accomplished."

"You don't think you're already proof? Just in how you live your life?"

Her mood brightened. "That sounds kind of cool."

"You're kind of cool. I'm curious why you need the degree before making a change." He held up one hand. "I get the thing with your family. You're concerned they won't believe you're different until they have tangible evidence. They will, of course, but you'll feel better to have something concrete. But Joyce has known all along. Why not start moving up the ranks?"

"I don't know. I just need to have my degree first." She thought about what he'd asked her before. If she was punishing her family or punishing herself. "This isn't very good foreplay."

"It wasn't supposed to be foreplay." One corner of his mouth turned up. "I promise, you'll know when I make my move."

"And you have condoms?"

"Yes. In case you're curious, the sheets are clean and I've already put out the do-not-disturb sign. Any other questions?"

She was trying to be sophisticated and brave, but it was

hard. She forced herself to take what she hoped was a non-chalant drink, then smiled.

"I'm good."

"Yes, you are. Tell me about your first time."

She blinked at the unexpected question. "You mean sex?"

He nodded. "I don't need details. Just who and when."

She took another sip. "I was eighteen and I'd moved out of my mom's house. I had the job at Happy Burger."

"A destiny you ignored."

"I know. I hope I don't regret it." She smiled. "I don't think I will. Anyway, his name was Cameron, he rode a motorcycle and he told me I was pretty." Her smile faded. "I was more interested in someone wanting me than caring about whether or not I wanted him."

"And you wanted to be like everyone else."

She stared at him. "Excuse me?"

"You were taller than all your classmates, two years older. You didn't fit in. You couldn't fix that, but you could stop being a virgin. At least there you could be just like everyone else."

She had a bad feeling she was still staring, but she couldn't stop. "I honestly don't know what to say."

"Then I'll tell you that I think you're pretty amazing. Strong and determined. Sexy as hell, but you already knew that."

Knew that she was sexy as hell? Um, no. She hadn't received that particular memo. Was there a way to get him to say it again? Or embroider it on a pillow?

Quinn stood, undid a couple of buttons on his shirt, then pulled it over his head. He let it fall to the ground before drawing her to her feet.

"I'm making my move," he murmured right before he kissed her.

She'd felt his mouth on hers before, the arousing combination of strength and confidence with just an edge of determination was so arousing. He kissed her purposefully, taking rather than offering, but not in a scary way.

He cupped her face in his large hands. She pressed her palms to his bare chest and felt the warmth of his skin and the muscles beneath. They met as equals—at least physically. She had a feeling that on the experience front, he was miles ahead.

He deepened the kiss and she welcomed the heat of his tongue against hers. She moved her hands to his shoulders and leaned into him, letting herself get lost in his deep kisses.

Need washed over her. Hunger and a desire to be closer. To know all of him. She wanted him touching her everywhere and she wanted to explore all his secrets. Patience, she told herself. The joining would be better for the waiting.

His hands slid along her upper arms, then down to her wrists and lower to her hips. His fingers toyed with the hem of her T-shirt. He tugged it up and over her head, then tossed it away.

He leaned in to kiss her again, but this time he pressed his mouth to her cheek, then her jaw. He moved slowly, drawing his lips across her skin, nibbling as he went. When he nipped right behind her ear, she felt her skin erupt in goose bumps. Then he straightened and took her hand in his.

He tugged slightly, urging her across the living room. They went into the bedroom. No lamps burned, but light filtered in from the living room. She saw the big bed and then Quinn turned her so she looked into his eyes.

"Second thoughts?" he asked.

"What? No. I want this." *You*, she thought. She should have said "I want you," but she wasn't quite there yet. That would require just a little more courage than she had at the moment.

"Good."

He unfastened his jeans and pushed them to the floor. He

wasn't wearing any underwear and he was already aroused. She allowed herself a moment of admiration at the size of him, then watched as he crossed to the nightstand and clicked on a light.

"Let's see those wings."

She laughed and turned her back to him. "Don't judge."

"I won't." He moved behind her and lightly traced the tattoo across her back. "It's beautiful. Do you feel free?"

"Sometimes."

He unfastened her bra. She let it slide off her arms. He reached around and undid her jeans, then pushed them past her hips along with her bikini panties. She stepped out of her clothes and started to turn to face him. He put a hand on her hip and held her in place.

"Not yet," he breathed, his mouth inches from her shoulder.

So she stood naked in the center of his bedroom. He was right behind her—she could sense his nearness. But he didn't touch her anywhere other than the hand on her hip. Not at first. Then he placed his fingertips on her shoulder blades and drew them down. Just the lightest of touches. The stroke made her shiver and her nipples tighten. He traced the words on the small of her back—words he'd written.

He put his hands on her hips and eased her around to face him. His eyes locked with hers and he cupped her small breasts in his hands. He touched them gently, smoothing the pads of his fingers over her nipples. Pleasure shot through her, taking a direct path to her groin. Excitement grew as he bent down and took one of her nipples in his mouth.

He sucked deeply, circling the tight tip with his tongue. Her breath caught and she had to hang on to him to steady herself. He repeated his actions on her other breast. Need hummed, pulsing in time with her heartbeat. She wanted what he offered. She wanted all of him.

He urged her to step back until she bumped into the bed. "Sit down," he told her.

She sat. He dropped to his knees in front of her. When he guided her to lie back, she did. He parted her legs before dipping his head to press his mouth against the most intimate part of her.

At the first stroke of his tongue, she exhaled slowly. With the second, she let her eyes sink closed as she gave herself over to the ministrations of a partner who knew exactly what to do.

He used his tongue to explore her from every angle. Top to bottom. Side to side. He circled her clit, slowly at first, then faster and faster. Just when the movements reached that perfect *this is the road to me coming* rhythm, he switched things up and pressed the flat of his tongue against her swollen center. She sank back a few levels and caught her breath.

He slipped a finger inside her and pushed in and up, finding what she would swear was the back of her clit. At the same time, he sucked on it, pulling it in and moving his finger and circling and—

She came without warning. One second there was only liquid pleasure, and the next she was shaking and panting through her release. She called out some weird nonword and tried to breathe as every cell in her body sang and her muscles convulsed and she lost complete control.

It took nearly a minute for her to finish, and even then she wasn't totally sure what had happened. She opened her eyes to find Quinn watching her—his hooded blue eyes, as always, unreadable.

"Just once I'd like to know what you're thinking," she complained.

He smiled. "You're welcome."

She laughed.

He stood and pulled her into a sitting position and then onto her feet. Together they drew back the covers. He took a package of condoms out of the nightstand. She got in the bed on one side and he got in on the other, then he pulled her close.

He lay on his side, next to her, supporting his head with one hand and resting the other on her belly.

"Can you come with me inside?" he asked.

She felt herself blush as she looked at everything but him. "Excuse me?"

"Some women find it easy, some don't. Can you? Do you want to learn how? Where are you in this?" As he spoke, he shifted his hand between her legs and began to rub her very swollen center.

"Um, I have a couple of times, but not very often," she admitted.

"What do they do wrong? Don't do it right? Don't last long enough? You're not aroused enough? You can't stop thinking?"

She swallowed hard, then looked into his eyes. For once, she was pretty sure she could guess what he was thinking. His expression was both kind and hungry. He was curious and interested in her response.

At the same time, he continued to rub her. Around and around and around, moving at the same speed, the same pressure, as if they weren't having a conversation at all.

"Do we have to talk about it?" she asked with a whimper. "Can't we just do it?"

"I want to know what makes it good for you."

"You already do. That bit before. That was good. Really good." She reached for him and drew him close. "Quinn, please."

He smiled. "I like when you say my name. Especially when you're coming."

"I didn't."

"Oh, yeah, you did."

She wanted to argue, but what he was doing felt too good. She was getting closer and closer. She could feel it. The rising tension, the promise that was just out of reach. Just a couple more seconds and—

"Give me your hand," he said.

She opened her eyes. "W-what?"

"Your hand." He took his away, then replaced it with her own. "Keep going. We don't want to lose ground."

"I… You…" Was he serious? She barely did that when she was by herself, let alone in front of another person.

He nudged her hand. "Keep going. I'm only going to need a second."

Before she could form enough words to actually protest, he'd rolled away and was reaching for a condom. She stayed where she was—frozen. But then she kind of circled a little, pressing her fingers down on her clit.

She was so swollen, she thought hazily. So ready for another orgasm. Her fingers stroked again and again, then found the rhythm that would get her over the edge.

"Just like that, baby."

Her eyes popped open. Quinn was watching her. His expression was predatory.

"I can't do this," she whispered.

"You already are."

He shifted until he was between her thighs, then eased into her. As he filled her completely, she told herself to stop touching herself. But she couldn't. Everything felt too good.

"What are you doing to me?" she asked, still rubbing herself.

His dark blue gaze locked with hers. "I want what I want."

"Which is?"

He pushed in deeper. She gasped and felt herself slipping

out of control. She couldn't help moving more quickly—pressing harder.

"That," he said, his voice hoarse.

He moved in and out. Faster and faster until she had no choice but to surrender. She cried out as she came, then wrapped her legs around his hips to pull him in deeper. She held on until he, too, gasped his release and was still.

She wasn't sure what to say afterward, or even how to act. Quinn solved the problem by pulling her close and kissing her.

"Want to stay the night?" he asked.

An unexpected question. "Yes."

"Good."

It was good, she thought as she snuggled next to him. Unexpected, but very, very good.

The house for sale was a small three-bedroom ranch. It had been built in the 1950s and had only minimal updates. According to the brochure, there was a peekaboo ocean view from one corner of the backyard, and the local elementary school was only three blocks away. Perfect for a growing family.

Sienna walked through the light, bright living room and into the kitchen. The countertops had been updated, but the painted cabinets looked original. They would be made of real wood, she thought. When stripped down and stained, they could be gorgeous. The stove was newish, maybe eight or ten years old. She wondered if the new owners would consider buying one of those vintage stoves. That would look great in this house.

She saw Jimmy talking to a young couple in the dining room. Their conversation seemed intense, so she didn't interrupt. When Jimmy caught sight of her, he winked.

She explored the bedrooms and the single bathroom. It retained its 1950s flare with medium blue-and-turquoise tiles.

Talk about retro. Although she had to admit she wasn't sure if she would want to change the look. It was oddly stylish. But the house did need a second bathroom.

She went out into the backyard. It was huge, with a few mature trees and a nice fence. A picnic table stood by a barbecue. She took a seat and allowed herself to simply be in the moment. There was no rushing, no hurrying to do something. Just sitting in the sun on a warm spring day.

Her mind raced with all kinds of thoughts. She ignored them and focused on her breathing. Gradually, she started to relax.

She hadn't meant to stop by the open house, but when she'd seen the signs with Jimmy's head shot on them, she'd found herself turning into the residential neighborhood and parking in front of the house. Now she was glad she had. These few minutes of quiet had renewed her.

She heard someone come up behind her.

"What do you think?" Jimmy asked.

"There's room for an addition," she said as she stood and smiled at him. "I'd add a master suite, which would mean an extra bathroom." She turned and pointed to the other side of the house. "There's room for a second addition there. A family room along with a half bath."

"You're practically doubling the square footage of the house. Are you sure that's a good idea?"

"Based on the sizes and prices of homes in this area, yes. It won't be the largest or the most expensive house in the neighborhood. Not even close."

Jimmy grinned at her. "You've learned well, grasshopper. Want a beer?"

"You drink at your open houses?"

"Naw. I'm just kidding. But I do have some lovely imported bottled water, if you're interested."

"Thanks."

She followed him back into the kitchen. The open-house signs were gone from the lawn and all the potential buyers had cleared out. She took the water he offered and unscrewed the top.

"You had a big crowd," she said.

"The whole three hours. We're going to get at least one offer on the place, maybe two."

"That's great."

He looked good, she thought as she studied him. Dressed for business, but not stuffy. He had on khakis and a light blue shirt with the sleeves rolled up. He wore a tie, but it was loose. He was a small-town success story.

"How were the waves?" she asked.

He grinned. "I haven't been surfing today. I had paper-work to do."

She gasped. "Say it isn't so."

"I wish I could. But a man's gotta do what a man's gotta do."

"I remember when surfing would have been the priority."

"We all grow up," he said easily. He nodded at her ring. "Congratulations."

Her good mood evaporated. "Thank you."

"Will you and David be buying a house in town?"

She took a drink of water. "I honestly have no idea."

"Do you want to stay in Los Lobos?"

That wasn't the right question, she thought. The right question was *what the hell were you thinking?* But no one seemed to be asking that. At least not to her face.

"I'm not sure what will happen," she said, evading the question.

Jimmy stepped toward her. His expression was intense, his eyes gentle. "Sienna, we've known each other a long time.

We're friends. I care about you. If you ever need me…for anything, I'm here. You just have to let me know."

"Thanks. I appreciate the reminder."

"Are you okay?"

She faked a smile. "Never better." She held up the bottle of water. "Thanks for this. I appreciate it. And I'll see you soon."

Jimmy looked as if he was going to say something, but in the end, he only nodded. "Say hi to your mom for me."

"I will."

15

COURTNEY WAS EXHAUSTED. Not from a lack of sleep. She'd gotten over that in a couple of days. No, her bigger problems were terror and faking it. Both had a way of draining a person.

It had been three days since her glorious night with Quinn. Three days of catching sight of him around the hotel and sharing a secret smile. Three days of sexy texts and a delivery of chocolate chip cookies, which was way better than flowers. Three days of thinking it wasn't that the intimacy had been so great, it was that she really *liked* him. A given for some people, but her past choices for lovers had been on a scale of bad to worse. Which was why she'd decided to give up on the whole boy-girl thing for a while. She didn't need the distraction.

But Quinn was different. If she was going to get weird about it all, she would say he was a positive force in her life. He wasn't the kind of guy who had to put a woman down to feel like a man. He was actually sweet and sexy, and the things he'd done to her body...

Don't think about that, she told herself firmly. Because her problem wasn't with Quinn—it was with his grandmother. Courtney was terrified everyone around her could see that she'd had amazing sex with Quinn and that so wasn't anything she wanted to discuss with Joyce.

For the most part, she'd been able to avoid her boss, but this afternoon was the first of many planning parties with Maggie about the wedding. It was being held in Joyce's spacious office, and there was no way Courtney couldn't attend. So she put on her best *why no, I didn't have sex with your grandson* face and tried very, very hard to pay attention to the wedding planning details.

They'd already settled on the location—the lawn by the grand pavilion. There would be tents, similar to those used for the engagement party. The wedding would be at the north end of the property, the reception at the south end.

The chairs would have a nice drapey cover on them. Courtney was to check into color availability. The menu was still up for discussion, as was the cake. Although a discussion on the latter was going to be about what kind and flavor, not where to get it.

"I checked with Gracie," Courtney said, consulting the notes on her tablet. "We're not giving her nearly enough notice, what with how popular she is. But there was a cancellation, so she can fit you in. I've made an appointment for a design and tasting meeting." She smiled at her mother. "I can come with you, if you want. Neil should be there, as well. And Gracie wants to know if you would like a groom's cake."

Maggie clapped her hands together. "I can't believe I'm going to have a wedding cake made by Gracie Whitefield. She's been in *People* magazine."

"I remember," Joyce said with a sigh. "No one loves cake like Gracie does."

Courtney offered a silent apology to Gracie. She was sure the other woman was perfectly nice and deserved to be left alone to live her life in peace. But that wasn't ever going to happen—not in Los Lobos.

Although Gracie was a few years older than Courtney, and the two knew each other only enough to say hello, the legend of Gracie lived on, even some twenty years after the fact.

When Gracie had been fourteen, she'd fallen deeply and totally in love with Riley Whitefield. He'd been a few years older and not the least bit interested. When Gracie had discovered he was seeing someone else, she'd done everything from putting a skunk in his car to nailing his doors and windows shut so he couldn't go on a date. When Riley's girlfriend had turned up pregnant and Riley had offered to do the right thing, Gracie had lain down on the road, in front of his car, and begged him to run her over. Because without him, life wasn't worth living.

Gracie had been sent away for the wedding and hadn't returned to town for nearly fourteen years. Courtney remembered some rumor about the girlfriend not being as pregnant as she thought, and the marriage had ended as quickly as it had begun. When Gracie had come back, Riley had been in town, as well. Somehow they'd gotten together. Courtney wasn't sure of all the details, but in the end, Gracie and Riley had married and she'd moved her wedding cake business to Los Lobos.

"Did you tell her the cake needs to be pink?" Maggie asked.

"I did." Courtney checked her notes. "She's going to show us a range of colors and styles and says she has some really fun ideas for you."

"Excellent." Maggie turned to Joyce. "What do you think of adult Otter Pops?"

Courtney pressed her lips together. Seriously? Was this a frat party?

"What are Otter Pops?" Joyce sounded confused.

Courtney described the frozen treat. "They come in a lot of different flavors. Mom's suggesting we add alcohol."

"Vodka," Maggie said cheerfully. "You inject them with a syringe, then freeze them. It's fun."

Courtney wasn't sure which part would be fun. And where exactly were they going to get syringes?

"I'll make a note of the idea," she said, entering the information on her tablet. "We're confirmed to have Judge Jill Strathern-Kendrick perform the ceremony."

"Oh, good." Maggie smiled. "I just love Jill. She and I serve on several community boards together. She's really pregnant, though. Is that going to be a problem?"

Courtney checked her notes. "She's not due until three weeks after the wedding and she was late with her last baby. Do you want me to arrange for a backup? It's probably a good idea. Just in case."

"No. I want Jill. I'm sure everything will be fine. Now, about the flowers…"

Courtney listened as the other two women discussed various choices. She offered suggestions as well, thinking the color scheme made it easy to have a range of options. Now, if her mother's colors had been shades of blue, they would have had to be more creative.

She had visions of the hotel overflowing with vases filled with water colored with food-based dyes and roses in a range of sky blue to violet. That would be interesting.

"I'm going to be away for a few days," Joyce was telling Maggie. "Just so you know. Courtney will be handling everything while I'm gone."

"With the wedding?" Maggie asked, her tone doubtful.

"Yes. She fills in where we need her and she's been handling a lot of events for us. She planned your engagement party and that turned out very well."

"That was a onetime thing." Maggie turned to her daughter. "I thought you were just a maid."

"Most days," Courtney said, reminding herself it was her choice not to say anything to her family. "I've also been known to serve tables, bartend and coordinate weddings. I go where I'm needed."

"She does an excellent job," Joyce added, looking pointedly at Courtney. "You should ask her about it."

Maggie nodded, still looking doubtful. "Yes, I would imagine after all this time you would be able to do a lot of things around the hotel. But you're still primarily a maid."

For a second Courtney thought her mother was going to say more. Suggest yet another course at a trade school. Soon, she promised herself. Soon she would be done with college and be able to tell everyone what she'd been doing.

She thought about what Quinn had said about external validation versus internal. Maybe she should—

No! She'd waited this long. She wanted to be able to slap her diploma down for everyone to see. She wanted it to be real and tangible. Until then, she was keeping her secret.

They finished up with their appointment, and Maggie left to go back to her office. Joyce walked out to the lobby with Courtney.

"You should tell her," the older woman said. "She worries about you."

"I will."

"You've accomplished so much. She'll be proud of you. Why make her wait any longer?"

"I'm not done."

"You're hurting them and I worry you're hurting yourself."

Shades of what Quinn had said about her punishing herself as well as her family. Was insightfulness genetic?

"I appreciate your concern," she said instead, "but this is how I want to do it."

Her boss smiled at her. "A very polite way of telling me to mind my own business. All right. I will. You have to decide for yourself."

"I know and I have. This is the right thing for me to do."

But even as she spoke, Courtney couldn't help wondering why she was the only one who could see that. And if everyone else thought differently, wasn't there the tiniest chance that maybe she was wrong?

The door to the bungalow swept open and a tall, handsome African American man walked in. He spread his arms out wide and announced, "I want to be the next Prince!"

Quinn pulled off his headphones. He stood and crossed to his client and friend.

"Tadeo," he said and held out his arms.

The two men hugged. Tadeo slapped him on the back.

"What are you doing here, bro? This town, it's not you."

"It grows on you."

"So does fungus. It's so small. There's no shopping or restaurants. What do you do for fun?"

Quinn flashed to Courtney. There was plenty of fun to be had with her, and a good portion of it didn't include sex. How often could a man say that about a woman?

"I get by."

Tadeo put down his guitar case. "I meant what I said about Prince."

"No, you didn't. What are you doing here? Are you and Leigh fighting again?"

"Why would you ask that?"

"What happened this time?"

Leigh and Tadeo's fights were legendary. They loved hard

and loud. Marriage and three kids hadn't changed that. Anyone hoping that time would mellow the passionate couple had been disappointed. Although Quinn had to admit they were never boring. But their relationship was a little too high-energy for him.

"She's trying to cramp my style," Tadeo complained as he sank into one of the club chairs. "If I write music all night, I can't get up and take the kids to school. She's got to be reasonable. I'm an artist, man."

"You're also a father."

"That's what she said." Tadeo glared at him. "Did she call you?"

"She didn't have to."

Tadeo shook his head. "I'm not going back. This time it's for good. I'm outta there. She keeps me on too tight a leash."

"You'd be lost without your leash." Quinn glanced at his watch. It was nearly one in the afternoon. "I'm going to order some lunch. You want something?"

"Sure."

Tadeo looked over the room service menu, then Quinn called in the order, including food for Wayne and Zealand, who were due back shortly.

"Zealand texted me about the new studio," Tadeo said. "I'm down with that. Show me the plans and I'll give you my ideas."

"What makes you think I want your ideas?"

Tadeo sat back in the chair. "I'm the artist here, bro. I get to have the attitude."

"I sign the checks."

"Oh. Yeah. I forgot that part."

Quinn chuckled, then got out the floor plan of the building. He explained the modifications they were going to make.

"There'll be rooms where we can write?" Tadeo asked. "I need to be writing and I can't do that at home."

"You're living in LA," Quinn pointed out. "Do you plan to commute up here?"

"I can stay in the hotel. It's nice. Leigh needs to remember I'm a man."

"She needs to kick your ass, which I'm going to guess will be happening soon enough. If she calls me, I'm not lying about where you are."

"You don't know where I am." Tadeo sounded smug.

"You're in my living room."

"I meant you don't know where I'm staying."

Quinn would guess the singer would get a room at the hotel, but he didn't bother stating the obvious. Nor did he continue the discussion. One thing he knew for sure—the more talented the artist, the bigger pain said artist was in his ass. Tadeo was one of the best. Marriage to Leigh had mellowed him, but not enough for the singer to ever be considered just like everyone else.

Quinn supposed he was a little strange himself, and he wasn't sure if that was good or bad. Before he could decide, someone knocked on the front door.

"Room service," a familiar voice called.

He opened the door to find Courtney pushing a large cart.

"Either you have company or you're seriously hungry," she told him.

He took a second to study her. The chef-style jacket suited her. He'd liked the bangs from day one and was pleased she'd kept them. The ponytail was practical and sexy—his kind of combination.

"You look good," he told her. "I miss you."

She blinked. "Wow. Right to the heart of things. You look

good, too, and I—" She glanced over his shoulder. "You do have company."

"Tadeo, this is Courtney," Quinn said without turning around. "She works for my grandmother. Courtney, Tadeo. He sings."

"Nice to meet you," Tadeo said, then cuffed Quinn in the arm. "I'm more than a singer. I'm a songwriter. An artist. I'm the next Prince."

"So you claim. I'm less sure."

Courtney laughed. "I can see you're really busy. Let me get this set up and I'll leave you to it."

"You don't have to rush away," Quinn told her as he helped her maneuver the cart into the bungalow.

"We had someone call in sick today, which is why I'm delivering food. I need to get back to that."

She went over the order, then held out the bill for him to sign.

"Tadeo is one of your clients?" she asked.

"I found him singing at some dive club in Riverside. He owes me everything."

Quinn was joking about that last part, but Tadeo looked up and nodded. "I do. The man even married me."

Courtney raised her eyebrows. "I didn't know you played for both teams."

Tadeo sniggered. "No. I mean he married me to my wife. She thinks you're gay, bro. That's a good one."

"Isn't it just?"

Courtney looked between them. "You're allowed to perform marriages?"

"Only in California. I took the online class and I have my license. You could tell Sienna."

She laughed. "I'll be sure to mention it."

Tadeo sighed. "Leigh and I were married on the beach at sunset."

"Here we go," Quinn murmured. "Next he'll start crying and then he'll go call her."

Tadeo glared at him. "It was a beautiful day."

"It was," Quinn agreed.

"Leigh was stunning." Tadeo sniffed. "I'm going to call her and see how she's doing."

"Probably for the best. Tell her you're sorry."

Tadeo held up his left hand, middle finger extended, but what Quinn heard before Tadeo closed the bedroom door behind him was "I'm sorry, baby. You still mad at me?"

"Have they always been like that?" Courtney asked.

"They have a passionate relationship that defies description." He took a step toward her. "I haven't seen much of you lately."

"I know. It's been crazy. But soon?"

He took another step and was about to pull her close when he heard Wayne and Zealand approaching outside the door.

"Soon," he told her. "Make that very soon."

Courtney worked the room service shift for two days. The pace was different than she was used to. There would be periods of inactivity when she would help out in the kitchen, then a flurry of orders would come in and she would be running all over.

The hotel was already ramping up for the busy summer season. July Fourth was less than a month away, which meant lots of vacationers coming to Los Lobos. The extra staff had been hired. Courtney was scheduled to train the temporary maids the following week. Servers would be added in the restaurant and bar. Her friend Kelly had been promoted to lead server.

Courtney dropped off a bottle of Drama Queen pinot grigio to room 312, then went downstairs and out into the cool evening. It was barely eight, so the sun was a few minutes from setting. She admired the reds and oranges staining the western horizon. The air smelled of ocean and barbecue. A seagull flew overhead. She let the calm wash over her.

These were the parts of her day she always enjoyed, those few minutes of peace between bouts of crazy. Although it was late enough that she would probably have only another half dozen room service deliveries for the night.

She found herself heading toward Quinn's bungalow. Not that she was going to knock or anything, but if the man happened to see her and invite her in…well, it would be rude to say no. She was still smiling at her slightly twisted logic when she rounded the corner of the hotel and saw him sitting in one of the patio chairs. He pulled the side table up close. As she watched, he played a couple of chords on the guitar he held, then made some notes.

He wore jeans and a ratty T-shirt. He was barefoot, slightly mussed and totally hot.

As she got closer, he looked up and smiled. "Hey."

"Hey, yourself," she said. "The guitar really works for you. But you already knew that."

"I've been told." He motioned to the chair next to his. "You can keep me company until your next delivery, if you want."

She sat down. "Thanks. It was a busy dinner service tonight." She touched the guitar. "What are you working on?"

"A couple of songs Tadeo brought me. He has good ideas but can't finish a song to save his life. I clean them up and flesh them out."

They'd talked about this before. How he did more than simply discover talent and push buttons in a recording studio. But she still had a hard time grasping the extent of his involvement with his artists.

"I didn't realize you played guitar."

"Piano, too. You can thank Joyce for that. She insisted. Music lessons started when I was about five. At first I hated them, but then I got good enough to do more than practice scales. When things were difficult with my mom, the lessons and practice gave me a place to escape." One corner of his mouth turned up. "Joyce put a piano in one of the small rooms on the ground floor. I would go practice there every day. I'm sure the guests in the nearby rooms loved that."

"It could be worse," she said with a laugh. "You could have been a drummer."

He chuckled. "I never had that great a sense of rhythm."

"I don't know about that."

He looked at her. "Don't tempt me. You're still working."

Tension crackled between them. She wondered how tacky it would be if she was seen kissing a guest. Or they could slip into his bungalow and—

Her phone chirped. She hung her head.

"What?" he asked.

"It's my mother. I gave her a special tone so I would know it's her texting me, what with the wedding and all, but now I'm thinking that wasn't a good idea. Maybe it's better if I don't brace myself."

"Are you arguing?"

"Oh, no. Nothing like that. It's more the constant flood of ideas." She glanced at the screen. "'Confetti drop with pompoms,'" she read.

He frowned. "Like cheerleader pom-poms? Wouldn't someone get hurt?"

She laughed and held out her phone so he could see the picture. "No. The little fuzzy ones. Instead of dropping confetti, we would drop little pom-poms. I can't decide if they would be easier or harder to clean. Probably easier. We could use the leaf vacuum to suck them all up."

She texted a quick Great idea! then put her phone back in her pocket. "I had no clue she was so creative. I think she's spending a little too much time on Pinterest. Did I tell you the colors of the wedding are basically shades of pink, with a little vanilla thrown in for contrast? So it's pink everything. Even pink champagne."

Quinn strummed a chord. "You mean rosé champagne."

"Oh, please. Don't start with me."

"There's a difference."

"Sure there is," she said sarcastically. "Enlighten me."

He smiled and began to strum a tune she recognized as one of Tadeo's hits.

"Cheap pink sparkling wine gets its color from food coloring. Rosé champagne, true champagne, gets its color from the skin of the grapes. Pinot noir grapes, to be exact."

Holy crap, she thought. How did he know that? Probably from dating some supermodel slash winemaker. "I am so out of my league with you."

He chuckled. "Not really, but I do have a talent for picking up odd facts. Never bet against me at trivia."

"I'll make a note. And tell my mother we need rosé champagne for sure."

"That will make her happy."

He continued to play the song.

"Did you write that?" she asked.

"Most of it. Tadeo helped." He grinned. "He would say it was the other way around."

"You have an interesting group of guys you hang out with," she said. "Zealand, Wayne, Tadeo." Zealand and Tadeo were involved in the music business, so they made sense, but Wayne was kind of an odd choice. The former marine and the playboy music executive. "How did you and Wayne start working together?"

Quinn stopped playing. His smile faded. "It's a long story."

"Oh. You don't have to tell me. I was just wondering, but it's no big deal."

He put down the guitar, and the quiet of the night crept in to surround them.

"It's all public. You can find out online." He leaned back in his chair. "Wayne's son, Casey, was also a marine. He was injured in a bomb blast. Badly injured. Stuck in a wheelchair and living with a brain injury. The doctors did the best they could, but there wasn't much hope. Wayne took care of him, but it's a hard job and he was doing it all alone. The only thing Casey still responded to was music. Specifically Tadeo's music."

Courtney thought about what she knew about the artist. He'd had multiple hits and was known for very loud, slightly crazy concerts.

"Wayne got concert tickets, but when he tried to get the stadium to make special accommodations for Casey, no one would help. He showed up during setup and made a fuss."

"What does that mean?"

"He punched one of the roadies." Quinn lifted a shoulder. "I happened to be there. He was brought to me, and the tour manager wanted to call the police. I asked what was going on and it all came out. Wayne was emotionally and physically at the end of his rope. He just wanted to get his son into the concert before he died. That was it. An easy enough request to fulfill."

"You made it happen," she said.

"Sure. Casey came to all three concerts. He met Tadeo. We made some calls and got Wayne help with his son and then we moved on to the next venue." He stared past her, as if seeing things she couldn't. "Two months later Casey died. Six months or so after that Wayne showed up in my office.

He looked like hell. He said he wanted to thank me for what I'd done. We talked for a while and then I hired him to be my assistant. That was about seven years ago."

Courtney's eyes filled with tears. She wasn't much of a crier, so they were kind of a shock. She sniffed, blinked them away, then glared at Quinn.

"You're really pissing me off," she told him.

"What did I do?"

Everything. Nothing. Before she could figure out what to say, her pager went off.

She stood. "I have to get back to the kitchen. There's a delivery. I'll see you later."

"Courtney. What's wrong?"

She waved off the question. Because what was she going to say? She already liked him. After the amazing sex, she was in danger of getting more involved. Now, hearing the story of how and why he'd hired Wayne, she could feel herself sinking in deeper.

She knew the danger. Love hurt. Always. Every kind. If you loved someone, you were going to get hurt. It was a given. She didn't want that. Not ever. The guys she'd been involved with before had all been borderline losers. Her heart had never been at risk. But Quinn was different. Something she would have to remember. If she wanted to get out of this unscathed, she was going to have to be a lot more careful.

16

SATURDAYS AT THE salon were always long. Rachel's new walking program had given her a little more energy, but by six o'clock, she was still dragging.

As she drove the few miles home after work, she went over the mental list of what had to get done on her two days off. There was laundry, grocery shopping, planning meals for the upcoming week—a chore that should probably come before grocery shopping—an afternoon of Crock-Pot cooking, salad making and the like to give her a jump start on the week.

Both bathrooms were desperately dirty, as was the kitchen. And the yard. She sighed. She didn't want to think about how horrible the lawn looked, not to mention the weeds.

She turned onto her street and saw Greg's truck parked in front of her house. For a second she felt almost giddy anticipation—reminiscent to what she'd felt at seventeen—then firmly squashed the ridiculous emotion. He'd had Josh all day. Of course he'd come by to drop off his son. He must have stayed because he wanted to talk about something. Fine. They would talk, then he would leave and she and her son would have a perfectly wonderful evening together.

But as she pulled into the driveway, she saw something even more unexpected than her ex-husband's truck. Her lawn had been mowed and the majority of the weeds were gone. As she got out of her SUV, Greg came around the side of the house, pushing the lawn mower. He waved when he saw her.

"You're home," he called. "Great timing. I just finished in back."

"You mowed my lawn?"

"Yup. Josh helped. Another year or so and he'll be able to handle it all himself. He's finishing up the weeding in back right now."

She wasn't sure her blood pressure could handle her preteen son using something as dangerous as a lawn mower, but she would deal with that later.

"Thank you," she told him. "Really. I don't like having to deal with the yard. I appreciate the help."

He grinned. "Then you'll be even happier to know you had a broken sprinkler head in the backyard. We fixed it."

"Thank you."

She felt as if she was repeating herself but didn't know what else to say.

"Let me get this cleaned up and in the garage," he told her. "I'll let Josh know you're home and we'll meet you inside. We stopped for Chinese. It's in the refrigerator."

Those last three sentences pretty much left her speechless. She had no idea which to tackle first. That he'd bought them dinner? That he was expecting to join them for said dinner? As if they did this all the time?

What was he doing and what did it all mean?

"You okay?" he asked.

"Um, sure. I'll meet you inside."

She might as well be confused indoors, she thought as she collected her purse and her work tote, then headed into the house.

She changed into jeans and a T-shirt. For a second she'd

had the ridiculous notion that she should touch up her makeup and wear something nice. She squashed that notion. She'd had a long week. She was hungry and tired and she wasn't trying to impress Greg.

She went into the kitchen and pulled the large bag of Chinese food out of the refrigerator. He'd brought all her favorites, which meant her job was going to be portion control. Oh, and she would have to remember not to weigh herself for at least three days, not to mention drink extra water tomorrow and add a mile to her walk. But aside from that, she was going to eat what she wanted without feeling guilty.

She was about to close the refrigerator door when she noticed Greg had also brought a bottle of her favorite chardonnay. What on earth?

"Hey, Mom."

She smiled at her son. "Hi. You worked hard today."

"I know, but the yard looks great." Josh grinned. "Dad says a man has to take pride in his house."

"Does he?"

Her eleven-year-old nodded with self-importance. "I'm going to go get cleaned up."

"Sure." She turned back to the refrigerator and pulled out the bottle of wine just as Greg walked into the kitchen.

"Let me wash up," he said, "then I'll set the table while you heat the food. I can open the wine, too." He pulled off his T-shirt and dropped it onto the counter.

She would have protested that he was taking charge and that wasn't necessary, but she found herself unable to speak.

Oh. My. God.

She'd forgotten. Genuinely forgotten that was what he did. After working in the yard or on the car, he would come into the house, pull off his shirt, then wash his hands and face. He would feel around for one of her perfectly clean dish towels and dry his face before wiping the towel across his chest and down his arms.

She remembered yelling at him about it. How he should learn to clean up in the bathroom. And what was with using her matching set of dish towels? Only, they'd been married then and she was used to seeing him half-dressed or undressed or naked.

But they weren't married now.

She found herself mesmerized by the sight of her ex-husband wearing soft, worn jeans, work boots and nothing else. His chest and back were broad and tanned. She could see the muscles his job required. He hadn't shaved in nearly a week, she would guess, and the dark, scruffy beard looked good on him.

As he turned off the water, she forced herself to look away. Serving dishes, she told herself. She needed to get out serving dishes.

As she crossed to the cupboards, she was aware of a strange pressure in her stomach. What on earth? She couldn't be getting her period. So why was she feeling heavy and—

Rachel wasn't one to swear, but several colorful options occurred to her as she realized she wasn't *cramping*, for heaven's sake. She was aroused. Talk about unfair!

It took only a few minutes to heat up the food. Greg pulled his T-shirt back on, then set the table and opened the wine. Josh appeared and sniffed the air.

"My favorites," he announced, then glanced longingly toward the family room. "So there's a really important Dodgers game on," he began.

Greg rolled his eyes and looked at Rachel. She was still trying to ignore her state of sexual arousal. The last thing she needed was for Josh to announce she was acting weird.

"Sure," she said brightly. "You can watch the game while you eat."

Josh pumped his arm. "Sweet. And soda?"

She hesitated. "Just this once."

"Woo-hoo!"

Greg raised his eyebrows. "That's new."

"We're having wine. It only seems fair."

She and her ex-husband sat across from each other—in the same chairs where they always had. She had an odd sense of past and present blurring until she wasn't sure what to think or say.

"What are you thinking?" he asked as he passed her egg rolls.

"That technically you invited yourself to dinner."

"Uh-huh. I also mowed the lawn without asking you."

"And why is that?"

"Remember that talk we had a few weeks ago at the baseball field?"

She willed herself not to blush. "I'm not sure I would call it a conversation, but sure."

He smiled. "After that, I made a decision. I always ask if I can help and you always tell me no. From now on, I'm going to simply step in and do whatever needs doing."

"Even if I don't want you to? That could get you into trouble."

"Sure, but I figure you'll be mad at me less than you have been and that's a win." He scooped up some kung pao shrimp. "Sienna still engaged to David?"

She elected to go with the change in topic. Probably safer for both of them. "As far as I know. That was the craziest thing. She wasn't happy about him proposing, but I don't know how much of that was the shock and how much was him asking in the first place."

"What number engagement is this? Four?"

"Three. Jimmy, then Hugh, then David."

"I didn't meet Hugh, but Jimmy's a good guy."

"What about David?" she asked, curious about his opinion.

"I guess he's okay. I just don't see them together. There's no chemistry. Maybe she's pregnant."

Rachel choked on her wine. "I'm fine," she gasped, holding up a hand. "Pregnant? No. She would have said something by now."

"It was just a thought."

Sienna pregnant. Rachel couldn't imagine it. Not with David. But of course they were having sex, and once you were doing it, there was always a risk.

She had learned that the hard way. Not that she regretted having Josh.

"You're right," she said slowly. "They could have an unexpected pregnancy."

"Dammit, Rachel." His voice was low, but forceful.

She looked at him. "What?"

"It's not your fault we had Josh before we'd planned. We were both in the bed, making love."

She glanced toward the family room, then back at him. "I know. But if I hadn't forgotten my birth control pills, it wouldn't have happened."

"Would you give up Josh if you could?"

"Of course not." She sipped her wine. "How did you know what I was thinking?"

"I know you."

Something that was both a blessing and a curse, she thought.

"Speaking of Josh," he said. "He's getting to the age where he needs to have chores and start earning an allowance."

"Probably a good idea," she admitted. "What do you think he should do around the house?"

Greg gave her an easy smile that, had she been standing, would have made her knees go weak. "You're the one who's taking care of him on a day-to-day basis. What drives you crazy the most?"

That was easy. "His bathroom. It's always a mess. He leaves towels everywhere. He doesn't wipe out the sink. I bought him some of that spray you use after every shower to keep the tiles clean, but he won't do it."

Greg got up and opened the junk drawer. He pulled out a pad of paper and a pen and returned to the table. "All right. Bathroom it is. What does he need to do on a daily basis versus a weekly basis?"

Thirty minutes later dinner was done, they were on their second glass of wine and they had a chore list for their son. From the family room came sounds of the baseball game.

"I'll put together a chart," Greg offered. "One we can put on the refrigerator. If he does everything he's supposed to for the entire week, he gets a bonus."

"I like that idea and I'm thrilled at the thought of not nagging him to pick up his towels every day."

"He's a capable kid. He can help."

She supposed that was true—it was just she'd never thought to ask. She'd always done everything.

"What about his summer camp?" Greg asked. "When does that start?"

"The Monday after school's out. He's signed up for science mornings and sports afternoons."

He typed the information into his phone. "Great. I'll get you my schedule and we'll figure out when I'm off and can take him there and back." He grinned. "Hell, I'll even make him lunch."

"Do you know how?"

He laughed. "I can figure it out. If I have any questions, Josh will talk me through it."

"Why are you doing this?"

He leaned across the table and lightly touched her hand. "He's my son, too. I should have been doing this all along."

His touch was distracting. She'd always liked the feel of Greg's body next to hers. She'd enjoyed everything they did together. She'd heard other women talk about how they hated their exes or were indifferent to them. She couldn't imagine being indifferent to Greg. No matter what. Probably the reason she hadn't dated since the divorce. What was the point? No man could do to her what he did.

"I wish you'd expected more of me."

His statement brought her back to the conversation. "I did expect more. You weren't willing to do it."

He straightened and dropped his hand to his lap. "You mean you asked once, I didn't bother and that was it."

She pressed her lips together. "I can't tell if you're blaming me or yourself."

"I'm blaming both of us, but mostly me. I know I've said it before, but I'm sorry. I'm sorry that I was willing to marry you but I wasn't willing to be a good husband. I loved you, Rachel, and I wanted us to be together, but I wasn't ready for the responsibilities of being married." He frowned. "I didn't want other women, just a little freedom. Which put the burden of everything on you."

She didn't know what to say to that. "Okay," she murmured.

"What I can't figure out," he continued, "is how much of what went wrong was because of me not being willing to be a grown-up and how much of it was you needing to be a martyr?" He looked at her. "Don't worry. I'm not expecting an answer."

He didn't sound mad. More curious, which was better than angry, but also confusing.

"I'm not sure we'll ever know," she said.

"Probably not." He stood. "Let me help you clear the table, then I'll get out of here. I'm sure you have things to do."

She'd had a plan for the evening, but she was a whole lot less interested in it than she'd been. She wanted Greg to stay. She wanted to curl up next to him on the sofa and watch a movie. Or talk. She wanted him to kiss her and hold her, then take her upstairs and make love to her.

Because she missed him, she thought sadly. What a tragic revelation over cartons of kung pao shrimp and egg rolls. Two years after the divorce, she was still in love with her ex-husband.

They worked in silence, then he went and said goodbye to Josh. She waited for him by the front door.

"Thanks for dinner," she told him. "And doing my lawn. I appreciate both."

"I'm glad. I like the plan we have for Josh."

"Me, too."

The door was open and the porch light on. The evening was still. Cool, but clear, and she could smell the salt air of the ocean only a few blocks away.

She wanted to say something clever or funny or interesting. Something that would make him laugh or wish they were still together. Something that would make him want to stay. But her mind was totally blank, so she could only cross her arms over her chest and smile tightly.

"Have a good rest of your evening."

"You, too."

He leaned in and brushed his mouth against hers. The act was so unexpected, so quick, she didn't have time to respond. Before she realized what had happened, he had straightened and was walking down the porch steps.

She closed the door and told herself it had been a friendly kiss. It had meant nothing at all. But that didn't stop the tiny bubble of hope that settled deep in her chest. She wasn't going to overthink the situation, she promised herself. She was simply going to go on with her life and wait to see what happened next.

Courtney stared at the box on her bed. It was addressed to her, with a Nordstrom's return address label. She hadn't ordered anything from Nordstrom. With paying for her car, her insurance and her college, she wasn't sure she could afford much more than a sock there. Not a pair—just a sock.

So why was there a Nordstrom box on her bed?

She had a feeling she already knew the answer, but there was only one way to be sure. She picked up the box and headed for the stairs. Two minutes later she was knocking on Quinn's bungalow's front door.

He opened it and smiled. "Oh, good. They arrived."

"What did you buy me?"

"Look inside and see."

She took the package over to the wet bar and opened it. Inside the shipping carton was a black shoe box. On the lid it said: Saint Laurent Paris.

She looked at him. "You bought me shoes?"

"So it would seem."

"From Paris?"

"Technically from Nordstrom's website, but I think they originally came from Paris, yes."

"How do you know my shoe size?" She winced. "You don't have a weird foot fetish, do you?"

He laughed. "No. I asked my grandmother to find out your size and she did."

She stared at the box. It was the most beautiful shoe box she'd ever seen—which made her nervous about what was inside. "Why did you buy me shoes?"

He put his hands on her shoulders and turned her until she faced him. "I've watched you walk. You hunch your shoulders as if you're trying to be smaller. Maybe even invisible."

"You noticed that?" Talk about humiliating. She sighed. "I'm very tall. Freakishly so. I don't want everyone to notice."

"It's impossible to miss. You need to embrace your height. You're beautiful and tall. Work with it."

Had he just called her the B-word? For real? Could he please, please say it again?

"Open the box."

Apparently, he wasn't going to repeat the compliment, but she would remember always. She turned back to the counter, sucked in a breath, then raised the lid.

All her air came rushing out as disappointment flooded her. Oh, not in the shoes. They were stunning. A pointed toe, peacock suede pump with what had to be a four-inch heel.

"I can't wear these," she said. "I can't."

One eyebrow rose.

"I'm already six feet tall." She pushed the box toward him. "I'm not interested in being six-four."

"Why not?"

"It's awful. I don't want to be that abnormal. Besides, I don't know how to wear heels."

"Have you ever tried?"

"No."

"Then it's past time. Put them on."

He pulled out one of the dining room chairs. The implication was clear. She sighed again and sat down, then pulled off her sensible flats. Quinn handed her the shoes.

They were gorgeous. They felt good just to hold. She slipped them on and found they fit kind of perfectly. And she had to admit, they looked good on her feet.

He held out his hand. "Ready to stand?"

She grabbed hold of him and rose. Her ankles wobbled and it took her a second to find her balance. "This isn't so bad."

She took a step and nearly toppled over. He caught her and laughed. "You weren't kidding about never walking in heels. Stagger this way."

She laughed and, leaning on him, was able to make her way into the bedroom. He led her to the full-length mirror by the bathroom.

"What do you think?" he asked.

She was in jeans and a shirt. Nothing fancy. But the shoes. They were exquisite. "I'll never be able to walk in them, but they are amazing. Thank you."

"You're going to keep them?"

She looked from her feet back to the mirror, then winced. "Look. I'm taller than you." She was by a couple of inches.

"It looks good on me."

She thought about the models he'd dated. They were all tall. And the man had ridden around with a poodle in the passenger seat of his Bentley. She supposed a little thing like height wouldn't bother him at all.

"I'll have to learn to walk in them," she said, tempted by the thought.

"When you've conquered the heels, you will have conquered your fears."

She laughed. "I'm terrified you're actually telling the truth. And here I thought I would have to grow as a person instead."

He put his arm around her. "Nothing that mundane."

17

COURTNEY WAS A big believer in tasting dinners before a big event like a wedding. The last thing the bride and groom wanted was to find out they didn't like the food being served. She and her mom had an appointment to meet with Gracie to decide on the cake, but just as important was the meal at the reception.

As her mother's wedding was slightly more of a family affair than most, she suggested Maggie also invite Rachel and Sienna to the tasting. There had been a brief discussion then about David, but Maggie had finally decided that as long as he and Sienna were engaged, he should be included. As a friend, honorary grandmother, not to mention owner of the hotel, Joyce had also been asked to come.

Because it was a Thursday evening, Courtney had been able to book one of the smaller dining rooms off the main restaurant. She'd stolen, um, requested, Matt, her favorite bartender, and Kelly was helping her serve.

Courtney had expected to be nervous, but she was way tenser than she'd anticipated. She'd done dozens of tasting dinners before—this was no different. Except for the fact that this was for her mother. She had to remind herself that if Maggie didn't like her suggestions, she was entitled to her opinion. She was a client, like any other, and her likes and dislikes weren't to be taken personally. Now if only she could convince herself to believe it.

Neil arrived alone. He greeted Courtney with a hug.

"Thank you so much for setting this up," he told her. "We're both excited to taste everything you've put together tonight."

"It's going to be a good time," she promised, then looked around. "Where's Mom?"

"Sienna and David are picking her up on the way."

They went over to the bar and Courtney explained about the different cocktail options—all of which were pink. "A signature drink can be fun for guests. One of the questions I'll have for you two is if you want your guests to have the option of getting a drink before the ceremony. There are arguments to be made on both sides."

Neil chose the cosmopolitan, and they walked to the large table set up in the center of the room. When they were seated, he took a taste.

"Nice. Not too sweet."

She smiled. "All the pink doesn't bother you?"

He looked at the pink-and-cream balloons anchored by small bouquets of small pink flowers. "I'm good with it. If Maggie's pleased, then I am, too." He winked. "I'm a big believer in that old saying—happy wife, happy life."

"An excellent quality in a man," she teased.

"I've been married most of my adult life. I've learned my lessons."

"You lost your first wife to cancer, didn't you?"

He put down his glass. "Yes. Karen and I were together for nearly twenty years. When she found that lump in her breast, we never thought it would be a big deal. Some surgery, a little chemo and she'd be right as rain."

His normally smiling face turned serious. "But it wasn't

like that, and when I lost her, I was devastated. We hadn't been blessed with children. I had my work and friends, but it wasn't the same. She'd been everything to me."

"I'm sorry," Courtney told him. She'd known that Neil was a widower, but not the details.

"After a couple of years, I started dating." He grimaced. "I was a disaster. I missed Karen and I couldn't seem to make a connection to anyone else. After a year or so, I gave up. I eventually started traveling to figure out where I would retire." He smiled. "I stopped here for a few days and stayed at this very hotel. Your mother was here for a client lunch. I saw her and couldn't take my eyes off her. The second her client left, I went up and introduced myself."

Courtney laughed. "I remember talking to her after that meeting. She couldn't figure out if you were the sweetest man ever or a serial killer."

He chuckled. "I know. I felt a spark and I knew she was the one. But I went slow so I wouldn't scare her off." He lightly patted her hand. "I'm pretty much a one-woman man. I want you and your sisters to know that. While I was married, I never even looked at another woman. I'm the same with your mother. She's my princess and I'm lucky to have her in my life. I never figured I was a lucky guy, but I know now that I'm about the luckiest SOB to ever walk the earth. Look at the two blessings I've been given."

Courtney felt a burning in the backs of her eyes. She leaned forward and hugged Neil. "We're so glad she's found you."

"I'm the one who's glad." He cleared his throat. "I make you this promise. I will take care of Maggie for the rest of my life and hers. She'll never want for anything. I give you my word."

"Thank you."

Courtney knew that Neil had recently sold a successful business, so she would guess he was reasonably well-off. Mag-

gie had done well with her accounting firm, so between the
two of them, she was sure they would have a comfortable life.

Neil glanced over her shoulder, and his face lit up. "Speaking of princesses…"

She turned and saw Maggie, Sienna and David making their
way to the table. Courtney doubted the princess remark referred to David. She stood and crossed to her sister.

"Thanks for doing this," Sienna said. She looked around.
"Cute decorations. You really went all out." She paused for
a second. "This is you, isn't it? Doing the work? Mom mentioned something about you handling the wedding."

"I've been helping out around the hotel," she said, side-
stepping the question. "What with this being a family affair,
I wanted to help."

David joined them. "If we get married here instead of in
St. Louis, we'll have to talk to you, Courtney. You know all
the ins and outs."

"You're thinking maybe of St. Louis?" she asked, surprised.

David nodded. "Or a destination wedding. We haven't
decided."

Courtney watched her sister as he spoke. Sienna was smiling, but there was a trapped look in her eyes. Or maybe Courtney was imagining things. She saw Rachel arrive and excused
herself.

"Hey, you," she said as she hugged her older sister.

"Hi, back. Wow—the room looks great. I can't wait to try
everything." She patted her stomach. "I walked two extra
miles yesterday and today, so I'm not going to think about
calories."

"You've lost weight, though. I can tell. You look great."

"Thank you. I hate to say this, but I'm feeling better. What
a nightmare. What if everything they say about exercise is
true? What if I have to do it forever?"

Courtney laughed. "There are worse things."

"Really? Like what?" Rachel pointed to the bar. "I want a cocktail. Lena dropped me off and Mom and Neil are taking me home, so I can indulge."

"You do that. I'm going to get everyone to the table, where we'll discuss how the evening is going to go."

Once everyone had drinks and had found a seat, Courtney explained how the evening would work and what they would be tasting.

"I have note cards and pens for each of you," she said, pointing to the paper at each place setting. "Go ahead and rate the food. There's also room for comments."

"Like what?" Maggie asked.

"Things like 'I like it, but it's hard to eat and I'm afraid I'm going to spill.'"

"Guests hate that," Sienna said. "No one wants to trash their good clothes."

Courtney had been bracing herself for a crack about "pulling a Courtney" and was surprised by the support. "You're, um, right. So we'll go in the traditional order of the meal. Appetizers, soups and salads, entrées and desserts. Portions are very small so we can sample as much as possible."

Her boss walked in with two trays. Courtney hurried over to help her. Joyce settled next to Maggie as Courtney passed around the tray.

"Caprese sticks," she said. "Grape tomatoes, mozzarella with basil and a balsamic reduction. If you like the flavor but not the presentation, we can do it in appetizer spoons. We can also replace the bruschetta topping with a chopped version."

Maggie took a bite and moaned. "These are fantastic. Neil, darling, you have to try one."

"I'll try two."

They continued with appetizers and worked their way

through soups and salads. While everyone was eating, Courtney set out wineglasses. Sienna counted.

"There are six glasses. We can't have that much wine and
drive."

David nodded. "I have to agree."

"We're tasting, not drinking," Courtney told him. "Two
whites and four reds, all from Joyce's favorite winery."

Joyce laughed. "I think you're going to be happy with
Courtney's suggestions for tonight. They're delicious and they
all have charming names that seem perfect for the wedding."

"Really?" Maggie looked intrigued. "Like what?"

"Rebel Red and Goodie Two Shoes pinot noir." Courtney
grinned. "The labels are so fun that we don't have to worry
about leaving out the bottles. The guests will love looking at
them. Look, Mom, the pink Goodie Two Shoes label even
matches your color scheme."

She held up a bottle.

"Middle Sister Wines?" Sienna said, raising a glass. "I like
it already!"

Rachel leaned toward Courtney and muttered, "I wonder
if the winemaker has a middle sister complex, too."

Courtney hid a smile.

"It's an intriguing story, actually," Joyce said. "The winery
is named after the middle daughter of one of the founder's
best friends. She said the girl is larger than life, a free spirit. I
always felt the same way about you, Sienna."

"Thank you, Joyce." Sienna stuck out her tongue at her
sisters.

"Don't worry about drinking too much," Rachel said.
"Greg's off tonight. He has Josh. I'll call him and he can
give everyone a ride home. You can pick up your cars in the
morning."

Courtney met her sister's gaze and raised her eyebrows.

Really? She and Greg were getting along that well? Obviously, there had been a shift in their relationship.

Courtney leaned close as she poured the first wine. "We are so talking later."

"There's nothing to talk about." But Rachel blushed as she spoke.

Courtney brought out trays with various entrée choices. She set a small ramekin in front of her mother, who wrinkled her nose. "What is this?"

"Chicken and spinach."

Maggie turned to her. "I hate spinach."

"I know, so I was surprised when you checked it off on the menu list. Remember? We texted about it."

"I suppose it sounded good at the time." She sighed. "Fine. I'll try it, but I won't like it."

Neil kissed her cheek. "I've always admired your maturity, my love."

Courtney didn't have much time to sit and eat, but she was pleased that everyone enjoyed the choices. Well, except for the spinach and chicken dish, which her mother didn't want on the menu. They decided to start with an antipasto platter of olives, roasted peppers and marinated mushrooms, paired with Drama Queen pinot grigio. For the entrée, guests would have a choice of steak paired with Rebel Red or grilled salmon paired with the Goodie Two Shoes pinot noir. They would top off the evening with a bubbly toast.

So far, so good, she thought, pleased to be nearly finished.

Coffee—both regular and decaf—was delivered right before the desserts. Sienna got up and poured herself a cup.

"This is going really well," she said, her voice laced with surprise. "You're not just filling in here and there, are you? You're actually planning weddings. Or at least this one."

"Sometimes," Courtney hedged. "A couple of summers

ago one of the wedding planners got sick and I helped out. I liked the work and I know everyone at the hotel. It makes sense for me to coordinate."

Sienna studied her. "What else aren't you telling us?" she asked.

Joyce interrupted then, saving Courtney from having to make up something.

"What are you two girls whispering about?"

"I was saying that Courtney's doing a great job with the wedding. It's nice to see."

Joyce's look was pointed. "Yes, it is."

Courtney smiled tightly, then returned to the table. "Desserts should be here any second. We have six choices."

Rachel groaned. "I'm already stuffed. I don't think I can taste dessert."

"You have to rally," Maggie told her. "I need everyone's opinions." She looked at Courtney. "Did you think any more about that massage school?"

Everyone turned to look at her. Sienna frowned. "Why would you go to massage school? You're working here."

"She needs more," Maggie said. "She's a maid." She held up a hand. "That's not bad, but, Courtney, honey, you could be so much more."

Neil touched her hand. "Maybe this isn't the time."

"I know." Maggie shook her head. "I'm feeling the wine. I'll stop. I promise. It's just I worry about you."

Courtney wanted to snap that she didn't. Not really. What she worried about was being proud of her daughters. Of being able to say something other than "my daughter's a maid."

She told herself to take the high ground—to let it go with a smile.

Joyce walked over and set her cup of coffee on the table. "Tell them."

Courtney held in a groan. Seriously? Her boss chose this exact second to break ranks?

Maggie looked between them. "Tell me what?"

"Nothing. Where are those desserts?" Courtney eyed the house phone by the door. "Let me check on them."

"Courtney Louise Watson, what is Joyce talking about?"

Ack! What was it with mothers and that stern tone? Her stomach clenched, her throat tightened and she felt about ten years old again.

"Mom, I'm fine," she said. "I love my job here. Let it go."

"Mom, stop." Rachel got up. "I'll get you some coffee. Neil, talk to her. This is a nice evening. Let's leave it that way. Courtney, you've done an excellent job. Congratulations."

Courtney dashed to the phone and dialed the kitchen. One of the servers picked up.

"We know, we know. One of the trays got dropped and we're trying to fix things."

Of course, she thought grimly. Because life was always about timing. "Bring what you have. Quickly, please. I beg you."

She turned back to the room, only to find her mother had cornered Joyce.

"What do you know?" her mother asked the other woman.

"We have a dessert crisis," Courtney said quickly. "But we'll have some samples to taste any second now. Mom, I know there's mousse, assuming it's not on the floor. Won't that be good?"

She was afraid she sounded frantic, mostly because she was. It was one thing for her boss to not volunteer information, but to lie when asked directly was another thing. Courtney got that. She also recognized the trouble had started with Joyce's comment, which left her in the unusual position of being angry with Joyce.

"There's something," Maggie insisted. "What is she keeping from me? What do you know that I don't? Dammit, Joyce, we're talking about my daughter."

"Don't try that tactic on me, Margaret," Joyce snapped back. "I'm sure you care, in your way, but you've never really been there for Courtney and we both know it. Of course she keeps secrets from you. Why wouldn't she? But in this case, I wish she wouldn't. If you knew what she'd done, what she's doing, you wouldn't treat her like an idiot. Because she's not. She's a smart, capable woman."

The room had gone silent. Even the canned music had faded to faint background noise. Courtney couldn't decide if she wanted the desserts to arrive or if it was better that no one she work with witness what was going to be one of her life's great disasters.

Her mother looked at her. Tears filled her eyes. "What's going on? What are you keeping from me?"

Anger was easy to resist, but hurt was something else. She could tell herself she hadn't done anything wrong, that they didn't deserve to know, but she wasn't sure she could make herself believe that. Not in her heart.

"I don't want to be a massage therapist," she said quietly. "Or a vet tech or any of the other jobs you've suggested over the years. I want to run a hotel."

"Go on," Joyce prompted. "Tell her what you've done."

In for a penny, she told herself. "I got my GED, then my AA. I'm two semesters away from getting my bachelor's in hotel management."

Joyce moved to her side and put her arm around her. "There's more. She just got invited into a special class. That's how much her instructors think of her. She's a straight-A student, and most of her college has been paid for by academic scholarships."

Maggie took a couple of steps back, reached behind herself and felt for a chair, then sank into it. Her face was white, her eyes wide.

Rachel stared at her. "You never said a word." She sounded breathless and hurt. "All this time, all the things we did together. You never hinted."

Courtney's stomach twisted and guilt filled her. "I'm sorry. I know you don't understand. I didn't plan this. It just kind of happened. I wanted to get my GED and surprise everyone. Then I kind of signed up for community college and decided to wait and see if I could really get my AA. When that happened, I wanted to be able to show you all what I'd done. I wanted to be able to hand you my degree."

Not hand it to them, she thought to herself. Throw it at them. She'd wanted proof that she wasn't what they thought.

"But you've been doing this for years," her mother breathed. "You've kept this from us for years. We're your family and you didn't tell us any of it."

She covered her face with her hands and started to cry. Neil rose and hurried to her. He crouched down and put his arms around her.

"I'm sure you had your reasons," he told Courtney. "But you've hurt your mother."

"You've hurt all of us," Rachel said. She stood. "I'm going to call Greg to come get us."

Sienna stood up. "What's wrong with all of you? So she didn't tell us. Look at what she's done. Courtney, good for you. You did the work and you have a lot to show for it. Mom, you have to see, this is a good thing. Courtney's not the loser you thought. She's going to be fine. I'm proud of her, and you should be, too."

No one said anything. Courtney knew she had to figure out something to explain or make the situation better, but she couldn't think of what. She wasn't going to apologize. She hadn't done anything wrong. But her mother was in tears, Rachel was upset and the tasting dinner had turned into a disaster.

"You should be proud of yourself," Joyce told her.

"I wish you hadn't said anything."

"It was time for them to know."

"That wasn't your decision to make. This was between me and my family. I wasn't ready."

Her boss didn't look the least bit contrite. "Based on how things were going, you were never going to be ready, dear. I just gave you a little push."

"You didn't have the right." She walked toward Rachel.

Her sister glared at her. "Whatever you have to say, I don't want to hear it. My God, Courtney, I've tried so hard to help you. All these years. I thought we were close. I thought we were the kind of sisters who could depend on each other. I can't believe how wrong I was about you."

She walked out. Maggie and Neil followed. Sienna and David stood, as well. Sienna paused.

"They'll get over it. You'll see." Sienna hugged her. "You go, girl."

Courtney nodded because she couldn't speak. Shock and guilt and a sick feeling combined into an impossible emotional stew. Joyce left with Sienna and David, leaving Courtney standing alone in the center of the room. Two seconds later one of the servers walked in with a tray of desserts.

"Where is everyone?" he asked. "Are we still tasting these?"

Courtney shook her head. "Not tonight."

18

QUINN WAS SURPRISED to find his grandmother and her dogs at his front door so early in the morning. He was just back from the gym and was about to start coffee.

For once, Joyce wasn't perfectly groomed. She looked tired and wasn't wearing makeup. Based on the dark circles under her eyes, she hadn't slept well. He stepped back to let her into the bungalow. Her two dogs followed.

"What's wrong?" he asked. "Are you all right?"

She twisted her hands together. "The tasting dinner didn't go well."

He knew that Courtney had worked hard to get the menu right. He'd helped her with the wines, and they'd talked about how she wanted the evening to go. He'd thought she might stop by afterward, but he hadn't heard from her. He'd assumed she'd been tired and had gone to bed.

"What happened?" He took her arm and led her to the sofa. "Tell me."

She perched on the edge of the cushion. Sarge and Pearl sniffed around the room before Pearl jumped onto one of the club chairs. Sarge joined her and they curled up together.

Joyce briefly closed her eyes. "I think it might be my fault."

"Why?"

"Her mother wanted to talk to her about massage school. We both know that's not what Courtney wants to do. I know that she wanted to wait to show them her degree, but enough's enough. I said to tell them what she was doing."

Quinn's sympathy faded. "You told them?"

"Why are you saying it like that? I was only trying to help."

Love for his grandmother blended with frustration and worry about Courtney. "It wasn't your secret to tell."

"I didn't." Joyce raised her chin. "Not exactly."

"If that's true, why are you here so early in the morning?"

Her lower lip began to quiver. "You're mad at me."

"No, I'm disappointed."

"Don't say that."

He leaned over and kissed the top of her head. "I love you. Nothing can change that. But you were wrong and you know it. I'm not going to tell you otherwise. The person you should be talking to is Courtney, not me."

"I c-can't."

"Then I will."

He left the bungalow and headed to the hotel. He figured there was a fifty-fifty chance that Courtney had started work, but he went to the fourth floor anyway and knocked on her door.

She answered almost immediately.

She had on her usual maid's uniform, with her hair pulled back in a ponytail. Her eyes were tired, her mouth drooping.

When she saw him, her shoulders pulled back a little. "If you've come here to plead Joyce's case, I don't want to hear it."

He stepped into the room. As she moved back, he cupped her face in his hands and kissed her.

"Why didn't you text me or come by?" he asked.

She sagged against him. "I needed to cry, and no guy wants to deal with that."

"I can deal with anything you have going on." He kissed her again. "Next time I want to be there. I don't care what time it is. Understand?"

She nodded and drew back. Tears filled her eyes, but she blinked them away. "What if you're busy having sex with some hot singer?"

"I won't be. I gave up singers a long time ago. Now I'm into college-going maids who look hot in khakis."

"That's a very limited subset."

"I'm a particular kind of guy."

She sucked in a breath. "They're all mad at me. No, not mad. Mad I could deal with. But they're hurt. I don't know how I feel about my mom, but I feel awful about Rachel. She and I have always been close."

"Did you talk to her?"

"I've left a couple of messages and texted her. She hasn't answered." She sniffed. "You want to know the weird part?"

He nodded.

"Sienna's the only one who gets it. She thought it was great and said she was proud of me. Who would have thought that would happen?"

"Family dynamics are always interesting."

"There's one word for it." She looked at him. "Just so you know, I'm really mad at Joyce."

"Good. I am, too."

"But she's your grandmother and you're not really involved."

"She upset you. That makes me involved."

"I honestly don't know what to say to that."

"Tell me what time you get off work. I'll take you to dinner, then bring you back here and help you forget about your troubles."

She managed a slight smile. "With a rousing game of Scrabble?"

"You read my mind."

She wrapped her arms around him. "Thank you."

He hugged her back. "Anytime."

"I have to get to work."

"I know. I'll see you soon."

As Courtney started down the stairs, Quinn thought about all that had happened. Joyce meddling wasn't news, although this time the consequences would be bigger than usual.

But the problem his grandmother had created wasn't what captured his attention. Instead, it was how he'd felt when he'd found out. And how he'd reacted. He'd wanted to protect Courtney. He'd wanted to be there for her.

Somehow she'd gotten under his skin. He supposed some of it was the juxtaposition of her lack of confidence and her complete bravery. Some of it was just her.

He'd moved back to Los Lobos to be closer to his grandmother, to get away from LA and to figure out what was next for him. Courtney was an unexpected gift. Now he had to figure out what he was going to do about her, his job, hell, his life, and if there was any possibility of finding his way to what the rest of the world considered normal.

"You shock me," Lena admitted as she pulled her car into the parking lot. "In a good way."

Rachel unfastened her seat belt. "I appreciate the invitation. You're right—it's time for me to get out a little."

When her friend had phoned to suggest they go out to a bar for the evening, Rachel had found herself wanting to accept the invitation. Josh was celebrating the end of school with a sleepover at a friend's house for the night. She'd thought she might hear from Greg, but she hadn't. She was still trying to work through what had happened at the tasting dinner two nights before. Going out with Lena had seemed like the perfect distraction.

They got out of the car. "Did I tell you that you look great?" her friend asked. "You do."

"Thanks." Rachel self-consciously smoothed the front of her dress. Her reduced calorie diet and morning walks were paying off. She'd lost ten pounds and was back in a dress she hadn't worn in maybe three years. Despite her long day at work, she felt good. She'd taken extra time with her hair and makeup. Not that she was interested in impressing anyone. Instead, she'd done it for herself.

Lena paused outside the entrance. "We need a game plan."

Rachel laughed. "We're going to go inside, have a couple of drinks, and then we're going home."

"What if you see a good-looking guy?"

"We'll giggle about it."

Lena groaned. "What if he asks if he can buy you a drink?"

"Not gonna happen."

"What if it does?"

She knew what her friend was trying to say. That it was time for Rachel to get back out there. She'd been divorced for nearly two years. She wasn't that old, so finding someone to spend the rest of her life with made sense. There was only one problem—she wasn't over Greg.

"I'll thank him and say no."

"I knew you were going to say that."

"Hey, at least I got dressed up and came out with you. Baby steps."

"You're right. I'll take what I can get."

She pulled open the door. Harry's Bar was located down by the pier. The clientele was a pretty even mix of locals and tourists. For Los Lobos, it was considered fairly upscale—with nice finishes and decent lighting. In addition to the usual drink selection, there was also a menu of light bites and a flatbread of the day.

They took a table by the windows. Rachel scanned the cocktail menu, then passed it to her friend.

"What looks good?" Lena asked.

"I'm going to try the blueberry mojito."

"Wild woman."

"I'm trying."

Rachel looked out at the hundred-plus-year-old pier where families and couples were enjoying the warm late-June evening. The beginning of tourist season. The town's population would swell, and businesses would be busy for everyone. Especially at the hotel.

Thinking about the hotel made her think of Courtney.

"Uh-oh," Lena said. "What?"

"I still can't wrap my mind around Courtney. About getting her GED and going to college. She and I talk nearly every day. We hang out. We've always been close. What happened?"

"I don't know," Lena admitted. "I can't imagine keeping something like that from my family or you. Have you talked to her?"

Rachel shook her head. "She's left me some messages and a few texts. At some point I'll have to answer. I honestly don't know what to say to her."

"I get you're upset. I would be, too. But don't stay mad too long. You two have a great relationship. I'd hate to see you lose that."

The server came by to take their drink orders. Rachel used the interruption to change the subject.

"How are the vacation plans coming?"

Lena and her family were planning a four-week road trip. It was Rachel's idea of hell, but she understood that some people enjoyed hours and hours together in the car.

"There are maps everywhere in our house," Lena said with a laugh. "Right now the discussion is about how long to spend with Toby's parents. I love my in-laws, but anything more than three nights is too much."

Lena spoke for a few more minutes, then excused herself to use the restroom. Rachel sat alone at the table and realized she wasn't sure she'd ever been in a bar by herself. She'd married so young. By the time she turned twenty-one, she was a mother. Going to bars didn't fit in with her lifestyle.

She felt her purse buzz and pulled out her cell phone. She had a text from Greg.

What are you up to tonight?

She studied the message. If only he'd asked a few hours ago. As it was...

I'm out with Lena. At Harry's Bar.

Want company?

She smiled. Lena *had* encouraged her to make contact with a handsome man. Greg certainly counted as good-looking, even if he violated the spirit of what her friend had meant.

Sure.

By the time she and Lena were halfway through their drinks and laughing about potential road trip disasters, the hairs on the back of her neck began to prickle.

"What?" Lena asked, then glanced toward the door. "You didn't."

"He texted me first," she said, knowing she sounded like a defensive teenager. "And you did tell me to talk to a man."

"I didn't. I asked what you would do if one wanted to buy you a drink. You're impossible. You know that, right?" Lena stood and hugged Greg. "You two make me crazy."

"Nice to see you, too," he said, kissing her cheek. He pulled out an empty chair. "What are you two ladies having?" He looked at Lena's strawberry daiquiri and her mojito, then grimaced. "Never mind."

"A beer," he told a passing waitress.

"You're such a guy," Rachel told him.

"I am what I am. So, who are we talking about?"

"What makes you think there's a who?" Lena asked.

"Because there always is."

Rachel was content to listen to the two of them chatting. She liked that her husband and best friend got along. They always had, just like she'd always liked Toby. The four of them had done a lot together. Their boys were friends. It had worked, until the divorce.

Funny how the feelings from Greg's and Courtney's secrets were so similar. A sense of betrayal, enough hurt that she didn't have room inside to hold it all. The sense that everything was just plain wrong. The emotions had been stronger two years ago, but these new ones still hurt.

The three of them talked for a while. The server returned to ask about a second round. Lena shook her head.

"I'm done. You two go ahead."

"What do you mean?" Rachel asked. "We're hanging out."

Lena raised her eyebrows. "Being with you two makes me want to go home and hang with Toby." She held up a hand. "Don't take that wrong. Greg will drive you home."

"Yes, I will," he said easily.

Rachel stood and hugged her friend. "I'll talk to you tomorrow."

"Of course. Have fun."

"That was strange," Rachel said after Lena left. "I don't know why she left."

"Don't you?"

Before she could answer, the server returned. "Have you decided if you want another round?"

"I'm game if you are," Greg told her.

"Sure," she said. "I'll have another."

"Great. Be right back."

Greg leaned close. "So what's going on? You have something on your mind. What is it?"

He'd always been able to read her, she thought. "It's Courtney." She told him about her sister and what she'd been doing.

"I don't get it," she admitted. "How could she not have told me?"

Greg shifted his chair closer and stared into her eyes. "It's not your fault."

"Her keeping secrets? I know that."

"No. That she had trouble learning to read. That she got held back. That wasn't you."

Rachel slumped in her seat. "I know."

"I'm not sure you do. You were a kid when your dad died. You did the best you could to hold everything together. You helped your mom. But you weren't the adult. Courtney was born the way she was born. You didn't make a learning disability happen. You weren't responsible for her being held back."

She nodded but was unable to completely believe him. "I was so hurt when I found out what she'd been doing," she admitted. "I keep thinking she blames me for not doing well in school."

"She doesn't. You're a good sister."

"I hope so." She sighed. "Let's talk about something else."

"Okay. I'd like to take Josh camping," he said. "Are you good with that?"

"Sure. He'll love it. Have you told him?"

"I wanted to talk to you first."

"Thank you. I say have a great time."

He grinned. "You want to come with us?"

"Not even for money."

He chuckled. "I knew you'd say that."

Their drinks arrived. They sat in the bar for nearly two more hours, talking about work and Josh and mutual friends. Around ten, Greg drove her home.

She'd been in his truck hundreds of times. She knew the route and how long the trip would take, and with each passing second, she found herself getting more and more nervous. Her mouth was dry, her hands trembled.

It was all his fault, she thought, trying to summon annoyance with the hope that it would counteract the growing tension. He thought he was so smart when it came to her. Sure, he was being really nice and helping more with Josh, but so what? It had only been a few weeks. It wasn't as if she could trust him.

Which wasn't really the problem, she admitted to herself. The problem was she missed him. Missed them. Greg had always been the only man in her life, and she didn't want that to change. She wanted them back together. She wanted what they'd had before the affair, only without the drama. She wanted a husband she could depend on and she wanted that man to be Greg.

Heat burned low in her belly. She recognized desire. It was brought on by too many months alone and the close proximity to the only man she'd ever been with. Whatever else had gone wrong between them, the sex had been right.

Indecision tore at her. She wanted to ask him in…ask him to stay. She wanted to make love with him. Fast and hot, then more slowly. She wanted to feel his body next to hers, his hands everywhere. She wanted to kiss him until she was wet and swollen and oh so ready to be taken.

But they were divorced and she just wasn't sure. What if she asked and he said no? For all she knew, he was sleeping with someone else.

The thought stabbed her, leaving her nearly breathless. She was still dealing with the possibility when he pulled into the driveway.

"Thanks for the drive home," she said and opened the passenger door.

"You okay?"

"Fine." She slid to the ground. He started to get out of his truck, but she waved him back in place. "I'm fine. I'll see you later."

"Rachel, what's up?"

"Nothing. Good night." She slammed the car door shut and practically ran to the house. Once inside, she leaned against the door.

What was wrong with her? So what if Greg was sleeping with someone else? They weren't together anymore. He could do what he wanted. With whomever he wanted. They were both used to having great sex. Unless she was fooling herself. After all, he'd been with at least one other woman and she'd only ever been with him. Maybe what she thought was great sex was just ordinary. Maybe it was better with other women and he would have told her no, anyway.

Thoughts swirled and danced, leaving her confused and with a headache. Not knowing what else to do, she started the long, lonely walk back to her solitary bedroom. The one she'd once shared with the only man she'd ever loved.

19

WHEN COURTNEY STILL hadn't heard from her mother five days after the dinner, she knew there was a problem. The question was how to deal with it. The wedding was less than two months away and details had to be finalized. Perhaps more to the point, they were still a family, and getting along seemed kind of important.

They'd gone longer without speaking, she reminded herself as she drove through town. The day she'd turned eighteen, she'd dropped out of high school, packed a bag and moved out. She hadn't spoken to her mother for nearly a year.

But this time was different. This time was her mother not answering *her*. She supposed there was some karmic payback in that and she probably shouldn't complain, but she couldn't help wondering…and maybe worrying.

Figuring the wedding would go on regardless of the family drama, she headed for the appointment with Gracie White-field, local celebrity and nationally famous cake decorator.

Courtney pulled onto the quiet street and was pleased to see her mother's car parked outside Gracie's house. The huge old mansion had once belonged to Gracie's husband's uncle. From what Courtney had heard, an entire wing had been turned into an industrial kitchen for Gracie's business.

Courtney parked behind her mom's car. She ran through possible greetings. The first one that came to mind was "you started it," but that was hardly mature. She knew that technically she had every right to not share any part of her life. But technicalities weren't always helpful—especially where mothers were concerned.

She and Maggie got out of their cars at the same time. They looked at each other.

Courtney drew in a breath and went with the obvious babble. "Hi, Mom. I'm glad you're here. I think you're really going to like Gracie's cakes. She's pretty gifted." She hesitated, knowing she had to address what had happened. "About last Thursday," she began. "I'm sorry if you're upset."

Just saying the words made her wince. Talk about a weaselly apology.

"I don't want to talk about it," her mother told her. "Let's just get this over with."

Courtney felt the emotional slap hit her cheek. So all was not forgiven, or even understood. "Is Neil joining us?"

"No. He was called away to a board meeting. He's selling his company."

"I thought he had already sold it."

"The deal is taking a while."

And it required a board meeting? Courtney thought he owned a couple of video game/pizza places. Would that really require a board of directors? Not anything they were going to talk about now.

They walked around to the side entrance to the house. Gracie opened the door as they approached. She was a pretty blonde, who greeted them with a friendly smile.

"I'm so excited about your cake!" She ushered them into her kitchen.

Gracie's kitchen was large, with high ceilings and what

seemed like miles of counter space. The decor was simple—white, painted cabinets, pale gray-and-white marble countertops and stainless-steel appliances. What could have seemed cold and impersonal was instead the perfect, plain backdrop for the extraordinary cakes being assembled.

There was a four-tier extravaganza partially covered in lavender-and-blue flowers. Another cake had tiny butterflies, poised to take flight. There were photographs on the walls and drawings leaning up against the subway-tile backsplash. In the corner was a pint-size table, littered with crayons and coloring books.

Gracie led them to a long table with eight chairs in a corner of the room. A sketch pad sat at one end. At the other were plates with slices of cake and a pot of coffee.

"I've been thinking about your colors," Gracie said when they were seated. "And the fact that you and Neil can't decide between vanilla and chocolate for your cake. So what about something like this?"

She opened the sketch pad and showed them a picture of a slice of cake. The inside was a checkerboard of vanilla and chocolate. The squares lined up perfectly.

Maggie's tense expression relaxed. "It's beautiful. Can you really do that?"

"Sure. It's actually not that difficult. There are special pans and once everything gets rotated..." Gracie waved her hand. "You don't want to hear the details, but yes, it can be done and it's really lovely."

She collected two plates and forks. Courtney saw that while the icing was yellow, the cake was the checkerboard pattern.

"Have a taste and tell me what you think."

Courtney took a bite. The flavors combined perfectly. "It's delicious," she said. "I've never seen anything like this, and there have been a lot of wedding cakes at the hotel."

"The hotel you're practically running?" Maggie asked, her voice sharp.

Courtney looked at her. "Mom, what do you think of Gracie's cake?"

Maggie shrugged and took a tiny bite. "It's fine."

Gracie glanced between them. "I have other flavors for you to try. Chocolate and vanilla, of course, and a really nice spice cake that's popular."

Maggie put down her plate. "This is fine."

Courtney felt herself getting tense. Obviously, this was the wrong time for the appointment. "We should reschedule," she began.

"Why?" Her mother turned to Gracie. "We're here. If we don't decide, we will have wasted your time. As I said, this cake is fine."

"All right," Gracie said cautiously. "Based on what you and I talked about on the phone, I've been looking at something relatively simple for the frosting. There's a technique called scratching. It creates a texture on the cake that's very beautiful."

She showed them several pictures of cakes with icing that looked as if it had been put on in rows and then partially smoothed.

"I would do a cascade of flowers from the top down one side." She put a sketch of a four-layer cake on the table. "This is fairly true to size and will serve three hundred easily. I believe that was the number you mentioned?"

Maggie glanced down at the sketch. "Is that the color?"

"The pale pink? It is if you like it. I would do the flowers in the colors you see. They would range from very pale to deep pink. Not magenta, though. Just true pinks."

"I'll take it. Thank you for your time." Maggie rose and walked to the door. Before Courtney could stop her, she was gone.

"I'm so sorry," Courtney told Gracie. "We're fighting. But I guess you figured that out."

Gracie smiled patiently. "It's okay. You'd be amazed by what I've seen happen at these appointments. It's never boring, that's for sure."

"The cake really is beautiful. I'll make sure it's what she wants and get back to you by the end of the week. Does that work?"

"Sure. I have your mother's wedding date in my schedule. I need the design nailed down by mid-July. Otherwise, we're good."

"Thank you."

Courtney expected her mother to have already left, but Maggie stood by her car. Courtney recognized the determined expression on her mother's face and braced herself for battle.

"I can't believe you kept this from me," her mother said as she approached. "For years. How could you lie to me? How could you not tell me what you were doing, day after day, year after year?"

There were a thousand different responses. Courtney considered several of them before her own anger took over. "How could you not care about me for all those years? I was held back in school twice, Mom. *Twice.* Do you know what that was like for me? Do you know how horrible school was?"

"You had a learning disability. That wasn't anyone's fault. You can't blame me for that."

"I don't. I blame you for not caring enough to get me tested earlier. I blame you for not noticing when I moved up from remedial classes into the mainstream ones. When I quit high school, I was getting As and Bs and you didn't know."

Her mother glared at her. "Of course. Make it my fault. I'd like to remind you I was doing my best to keep my family afloat. Your father left us destitute. You have no idea what I had to go through to save us."

"You have no idea what I went through, either. The difference is I was the kid and you were my mom. You were supposed to be there for me and you weren't. You didn't see me at all except to tell me to try harder. I grew up knowing I was a disappointment and a failure in your eyes."

Her mother began to cry. "That's not true! How can you say that to me? I love you."

"I know you do, but that's different than believing in me. The reason I didn't tell you what I was doing was because I had something to prove. I thought if I could hand you my diploma, you'd finally think I was good enough."

"I do think that."

"No, you don't. You're always trying to get me to try something else. You're ashamed of me and what I do."

"I thought you were just a maid. It's not wrong to want more for my child."

"No, and it's not wrong for me to want to do it myself. You've never talked about me the way you talk about Rachel and Sienna. Even at the engagement party, you said 'I'm so proud of my daughters...and Courtney.' I've always been an afterthought."

"That's not true. I never said that."

"Mom, there's a video."

The tears flowed faster. Maggie's mouth trembled. She seemed to shrink a little. "Why are you doing this? Why are you so cruel?"

"I'm not. I'm trying to explain. I just wanted to do it on my own."

"Without me."

She wasn't asking a question, so Courtney didn't answer.

Instead, she said, "I never meant to hurt you. I'm sorry that happened."

"But you're not sorry for what you did?"

"Getting my GED, my AA, and being a year away from my bachelor's? No. I'm not sorry for that."

"I would have helped you."

"I wanted to do it on my own."

Her mother brushed the moisture from her face. "No. You didn't want me to be a part of it. There's a difference."

With that she turned and got in her car. Courtney watched her drive away. She felt sick and shaky. This wasn't the end of it, she thought grimly. Not even close.

Sienna slid into the booth across from her sister. Courtney looked at her warily.

"So this is just lunch?" she asked.

Sienna frowned. "Sure. What else would it be?"

"Everyone is mad at me. Just checking you're not."

"No way. Like I said before, I think you're to be commended for what you did." She smiled. "We all know that if I'd been getting my GED and everything else, I would have been taking out ads in the local paper."

Courtney relaxed. "Thanks. I need someone to not be mad at me."

"I'm your girl."

They were having lunch at Treats 'n Eats near the pier. Sienna had texted her sister impulsively and now she was really glad she'd suggested getting together. Funny how Courtney's revelation had shifted everything. She was sorry her sister was having trouble with Rachel and their mom, but Sienna was happy to discover they were more alike than she'd thought.

"It's the secret thing," she said now. "Mom feels stupid for not knowing and Rachel feels betrayed."

Courtney groaned. "Thanks for that slightly painful recap."

"I didn't mean it in a bad way. We all have secrets. It's just yours are more interesting than most."

Their server arrived. They both ordered diet soda and promised to look at the menu. Not that they needed to, Sienna thought. They'd been coming to Treats 'n Eats since they were kids and pretty much had the offerings memorized.

"So what are yours?" Courtney asked.

"My what?"

"Secrets."

There were so many to choose from, Sienna thought. Her ambivalence about David—although that might be more widely known than she suspected.

"My engagement to Hugh," she said impulsively, then wondered why she'd gone *there*.

"What about it?"

"Why it ended."

Her sister leaned toward her. "You said you realized when you got to Chicago that it wasn't going to work."

"Yeah, that's what I said. What really happened was, when I got to Chicago, Hugh decided I wasn't good enough. I think his family had something to do with it, but in the end, he dumped me."

Courtney stared at her. "You? He let you go? But you're beautiful and smart, and WTF! Did he think he could do better?"

Hearing her sister's outrage was both surprising and gratifying. "Thank you. That's really nice. I like to think it was his loss, but at the time, I was devastated."

"I'm sure. What an idiot. David knows you're a prize, right?"

"Yes. He's clear on that." Her problems with David were different. Or maybe they existed entirely in her head. He was sweet and attentive. So why couldn't she see them together for the next fifty years?

"My point," Sienna continued, "isn't about the engagement. It's about secrets. We all have them. They make us feel safe. They get us through."

"I was afraid everyone would tell me I couldn't do it," Courtney admitted.

"I would have." Sienna raised a shoulder. "I thought you were...challenged."

"Retarded," Courtney corrected.

"We don't use that word anymore, but kind of. When you were younger. But what you're doing now is amazing. Not just because it's hard to work and go to school, but because of what you had to overcome. There's no way you could have gone through what you did and not have some emotional scars."

Sienna had been thinking a lot about Courtney over the past several days, ever since the tasting dinner. She'd never thought about her sister's life from her point of view. Not really. But to have been held back and then be so tall. It had to have been hard. Or even impossible. But here she was. A success.

"I've never said this before and I hope you take it in the right way, but I'm really proud of you."

Courtney smiled. "Thank you. That means a lot."

Sienna smiled back. "Good. Now, what happened with Mom? I asked her about the wedding cake and she couldn't tell me anything beyond the fact that it's pink. Did you really have a fight in Gracie's kitchen?"

"Oh, no. That would be classy. We had a fight on the street. In front of the neighbors."

Sienna grinned. "That's my girl. Tell me everything."

Courtney carefully wiped down the bathroom counter before double-checking that she'd left the correct number of towels. She scanned the room for any supplies she might have forgotten on a tabletop or nightstand, then walked out of the room and closed the door behind her. She turned toward her cart and jumped when she saw Joyce hovering in the hall.

They hadn't really seen each other since the tasting. Joyce looked older and tired—as if she hadn't been sleeping.

"Hello," Courtney said politely, then reached for her clipboard to make her notes on the cleaning.

"I wanted to talk to you."

"Of course. Let me return the cart to the utility room and I'll be right down to your office."

Joyce twisted her hands together. "Courtney, don't."

Courtney tilted her head. "I don't understand."

"Don't talk to me like I'm your boss."

"You *are* my boss."

"We're friends, too. I care about you. Maggie and I have always gotten along, but you and I have a much closer relationship. I don't want to lose that."

You should have thought of that before, she thought angrily. She had to concentrate on pressing her lips together to keep from saying something she would regret.

"You're still mad at me," Joyce said helplessly. "Please don't be. I'm sorry for what I said. I didn't mean to start trouble between you and your mother."

Perhaps not, but she had meant to push things along. Joyce had grown impatient and had taken matters into her own hands, so to speak. Not that stating the obvious would help either of them, Courtney thought. And even though she did consider Joyce a friend, the fact was the other woman was her boss. Not something she could forget.

She needed this job. Not only the pay, but also her living situation made her life convenient. She liked the hotel. She liked being around different people all the time. The hours made it easy for her to study. All of which meant she couldn't lash out—not without accepting possible consequences.

"I'm sure you had the best of intentions," she said at last. "Everyone knows now. I'm sure it will all turn out fine."

"But you're still angry."

"I need a little time."

"Courtney, I've known you since you were a little girl. We have to make this right between us."

"We have. It's fine." Courtney held in a groan. Now she sounded like her mother.

"Are you sure?" Joyce's voice was small as she spoke.

"Yes, of course."

"I don't believe you." Joyce shook her head. "All right, then. I'll leave you to your work."

She walked away. Courtney headed in the other direction. She restocked her cart for the next day, signed out and started for her room. Halfway there, she changed direction and walked to Quinn's bungalow. He answered her knock.

"What's up?" he asked as he let her in.

"I'm crabby and mad at the world. Your grandmother wants everything to be all right between us. She's my boss, so I can't say what I really think. Not if I want to keep my job. My mom is hurt and angry, and suddenly Sienna and I are hanging out. Rachel's still not talking to me and she's the one I feel the worst about. Aside from that, I'm great. How are you?"

Quinn studied her for a second, then went into his bedroom. She followed, not sure what he was going to do. While she wasn't exactly in the mood for sex, she was pretty sure Quinn knew which buttons to push to change that.

But instead of getting naked, he pulled a box out of his closet and handed it to her. She sank onto a chair when she saw what it was.

"Those high heels? Really?"

"Put them on and walk around. Trust me."

She was well aware of how ridiculous she would look prancing around in Saint Laurent high heels in her khakis and polo shirt. But she also knew Quinn well enough to trust him. Crazy, but true. She pulled off her athletic shoes and white socks, then slipped on the pumps.

It took her a second to find her balance. Once she did, she walked the length of the bungalow and back. She felt the tension leave her body. Her shoulders eased and she was able to pull them back. Her breathing slowed and her mind stopped racing.

Quinn moved into the living room and she joined him.

"Better?" he asked.

"Yes."

He gave her that *I'm a star* smile and sank onto the sofa. "It's hard being more than a pretty face, but I do my best."

"Your best is damned good." She sat opposite him. "I don't like being mad at Joyce."

"Then don't be."

"As simple as that?"

"Why does it have to be complicated?"

"Because relationships usually are."

"Only if you let them be. She was wrong. You know she's sorry for the results, but it's unlikely she's sorry for what she did. If you can accept that, then you forgive her and move on. If not, then you stay mad."

"Where are you on that spectrum?"

"I'm punishing her."

"How is that different?"

"She's my grandmother. She's not going to fire me. I'll let her off soon enough, but for now I want her to think about what she did. She hurt you. I don't like that."

He spoke matter-of-factly, as if discussing the weather.

Only, they were talking about her and he sounded…well, protective.

She didn't know what to do with that information. Part of her wanted to hug it close and relive this moment over and over. Part of her wanted… Nope, she thought. There was no other part. There was just the hanging on. Because it had been a long time since anyone had looked out for her. She would guess the last person was Rachel, and they'd both been kids then.

"Thank you," she whispered, thinking that she wasn't going to ask why. Just in case the reason was he felt sorry for her. Better to simply hang on to the cuddling feeling.

"No problem. So what are you going to do?"

She looked at the shoes. She'd told herself she'd left them at Quinn's because she wasn't sure she was going to accept the gift. But the truth was she hadn't taken them home because she wasn't sure she was worthy. Whoever wore these shoes needed some attitude and a lot more confidence than she had.

"I'm going to tell her we're fine. She did what she did. I know why and I understand it. I'm going to tell her I don't agree with her actions and I don't want her to do it again. Then I'm going to hug her."

"Sounds like you have a plan."

"Always a good thing, right?" She stood. "Thank you for listening to me."

"Always."

"Want to help me stop being mad at my mother?"

He held up both hands. "Even I have limitations."

"Chicken."

"I prefer prudent."

"Cluck, cluck, cluck."

He chuckled and wrapped his arms around her waist, pulling her close. In the heels, she was a couple of inches taller. She kind of liked how easy it was to rest her arms on his shoulders and lean in to kiss him. When they finally drew apart, she smiled.

"I do feel powerful. Next time we make love, I want to be on top."

"Another fantasy realized."

She laughed. "You're easy."

"I'm glad you think so." He touched her cheek. "You okay?"

"I'm better."

"You going to take the shoes with you?"

Had he guessed why she'd kept them here? She wasn't sure, then decided it didn't matter. "I am. They're beautiful, and despite your pretty face, they don't suit you at all."

20

QUINN SAT ON the sofa, his feet on the coffee table, his laptop open. Pearl was stretched out next to him, while Sarge was on the club chair. Wayne sat at the dining room table, several stacks of paper in front of him.

"You have your lawyer look at these?" his assistant asked.

"Twice."

"Then why am I reading them?"

"You'll bug me about them if I don't let you," Quinn said easily as he deleted an email. "You don't trust my lawyer."

"No one trusts lawyers."

"What if she's former military?"

Wayne didn't bother looking up. "She's not."

Quinn's cell rang. He looked at the screen and saw a familiar album cover pop up. "You check the news this morning?"

That got Wayne's attention. "Sure. Nothing about our crew. Why? What's happened?"

"Nothing yet. Just want to know before I answer the call." He pushed the speaker button. "Yes?"

"Hey, Quinn, it's us."

Bryan, Quinn thought wearily.

"Where are you? We're at your place and no one's here." Collins's voice was clear despite their being on speakerphone.

"You're not dead, are you?" That was Peter.

"He answered the phone," Bryan pointed out. "He can't be dead."

"Maybe we called the great beyond. It happens. Don't you watch sci-fi?"

Quinn felt the beginnings of a headache. As a rule, he avoided bands. In the beginning, he hadn't had much choice. He'd taken talent wherever he could find it. But as he'd gotten more successful, he'd been able to pick and choose. He could turn over a promising group to other people in his organization.

It wasn't that bands couldn't be brilliant. Of course they could. The real problem was the mix of personalities. Look at Tadeo. He was one guy, but between his wife and kids and entourage, dealing with him was like a meeting at the UN. With a band, you multiplied that number by all the members, plus twenty.

Even knowing all that, a few years ago he'd been sucked in by a group of teenage boys with amazing talent. He'd told himself it wouldn't be so bad. That Bryan, Peter and Collins were different. Which was how he'd ended up producing music for And Then.

Their first three albums had gone triple platinum, with a string of eight number-one hits. But honest to God, he wasn't sure it was worth it.

"Why are you calling me?" he asked.

Bryan, the singer for And Then, made a *tsking* sound. "Quinn, is that any way to talk to us? We know we're your favorite."

"Did you consider the fact that there's a reason you don't know where I am?"

Peter, the very handsome but not bright drummer, spoke next. "Are you dead? Is it cool being dead?"

"I'm not dead."

"You sure? Because you're not here."

Quinn looked at Wayne, who was slowly shaking his head. "Peter, there are other places than here."

"Like where?"

Quinn didn't know if the twenty-four-year-old had been dropped on his head or had done too many drugs. Maybe it was a combination of both. Regardless, he was the best drummer in the business, and And Then owed a lot of their success to him.

"We want to write with you," Bryan said. "Tell me where you are and we'll be there today."

"That's what I'm afraid of."

"Look, you know you're going to give in. Why go through all the trouble of pretending you're not?"

Bryan had not been dropped on his head. He was the front man and the brains of the operation. Collins played lead guitar and, like Zealand, rarely spoke. But he wrote music like an angel.

"Los Lobos."

"Is he speaking Spanish?" Peter asked. "*Hasta la vista*, baby." The other man laughed. "That's from a movie. I can't remember which one."

Wayne pressed his forehead to the table. Quinn hoped he wasn't going to start hitting his head. He needed Wayne to stay conscious.

"I'm *in* Los Lobos," Quinn clarified. "You can drive here. There's a hotel. If you get rooms here, act nice. This is my town, and my grandmother owns the hotel. I will let Wayne shoot the three of you if you don't behave. Understand?"

"Yeah, man." Collins sounded more amused than worried. "That would make Wayne happy, but our fans would eat you alive."

"There are worse ways to go."

"We'll be there. I've got some good ideas I want to talk to you about."

That piqued Quinn's interest. "How many songs are we talking about?"

"Eight, maybe ten."

For most artists, that meant at most two of three would be viable. But with Collins, each one could be a hit.

"I look forward to hearing what you have."

"Good. Thanks, Quinn."

"Yeah, thanks, Quinn," the other two yelled before hanging up.

"I have to go back to LA," Wayne announced. "Right now."

"No, you don't."

"I want a raise."

"Fine."

"You don't know how much I want."

"I don't care how much. You can have it."

His assistant glared at him. "I hate it when you give in to me."

"I know. That's part of why I do it."

Before Wayne could say anything else, the phone rang again.

Quinn picked it up. "Go away."

"W-what?" The female voice was soft and trembling.

"Joyce?" Quinn dropped his feet to the floor. "What's wrong?" His grandmother had gone out with one of her friends for lunch.

"It's so s-silly," she said. "I slipped in the restaurant. I'm in the emergency room. I'm sure I'm fine, but could you come be with me?"

"Give me fifteen minutes. I'm on my way."

★ ★ ★

"You won't believe it," Belinda continued. "He told Ellie that she could get a tattoo!"

Rachel carefully applied the color to the strand of Belinda's hair, then expertly folded the foil into a neat packet. "But she's only fifteen."

"I know. I should kill him. Seriously, just back the car over him. Maybe twice. Now I have to be the one to tell her no. So he's the cool dad and I'm the terrible mother. How is that fair?"

Belinda continued to rant. Rachel couldn't blame her for being upset. How on earth did something like that happen? What had her husband been thinking? Thank goodness Greg never did anything like that to her. Even at his worst—when he'd been more interested in hanging with his friends than being a husband and father—he'd never deliberately undermined her. And lately, well, she wasn't sure what was happening lately.

He was around so much more than he ever had been. He was cooperative, nice and understanding. It was as if he'd made the decision to grow up. If only that had happened while they'd been married.

Sometimes she wondered why he was trying so hard. Did he want them to get back together? Did she? She missed him, of course. Missed them. But to let him back in her life. Could she trust him? He'd cheated. There was no forgiving that. That was what she'd always thought. But maybe, just maybe, she'd been wrong.

She rotated the chair to finish up a few more foils on the side of Belinda's head.

"Give this twenty minutes and we'll get you shampooed," she said when she was done. "Do you need any more magazines? Or something to drink?"

Belinda picked up the latest copy of *Vogue*. "I'm good.

Coming here is a break from four kids. Twenty minutes to just sit and read is heaven."

Rachel smiled at her and cleared away her bowls and brush. She went into the back room and cleaned up, then drank some water. She was about to go check on her client when Martina, the receptionist, hurried toward her.

"You had a call," she said quickly. "It was dispatch. Something happened to Greg."

Rachel went cold. It was the call every firefighter's wife dreaded.

She rushed to the phone on the wall and dialed a number she'd never forgotten.

"Dispatch."

She fought to keep her voice calm. "It's Rachel Halcomb. I'm calling about Greg."

"Hey, Rachel. Greg was injured on scene. I don't have the details, but he was conscious when he was taken to the hospital. That's all I know. Are you heading over?"

"Right now."

She pressed a hand to her chest as she spoke. Her heart pounded so hard and so fast. She wanted to cry, but there was no way she could give in, she told herself. She had to stay strong. Who knew what was going to happen or what she would have to deal with?

She hung up and headed directly for her locker to collect her purse. She went into the break room, where Sara was working on her laptop.

"Greg's been taken to the hospital," she told her coworker. "I don't know how bad it is, but I need to get over there. Can you finish up with Belinda?"

Sara looked up. "Sure. Is he okay? Are you?"

"I don't know. I'm having a little trouble breathing, but that should pass. Her color will be done in about five minutes. She gets a simple layered cut. Nothing you haven't done a million times. Thanks so much. I owe you."

Sara stood and hugged her. "Don't worry. I'll deal. Go be with Greg."

Rachel hurried out to explain the situation to Belinda, then raced to her car. She had no idea what had happened, but her imagination was able to produce dozens of scenarios, each worse than the one before. He could have been hit by a car at a car accident or burned in a fire. He could have fallen through a roof or been attacked by a crazy person.

By the time she got to the hospital, she was nearly hysterical. What was she going to tell Josh? How would she survive as a single parent? While she thought of herself that way now, in reality Greg was around, helping. He couldn't be gone, he couldn't!

She rushed into the ER. There were a handful of patients waiting, a few nurses and someone at the reception desk.

"I'm Rachel Halcomb. My husband, Greg, was brought in. He's a firefighter."

The receptionist scanned her computer screen. "He's in exam room four. You can go right in. It's that way." She pointed to her left.

Rachel thanked her, then jogged down the hallway. She felt sick to her stomach and a little dizzy. She slowed for a second, startled to see Quinn pushing his grandmother in a wheelchair. She started to stop to ask if Joyce was all right, then simply waved and kept going. There were a couple of firefighters standing in the hallway by Greg's exam room. She knew them all, had had them over for dinner, been on picnics with their families. The tallest of the three, Zack, smiled when he saw her.

"Hey, Rach, don't worry. He's fine. One of the rookies got into trouble at a fire and Greg helped him out. Unfortunately, he got a cut on his arm in the process. It was bleeding pretty bad, so we brought him here. He's going to be okay." Zack winked. "He'll have a scar, but chicks dig scars, right?"

She forced herself to smile. "We do." She drew back the curtain of the exam room. As she did, she saw Greg lying on the bed. There was a makeshift pressure bandage around his biceps...and a gorgeous redhead holding his hand. They both looked at her.

Rachel stood immobile for two whole beats of her heart, then turned on her heel and walked back the way she'd come.

"Rachel! Rachel, wait!"

She ignored Greg's voice and everyone around her. She kept her head high and her pace brisk. It wasn't until she was back in her car that she gave in to tears.

She was a fool, she thought bitterly. A pathetic ex-wife turned laughingstock. Greg wasn't trying to get her back. She didn't know what his game was, but it wasn't that for sure. He was probably just trying to be a better father to Josh. He didn't want her getting in the way of that. So he'd played her. And she'd let him.

Not again, she told herself angrily as she wiped the tears from her face. Fool me once and all that. She was going to get back to work, do her job, then go home. Tonight she would walk an extra two miles. She would find an exercise class and start lifting weights. She would get so incredibly fit and hot, she would attract some amazing man and they would fall madly in love. Wasn't there an old saying about living well being the best revenge? As of this moment, she was all about revenge. At least on the inside. Screw Greg and his bimbo redhead. She was going to be just fine.

By the time she was cleaning up her station for the night, her hurt and anger had faded a little and she'd had a chance to think about all that had happened with Greg. Or hadn't happened.

She hadn't bothered to actually talk to him and see that he was okay herself. She hadn't let him explain. And maybe, just maybe, she'd overreacted to the situation.

She had no idea who the redhead was, but chances were if her ex was dating, she would know about it. As for thinking she'd been played—she honestly had no idea if that was true. Because whatever she and Greg were doing, they weren't talking about it and that was as much her fault as his.

She drove to camp to pick up Josh. He stood by the curb wearing swim trunks and a T-shirt.

"Hey, Mom," he said as he slid into the passenger seat and fastened his seat belt. "We went swimming today."

"I never would have guessed."

He grinned at her. "It was fun. We're learning how to play water polo. It's really hard. You have to swim the whole time *and* get the ball in the goal." He frowned. "I guess it's like soccer, but in the water and with hands, not feet."

"So nothing like soccer?"

He laughed. "I guess I'll have to learn more before I can tell you for sure."

She hesitated, not sure if she should mention what had happened to his dad. She still didn't know any details. Before she could decide, they rounded the corner and she saw Greg's truck parked in the driveway. She wasn't sure what to make of that except she now knew he'd been released from the hospital.

"Dad's here!"

She reached for her son's arm, holding him in his seat. "Your dad had an accident on the job today. He's okay, but go easy on him."

Josh's smile faded. "What happened?"

"He was helping one of the rookies and he hurt his arm."

Josh was out of the car before she could stop him, and racing to the house. "Dad! Dad!"

Rachel followed more slowly. Greg sat in the living room, a thick bandage on his arm and looking almost gray. Josh stared at his dad.

"Is he okay?" Josh asked in a whisper.

Greg smiled and held open his good arm. "I'm great. Come here and give me a hug."

Josh raced to his dad and dived at his uninjured side. Greg pulled him close.

"I'm okay. I promise."

"Good." Josh stood. "I'm gonna take a shower. Then can we have pizza? Because, you know, Dad's hurt."

Rachel nodded. "Sure. I'll wait until you're out before I order."

Josh whooped and ran down the hall. She waited until she heard his bedroom door slam shut before looking at Greg.

"I didn't expect to see you here."

He shifted on the sofa and winced. "I wanted to talk to you. The way you took off... I knew what you were thinking, and I knew it was bad." His dark gaze settled on her face. "That was Heidi. She's Tommy's fiancée, that rookie I helped out. He was in surgery and she was totally freaked, so I was trying to calm her down. You know what it's like to worry, but it's new to her. And with him getting hurt..." He shook his head. "She wasn't handling it well."

He stood and swayed a little. "I don't want you to think there was something going on, Rachel. There hasn't been anyone but you. There was that one night, but that was the only time, I swear. I wish you'd stayed so you could have met Heidi."

"Me, too. I should have stayed. Or at least not run away." Which was the same thing, but she couldn't seem to help saying stupid things. "You look terrible. Are you up for staying for dinner, or should I drive you home?"

"I want to stay with you."

He meant for dinner. She knew that. But part of her wanted to believe he was saying something else. That he was telling her he missed being with her in every sense of the word.

"Greg, I—"

She never got to finish her sentence. He took a step toward her, then staggered a little. She reached to steady him, only to find herself in his arms. She wasn't sure if they were embracing or he was holding her up. Then it didn't matter because his mouth found hers and they were kissing.

For a second she felt nothing. Just pressure. No heat, no desire. For that single heartbeat, she could have pulled away. Maybe she should have. But she waited too long. Because in the next second, she felt *everything*. The soft firmness of his mouth on hers. His hands on her arms.

In that second, she remembered everything about them being together. Their kissing, their touching. The feel of his hands on every inch of her body. The way he always stared deeply into her eyes as he entered her. How he called out, "Come for me, baby," when she was close. How they were always trying different things and sometimes the awkwardness of that made them laugh so hard they had to stop and simply touch each other until the laughter faded.

She remembered countless stolen moments. In a restaurant bathroom on their only trip to Hawaii. That time at her mom's, when they'd arrived a few minutes early for dinner and had sneaked into the house to take advantage of one of the guest rooms. They were experts at doing it in the backseat of the car, because when you had a kid in the house, you had to find your moments.

He drew back and looked at her. "What are you thinking?"

That I never stopped loving you. That I'm sorry we got a divorce. That I want you back.

But she couldn't say that. She couldn't admit to the weakness. She had to be strong and remember what he'd done to her. Not the good stuff, but the rest of it.

"Josh is going to be done in a second. I'll find out what pizza he wants. You need to get some sleep," she told him. "You're injured and totally exhausted. In the morning, you won't remember any of this."

"I'll remember," he told her. "Rachel, I miss us. I miss you and Josh. I miss what we were together. We need to talk."

"We do. Just not tonight. You're drugged and I'm..." Scared, she thought. Terrified. Of what she wanted and of taking a chance on him again. She'd barely survived before. If she gave herself to him again, and he betrayed her, she would be lost forever.

"Not tonight," she repeated. Later she would be brave, but not just yet.

21

COURTNEY HURRIED ACROSS the hotel lawn, Pearl and Sarge keeping pace easily, as if they, too, had been worried. Quinn had called from the hospital and explained that his grandmother had slipped in a restaurant and twisted her ankle. She was going to be fine but had to take it easy for a few days.

At the front door of Joyce's bungalow, she knocked once then entered, announcing herself as she did. She found Joyce sitting in a club chair, her wrapped foot propped up on an ottoman. When Courtney saw her, all her irritation fled. Joyce looked delicate and a little broken. Not at all the powerful woman who ran the hotel so successfully.

"What happened?" she asked as she hurried over. The dogs beat her to Joyce. Pearl nudged her arm to get a pat, and Sarge jumped directly onto her lap.

"I was clumsy," Joyce said. "There was a bit of water on the floor. My foot slipped out from under me. I feel so foolish."

Quinn stood by her chair. "She's going to be sore and swollen for a couple of days. She has to stay off her feet until that ankle feels better, but she should be fine."

Joyce pressed her lips together, as if holding in emotion. "I didn't do it on purpose. I want to be clear about that."

Courtney smiled. "No one thinks you deliberately fell just so I wouldn't be mad at you anymore."

"Oh, I don't know," Quinn said drily. "I wouldn't put it past her."

Joyce stroked her dogs. "I am sorry about what happened and what I did. While I was lying there, waiting for the ambulance, all I could think was that I didn't want you angry at me anymore." Her lower lip trembled. "Courtney, you're family."

Courtney crossed to her and dropped to her knees. She hugged the older woman. "You are to me, too," she told her. "I admire you and want to be like you."

"You're just saying that."

"I'm not. I promise."

They hugged again. Over Joyce's head, she saw Quinn looking at her. She had no idea what he was thinking. Was forgiveness a sign of strength or weakness in his mind? He'd encouraged her to make up with Joyce, but was that just for her or something he genuinely believed? She supposed it didn't matter. She loved Joyce and she couldn't stay angry with her. If that made her spineless, she could live with the label.

"I have a surprise for you," David said as he pulled his car into the garage of his town house. "I can't wait to see your reaction."

He sounded excited and happy. Sienna hoped she would feel the same when she found out what the surprise was. She'd been longing for a quiet Fourth of July weekend, but David had insisted he had special plans for her and had picked her up just after nine on Saturday morning.

"You're not going to give me a hint?" she asked.

"Just a couple more minutes."

They got out of the car. He came around to her side and took her hand in his. "I love you, Sienna. You've made me so happy. We're going to have a great life together."

She smiled because saying "I hope so" seemed mean and

saying "I know" wasn't exactly true. She had to remember that she was getting a second, or in her case, a third chance to make the right decision. She was going to simply keep moving forward and enjoy being with him. It wasn't as if they were getting married tomorrow. In fact, David hadn't said anything about setting a date for a couple of weeks now. They had time to figure it out.

He led her inside through the rear foyer of the town house and up the stairs to the main living floor.

"We're back," he called as they reached the landing.

She turned to him. "Someone's here?"

He grinned and pointed. Sienna turned in that direction and saw a short, plump, middle-aged woman hurrying toward them. Her dark hair was styled in kind of a bubble, and she had on a lot of makeup.

"Finally!" she said, holding open her arms. Several charm bracelets jangled as she moved. "Sienna! Welcome to the family."

David released her hand and Sienna found herself being hugged by the woman. "Who is she?" she mouthed over the other woman's head.

"My mother," he said with a laugh. "Linda. Mom, this is Sienna."

His mother was visiting and he hadn't told her?

Linda straightened but kept hold of Sienna's upper arms. "Oh, my, you are tall! David said you were, but I wasn't expecting all this." She shook her head. "I hope your children aren't going to take after you in that respect. They'll look so peculiar in family photos."

Sienna opened her mouth, then closed it. "It's, um, very nice to meet you, Mrs. Van Horn."

Linda released her, then waved a hand. "Call me Linda. Or Mom. We're family now, dear." She looked up. "Is that your natural color? The blond is pretty enough, I suppose. Now, we have so much to discuss. I'm only here for a couple days, and there's all the planning to do before I fly back to spend the Fourth with our family."

Sienna found herself guided into the living room, where a large suitcase lay on the floor. While she wasn't usually afraid of luggage, she found herself sidling away from it as she moved to the sofa.

"Planning?"

"The wedding," Linda said, settling next to her and smiling. "David keeps mentioning Christmas, but I just don't see how that could possibly happen. Plus, the weather in St. Louis is a little iffy in December. Spring would be better, as long as there isn't a tornado."

"Or flooding," David added.

Tornadoes and floods? "I didn't know the weather was so bad in the Midwest," Sienna murmured.

"You get used to it," Linda assured her. "Once you've lived there a few years, you won't think anything of it."

Lived there? As in…lived there?

"Now, Mom, you know I told you that Sienna and I haven't decided what we're going to do about living arrangements."

Linda shook her head. "Of course you'll come home, David." She turned to Sienna. "There are so many opportunities there for him now that he has the right kind of experience. Plus, St. Louis is a much better place to raise children than California. Everybody knows that."

Instead of looking panicked, David seemed pleased. Had this been his plan all along? They'd talked about the possibility of moving someday, but she hadn't thought it was anything but just that—talk.

"I had no idea you were coming for a visit. David, you're just full of surprises."

"Mom called me a few days ago."

"I told him I had to meet the woman who had stolen his

heart," Linda confirmed. "With the long weekend, this seemed like the perfect time. I flew in last night and I'll head home tomorrow. I'm such a jet-setter." She smiled. "Oh, we need to take lots of pictures so everyone can see what you look like."

"That will be great," Sienna said faintly.

"Did I mention we've already set up a Facebook page for the wedding? Everyone is so excited. The entire family wants to be a part of things. Oh, and speaking of that." Linda pointed to the suitcase. "That's for you."

"You bought me luggage?"

Linda laughed. "Of course not. Open it. Your gift is inside."

Sienna stood and walked around the coffee table. David nodded encouragingly.

"Do you know what it is?" she asked.

"Not a clue."

She knelt on the floor and unzipped the case, then slowly opened the top. Inside were several layers of tissue paper. She folded them back, then stared at what looked like a white dress. No, not a dress. A wedding gown.

"It was my mother's," Linda said proudly. "I was hoping I would have a daughter to wear it, but I only had boys."

Sienna pulled out the dress. It was enormous and heavy, with long sleeves and a full skirt. Lace covered every inch of the gown, and as for it being the right size...

"My mother was a larger woman," Linda said. "We might have to take it in a bit."

A bit? Sienna stood and held the dress in front of her. It was at least eight sizes too large. It was also about six inches too short.

"You are tall," Linda mused. "That could be a problem."

So was the fact that the dress was ugly. Wasn't the engagement ring enough? Why was she being punished?

"Did you wear this on your wedding day?" Sienna asked.

"Goodness no. I wanted something new. But you'll like this, I'm sure."

Sienna looked at David, who shrugged.

"We'll consider it," he promised. "But Sienna needs to make her own choice when it comes to her dress."

"Of course," Linda said. "Still, I'm sure she'll also want to please her husband-to-be. Isn't that right, dear?"

"More than words can say," Sienna murmured before letting the dress sink back into the suitcase. "I'm going to get some coffee. Is the pot on?"

David nodded.

Sienna escaped to the kitchen, where she clutched the counter and told herself to keep breathing. There was no way in hell she was wearing that ugly dress. Even if she loved it, what would they do about it being too short? And what was with Linda's obsession with her height?

Before she could do any more mental ranting, her future mother-in-law joined her. Sienna quickly pulled a mug from the cupboard, then forced herself to smile as she asked, "Would you like coffee, too, Linda?"

"I'm fine, dear." Linda waited while she poured. "David's father and I are so pleased he's found someone to make him happy. A good marriage is a blessing—don't you agree?"

"I do."

"David tells me you've been engaged before and it didn't work out. You're not going to run out on him, are you?"

Talk about cutting to the heart of the matter, she thought. "Of course not. David is a great guy. I'm lucky to have him."

"That's what I thought." Linda smiled. "I understand you work for a nonprofit and that you're raising money to buy a bungalow. Is that right?"

The change in subject was confusing, but sure. "We are. We provide housing for women escaping an abusive relationship. It helps if they have a secure place to settle that's some distance from where they were."

"That makes sense. David's father and I want you to know that we'll be happy to contribute to your organization. After the wedding. The check will be enough to make sure the purchase can go through."

Sienna got the milk out of the refrigerator, then poured a large splash into her mug. She stirred while she tried to figure out what to say.

Why on earth did David's mother feel she had to offer a bribe? How could Sienna tell her no thanks without sounding ungracious? And shouldn't she accept the check on behalf of The Helping Store? That was kind of her job. Not that Seth would expect her to sell herself in the name of raising funds. But if she was going to marry David anyway, did it matter?

She supposed that was what it came down to. Was she going to marry David? Because one broken engagement could happen to anyone, and two, well, they could be explained, but three was more than was normal. It wasn't so much that people would talk, as how breaking this engagement would make a statement about her. But what was the alternative? To get married so people didn't talk?

"You're very generous," she told Linda. "Thank you."

Her future mother-in-law beamed. "I knew I was going to like you."

"I feel exactly the same way."

As Sienna sipped her coffee, she wondered if they were both lying, or just her.

Central casting couldn't have done a better job putting together the perfect boy band, Quinn thought as the members of And Then arrived at his bungalow with Wayne on their heels. Bryan, the lead singer, was African American, Peter, the drummer, was blond and blue-eyed and Collins was mixed race leaning toward Asian. They were all close to six feet tall, lean and fit and good-looking enough to get girls across the world screaming every time they walked into a room.

He'd been interested in them because they were brilliant enough to make him overlook his usual band aversion, but the "it" factor sure didn't hurt. The contrast between their prettiness and Wayne's slightly bulldog appearance made him grin.

"Wayne bought us a house," Peter said proudly.

"I didn't *buy* you a house," Wayne corrected. "I rented you a house." He glanced at Quinn. "A vacation rental. I tripled the damage deposit."

"We're cool," Bryan said. "We're not going to trash the place."

"Can I have that in writing?" Quinn shook hands with all of them. "You three ready to work?"

Peter looked startled. "I thought I was going to surf. The waves look good and I brought my wet suit."

Collins patted his shoulder. "You can surf. Quinn and I are going to write. Bryan wants to help."

"Will I be missing out?" Peter asked, sounding worried.

"Not on anything fun."

"Okay, then I'll surf."

Quinn was pleased that order had been restored. Bryan walked over to the dining room table.

"These the plans for the studio?" he asked. "It's big."

"It's a warehouse." Quinn walked to the table. "Recording studios here. Rooms for writing here. Offices and a couple of places to crash upstairs."

Peter wandered over to Wayne. "You want to go surfing with me?"

"No."

"You sure? I could teach you."

Wayne shot Quinn a *help me* look, but Quinn figured the big, bad marine could handle the kid himself.

"No, thanks."

"We could go to dinner later. You know, hang out."

Wayne's brows drew together. "Why?"

"To just talk about stuff."

Quinn held in a smile. Despite their good looks and success as a band, when he'd discovered them, they'd been living in a van. Each of them was dealing with a difficult past. Peter had been born a crack baby and had lived in foster care all his life. Bryan had lost his mom in a drive-by shooting. Collins had never much talked about his past. None of them had ever known a father, and for reasons that made perfect sense to Quinn, they had adopted Wayne. While they worked with Quinn, they wanted to hang out with his assistant. Wayne's was the opinion that mattered.

Wayne sighed heavily. "I'll meet you for dinner later," he grumbled.

"Count me in," Bryan said quickly.

"Me, too," Collins added.

Quinn chuckled at Wayne's *kill me now* look as he stalked out of the bungalow. This was shaping up to be a very good day.

Rachel hesitated before going into the coffee shop. While her self-actualization plan was moving forward, she felt as if her newfound strength was a lot more flash than substance. She was doing a great job walking every day, and she would say she was about eighty percent on her new food plan. Her pants were looser, her stomach a little flatter, and most important, she felt better about herself.

But she suspected it wouldn't take much to derail her. The evening with Greg was proof of that. After their kiss, she'd felt shaky and fragile for a couple of days. She'd just gotten over that when Courtney had texted her, yet again, suggesting they get together to talk.

Avoiding her sister seemed so much easier than discussing what had happened, but the truth was, with their mom getting married, avoidance, however cheerful a thought, wasn't an option.

Which was why she found herself wanting an extra shot of mocha syrup with her latte. Sugar could always be counted on to help her be brave.

She took her drink—sans chocolate—to one of the small tables to wait. She was a few minutes early. She and Courtney had exactly thirty minutes to solve their problem. Then both of them had to meet Sienna at the bridal shop to pick out bridesmaid dresses. Last she'd heard, there were two choices on the table. The same style in different colors, or different styles in the same color.

Betty Grable had sent several pictures for them to consider. Rachel sipped her coffee as she scrolled through them. The styles weren't bad, but the colors... Seriously? Shades of pink? Did they have to?

"Hi."

She looked up as Courtney sat down across from her. Her baby sister looked both anxious and hopeful. Fierce love flooded Rachel, washing away the hurt. For so many years, she'd been the fill-in mom for her youngest sister. She'd been the one to make Courtney's lunch and make sure her homework was at least attempted. She'd tried and tried to help Courtney learn how to read, but nothing she'd done had worked. It had taken a reading disabilities expert to make that happen.

Rachel knew her sister being left behind two grades hadn't

been her fault, but she still felt guilty about it. Ridiculous, but true.

"I'm sorry," Courtney told her. "I should have told you. At first I was afraid to tell anyone because I was so sure I was going to be a disaster. That I wouldn't be able to even get my GED. But then I did and my teacher suggested I apply to community college. That floored me. So I got the idea of surprising everyone with a diploma. It just kind of grew from there."

She swallowed. "It's just that I spent so long being the problem child. You know? I wanted to be the successful one. Just once."

Rachel knew her well enough to read between the lines. She remembered all the times she'd tried to comfort a devastated Courtney when her sister had come home from school, crying because the kids had called her stupid or retarded. She'd been so incredibly frustrated herself—unable to understand what was wrong. What must her sister have gone through?

"I know I hurt you," Courtney continued. "I'm so sorry about that. I honestly never thought about it from anyone's perspective but mine."

Rachel stood and held open her arms. Courtney rushed to her and hung on so tight, Rachel could barely breathe. But that was okay. Better to have a sister than air.

"I'm sorry, too," Rachel said. "But also happy and proud. Really proud. Look at you."

Courtney drew back, her expression apprehensive. "What about being mad?"

"I'm still a little mad, but I'll get over it."

Courtney got a latte for herself, then rejoined Rachel at the table. They smiled at each other.

"Better," Rachel admitted. "With everything going on, I've really missed you."

As soon as she spoke, she wanted to call back the words.

Courtney wasn't the only one keeping secrets. Rachel had yet to share with anyone how her feelings for Greg confused her. She wasn't sure if she should start now or not.

"What's going on?" Courtney asked.

"Nothing. Everything." Rachel looked at her coffee, then back at her sister. "I'm losing weight. Walking and eating better. That's good. There are still times I would kill for a muffin, but even when I eat one, I tell myself it's okay, as long as I get back to my program."

"Good for you. I should eat better." Courtney wrinkled her nose. "Or exercise."

"Your job is exercise."

"Kind of. But you're on your feet, too."

"Standing, not moving around. There's a difference. Anyway, that's part of it. I'm also having trouble with one of the baseball moms. She's not showing up when she says. It's frustrating."

"Have you talked to her?"

Rachel laughed. "You mean in a mature, mother-to-mother kind of way, telling her why I'm upset that she's not doing what she signed up to do?"

"I'm guessing that's a no."

"It is. I've tried, but she always has an excuse. So I hate her in my heart and glare at her. I'm starting to think I might have some serious passive-aggressive issues."

"You think?"

"Hey! You're still in trouble. You have to be nice."

Courtney grinned. "I think you're more aggressive than passive."

"I hope so."

"So what else is going on?"

"Just stuff. It's summer. Josh has a million activities and either Greg or I have to take him there. Thank goodness he's a social kid. He's also hanging out with his friends a lot, so that's good."

She tried to speak as casually as she could so Courtney wouldn't suspect that the real problem was her ex rather than her son.

"Greg's helping?"

Rachel picked up her latte. "Uh-huh. He's, um, coordinating his schedule to be around as much as possible, which is great for Josh. He needs his dad, especially as he gets older."

Courtney's blue eyes focused on Rachel's face. "You two are getting along?"

"Sure. We always have."

"Not after you first threw him out." She hesitated. "What Greg did was horrible, but I always felt bad that you two couldn't have worked it out. You were so good together. The way he would look at you when you weren't paying attention..." She sighed. "I always envied that."

Rachel had no idea what she meant and didn't know how to ask. "We married young. He wasn't ready to be a husband and father, and I wasn't interested in giving him room and time to grow up. I'm not sure we weren't doomed from the start."

"That's too bad. At least you're getting along better now."

Rachel thought about the other night, when Greg had shown up at her house to make sure she understood he wasn't dating anyone else. They were divorced. Why should he care what she thought?

"We are," she murmured, then glanced at her watch. "We need to get going. Sienna's meeting us at the store. We have to make a decision today. Betty told me that all the dresses we're considering are available in different stores around the country, so they'll be here in time, but we don't want to wait any longer."

Courtney sighed. "Okay—here we go. Into the dress lion's den." She frowned. "That sounded a lot better in my head."

Rachel laughed. "I know what you mean. Don't worry."

They walked out together and headed around the corner to the dress shop. Sienna hurried in behind them.

"Oh, good. I'm not late," she said and hugged them both. "Thank God. Normal, rational family. I'm so grateful."

Rachel raised her eyebrows. "What does that mean?"

Sienna covered her face with her hands, then dropped her arms to her sides. "David's mother flew in for a couple of days over the holiday weekend. It was horrible. She's obsessed with my height and I don't know why. David is a few inches taller than me. But she kept going on and on about it. Worse, she brought me his grandmother's wedding gown. It's hideous and huge and too short and she expects me to wear it. David said I didn't have to, but still. It's there. In his house. I hear it mocking me every time I walk into the living room. Oh, and she's set up a Facebook page for the family and she expects us to move to St. Louis."

Sienna paused for breath. "It's not that he isn't a great guy and all, it's just I'm so confused about everything."

"Including whether or not you love David?" Rachel asked, recognizing the panic in her sister's voice and eyes.

Sienna stared. "What? No. I love him. At least I'm pretty sure I do. I mean, of course I do. It's just everything happened so fast and there's the haunting dress to consider."

Rachel patted her arm. "It's a little early to drink, but I think come five o'clock, you need some serious margarita time."

"Tell me about it."

22

THIRTY MINUTES LATER Sienna seemed calmer, the sisters had viewed the color and style choices in the bridesmaid dresses and now had to make a decision. Courtney knew which one she wanted, but it wasn't up to only her.

"Your mother has settled on a pale pink wedding gown," Betty told them. "She said your choices are white, ivory, a darker pink or black."

"Black," Sienna and Rachel said together.

Courtney nodded. "Black." White or ivory would be too weird and dark pink, well, given what had already been ordered for the wedding, no one wanted to go there.

"So black dresses in similar styles, but slightly different?" Betty asked.

They all nodded.

"Excellent. Let's see what we have."

They walked back to the racks of bridesmaid dresses. She showed them various options. They settled on a designer that had three dresses in the same fabric. They were similar, with just enough variation to keep things interesting.

Each of them took a dress into a changing room. Courtney had barely pulled off her jeans when her phone chirped. She glanced at the message.

"Uh-oh."

"What?" Rachel called from her room.

"It's Mom," Courtney told her. "She wants to know if we have a DJ request list."

"Do we?"

"Last I heard, we weren't using a DJ."

"We are now," Sienna said from her room. "I know a great guy we use all the time at fund-raisers. Want me to get in touch with him?"

"Yes, please." Courtney replied to her mother. They were texting now. Not speaking all that much, but there was communication. She supposed that was an improvement.

She pulled off her T-shirt, then slipped on the dress. As soon as it settled on her, she realized her bra wasn't going to work at all, so she removed that, as well.

"I'm going to need a strapless bra with this," she said.

"Me, too," Sienna called.

"Me, three."

Courtney's dress was simple. It had a fitted sweetheart bodice, with spaghetti straps. The skirt followed the shape of her body through her hips before falling to the floor. The fabric was flowy without being overwhelming. The cut was flattering and comfortable.

She stepped out of the dressing room. Her sisters did the same. Sienna's dress was a wrapped bodice, strapless style, while Rachel's was an off-the-shoulder style. They were all long and fitted to the hips. The black fabric emphasized their blond hair and fair coloring.

The three of them stood on the low dais, in front of the large mirror. Sienna tossed her head.

"We look good."

"We do," Rachel agreed, her tone slightly bemused. "I have a great body. I need to appreciate that more."

"Modest much?" Courtney teased.

"Hey, I've been suffering in a muffin-less world. Get off me."

"Girls," Sienna said. "Let's play nice and take a moment to admire us."

Courtney thought of the high heels Quinn had bought her. While the color wouldn't work, knowing she had them made her want to buy a pair for this dress. This bridesmaid gown deserved killer heels.

Betty walked in and clapped her hands together. "You're more stunning than I'd imagined. Impressive. If you don't order those dresses, I'm going to be disappointed."

"I think these are the ones," Sienna said. "You both agree?"

"Uh-huh."

"I want this one," Rachel said, turning so she could see herself from the side. "I can't remember the last time I felt hot. I think it was before I had Josh. This is great. Do you think it would be tacky to wear this dress to work after the wedding?"

They laughed, then stepped down and went back into their dressing rooms.

Courtney pulled on her jeans and felt decidedly less glamorous than she had before. Funny how she'd never thought much about clothes before. They were something she wore, but nothing to care about. But those stupid high heels had changed everything. Or maybe it was just the way Quinn looked at her when she wore them.

Her phone rang. She picked it up.

"Hello?"

"Courtney? It's Jill Strathern-Kendrick. I'm officiating at your mother's wedding?"

"Of course." She couldn't think of a single reason for the judge to be calling, unless... "Is there a problem?"

"I hope not. You know I'm pregnant, right?"

"Yes." Courtney held in a groan. Was Jill going to have to be on bed rest or something?

"It seems my due date has changed. The doctor just moved it up a couple of weeks." Jill gave a strangled laugh. "It's, ah, technically the day of the wedding."

"Yikes. That's not good."

"I wanted you to know, in case you wanted to make other plans. But to be honest, I was more than two weeks late the first time, so there's no reason to think I won't be late again. It's your call. I'll totally understand if you want to get someone else."

Courtney hesitated. "Mom really wants you to perform the ceremony. She's known your dad forever. He was very nice to her after she lost my father. I'll talk to her about it, but I'm going to say we're hoping for the best where you're concerned."

"Oh, good. I'd love to be the one to officiate. Your mom is a real sweetie. I plan to be there."

"That's great. Thanks for letting me know, Jill."

Sienna and Rachel walked into the dressing room.

"We heard," Sienna said. "What are you going to do?"

"Talk to Mom, even though I'm sure she's going to want to keep Jill. I'll check around for a backup person in case Jill goes into labor. It will be fine."

Sienna smiled at her. "You really do have all this under control, don't you?"

"I'm trying."

"No. You're doing a lot more than that."

Quinn and Joyce sat out in the shade on the patio of her bungalow. It was midafternoon, with the temperature near eighty. A light breeze off the ocean kept them cool, as did the crisp Washington chardonnay she'd poured. There was a plate of fruit and cheese, along with two very attentive dogs waiting for anything that fell.

Joyce sat on a chaise with her wrapped foot propped up on a pillow. Sarge sat on her lap, watching every bite she took. Pearl had staked her hopes on Quinn. She'd positioned herself in front of him. He wasn't sure how he was supposed to refuse those big brown eyes.

"When do you close on your building?" she asked.

"The end of the week." There were advantages to paying cash. "Wayne has contractors lined up to give bids. We should be able to start construction by the end of the month."

He was going to say more when he saw Maggie approaching. He knew from what Courtney had told him that their reconciliation had been halfhearted at best. While he understood that Maggie was still smarting from what she'd found out, he was Team Courtney all the way.

He started to stand, but Joyce put a hand on his arm. She didn't say anything, but he heard the message all the same. She wanted him to stay in case things got difficult. Maggie gave him a quick smile, then turned her attention to Joyce.

"I just found out about your accident. How are you?"

Joyce waved her into a chair. "I'm fine. It was a silly thing and I'll be up and about in the next day or two. I'm lucky it was just a sprain. At my age, you don't want to break a bone."

"No, you don't."

Quinn poured Maggie a glass of chardonnay and passed it to her.

"Thank you." She took a sip. "I wanted to talk to you about Courtney."

"I thought maybe you did." Joyce gave Sarge a piece of cheese. "I'm sorry. I was wrong to say what I did. I shouldn't have pushed Courtney like that. It wasn't my secret to share."

Maggie's mouth turned down. "What I don't understand

is why she had a secret in the first place. She's my daughter, but she's so much closer to you than to me." Her lower lip trembled. "Everything was so difficult after Phil died. I know I focused on work, but I thought the girls were fine. I never meant to hurt them."

"You got through it," Joyce assured her, her tone warm. "Maggie, you had a high school education and minimal training. You lost your husband, your house, and had three young girls to raise. Look at all you did and where you are now."

"But at what price? Maybe if I'd paid more attention to my girls, they wouldn't hate me so much."

"Now you're being silly. No one hates you. Courtney's doing everything she can to make your wedding wonderful. It makes her happy to see it all come together."

Maggie's expression turned hopeful. "You think so?"

"I know so."

Quinn gave Pearl some watermelon, then stroked her long, silky ears. Not that anyone was asking him, but in his opinion, everything about this conversation was wrong. If Maggie was so upset, why wasn't she talking to Courtney or her other daughters rather than Joyce? And what about all Courtney had been through? Where was the regret for that?

He remembered what she'd told him about being held back twice and the fact that her mother had barely noticed. How she'd moved out when she turned eighteen rather than face being the freak at school. He recalled the tattoo on her lower back, how it was a promise to herself. She wasn't going to give in. She was going to keep fighting.

But he didn't say any of that. He wasn't part of the conversation.

"Did she mention we're going to have a DJ?" Maggie asked.

"No. That will be wonderful."

"I've been thinking about the decorations. Don't you think it would be nice to have some kind of blooming tree brought in?"

Quinn fed Pearl some cheese. He needed the distraction to keep from rolling his eyes. Apparently, Maggie's pain was fairly short-lived.

"Trees are difficult to move around," Joyce mused. "But what if we did something that offered the same kind of visual interest? Just the other day I was talking to someone about Astrantia. It's so beautiful. We could pair it with cherry blossoms." She turned to Quinn. "Be a dear and get my laptop. I want to show Maggie what an Astrantia looks like."

He stood and kissed her cheek. "I live to serve."

She laughed. "If only that were true."

"You know I'm busy, right?" Courtney said as Quinn let her into his bungalow. It was Sunday and technically she wasn't on duty, but that didn't mean she wasn't busy. "The wedding is getting closer by the day."

"Time does march on," he murmured, shutting the door behind her.

"Ha-ha. There's some new weird flower combo I have to find and get delivered. Apparently, my mother and I are now speaking, even though we never had anything close to a reconciliation talk. Suddenly, there are texts and phone calls. She wants cake pops."

Quinn raised an eyebrow. "Like at Starbucks?"

"Yes. Little round cakes on a stick. Pink, of course. The tablecloths are pink and copper, so of course we need copper chargers on the table." She glared at him. "Do you know what chargers are?"

"Decorative large plates you put out before the dinner. Then they get taken away before anyone eats. It's very confusing. Your point being?"

"I'm busy! Why am I here?"

He'd texted her and asked her to stop by. Not that she wasn't happy to see him. He looked good, as always. Faded jeans, an untucked gauzy white shirt rolled up to the elbows. He hadn't shaved that morning, and the faint stubble looked nice. Sexy.

Don't think about that! She didn't have time for sexual daydreams, let alone actual sex. There were about five thousand things on her to-do list.

"And the shoes," she added.

"Excuse me?"

"We've ordered our bridesmaid dresses. They're black, which I like. But because of you, I keep thinking I want to wear high heels. I can't wear the blue ones. So I'm going to have to buy some. This is Los Lobos. Where am I supposed to buy a pair of nice black heels?"

He walked toward her. "They're not 'blue ones,'" he said with air quotes. "They're Saint Laurent suede pumps. I'll buy you black heels. Maybe Jimmy Choo." He reached around her to lock the door.

She was both intrigued and stressed. "I don't have time for sex."

One corner of his mouth turned up. "Good. We're not going to have sex. Come here."

He led her to the chair by the sofa and told her to sit. She saw a tray on the end table with a couple of small bottles with narrow tips, a washcloth and liquid in a bowl.

"What are you up to?" she asked as she took her seat.

"Henna."

"Huh?"

He pulled a rolling stool over from the corner and sat down, then wiped the back of her hand with the cloth. "I'm going to do a henna design on the backs of your hands."

He could have said he was heading off to Jupiter and she

wouldn't have been any more surprised. "Why would you do that?"

He glanced at her, then returned his attention to her hand. "Why not?"

Honest to God, it was a question she couldn't answer. "Did I mention being busy?"

"You did. Think of this as a mental vacation."

He picked up one of the small bottles and began squeezing the thick liquid on her skin. He worked quickly, creating a swirly design that was both simple and beautiful. More impressive, he was doing it freehand, without a template or a picture or anything.

"You've done this before," she said.

"A few times. I like to be creative from time to time. I've designed a few record covers. It's a nice change."

She watched as he took the design past her wrist. With all she had going on, it was kind of nice to just sit for a few minutes.

"What do I have to do to this?" she asked.

"Nothing. Once it dries, you brush off the henna and the design remains. Depending on your skin chemistry, it will last around ten days, maybe longer."

"Fun."

He finished with her right hand and rolled the stool to the other side of her chair to start on her left. She closed her eyes as he worked. The past few nights she'd covered the late shift on the registration desk and then had cleaned rooms in the morning. The wedding was only a month away and there were a thousand things to do.

"Joyce showed my mother some flower I have to find, along with cherry blossoms, which are not, by the way, in season. But does that matter to anyone? Of course not. Oh, and she found napkins that match the texture on the wedding cake. I get to order those, as well."

"You're busy."

"I am. What about you?"

"Things are good."

"How's the boy band?"

"Annoying Wayne."

She smiled. "Which you enjoy."

"I do." He tapped her knee. "I'm done."

She opened her eyes and looked at the swirling and curved lines covering the backs of her hands. "It's beautiful. So how long does it take to dry?"

"Two hours."

"Two hours!" She came to her feet. "What part of 'I'm busy' wasn't clear to you? I can't sit here for two hours."

He smiled as he rose. "You're going to have to. You can't get anything on the henna or it will be ruined. You don't want a smudge on the pattern, do you?"

"Are you insane? I have to go and do things."

"Sorry. I guess you're stuck."

He didn't sound sorry at all.

She glared at him. "If I didn't have henna on my hands, I would so hit you."

He grinned. "But you do and you can't. Two long hours. Whatever are we going to do?"

His tone caught her attention before the words sank in. When both connected in her brain, she felt her insides start to melt.

"Quinn," she began, not sure if she was annoyed or impressed. Probably the latter, she admitted, but only to herself. "Seriously, the time thing."

"You're stuck. That's my bad. I'm going to have to make it

up to you." He looked her up and down. "How should I do that?" He reached for the front of her jeans. "I know."

He unfastened her jeans and worked on the zipper. She reached to push him away, remembered her hands and was able to only stand there awkwardly as he lowered her jeans to the floor. She stepped out of them. Her panties followed. She was naked from the waist down, in the living room of his bungalow. It was a very strange afternoon.

He pushed her clothes to the side and moved close, then cupped her face. She had only a second to brace herself for the impact of his kiss before he claimed her.

She parted the second his mouth touched hers. Their tongues tangled as heat and need surged through her. The awkward thing went away, and anticipation took its place. This was Quinn, she thought hazily. Whatever else might be going on in her life, she trusted him, trusted *them*. Being with him was exciting and challenging and satisfying, but always, always safe. Whatever happened, he would have her back.

He moved his hands down to her shoulders, then lower onto her hips. They settled on her bare butt, where he squeezed her curves.

"If you'd rather, I can get you a magazine."

She laughed, then leaned in and nipped his bottom lip. "I think you'll be more interesting."

"If you're sure. I have the latest issue of *Rolling Stone*."

"And while that's tempting, I think this is better."

He moved his hands to her belly, then drew them to her breasts. He brushed his fingertips against her tight nipples. Even through the layer of her bra and T-shirt, she felt his sure touch. Tension and fire flowed from her breasts to her groin and back.

"Sit," he told her.

She sat on the chair. He knelt in front of her and shifted her until her butt was barely resting on the edge of the cushion. He pushed her thighs apart, exposing the very essence of her to him. He rested his hand flat on her stomach and pressed his thumb against her clit.

The pleasure was instant. She sank back against the chair and closed her eyes. Whatever he was going to do to her, she knew it would be magical. She was simply going to go along for the ride.

Quinn didn't disappoint. He continued to rub her clit until he had her moving her hips in time with his actions. She spread her legs wider still, knowing there would be more and wanting it all. She felt him shift, but she didn't look. She wanted to be surprised. For a second there was nothing, then, without warning, he pressed his warm tongue against her swollen center.

She gasped as tendrils of pleasure radiated out from her core. Her toes curled, her thighs tightened and she let her head fall back.

The man knew what he was doing, she thought as he circled her a couple of times before settling into a steady rhythm that had her hips pulsing in time with his ministrations. He licked and sucked until she was gasping and reaching for her release. At the same time, he pushed two fingers into her. He moved them in tandem with his tongue, then curled them so he could stimulate her G-spot.

Courtney grabbed on to the arms of the chair and dug her fingers into the fabric. Her entire body was focused on the places he touched and the ecstasy he promised. Her muscles tightened, her breathing quickened as she pushed toward her release. It remained tantalizingly out of reach until it suddenly exploded, causing her to shudder against him.

She felt herself pulsing against his fingers. He rubbed her clit from underneath even as he moved his tongue back and forth. She came and came for what felt like hours as every ounce of pleasure drained from her.

When she was done, she lay there, legs spread, eyes closed. She couldn't do much more than try to catch her breath. She heard movements and a rustling sound, then felt his hands on her thighs.

She opened her eyes in time to watch him push into her. His erection was huge, his expression intense. He pushed in, then withdrew. She shifted so she could wrap her legs around his hips. He shoved his hands under her T-shirt and massaged her breasts.

He pushed in and out, finding a fast road to his release. At the same time, he lightly pinched her nipples. She was so sensitized from all he'd done before that she found herself arching into the contact, wanting more and more.

She started to reach for him, remembered the henna, then grabbed the arms of the chair.

The combination of him filling her and his fingers and thumbs on her nipples was pushing her closer. "Harder," she gasped, not sure which she needed more of, then realizing it didn't much matter.

He shoved in deeper even as he squeezed her nipples more tightly. She came again with a shriek.

He pumped in and out of her faster and faster, carrying her on her orgasm until they were both gasping for air. He dropped his hands to her hips, held her still and pushed in one last time before climaxing himself.

They stayed like that—him inside her, his hands on her hips, while they caught their breath. His eyes were dark, his gaze direct. They watched each other. It was as if having just shared physical intimacy, now they wanted an emotional connection. She let herself get lost in looking at him.

"You okay?" he asked.

She smiled. "The henna thing really works for me."

He grinned. "I had a feeling you'd like it. We'll have to try it again sometime."

23

"DO YOU LIKE the dresses you and your sisters picked out for your mom's wedding?" David asked.

"We do. They're black, which is going to be great against all the pink, and the style is pretty classic. I'm going to take mine to a tailor after the wedding to get it cut off. I can use a knee-length dress a lot more."

They were having dinner at Audrey's on the Pier, a nice seafood restaurant on the waterfront. Sienna was doing her best to relax. Over the past few days, she'd had a sense of impending doom. If she had to guess, she would say it started when David's mother had shown up so unexpectedly.

"Did it kill you to pay retail?" he asked, his voice teasing. "I know you love a bargain."

"I do. I can't help it. Plus, I work right next to an amazing thrift store. Why not take advantage of that?"

They'd already ordered, and the server had brought them each a glass of chardonnay. She sipped hers.

"I was thinking," David said, leaning toward her. "We should go wedding gown shopping together."

"What?"

"Hear me out. I want you to know what I like. I'm going to want your opinion on my tux, so it's only fair." He smiled engagingly as he pushed up his glasses. "You're going to be beautiful no matter what, but I'd like a say."

In her wedding gown? "I thought it was supposed to be a surprise."

"It will be. I don't want to know which dress you buy. Just maybe offer some guidance."

He thought she needed guidance? "Okay," she said slowly. "As long as we don't deal with this until after Mom's wedding. There's so much going on. I want to be available to help Courtney."

"She's probably going to need it."

Her gaze sharpened. "What does that mean?"

He looked confused. "What? You're the one always saying she's incompetent and clumsy. I'm just repeating what you said before."

"Oh." He probably had a point. Until recently, she'd seen her younger sister as something of a disaster, but all that had changed. "She's got her act together, believe me. We should all be doing so well. As for the wedding, it's not that Mom's changing her mind so much as she's adding things. Regardless, I want to be around to help."

"I always knew you were more than a pretty face."

She smiled at him, knowing he meant the words kindly, but on the inside, she felt the need to slap him. Did everything have to be about her appearance? Of course, she could be overly sensitive. Maybe he didn't mean it that way at all, and she was reading too much into his words.

"We are going to have to talk about where we're having the wedding," he said as the server brought their salads. "St. Louis would be really nice."

"Except for the tornadoes and floods," she murmured.

"We can work around those. I have a big family. It would be easier for them to have it there."

She wanted to point out it would be easier for her family to have it here. Not to mention her. If the wedding was in David's hometown, she had a bad feeling it would be planned by David's mother. Which meant Sienna would be fighting Linda on every detail. While the other woman had been perfectly pleasant during her visit, she seemed to have a lot of firm opinions.

"Let's talk about this after the wedding," she said. "There's a lot to consider and I can't deal with that now."

"Not a problem." He winked. "How about an easier topic? The honeymoon. I've been thinking we should go somewhere exotic. Jennifer and Justin went to the Four Seasons in Bora Bora. We could go there. You'd look just as good in a bikini and we'd have great pictures to show everyone."

She knew her mouth had dropped open. She consciously closed it, then put down her fork. "Who are Justin and Jennifer?"

"Jennifer Aniston. I can't think of his last name. Didn't you see the pictures in *People* magazine?"

"I honestly can't remember." She took a steadying breath. "David, why do you care about going to the same place some celebrity did?"

"I thought it would be fun. Something we could talk about with our friends."

They didn't have any mutual friends, and her friends wouldn't care about a celebrity honeymoon. Why on earth did David? "I think it's kind of far. There are a lot of really nice tropical resorts much closer."

"I guess. We have time to discuss it. But I do want to honeymoon somewhere by the beach. Everyone needs to see how hot my wife looks in a bikini for sure."

She frowned. "That's about the fourth time you've mentioned my appearance tonight."

"Is it?" He laughed. "I think you're attractive. That's not a bad thing."

"No." It wasn't, she told herself firmly. "It's just I worry that's all you like about me. I'm not going to look this way forever."

"Of course not. You'll get old." He grinned. "Of course, there's always plastic surgery."

Sienna felt her eyes widen. "Excuse me? Did you just say that?" She started to rise.

David's expression immediately turned contrite and he reached across the table to grab her forearm. "Sienna, I'm sorry. I was making a joke, but it was a bad one." He released her. "I apologize. That was a terrible thing to say."

She sank back into her seat but didn't speak. The sting of his words lingered, as did her need to bolt. But she told herself to hear him out.

"Of course I love all of you," he continued. "You're smart and caring. That was what I noticed first about you. How much you care about the women you help. Please forgive me."

She nodded because it was the right thing to do. And his apology had been exactly right. Still, she couldn't shake the feeling that the plastic surgery comment had been the most honest thing he'd said. But was that really true, or was she simply looking for an excuse to run?

There was nothing that took the edge off a day like the sound of margarita ingredients mixing in a good-quality blender. Courtney moved her hips in time with the music flowing out of her mother's built-in speakers, then flipped the switch on the blender.

When Maggie had called for an impromptu girls' night in at her place, Courtney had taken the invitation as a peace offering. She'd rearranged her schedule to be there. Rachel and

Sienna had come, as well. Neil had gone to Los Angeles for a couple of days, so it was girls only. Probably for the last time until after the wedding.

She turned off the blender and poured the slushy mixture into four salt-rimmed glasses. Her mother took the first one and smiled at her. Courtney smiled back.

Yes, there were things to say. Maybe things that might never be said. Was it better to get everything in the open and deal with it? Probably, but so what? Every family had problems. To be honest, she could go her whole life without having to deal with who did what and when. Better to just accept there had been a problem and move on.

"I got takeout," Maggie announced as they took seats around the island. "Mexican from Bill's."

"Appropriate." Sienna took a long drink of her margarita. "Did you know that alcohol enhances the aging process?"

They all stared at her.

"That was cheerful," Rachel told her. "Are you okay?"

"I'm fine. Better than fine, because you know what? If I start to look old, I can get plastic surgery."

Courtney moved close and touched her sister's arm. "What's going on?"

For a second Sienna looked as if she was going to cry. Then she tossed her head. "Nothing. I'm fine. Just being weird. Ignore me." She turned to their mother. "Let's talk about the wedding. Mom, what's new with that?"

Maggie grinned. "Well, there are a few things I can show you."

"I want to see them all," Sienna told her.

Maggie got up and hurried from the room. Rachel got a large bowl and dumped chips in it while Courtney collected the take-out containers of salsa and guacamole. By the time

Maggie returned with a couple of boxes, they were passing the bowls along the island.

"I have sneakers," she said, opening the first box. "I love the internet. Have I mentioned that? Did you know you can order custom sneakers on the Converse website and that they have special wedding ones?"

She held up a pair that were white and trimmed in pink. On the heel, one shoe said "Maggie" and the other said "Neil."

"Too cute," Rachel told her. "What else?"

Their mother showed them etched champagne glasses for the bride and groom, along with a custom garter.

"I'm not going to have Neil throw it," she said, closing the box. "I'm a little old to be flashing that much thigh, but we'll know it's there and that's what matters." She looked at Courtney. "You're doing a wonderful job with the wedding. Thank you for that, darling. It's going to be an amazing day."

"I think it is." Courtney thought about mentioning Jill's due date concerns, but when she'd told her mother about the change, Maggie had insisted on keeping Jill as her first choice for an officiate. So Courtney had found a backup minister.

Maggie pushed the boxes to the far end of the island. "So how is everyone doing? I feel like we're all so busy these days. Rachel, honey, you're looking so good."

"Thanks." Rachel raised her margarita. "Tonight I sin, but in the morning, I will walk." She shrugged. "I'm taking care of myself and it's really helping me feel better."

"How's Greg?"

Rachel stiffened. "Why would you ask me that?"

Maggie shrugged. "I don't know. I think about him. You two were so good together. I'm sorry he was an idiot."

"Me, too," Rachel admitted. "At least we're getting along and he's being such a good dad to Josh."

Courtney studied her sister. The words were all correct,

but there was something in Rachel's tone. Nothing bad. Was it wistfulness? She'd said that Greg was around more, helping and hanging out with his son. Was there more going on?

"Any sparks?" Sienna asked, cutting right to the chase.

"What?" Rachel looked away. "Of course not. We're divorced. Sure, we can be friends, but that's all. I'm sure he's dating a million other people."

"I haven't seen him with anyone," Sienna said.

"Me, either." Maggie sipped her drink. "I won't push. You had every right to throw him out. It's just…well, enough about that. Sienna, how's David?"

"Good. Fine. We're putting off planning our wedding until after yours, but I'm paying attention so I can steal all the best ideas."

Courtney wasn't sure that happy statement could have sounded more wooden. "What's up?" she asked.

"Nothing." Sienna beamed. "I'm happily engaged."

Rachel rolled her eyes. "No one believes that. You want to talk about it?"

Sienna drained her glass. "What I would love is a refill." She walked to the blender and poured. "Courtney, your turn. How's your love life?"

"I don't have one."

Everyone laughed. "Of course you do," her mother said. "You're seeing Quinn."

"Sure, but it's just fun." And hot and amazing, she thought, glancing at the henna on the backs of her hands. "He's not the settling-down kind. I mean, look at him. He's dated all kinds of famous women. Actresses and models. He wouldn't be interested in me."

"Of course he would," Rachel told her. "He'd be lucky to have you."

"Thanks, but let's be real." She reached for a chip. "However this ends, he's been so great to me. He's helped with a lot of things." Like her worrying about being too tall, and he'd been there after Joyce had outed her about her education. "I like him. He's been an amazing summer fling. When it ends, and it will, I'll be crushed, but I'll move on."

"I'd really like to see you married," Maggie said, then frowned. "All of you. Dear God, I just realized, you're all single."

"I'm engaged," Sienna said, waving her left hand. "Look. I have a ring and everything."

"Yes, but none of you are married. I'm a horrible mother."

Now Courtney was the one to roll her eyes. "Mom, shocking, but true—not everything is about you."

Maggie laughed. "You're right, but it should be. Don't you agree? Now, who wants dinner?"

Josh bolted from the kitchen for his Tuesday night video game session. One of the new rules for summer was limiting his computer playtime to three nights a week. Greg stared after him.

"Are those skid marks on the floor?" he asked with a laugh.

"Absolutely. I always plan to entertain myself on video game nights."

He turned back to the dishwasher and loaded the last of the dishes. When Greg had brought Josh home from camp, they'd stopped for takeout, and somehow her ex had ended up staying for dinner. With Josh at the table, she hadn't worried about feeling awkward, but now they were alone and she had no idea what to say.

"How's your arm?" she asked, then wondered if she shouldn't have. Maybe it was better to ignore what had happened before.

"Nearly healed. The stitches are dissolving, so I just have to keep it dry a few more days and I'll be good as new."

She wiped down the counter. "Good. And that other guy, Tommy? How's he doing?"

"He'll be back to work tomorrow."

She rinsed off her hands and dried them. Okay, time to get Greg to leave. Only, she wasn't sure how without being rude. Before she could figure something out, he'd crossed to the Keurig and turned it on.

"I'd like a decaf," he said. "What about you?"

"Sure. Thank you."

He knew where everything was. As he collected the pods and mugs, she went into the living room and settled in one of the chairs. On purpose. With the sofa, she would worry about where to sit. One end? The middle? A chair was much safer.

Greg brought in their coffees a few minutes later. He sat on the end of the sofa closest to her.

"My mom was telling me I don't bring you around enough," he told her.

"I'll have to stop in and see her the next time I pick up Josh." Rachel had always liked Greg's parents. "How's it going living with them?" Because he'd moved in with them after the divorce.

"Not bad. They mostly leave me alone."

"You ever think about getting a place of your own?"

"Sometimes. I'm waiting."

That got her attention. Waiting for what? For them? Her heart began to beat faster in her chest. Was this it? Were they going to talk about their relationship now? She opened her mouth, closed it, then decided to let him bring it up.

"How is it going with Josh and his chores?" he asked.

Okay, not the subject she'd been expecting. "I haven't done much with that," she admitted.

"I could tell from the chart on the refrigerator. Why don't you want him doing chores?"

"I do."

"But?"

She shifted on her seat. "I don't know. It's easier to do it myself. Then I know it's done right."

"I thought you hated cleaning up after him in the bathroom."

"Well, if you're going to use logic," she murmured, then sighed. "You're right. I need to get him to clean his bathroom."

Greg's dark gaze was steady. "You really have trouble asking for help, don't you? How much of that is about me, and how much of it is your dad?"

She stiffened. "I don't want to talk about this."

"I'm sure you don't, but you should. Come on, Rachel, you've always had trouble letting other people do things for you. Help me understand why that is."

"I just…" She picked up her coffee, then put it back on the coffee table. "I've always been that way." She could remember her mother crouched in front of her, tears in her eyes. "Be a good girl for me, Rachel. Please. I need you to take care of things."

"You took on a lot when your dad died," Greg said gently. "Too much."

"My mom depended on me."

"You did her proud, I'm sure. Then you married me and I was in no way ready for that kind of responsibility. So once again you got stuck doing it all. What was the lesson you learned? That if you depend on someone, they'll let you down?"

"Someone's been reading a lot of self-help books."

"True, but that doesn't answer the question."

She'd been hoping he wouldn't notice. "I am afraid," she admitted. "I trusted you, Greg. With everything I had, and you let me down."

"I know. I'm sorry. If I could take that back, I would. I was wrong. No matter what was happening between us, I didn't have the right to do that. But I hope you understand my cheating was a symptom, not a goal."

"You were angry and frustrated," she admitted. "I knew that. I felt like I couldn't get your attention and you thought I was never happy."

Which she hadn't been, she thought to her herself. Not at the end.

"I wish you'd think about trusting me now," he said quietly. "I'm doing my best to show you that you can. I meant what I said before. There isn't anyone else. There hasn't been."

"For, ah, me, either."

He smiled. "Good. I'm glad you believe me." He glanced at his watch. "I have an early start tomorrow. I need to get home."

Just like that? Didn't he want to stay and maybe make out with her? Obviously not.

She rose. "Thanks for bringing dinner."

"You're welcome. Get on Josh about doing his chores. He's a capable kid. Have a little faith."

"I will."

"I hope that's true, Rachel. More than you know."

24

"THEY'RE ALL BALLADS." Collins spoke defiantly, as if expecting an argument.

Bryan sucked in a breath. "Dude."

"I couldn't help it," Collins said. "That's what they are."

Quinn studied the music. Collins preferred to get the melody nailed down before he added lyrics. Quinn could work any way his artists wanted. But he was known to not appreciate a ballad, no matter how well they sold.

"Ballads are fine," he said easily, reaching for his guitar.

Collins and Bryan stared at him.

"You sure?" Collins asked.

"Yup."

"You're mellowing." Bryan picked up a pad of paper. "Is it an age thing?"

"Don't make me have Wayne beat the crap out of you, kid."

Bryan chuckled. "I'm glad you said it that way, because I'm pretty sure I could take you, old man."

"In your dreams. And it's not an age thing."

If he had to guess, he would say it was a Courtney thing, along with a coming-home thing. Being back felt right. He liked the pace of life here. He didn't miss any part of his life in LA—except maybe the view. That had been damned nice. But he could make do.

He liked being close to his grandmother. He liked the building his company had bought and how it was going to be when it was finished. He liked being with Courtney. She was that unique combination of challenging and restful. There had been a lot of women in his life. More than most men had. He wasn't sure if that was good or bad—the volume simply was. He was ready to let that go, as well.

The change had started a couple of years ago—when he'd been seeing Shannon. Before he had realized his feelings had changed, she'd fallen for someone else. He didn't think she was the one who'd gotten away, but he recognized he'd lost an opportunity. He wasn't going to let that happen again. He wanted more. He wanted permanent. Traditional. A wife. Kids. A couple of dogs—although they would never be as glorious and special as Sarge and Pearl.

"You ready?" Collins asked, drawing him back to the present.

"Let's make it happen."

Collins played several chords. Quinn listened, breathing in the sounds and letting them sink in deep. He didn't say anything. Collins played them again and again. On the fourth pass, Quinn played along, then made a few changes. Bryan scribbled the new chords.

Quinn played the whole thing while Collins listened, and so it went, back and forth until they had the melody nailed. They moved on to the lyrics. Quinn read through the lines.

"I think it's *over before it began* rather than *over when it began*," he said.

"That's better." Bryan played the melody and sang along.

Two hours later they had a song. It would need tweaking

before it was ready, but Quinn was excited. This one had the potential to be a hit.

The guys collected their stuff. Leigh, Tadeo's wife, had come to town and was having the band over for barbecue. He'd declined the invitation but had heard Wayne was going. As much as his assistant pretended to dislike And Then, hanging out with them was good for him. And for them.

As Collins and Bryan left, he saw Courtney walk toward the bungalow. She had Sarge and Pearl each on a leash. She waved at him.

"We're going for a walk," she called. "Want to come with?"

She still had her bangs. He suspected she kept them because they suited her face and not because they made her sexy as hell. Even in jeans and a T-shirt she got to him. She was a walking, breathing fantasy, and she had absolutely no clue. How could he resist that?

"A walk sounds great." He grabbed the bungalow key and his cell phone, shut the front door and stepped out onto the path. He greeted both dogs, then took Pearl's leash and fell into step with Courtney.

"How's it going?" he asked.

"Good. T minus three weeks and counting." She drew her brows together. "Why do we say *T*? Does it mean time?"

"I think so. We can look it up online if you'd like."

"I expected you to just know. You seem to have a lot of knowledge at your fingertips." She looked at him out of the corner of her eye. "Like your skill with henna."

He grinned. "That was fun."

"It was."

They walked west, toward the path down to the beach. The late afternoon was warm, the sky clear. Once they reached the edge of the property, there was a stone path that led down the cliff to the rocky beach below. The air tasted of salt, and the sound of the waves grew louder as they started down.

"I have to go to LA in a few days," he told her. "I need to check on a couple of things at the house before I list it. I'm also thinking of having a party. A last hurrah."

"You really doing it? Really moving to Los Lobos?"

"I am. I'm going to start looking for a place here."

"I don't know what to make of that. Won't you miss being around industry people?"

"No, and anyone who wants to see me can come here. About the party. Want to come with me as my date?"

She looked at him. "Go to LA with you to attend a fancy music industry party?"

He grinned. "I can even promise you a few movie stars."

"I've never been to a party like that. What if I don't fit in?"

"You'll be with me."

That made her laugh. "Because if I'm with you, I'm one of the in people."

"You know it, babe. Stick with me."

"Did you just call me babe?"

"I did and you liked it."

The smile returned. "Maybe. A little. Okay. I'm game." She came to a stop and faced him. Her expression was serious. "I'm going because of you, Quinn. Not the party."

He liked that she felt the need to clarify her position. "I figured, but thanks for making it clear."

"I don't have a thing to wear."

"It's Los Angeles. We can fix that."

"Are you going to want me in heels?"

He mostly wanted her naked, but that wouldn't be appropriate. "Only if it makes you happy."

She thought for a second. "I'm pretty sure I'm ready for the challenge. I just hope I don't fall."

"Don't worry. I'll catch you if you do."

"Can't I use paper towels?" Josh asked as Rachel showed him how to spray the counters and sink and then wipe them down.

"Microfiber cloths are better. They're reusable. I wash them every week so they're clean for next time."

Her eleven-year-old son sighed heavily. "I know. It saves money and protects the environment. I think I'd like cleaning the bathroom better if I could use paper towels."

"I don't think you'll ever like cleaning the bathroom, but that's okay. You just have to do it."

"Kind of like some of the drills for baseball. They're boring, but they make us better players."

"Something like that."

She showed him how to empty the water out of the toilet bowl and then use the long-handled scrubber.

"That's totally gross." He sounded oddly pleased by the fact. "I never thought that you have to clean a toilet."

"Did you think it never got dirty?"

He giggled. "It has to get dirty, Mom. It's full of poop."

What was it about boys and bodily functions? Especially the less socially acceptable ones? She told herself to be grateful he was still saying *poop* instead of other words.

They'd already cleaned out the shower, which left only the floor.

"You know where the stick vacuum is, right?" she asked as she shifted to get more comfortable. Her back was bothering her again.

"Uh-huh. In the laundry room."

"Go get that. You're going to vacuum first, then use a microfiber pad to clean the floor."

"You really like microfiber stuff."

"I do. It gets things cleaned and we don't have to use a lot of harsh chemicals."

"You sound like a commercial."

She smiled. "Then you should be paying me."

He laughed and went to get the vacuum. She watched as he moved it across the small floor.

"Do behind the toilet," she called over the loud roar. "And the corners."

He did as she requested, then wet down the microfiber pad that attached to the end of the mop.

"You have to squeeze it first," she told him. "Or it will leave the floor too wet."

He looked at her. "You're not going to be standing there every time I clean the bathroom, are you?"

She wanted to say she was. That if she wasn't, he wouldn't do it right. That he would cut corners or forget or... She thought about Greg's comments that she was unable to ask for help. That she hadn't bothered to get Josh going on his chores for nearly half the summer.

In her heart, she knew that the bathroom didn't have to be cleaned perfectly every time. That Josh learning about helping around the house was the more important lesson. He was old enough now to have responsibilities. Plus, it gave her a break. But letting go was hard.

"I'm going to make a master list," she said reluctantly. "It will help you remember everything you're supposed to do. But you'll be on your own unless you come ask for help."

"Sweet."

He dropped the mop to the floor and began moving it back and forth. She was about to remind him to do behind the toilet, then stopped herself.

"Put out clean towels when you're done," she said instead.

"I will."

"You know where they are?"

"Mo-om!"

"Fine." She deliberately turned her back on the bathroom and walked away.

"Do you really have to work late, or are you still angry with me?" David asked.

A legitimate question, Sienna thought as she shuffled through the piles of paper on her desk. She shifted the phone so she could cradle it between her shoulder and her ear. She was still at work and busy—so the last thing she needed was a call from David.

"I'm dealing with a lot right now."

"But you're still angry."

"*Angry* isn't the right word," she admitted. "I'm hurt. I worry about why you want to marry me." And maybe why she'd agreed to marry him.

"I was wrong," he told her. "I've apologized more than once. I don't know what else to do. I never meant to hurt you or imply I'm only interested in your looks. I love you, Sienna. All of you. I want us to be together always. I want to have children with you and watch them grow. I want to make you happy."

All the right words, she thought. So why couldn't she believe them?

"David, I just don't know. I worry things are happening too fast."

"Then we'll slow it down. Whatever it takes. I don't want to lose you, Sienna. Was my mom visiting a problem? I know she has a big personality."

"The dress didn't help," she admitted.

"We already talked about us going wedding gown shopping

together. I thought that meant you knew I wasn't expecting you to wear that dress."

He had a point there. "What if I don't want to get married in St. Louis? That's really important to you."

"It is, but there are ways to make it work. We could have two receptions. One here and one there. Or what we talked about before—a destination wedding." He paused. "Sienna, this is about us. I've been focused on the wedding too much. You and I being together is the important part. You're right. Things have been moving too fast. Let's put wedding talk on hold for a while and focus on each other. Let's get us right first."

Her throat got a little tight and her eyes burned. Finally, she thought with some relief. "I didn't know that was what I needed you to say, but now that you have, I realize that's what's been missing. I need there to be more us."

"Then there will be. I love you, Sienna. I mean that."

"I love you, too."

"Good. Now go do your work. If you're not too late, call me and we'll get dinner or something."

"Okay. Bye."

Two hours later she'd nearly caught up with her quarterly reports. All she needed was a quick check of her email and she could leave. Maybe she would call David so they could grab dinner after all.

Their conversation had helped, she thought. She felt better—less weight of the world and more like herself. Her cell phone rang.

She glanced at the unfamiliar number before answering. "Hello?"

"It's Erika Trowbridge. Don't hang up. I need your help."

Sienna thought of her high school frenemy and knew the situation had to be bad for Erika to reach out to her. "Where are you? Do you need either police or emergency medical aid? I can call 911 for you or come there directly myself."

"Okay, wow. I was thinking maybe I could ask you some questions. I'm outside your office."

Sienna was already moving. The familiar worry/panic threatened, but she told herself to focus on the task at hand. "I'll be at the front door in ten seconds. Stay on the line with me."

"I'm fine. No one's hurt me."

Sienna ran to the main hall and to the foyer. She unlocked the door. Only when she saw Erika standing there did she hang up on the call.

"What's going on?"

The other woman stared at her. "You take this stuff really seriously."

"It's my job." Sienna looked her over. "You're all right? No one's hurt you?"

"I'm fine. Sorry. I didn't mean to start anything. I just wanted to talk about someone I know. I think she's in trouble."

"It's not you?"

"No." Erika's mouth twisted. "I'm sure you find that upsetting."

Sienna drew in a breath. Her heart rate slowed to normal and the panic faded. "I'm glad you're all right. You can believe me or not."

"Were you really going to call the police or an ambulance?"

"Of course. That's what we do here. We help women in trouble. The thrift store is simply a means to help with the funding."

She closed and locked the front door, then led the way to the lunch room. She opened the refrigerator and had Erika choose a drink. She pulled a bottle of iced tea out for herself, then motioned to the sofa and chairs set up in the corner.

The furniture was worn but comfortable. As a rule, clients didn't come to the offices, but when they did, the conversations generally went better when people were more relaxed. Desks with computers could be intimidating as a backdrop.

When they were seated, Sienna tucked her legs under her, then opened her iced tea.

"Tell me what's going on."

Erika tucked a strand of red hair behind her ear, then clutched her bottle of water. "This isn't going anywhere, is it? You won't tell anyone?"

"If you share something that makes me think someone's life is in danger, I'm required to report that. Otherwise, I'm basically like talking to a lawyer. I keep your secrets." She smiled. "Without charging by the hour."

"Okay." Erika set her water on the coffee table, then grabbed it again. "It's my cousin. Her boyfriend's beating the crap out of her and I don't know how to make her leave him."

"How long have they been together?"

"Two years."

"What does beating the crap out of her mean? Bruises? Broken bones?"

"He hits her every now and then. I don't think he's broken anything, but she's had a black eye a few times. I've met him and he seems really nice, but apparently he has a temper. I've told her to just walk away, but she won't." Erika shook her head. "That's the part I don't get. She's this great person. Why does she put up with that?"

Sienna stood and walked to a small desk on the far wall. She opened a drawer and pulled out several sheets of paper, along with a brochure. She took them back to Erika.

"You need to read these," she said as she took her seat again.

"You're giving me homework?"

"Yes. Look at the brochure first. Items three and five are

the most important right now." Sienna held up one finger. "Help your cousin design a safety plan. She needs to know what to do if it gets bad." She held up a second finger. "Don't intervene. You'll only make her situation worse."

Erika wrinkled her nose. "What makes you think I'd do that?"

"I've known you since we were kids. You love wading into the middle of trouble. This is not the time to do that. If you try to fix this yourself, you could get your cousin killed."

Erika's eyes widened. "Are you serious?"

"Completely. You're smart and capable and you are totally out of your league on this one. You don't have to like me, but you do have to trust me." She motioned to the papers. "Read those," she repeated. "Go online and educate yourself. While no two situations are exactly the same, they do tend to follow a pattern. He will escalate the abuse. If you want to help your cousin, you have to do it on her terms in a way that supports her."

"Okay. Thank you. I appreciate the information. What if she wants to leave?"

"Then we can help. Where does she live?"

"Sacramento."

"Good. That's far enough away that coming here would make sense. You have my number. If she leaves, call me anytime, day or night. I'll get her to a safe place."

"Is that your job?"

Sienna smiled. "No, I raise money for the organization. But things will go more smoothly if you can reassure your cousin that you have a personal relationship with me. I've done it before. Once your cousin is here and settled, I'll introduce her to our support staff."

"Just like that?"

"Like I said—it's what we do."

Erika took a drink of her water. "Okay. Thank you. I'll read this and then talk to her. It's been pretty awful and I really didn't know what to say."

"For what it's worth, those of us who haven't been in the situation usually can't understand why they stay. The material will help with that."

Erika leaned back against the sofa. "Now I have to feel guilty about not giving you my great-grandmother's kitchen stuff."

"Yes, you do. You should write a generous check to make up for that."

Erika laughed. "Maybe I will." Her humor faded. "Why do you do this? Work here? Why aren't you working for a fashion magazine in New York or something?"

"You mean why isn't my work more shallow?"

"Yeah."

She raised one shoulder. "I was a marketing major my first year at college. I got a summer job at a travel magazine. One of the staff members was being abused by her husband. When she left, she came to me for help. I was nineteen and had no idea what to do, but I found a women's shelter in the phone book and arranged for her to go to them. The next year I started volunteering there. Then I changed my major and ended up here."

Sienna leaned forward. "Now it's my turn. Why have you always hated me? It can't be because of Jimmy. You didn't really want him."

"You still stole him."

"Okay, and I'm sorry for that. But it's not why you hate me."

"I don't hate you." Erika stared at her. "You never saw me. In high school, you were the princess and I was invisible. I wanted to be your friend and you never noticed me. You ignored everyone who wasn't in your privileged circle."

Sienna wanted to protest that wasn't true, but she was pretty sure it was. "Did I do or say something to hurt your feelings?"

"No. That would have required more than there was."

"I'm sorry you were invisible."

"I'm sorry I hated you."

Awkward silence filled the room. Sienna looked at the clock and saw it was close to seven. "Want to go get dinner?"

Erika thought for a second. "All right. Sure. That would be nice. I'll even buy."

Sienna shook her head. "This isn't going to be about work. This is friends spending time together. Why don't we split the check?"

"You're on."

25

"SO WHAT EXACTLY is happening at this big LA party?" Sienna asked.

"I have no idea." Courtney thought about what Quinn had told her about their upcoming trip to Los Angeles. "I know it's going to be at his house on Thursday night."

"I need more details. When you get back, you're going to have to tell me everything in real time. Do you have anything to wear?"

"No, but he said we'll shop for that once we get to LA."

"Okay, so you need something cute for the trip down and maybe a dinner out." Rachel grinned. "I'm sure you're having lots of sex, but you don't need clothes for that. Unless you're doing role-playing, in which case you're on your own. We don't need to know that you get off on being a lion tamer."

Courtney blinked at her sister. "A lion tamer? What on earth did you and Greg used to do?"

"Not that. I'm just saying you don't need clothes for the naked part."

Sienna shook her head. "Just when you think you know a person…"

They were in the middle of the thrift store. Both her sisters had agreed to help her get a few new-to-her things for her trip. Courtney wanted to look good for her time with Quinn. They would be hanging out with trendy people. She didn't think her jeans and T-shirts were going to cut it.

"Dresses," Rachel said. "They are easy to wear, easy to pack, and you can use accessories to fit any occasion."

"I agree." Sienna pointed to a rack at the other end of the store. "Let me go pull a few. I'll be right back."

"Lion tamer?" Courtney repeated when Sienna had left.

Rachel laughed. "I meant it as an example, not a suggestion. You're young and in love. Heaven knows what you're doing with that man."

Courtney felt herself stiffen. "We're not in love. We're having fun. Quinn's great and all, but it's not serious. He's not the serious type."

In love? Why would anyone think that? There was no love. There couldn't be. Love meant being hurt, and when she was around Quinn, she only felt good.

Rachel held up her hands in the shape of a T. "I meant it as a figure of speech. Don't bite off my head. You two are together a lot and it's fun. That's all."

"Okay. Sorry. We are enjoying ourselves. He's nice. I wouldn't have expected that, but he is."

"Everyone's having sex but me," Rachel complained as she looked through a rack of shirts. "It's depressing."

"Sex would be easier if you were dating."

"I don't want to date."

Not a surprise, Courtney thought. Since the divorce, Rachel had kept to herself. "Do you want to get back together with Greg?"

Her sister swung around and glared at her. "Why would you say that?"

"I'm just asking." Overreacting seemed to be in the air.

"You and he are getting along. He's a great guy, you're fantastic. Stranger things have happened."

"I know. Sorry. Greg confuses me."

Sienna returned with several dresses. "How does he confuse you?"

"He's being nice."

"That bastard!"

Rachel rolled her eyes. "He's stepping up with Josh. He's doing everything I ask. Why couldn't he have done that before the divorce? Why now?"

"Maybe he needed time to figure out what was important," Sienna offered. "Time to see what he'd lost."

Courtney nodded. "Once he lost you and Josh, he was able to see how much you meant to him. Rachel, you have to do what's right for you. I'm only pointing out that no one is going to judge you if you want to give things another try."

"Greg's not interested in that."

"How can you be sure? Have you talked about it?"

Rachel shifted from foot to foot. "No, but he hasn't said anything about us getting back together."

"Someone has to take the first step," Sienna reminded her. "Maybe it could be you."

Rachel grabbed the dresses and shoved them at Courtney. "You need to try these on so we can go meet Neil. Now hurry."

"That wasn't even subtle," Courtney pointed out as the three of them walked back to the dressing rooms.

They did have to keep an eye on the clock. Their mother's fiancé had asked to meet them for coffee.

Courtney tried on the five dresses Sienna had picked out. Two weren't for her, but the other three had possibilities. One was a slim-fitting sheath in a red-and-white swirl pattern.

"Hold on," Sienna told her and raced off. A minute later she was back with a skinny white belt. "Try this on."

The belt was perfect.

"Wear your hair up," Rachel told her. "And you need really great sandals. Not white. Maybe nude and with a heel."

"Nude pumps would totally work," Sienna added.

There was a light blue sundress they all decided would be perfect for the drive down, and a casual open-weave number that would work for a beach cover-up.

Courtney bought the three dresses for a total of thirty-seven dollars, then the three of them headed for Rachel's SUV. They were meeting Neil at Polly's Pie Parlor. Yes, they would have gone anywhere to join him for coffee, but the added incentive of a slice of pie didn't hurt.

"Do you know about the kazoos?" Rachel asked as she drove through town.

Courtney was glad she was in the backseat. There was less to bang her head on. "He mentioned them before. I hoped he was kidding."

"He wasn't. When he called to ask me to meet him, he played one for me. It's gonna be loud."

Sienna turned in her seat and grinned. "Be grateful there aren't going to be swans. They might think the kazoos are a mating call and start attacking guests."

"Aren't you the funny one." She would have to look at her timeline to figure out where they would be—event-wise—when the kazoos came out. If it was after ten, they would be violating the noise policy, not to mention disturbing the other guests.

"I wish we could stop with the surprises," Courtney said. "And buying things for the wedding. Mom ordered custom chair covers. They're embroidered with her and Neil's initials.

They're lovely and there are three hundred of them. Whatever will they do with them afterward?"

"Probably let us take them home as souvenirs," Rachel offered cheerfully. "Let it go, Courtney. This wedding is bigger than all of us. You simply need to surrender to the inevitable. At least Mom's happy."

Courtney leaned against the door. "You're right. I'll focus on that. And the meal will be great. We have excellent wine, and the rest of it will take care of itself."

There were a couple of minutes of silence, then Sienna said, "I don't remember Dad much. Do you, Rach?"

Courtney looked at her older sister. Rachel stared out the front window. "Some. I have images of him. Snippets, really. The sound of his laugh. How it felt when he hugged me and told me I would always be his princess. But not much more than that."

"I don't remember anything," Courtney admitted.

"You were a lot younger," Rachel said. "I should have more memories."

"It's been a long time," Sienna said. "We should be happy Neil came along."

Courtney was glad her mother had someone in her life, but she had no sense of Neil as a father. She'd seen other women with their fathers. Friends and coworkers. There were plenty of fathers and daughters at the hotel. But all that was outside her. She couldn't relate to it. As for missing her father—she found it hard to miss what she'd never had.

They pulled up in front of the restaurant and got out of the car.

"No talk about Dad," Rachel said as they walked inside.

"I don't mind if you talk about your father."

They all jumped and turned to find Neil had come in right behind them. He smiled at them.

"Phil was an important part of your mother's life, and yours, as well." He pointed to an open table. "Shall we?"

Courtney and her sisters exchanged glances. None of them seemed to know what to say, so they followed Neil to the table and took seats.

He wasn't a classically handsome man, Courtney thought as she looked at him. He was a little short and a little round. Balding. But there was a kindness in his eyes. A gentleness that made her feel, in her gut, that her mom was going to do very well with Neil.

Now he leaned forward, his hands on the table. "I have a few things to say and then we'll eat pie."

They waited.

"I was very lucky to find your mother. I've told you before, I lost my first wife to cancer and it took me years to get over the loss. I didn't want to be alone, but I couldn't imagine loving anyone the way I'd loved her."

He drew in a breath. "And here's the funny thing. I don't love Maggie the same. I love her differently. It's just as wonderful, just as deep, but I don't for a moment think I'm marrying someone who's similar. Maggie is her own person."

He smiled at them. "So don't worry that I expect you to see me as your father. I hope, over time, we'll be close. That you'll see me as someone you can come to, a man you can trust. But I'm not your father and I don't expect to replace him."

Sienna nodded. "Thank you for saying that. You never had children?"

"No. We weren't blessed. I hope you girls don't mind if I sometimes think of you as mine. Just because it makes me happy."

"That would be all right," Rachel told him.

"Good. I'm hoping I can convince your mother to sell her business and travel with me, but if she wants to work awhile longer, I'll keep myself busy. I also want you to know that I did all right in my business. I've put aside some money for your mother. It's in a trust fund. If I go first, she'll be taken care of. I don't want you to worry."

Courtney might not remember much about her father, but she did remember her mother worrying about how things were going to work out. Even after she was successful and the family was back in a house, she'd made comments from time to time that had made it clear that the fear of losing everything hadn't gone away. Courtney couldn't recall the man, but the pain his passing had caused had stayed with her. She and Maggie had their differences. Maybe they would always clash, but even so, she was happy to know there was a wonderful man who had her mother's back.

Without thinking, she rose and walked around the table. She leaned over and hugged Neil.

"Thank you," she told him. "For loving her. I hope you'll be very happy together."

"Thank you, my dear."

Courtney returned to her seat. Neil cleared his throat.

"Now that we have that out of the way, I thought I'd get your opinions on taking your mother to Vail for our honeymoon. There are some lovely resorts. This time of year, it's relatively quiet. There's enough nature to be beautiful, but also shopping and lots of restaurants."

"It sounds lovely," Rachel told him.

Sienna fluffed her short hair. "Jennifer Aniston honeymooned in Bora Bora. You could go there."

Neil smiled. "I'm not really the swimsuit type."

Courtney leaned toward her sister. "Since when did you care where Jennifer Aniston honeymooned?"

Sienna laughed. "I don't. I have no idea why I mentioned it."

"It's a lovely suggestion," Neil told her, "but I think we'll stick to Vail." He reached for the menus at the center of the table and handed them around. "Now, I understand the peach pie is not to be missed. Who will join me in a piece?"

The house was definitely a starter home—small, old and far from the beach. But the garden was pretty and there were a lot of windows to let in light.

Sienna had seen the open-house signs as she'd driven back to the office. She'd been at a women's business group luncheon, talking about what The Helping Store did for women in need. She'd ignored the first sign but had turned when she'd seen the second.

Despite the fact that it was a Tuesday afternoon and the open house was due to close in a few minutes, there were three other cars parked in front. She pulled in behind a young couple and followed them inside. Jimmy winked when he saw her. He handed all three of them flyers.

"New on the market," he said with an easy, welcoming smile. "The sellers are motivated. I've had a lot of interest and I expect this one to go quickly. Please let me know if you have any questions."

She murmured her thanks and walked from the surprisingly large living room to the kitchen in back. It was smaller and in need of updating, but it had that look of being well loved. There were stencils up by the ceiling, and the tiles were carefully scrubbed.

She checked out the two tiny bedrooms and the single bath, then went out into the backyard. It was a decent size, with a fence. No view—not this far east of the ocean.

All the windows were open and she could hear the other couples talking.

"I like it, too," a man said. "But, sweetie, could you be happy in this kitchen? You love to cook, and the right layout is important to you. We couldn't afford to remodel for a few years."

There was genuine concern in his voice. Love, she thought wistfully. He cared about her. Wanted her to be excited about their first home.

She went back inside and found her way to the small dining room. Jimmy had placed a notebook there with different pictures of the house along with information about the area, including schools and local restaurants and shopping. With three large companies moving to the area, they were getting plenty of relocations. The town was growing fast.

She sat at the table and looked through the notebook. Although she studied the pages, she didn't read the words. Instead of pictures, she saw David's face and wondered if anyone could hear love in his voice.

Their relationship confused her. On the one hand, he was sweet and supportive. On the other, she worried he was obsessed with her looks. Even more troubling, she couldn't pin down what she felt. Sometimes she was convinced she barely liked him, and other times she really wanted to be with him.

Was that love? It didn't sound like any of the definitions she'd ever heard, but maybe it was different for everyone. Maybe this was her version of love.

It wasn't like what her mom had with Neil. Just looking at them she could see they belonged together. They were happy. She would have put Rachel and Greg in that category, but they were divorced now. Even so, there had been a rightness to their marriage. Courtney had always avoided long-term commitments. Maybe that was going to change with Quinn. As for herself—she still had more questions than answers.

A few minutes later the last of the prospective buyers left, and Jimmy joined her at the table.

"Successful?" she asked.

"I'm expecting an offer in the next day or so. Maybe more than one."

"You do good work."

"Thanks." He studied her. "You okay?"

"I'm fine. A little introspective, but it will pass."

He took a bottle of water from the collection at the center of the table and opened it. "Want to talk about it?"

Discuss David with Jimmy? That would be awkward. "Have you ever been in love?"

He paused in the act of taking a drink. "You *are* introspective." He put the bottle down and considered the question. "Once, there was this girl. She was blonde and funny, and when she smiled, it was like the best thing in my world." He shrugged. "But we were young and it didn't work out."

"There has to have been someone other than me," she told him. "Not that I don't appreciate the compliment."

"I'm pretty sure you were the only one I could say I loved. There have been other women, but it wasn't the same." He took a drink. "I'm not worried. The right one will come along."

"You are a catch."

He flashed her a grin. "So they tell me. What about you? Besides me, of course. That Chicago guy and David. Anyone else?"

"No." She wasn't even sure about Hugh anymore. Had she loved him, or had she loved what he represented? And David…

"Are you coming to my mom's wedding?" she asked, not wanting to talk about love anymore.

"You know it. I got my invitation the other day. I've already RSVP'd." He frowned. "It was very pink."

"The invitation? I saw." She laughed. "You might want to brace yourself. There's going to be a lot of pink at the reception. Are you bringing a date?"

"Nope. I'm going to be cruising the single ladies, though. Maybe I can hook up with one of the bridesmaids."

"Unlikely. It's me, Courtney and Rachel. I honestly can't see you wanting to sleep with one of my sisters."

"That's true." He winked at her.

Oh! Did he mean to imply…her? The thought hit her low in the belly. But she was with David and they were engaged.

"I'm teasing," Jimmy told her. "Don't panic."

"I wasn't."

"You looked ready to run."

Maybe, but not for the reasons he thought. She reached for a bottle of water. "Want me to save you a dance?"

"Absolutely."

Courtney had been to Los Angeles before. There had been a couple of trips to Disneyland—which was technically Orange County, but close enough—along with Universal Studios. She'd spent a weekend with a girlfriend in Mischief Bay. But her only knowledge of Malibu came from what she'd seen in magazines or on TV.

The drive along Pacific Coast Highway was amazing. The ocean stretched on forever. The sky was clear, the temperature warm. There was heavy traffic, but she didn't mind that they had to go slow. That meant more time for her to gape at everything.

Quinn turned down a residential street. She was a little surprised to see walls and garage doors rather than houses. There were no high roofs and mansions, at least not that she could see.

He stopped in front of a closed wrought-iron gate and pushed a button on the underside of his rearview mirror. The gate swung open. Courtney saw a relatively short driveway with a four-car garage at the other end. There was a pathway leading to a modest-looking solid front door.

Quinn parked in the driveway and collected both of their bags. They walked to the front door, where he used a keypad to let them in. She stepped inside and realized the outside had been deliberately misleading.

The house was huge. She stood in a massive foyer. The floors were marble and the chandelier looked as if it might be Italian. She wasn't sure. There was an open living room with multiple seating areas. A giant dining room that could easily seat twenty was to the left, and stairs leading down were to the right. She had the impression of expensive artwork and the studied casual air of a room designed by someone who knew what they were doing. But what really caught her attention was the view.

The entire west wall was floor-to-ceiling windows. She could see down to the beach and the ocean beyond. There was a big deck and outside stairs leading to the sand.

Quinn led the way downstairs. She followed. The second level was more living space, but this seemed to be where he might actually spend his time. There was a restaurant-size kitchen, a comfortable living room and what looked like a den. Complicated electronics filled a glass-fronted cabinet. She noticed built-in speakers everywhere, which made sense, given what he did for a living.

Again, the view dominated everything. Light spilled into the house, and she knew if she opened a sliding glass door she would hear the sound of the ocean, along with the cries of the seagulls.

They went down one more floor. She saw a nice-size guest room and the master bedroom. The latter was big, with a fireplace and a luxury bathroom. The tub was large enough for five, as was the shower. On this level, the beach was right outside. There was a huge patio and seating. She looked from him to the window and back.

"Seriously? You're leaving all this to live in Los Lobos?"

"After a while, you stop seeing the view."

"Then you should get your eyes checked. This is incredible."

He chuckled and put both bags on the bed. "I assume you're sleeping with me," he said easily. "There's the guest room if you prefer."

She tilted her head. "Really? Why would I want that? Although it's very polite of you to offer. Your grandmother would be so proud."

He winced. "Let's not tell her."

"I'm sure she wants to hear about your sex life about as much as you want to talk about it." She turned in a slow circle. "You're really going to sell this place?"

"That's the plan. It goes on the market next week."

"You're not going to find anything like this in Los Lobos."

"I don't want anything like this. I'm ready to move on." He crossed to her and pulled her close. "About our few days here. I have a plan."

"I like it already."

He kissed her lightly. "We'll unpack, make love, then go shopping. Tonight we'll eat in and tomorrow I'll show you the sights. Thursday night is the party, then we'll drive home Friday."

She gazed at him, taking in the lines of his face. Passion flared in his eyes. He was tall and powerful, and when she was around him, she felt better about herself. As if she could do anything.

She smiled. "So we're just having sex the one time?"

He laughed. "I think we can do it a second time, if it's important to you."

She loved how he teased her. Well, two could play at that. "You're old. I don't want to strain your heart."

He kissed her again. "You're young. I don't want to shock you with my debauched ways."

"Are you debauched?"

"I might have been, once or twice." He straightened. "Courtney, you know there have been other women in my life."

Not a question, she thought, unclear on the message. "I was clear that you weren't a virgin, yes."

"At the party," he began, then hesitated.

She couldn't remember a time when Quinn hadn't known what to say. She put her hands flat on his chest.

"I get the mean girl thing. They'll want me to know why I don't belong or tell me you really don't care. It won't be about me." She thought about what it had been like when she'd been the oldest and tallest girl in her class. "I've been through a lot worse. I'll be fine."

"I never doubted that for a second."

26

WEDNESDAY NIGHT SIENNA met David at his house. She'd asked him to see her after work, although she hadn't said what she wanted to talk about. She felt as if she was going to throw up, but she knew she was doing the right thing.

She sat across from him in his living room. The suitcase was mercifully gone, but memories of that day lingered. His family had indeed created a Facebook page for their wedding. She'd received friend requests from cousins twice removed. As she looked at her fiancé, she acknowledged that while she couldn't put her finger on what exactly was wrong, he wasn't the one for her.

She swallowed hard, sucked in a breath for courage, then carefully removed her engagement ring from her finger.

"David, I'm sorry, but I can't marry you. I think you're wonderful and you deserve every happiness. I wish it could be with me, but it can't." She hesitated. "I'm afraid I'm not in love with you."

She forced herself to stop talking. While her natural instinct was to keep going, she knew she had to give him a second to process what she'd told him. He was going to be angry. She had to be prepared for that. No one wanted to be rejected this way.

Regardless, she knew she was making the right decision. Whatever she felt for David, it wasn't love. It couldn't be. Yes, she was afraid of what everyone would say, but so what? This was her life and she had to get it right.

He looked at her for a long time, then stood and crossed to her before pulling her to her feet. His expression was understanding, even kind. He didn't seem angry at all.

"Oh, Sienna, I've been expecting this for a while."

"What?"

He drew her against him and wrapped his arms around her. "You've been through a lot. I'm sorry for all the questions and worry. Poor you."

She didn't understand. This was not the traditional *I just broke up with you* reaction.

She drew back. "I'm breaking off our engagement. Did you get that?"

He cupped her face in his hands. "No, you're not."

"I am. I just did."

He smiled tenderly. "You're scared that you don't love me. You're concerned that you're making the wrong choice. You don't know what you're supposed to be feeling, but panic shouldn't be part of it."

"I, ah, maybe." How could he have figured all that out? She barely knew what was going on. How could he be more in tune with her than she was with herself?

"It's your dad," he said quietly. "You were so young when he died, and you and your family went through a difficult time. That scarred you. Not just you—all your sisters. You're each reacting differently, but you're all dealing with the ramifications. I know that's why you broke off the other engagements. You got scared and you're scared now. I believe the traditional term is *cold feet*." He smiled. "You have cold feet, nothing more."

"I do?"

"Yes." He stared into her eyes. "Sienna, you're the best thing to ever happen to me. Every day I'm so grateful I didn't settle. I waited, knowing the right person was out there, and then I met you. I knew from the start you were the one." He dropped his hands to her shoulders. "It's okay to be scared. It's okay to have questions. But as you go through this, please know I love you and I'll always be here for you."

She'd imagined the conversation going any number of ways, but she'd never pictured anything like this.

"I am frightened," she admitted. "About us getting married, about moving to St. Louis."

"I think those are just symptoms. I think what you're really frightened of is losing again. Of losing everything like you did before."

She hadn't thought about it that way, but it sounded kind of right. Of course her father's death would have affected them all.

David led her to the sofa and sat down next to her. He angled toward her and stroked her hand. "Sienna Watson, you are the woman I love. Give us a chance. Please. Just consider the possibility that your uncertainty has nothing to do with how you feel about me. That hanging on will be worth it. That when all this is behind us and we're married, you'll see that we belong together. Let me spend the rest of my life making you happy."

He was right, she thought, feeling dazed. She was letting her fears overtake her. David loved her. She should trust that. Trust him. Maybe in doing that, she would learn to trust herself.

She flung her arms around his neck and hung on. Just like he'd asked her to.

Courtney had seen dozens of parties at the hotel, but none of them compared to the one Quinn threw in Malibu. The caterer started setting up at eight in the morning. Food was delivered in trucks, as were flowers. The plates, glasses and flatware were enough to supply half the city.

Quinn had offered her the use of a stylist if she wanted. She'd accepted because, hey, when was that ever going to happen again? So she spent the afternoon at an exclusive Malibu spa. She was buffed, waxed and spray-tanned. Her hair was glossed, trimmed and curled into casual, beachy waves that took over an hour to achieve. Makeup, including false eyelashes, followed.

She'd brought her dress with her—the one she and Quinn had bought the previous afternoon. It was an off-the-shoulder fitted scrap of blue lace that cost more than her car. Fortunately, it was the exact color of her Saint Laurent heels, so she could wear them.

She put on the dress, then the shoes, packed up the shorts and T-shirt she'd worn in, then realized she wasn't sure how to get back to the house. Quinn had dropped her off at the spa, but he would be busy with party stuff now.

The spa receptionist approached. "Your car is here, Ms. Watson."

She had a car? "Thank you. Um, about the bill…"

"Oh, that's been taken care of. Along with a very generous tip for everyone who assisted you today."

Quinn, Courtney thought. She shouldn't be surprised. He'd treated her to the dress, as well. The man was just plain nice.

She stepped outside and saw a long, black limo waiting for her. Seriously? For a two-mile drive? She was still laughing when they pulled up in front of the house.

Inside she found controlled chaos. The caterer was in the final stages of prep. Courtney slipped off her shoes and walked barefoot to the bottom floor, where she saw Quinn buttoning up a solid black shirt.

The dark color contrasted with his blue eyes and blond hair. He looked sexy and dangerous, not to mention powerful. When he saw her, he smiled slowly.

"You look beautiful."

"Thank you." She crossed to him. "For everything. The dress, the spa day. This has been an amazing trip."

"I like making you happy."

"You know that doesn't require stuff, right?"

"I do, but sometimes stuff is fun. How were the treatments?"

She grinned. "Interesting. I have something to show you later."

"What does that mean?"

She pointed to her crotch. "I've always kept things trimmed, but this time I went for it. Full-on waxing." Her smile faded. "Wow, does that hurt."

"You okay?"

"I'm fine and later we'll have to take me for a test drive."

He pulled her against him. "I'd like that. But first I want to show you off."

She laughed. "That's just what I was thinking about you."

The party didn't get started until after nine. Courtney would guess that none of these people had jobs that required them to be at a desk at seven in the morning.

She spent most of her time on the deck, observing the beautiful people. Quinn kept finding her and bringing her back inside, where he introduced her to everyone. Then she would slip away again.

This wasn't her thing. Not really. While it was fun to watch celebrities and actors and singers mingle, she didn't know what to say to them. No, she hadn't seen their latest movie or TV show, nor had she listened to their latest song. Until this summer, she'd been working full-time and going to college. She didn't have time for much more than that. She wasn't interested in the industry gossip or who was sleeping with whom. Sure, it was fun to be here for the day, but any more than that would be tedious.

But for now she was going to take it all in and enjoy every second. The champagne was delicious, as was the food, and watching Quinn, well, that was always the best show possible. The man was beautiful in the most masculine sense of the word. She liked how he listened patiently, even when he wasn't interested in what the other person was saying. She was surprised no one else could read his body language, but it was sure clear to her.

She leaned against the railing and let the cool night air wash over her. Music played from hidden speakers. A tall, slender brunette walked over to her. Courtney tried to place her and honestly couldn't. Model, maybe? Actress? The dress was stunning, as was the body. Courtney had never had much on top, but this woman had fantastic breasts.

"Who are you?" the woman asked.

"Courtney."

The woman glared at her. "I don't care about your name. Who are you to Quinn? Why are you here?"

OMG! Was she really going to have a mean girl moment? Could someone video it so she could enjoy it later?

"Shouldn't you be asking Quinn that?" Courtney asked, hoping she sounded slightly bored instead of superexcited.

"I'm asking you."

"I'm his lover," she announced, then did her best not to spoil the haughtiness in her voice by giggling.

The other woman sniffed. Actually sniffed! "You're not his type."

"And you are?" Courtney sipped her champagne before giving her best dismissive smile. "I don't think so."

The brunette took a step back. "You can't speak to me like that. Do you know who I am?"

This was fantastic. It was like live theater. Okay, bad theater, but still. "I have no idea who you are. Nor do I care."

"Bitch."

Courtney held up her free hand. "Seriously? Bitch? That's the best you can do? At least put a little effort into this. Call me the C-word or something. Come on. I'm never going to attend a party like this again. You're the best thing to happen to me all night. Let's start over. Tell me how horrible I am. Oh, I know. Tell me I'm ugly and that I won't last a week with him. That's always good."

"He'll come back to me," the other woman told her. "He always does."

She turned and walked away. Courtney trailed after her. "You'll never steal him from me. You'll see. I'm going to have it all."

The other woman gave her the finger before retreating to the house. Quinn appeared at one of the other sliding doors. He raised one brow. "Want to talk about it?"

"I had a mean girl moment. It was fantastic, although she was disappointing. She didn't tell me I was ugly or that you were using me. Doesn't she watch teen movies? There's a way to do that sort of thing right."

He stared at her.

"What?" she asked. "Are you mad? Was I supposed to take it seriously?"

He laughed. "No, Courtney. You did everything exactly the way you were supposed to."

"You all right?" Greg asked quietly as the rest of the people at the table talked.

"Great." Rachel smiled brightly.

She was still playing catch-up. Her mother had called the previous day with a last-minute dinner invitation. Lena had taken Josh for the evening so he could hang out with his friend. Maggie had mentioned Sienna and David would be joining them at the hotel's restaurant. Courtney was still in LA. The one person Rachel hadn't expected to see was Greg.

"She really did run into me at the grocery store yesterday," he said in a low voice. "This wasn't an ambush."

"I believe you."

She did. It was just so strange. She and Greg were divorced. Why would her mother invite him to what was meant to be a family dinner? Sure, David was there, but he and Sienna were engaged.

"Do you want me to leave?" he asked.

"What? No! Of course not." She leaned toward him. "Greg, I'm fine with this. Despite the divorce, you're still family. Don't worry about it."

"You're sure?"

"Of course."

The problem wasn't that she felt awkward around him, she thought ruefully. It was that she didn't. They'd spent more time together this summer than they had in the past six months. They'd also gotten along better than they had in years. He was different, but maybe she was, as well. Over-hearing that conversation at the engagement party had been a real wake-up call for her.

Maggie waited until their server had poured them all wine, then she raised her glass. "Thank you for joining us tonight," she said. "I'm sorry Courtney isn't here, but we'll toast her in her absence."

Everyone raised their glasses and drank.

They were at a round table for six. Neil was on one side of

Rachel, with Greg on the other. Sienna was between Greg and David.

"Josh's baseball game was very exciting last weekend," Maggie said, putting down her wineglass. "He's quite athletic." She smiled at Rachel. "I'm sorry, my dear, but I suspect he gets that from his father."

Rachel held out both her hands, palms up. "I'm not going to argue, Mom. I was never interested in sports."

"Oh, he gets all the good stuff from me," Greg said with a wink.

"Not all," Maggie pointed out. She turned back to Rachel. "You have a lot to do at the games. I saw you with the water and the snacks. There should be more than one team mom."

Rachel felt Greg watching her. They'd discussed Heather's consistent no-show.

"There is," she said now. "I've been meaning to talk to her about blowing off her responsibilities."

"I should think so." Maggie smiled approvingly.

"Really?" Greg asked quietly.

"Glaring at her isn't much of a strategy if she isn't there," Rachel admitted. "I don't like the idea of confronting her, but yes, it's time."

Their server placed bread on the table. Rachel considered the warm rolls for a second, then shook her head. She was trying to keep her indulgences to things she really loved. While bread was nice, it wasn't as thrilling as a glass of wine or a great dessert. She was saving her calories for the chocolate mousse torte they had here.

She handed Neil the basket. As she turned, she felt a familiar twinge in her lower back. All the walking and other exercises had been helping, but lately she'd been feeling the telltale electric jabs on her right side. She would have to be more diligent about her stretches or else she would be facing a full-on back episode.

"Does Josh play any other sports?" Neil asked.

"He likes basketball," Rachel answered. "He's played soccer in the past, but he doesn't love it. I think he's a baseball guy."

"Better that than football," Sienna added. "You won't have to worry about so many injuries." She smiled at Greg. "Not that you weren't amazing when you were captain of the football team."

"I was pretty dreamy."

Everyone laughed.

"I played football for a year," David said. "Then I quit to focus on my studies."

There was a moment of awkward silence after that. Rachel told herself not to judge. Just because she couldn't see what her sister found appealing didn't mean David didn't have great qualities.

"I like that he's the kind of kid who wants to be outside," Rachel admitted, hoping to get conversation going again. "We limit his video game time and he's mostly fine with it. I would worry if he wanted to play for hours at a time."

"I agree." Neil nodded at her. "That's why Barrels offered so many other ways to play. Video games are fine in their place, but children need to be moving around. There was a lot of concern when I introduced laser tag, but it was successful from the start." His expression turned wistful. "I always wanted to have a paintball section, but that would have required too big a footprint."

Rachel did her best to figure out exactly what Neil was talking about. She knew that Neil had owned some kind of video arcade, but she'd assumed it was a single location. Barrels was a nationwide franchise with a unique business model. The name—Barrels—referred to its dual purpose. Barrels of fun for kids during the day and barrels as in wine and whis-key barrels at night.

Sienna looked equally confused. "You owned a franchise?"

"Barrels wasn't a franchise. The corporation owns every store across the country."

Maggie patted her fiancé's hand. "I thought I'd told you girls. Neil created Barrels. He opened the first one when he was in his twenties and grew it from there. He sold the whole thing last year."

Rachel looked at her sister. Sienna's mouth was hanging open.

Sienna recovered first. "Um, no, Mom, you didn't tell us that at all. You said Neil owned a video game arcade."

"Did I?" Maggie looked a little smug. "I suppose I didn't want to brag."

"Selling Barrels is a big deal," Rachel managed to say. "It had to go for millions." Or billions!

Neil's smile was modest. "I was very lucky. As I told you before, I'm going to make sure your mother is taken care of for the rest of her life."

"I guess," Sienna murmured.

Rachel had never been worried about Maggie's financial future, but it was nice to know there wasn't ever going to be a problem. Barrels. Now, that was a shock.

"You didn't know?" Greg asked.

"No. Did you?"

"Sure. When your mom started dating him, I looked him up online." He turned to Neil. "No offense."

"None taken. I'm delighted to know my fiancée has so many people looking out for her."

"You should hit him up for money," David told Sienna. "For that duplex."

Sienna flushed. "I don't ask my family to participate in any of my projects, David. You know that."

She was telling the truth, Rachel thought. When Sienna had started working for the nonprofit, she'd come up with the rule herself. That way she was free to talk about her work without anyone feeling they were being solicited. David should respect that.

"You can certainly talk to me," Neil told her. "I'd be happy to help."

"You're very kind. Someone change the subject."

"I'm pregnant," Rachel announced.

The table went silent as everyone looked at her. Well, everyone but Greg, who only looked amused.

She picked up her glass and grinned. "Just kidding." She smiled at her sister. "You owe me."

"I do and I'm grateful."

"Another baby would be nice," her mother told her. "I'd like more grandchildren."

"Me, too," Neil added.

Greg leaned close. "You started this, so it's your own fault."

"Thanks for the support." She turned back to her mother. "It was a joke. I'm not seeing anyone, so it would be challenging for me to get pregnant."

As soon as she said the words, she wondered why she hadn't mentioned she was long past that. She was in her thirties. Did she want to have more kids now?

The server appeared with their salads.

"There's the annual summer firefighter's family picnic this weekend," Greg said. "Want to go?"

The invitation surprised her. Rachel hadn't gone to the last one because of the divorce. Still, she'd always enjoyed hanging out with Greg's coworkers and the other wives.

"That would be fun. Thank you."

He smiled at her. For a second the rest of the world seemed to fade away and it was only the two of them. She found herself wanting to lean toward him, to be in his arms. Not just for sex, although that would be wonderful, but also simply to be held. She'd missed her Greg hugs. Actually, she missed nearly everything about being married to him.

For the thousandth time, she wished he could have been the way he was now back when they'd been married. She would have been the happiest woman ever.

27

SIENNA FORCED HERSELF to take small bites and chew. She was still upset about David's thoughtless suggestion that she "hit Neil up for money." What was that? Sure, it was stunning to find out her future stepfather was a multi-multi-millionaire, but so what? That didn't give her the right to demand he fund anything.

Asking for donations required tact and understanding. It was a delicate dance. Some people mistakenly believed that if you had money, you should just give. It wasn't always that simple.

Conversation had resumed around the table. She joined in, hoping no one noticed she was upset. Partway through the salad course, her phone chirped. "Oh, sorry," she said as she pulled it out of her bag. "I must have forgotten to put it on silent mode."

She glanced at the screen and saw a text from Erika.

My cousin is here. She's in bad shape and we need help. What do I do?

Sienna put her napkin on the table and rose. "I'll be right back."

"What is it?" David asked.

"Work. Excuse me."

She walked out into the hotel foyer and dialed Erika.

"Does she need medical help?" Sienna asked by way of greeting.

"She says not. She's banged up but swears she's okay. I can put her up at my place, but everything I've read said that's a bad idea. What if he comes looking for her here?"

"You're right. You don't want to get involved in this. It won't go well." Sienna was already walking toward the front desk. "Give me five minutes and I'll call you back."

She recognized the clerk behind the desk. "Hi, Cliff. I'm checking in for Anna Fields."

Cliff, the college-aged kid, looked confused for a moment. "Hey, Sienna. You have a friend coming in?"

"Kind of. Look for a permanent reservation for Anna Fields." She smiled. "It will be there."

Because Joyce's commitment to The Helping Store was to hold a small room available. Like Courtney's room, it wasn't especially large or desirable, but it was a safe haven until space could be made at one of the regular houses.

Cliff typed into his computer, then nodded. "I see it. There's no charge and I'm not supposed to ask questions. I've never seen a reservation like that before. What is it?"

She raised her brows. "Remember the part about not asking questions?"

"Oh. Sorry. Sure."

He made two keys and handed them over.

"Thank you," she said and reached for her phone. Two minutes later she hung up. Erika and her cousin were on their way to the hotel.

Once they arrived, Sienna could assess the situation. If Erika's cousin seemed okay, Sienna would have one of the volunteer social workers meet with her in the morning. If things were more dire, Sienna would call one in tonight.

She went upstairs and checked on the room. It was simply furnished with two twin beds. There was a small kitchenette with a tiny refrigerator, a two-burner stove and a microwave. The door had a double lock, to make guests feel more secure.

She used the notepad by the nightstand lamp to start a list. Food, she thought. Food and other things to get her through the next couple of days.

She returned to the lobby. David walked out of the dining room and crossed to her. "What's going on?" he asked, sounding annoyed. "You disappeared."

"Sorry. There's been an emergency at work. I was just on my way back to explain. I'm going to be busy for a couple of hours."

He looked skeptical. "What could you be doing that couldn't wait? Someone's check didn't clear?"

The dismissive tone caught her off guard, as did his words. "Excuse me?"

He rolled his eyes. "Come on, Sienna. Work? Really? You raise money. You don't actually help with the battered women. It's not like what you do can't wait. I'm heading out of town tomorrow for my business trip. This is our last night together for a while and you're ruining it."

She felt as if he'd slapped her. No, as if he'd taken everything important to her and ground it under his heel. "David, startling as it may be to accept, I *do* help with the battered women when it's appropriate. I can't go into detail right now except to say someone needs me and I'm going to help her. I need you to respect that."

"Not until you respect me. You can't just disappear from dinner and expect me to be okay with it."

"Why are you being like this? What's wrong with you? I

have a work emergency. When I can tell you more, I will, but right now I need you to trust me."

"If you're not going to stay for dinner, neither am I."

He had to be kidding. This all had to be some hideous joke—only, neither of them was laughing.

"David, please."

"Are you coming back to dinner or not?"

"I'm not."

"Then I'm leaving."

He turned and walked out of the hotel. Great. Not that she had time to deal with this. Later, she promised herself.

She hurried back to the dining room and explained there was a problem with work. Her mother, Rachel and Greg nodded in understanding, while Neil looked confused.

"I'll explain it in a minute," Maggie promised him, then looked at her. "Can we help?"

"I think I have everything under control." She collected her bag, then kissed her mother on the cheek. "Sorry I have to run."

"It's fine, dear. I'll talk to you soon."

Sienna waved and headed back to the lobby to wait for Erika. She spotted Jimmy with a young couple she would guess were clients but didn't try to catch his eye. Instead, she went out front to wait.

Less than five minutes later Erika arrived with a petite brunette at her side.

"This is Jessie," Erika said. "Jessie, my friend Sienna."

"Hi."

Jessie's voice was soft. She wore dark sunglasses and had a sling supporting her broken left arm. She looked tiny and defenseless. Sienna pushed down the anger that bubbled through her. This wasn't the time.

"Hi, Jessie. Nice to meet you. Let's get inside."

She got them all upstairs to the room, then handed over the keys and a card with several phone numbers on it.

"This room is yours for seventy-two hours," she began. "I can get you medical care, counseling, a job or a ticket home."

"I'm never going back," Jessie said flatly. She pulled off her sunglasses, revealing two black eyes. "He's hit me before, but never like this. I thought he was going to kill me." Tears filled her eyes, but she blinked them away. "I'm done with him. I want help to get away from him. Can you get me a lawyer?"

"I can."

"I'm staying with her," Erika said. "For as long as she needs me."

"Good. What did you bring with you?"

Jessie grimaced and held up her cast. "I left everything except my driver's license, some cash and my cell phone. Once I called Erika to tell her I was coming on the bus, I destroyed my phone so he couldn't track me. After paying for the bus ticket, I have thirty-two dollars."

Sienna smiled. "Don't worry. Everything is replaceable. You'll be fine."

"I can help with the money," Erika said quickly. "I'll pay for whatever she needs." She smiled at her cousin. "You can pay me back whenever. It's no big deal."

"Thanks."

Sienna knew having a support system would help Jessie. She hoped Jessie meant what she said about not going back to her abusive relationship. Time would tell.

"I need to go get you some supplies," she said. "Erika, can you stay with her until I get back?"

"Of course," Erika told her. "Like I said, I'm staying here. With Jessie. I don't want her to be alone."

"Jessie, you okay with that?"

She nodded. "Thank you. For everything."

"I'll be back in an hour," Sienna promised, then looked at Erika. "You have my cell number."

"I do."

Sienna left them and went out into the hall. She paused to write *cell phone* on her list before heading downstairs. It wasn't until she reached the lobby that she realized she didn't have a car. David had driven her to dinner. Well, damn. She was going to have to get her sister or Mom to—

"Hi, Sienna."

She looked up and saw Jimmy walking out of the bar.

"Hi, yourself. Client meeting?"

"Yup. We were celebrating the fact that their offer was accepted. What are you doing here?"

"I was having dinner with my family when something came up. Can you give me a ride home?"

"Sure." He pointed to the back of the hotel. "I'm that way."

They started walking.

"What's going on?" he asked.

"A work thing." She braced herself for David-like questions, but he only nodded.

"You need to go to the office?"

"Yes, then back here."

"I'll drive you," he told her. "Why waste time going home and getting your car? I don't mind."

"I might be a while."

"I can wait."

She was going to tell him that she was fine—she only needed a ride home. But to be honest, she would really like the company.

He held open the passenger door for her. She slid inside. Once they were on the road, he glanced at her.

"Is it hard when they leave?"

"For me or for them?"

"Both."

"Yes. They're scared and I'm scared for them. Sometimes it's difficult to see what they've been through." Like Jessie's broken arm and black eyes. Not that she would tell him that. They could talk only in generalities.

"You're a good person," he told her.

"Don't give me too much credit. I'm helping a friend of a friend. Usually a social worker would be handling this."

"Why didn't you call one?"

"I will if it becomes necessary. But for the basic stuff—like getting her settled—I'm qualified."

Jimmy parked in front of her office and went inside with her. Sienna walked to the storeroom, where they kept kits on hand for nights such as this. They were filled with the basics needed for the first few days. Most women leaving walked away with nothing.

The backpack contained everything from toiletries to socks, slippers and a couple of books. There was also a basic first-aid kit, feminine hygiene supplies and snacks.

Jimmy took the backpack from her and slung it over one shoulder. From another shelf she got a large tote bag, then filled it with underwear, a nightgown, a few T-shirts and a light brown teddy bear.

"Nice," he said. "Everybody needs someone to hug."

"Exactly."

There were packages with cell phones. She took one of those, along with a grocery bag filled with nonperishables.

"I need to get a few things from the refrigerator," she told him.

"I'll take all this to my car and meet you out front."

"Thank you."

In the break room refrigerator were a few staples. Milk, cheese, eggs and lunch meat. Bread and a few frozen dinners from the freezer went in a second bag. She added a couple of candy bars, then turned out the lights and joined Jimmy.

"Back to the hotel?" he asked.

She nodded.

He started the car and eased back onto the road. As they passed under a streetlamp, her engagement ring caught the light. The tiny flash made her think of David. Her fiancé had walked out on her. He hadn't bothered to consider how she was going to get home or what she might have to do to help someone. All he cared about was himself.

He'd told her that her doubts were just cold feet. That she was reacting to something in her past rather than to him. Now, as Jimmy drove her back to the hotel, she knew he was wrong. Her heart had been telling her something all along and she simply hadn't been strong enough to listen.

Quinn and Courtney had decided to take Pacific Coast Highway home to Los Lobos. The drive would be longer, but more scenic. Adding to that, he was in no hurry for their few days together to end.

She sat next to him in the Bentley, her bare feet up on the dash. Her hair was pulled back in a simple ponytail and she wore sunglasses. They'd stopped for lunch at In-N-Out Burger before heading north.

They'd had a good time together. He liked how she'd been able to hold her own at the party. She'd admitted to feeling totally out of her element, but she had stood her ground when necessary. Her reaction to the "mean girl" moment still made him chuckle.

He'd spent a lot of his life with something to prove. Maybe that need had come from the fact that his father hadn't bothered to stay much past conception or that his mother had also abandoned him. Maybe it was in his DNA. For whatever reasons, he'd given his all to his work and used the parade of beautiful women that followed to satisfy himself.

He'd been careful to not get involved until a few years ago when he'd started to realize he wanted something more. For a while he'd considered taking things to the next level with Shannon, but when she'd found love with another man, he'd moved on. Until he'd met Courtney.

She was everything he could have wanted and a thousand times more. Which kind of led him to the next obvious question. Where was he going with this?

A few years ago any talk like that would have him carefully showing the lady in question to the door. But now… now he had other plans.

Courtney stretched her arms out in front of her and pointed to the Los Lobos sign. "We're almost there. I had a great time, but I have to say, a little of that city goes a long way."

"For me, too."

"It didn't used to."

"People change."

She looked at him. "You sure did. Are you sure you're ready to give up that house and the—" she made air quotes "—'beautiful people'?"

"I am. The house was nice, but I can build another one just like it, here." Not that he wanted to. He was thinking more of a family home. With a big backyard and plenty of bedrooms.

"They sure want you back," she said.

"Who?"

"Those women."

He dismissed them with a shrug. "They want what I represent. For most of them, I could be anyone. It's the same with the men trying to get into the industry. I'm a means to an end. They want power and prestige and think I can make that happen."

"That doesn't bother you? Them using you?"

"I don't care about them. I care about my people and the music. The rest of it is simply part of the landscape."

She pulled her knees to her chest and wrapped her arms around her legs. "I can see that. I know I tease you about living in Los Lobos, but you really fit in. Wayne complains about the small-town stuff, but I can't see him in Los Angeles." She laughed. "He would never have survived at that party."

"It's not his thing."

"Mine, either. All the mean girl stuff was kind of fun, though. Weird, but interesting." She lowered her feet to the carpet. "Thanks for taking me. I've never been a flavor of the month before. It's been a wonderful experience."

He turned off PCH and drove toward town. "What are you talking about? You're not a flavor of the month."

She waved her hand. "Whatever you want to call it. I get it, Quinn. I don't want you worrying. Being together has been fun and I'm not looking to end things, but I know you're not..." She paused and pressed her lips together. "Okay, this got awkward fast. What I'm trying to say is that you're..."

They were nearly at the hotel. He pulled off the road and put the Bentley in Park, then turned toward her.

"Is that what you think?" he asked. "That I'm using you because you're handy and then I'm done?"

She pulled off her sunglasses. "No. That makes you sound awful. I'm sorry. I wasn't trying to make trouble or send us somewhere we didn't want to go. You've been so great to me and we have a wonderful time together." She flushed slightly but didn't turn away. "I like you and you like me. I appreciate that. As for the rest of it—" She swore under her breath. "Can we talk about something else?"

She liked him? That was it? He couldn't tell if she was trying to be cool or if she genuinely didn't care. Not knowing what a woman was thinking was unusual for him. And disconcerting.

"We should talk about this," he said.

Courtney wanted to stick her fingers in her ears and hum loudly. "I don't think that's necessary," she said. "Really." She pointed at the hotel. "Oh, look. We're almost there. Why don't we unpack and talk later?" Like never.

She didn't know why she was so uncomfortable. Her skin felt hot and tight. Her stomach was very unhappy and she was oddly breathless. Quinn was great. Being around him made her happy. She didn't want anything to change, and she had a horrible feeling that if he kept talking, everything would.

"Courtney," he began.

"Don't. Please. Let's just do what we've been doing. Talking and hanging out and the henna thing. That was great."

"That *was* great. But that's not all I want." He removed his sunglasses and looked into her eyes. "Courtney, I'm in love with you."

The words hit her with the power of a freight train. She felt physically battered and trapped. Definitely trapped. But she was in a car and there was nowhere to go.

"No," she said firmly. "No, you're not. You can't be. This isn't love. Love hurts and you don't hurt me. We're good together. Don't do this, please."

She tried to scramble away, but she couldn't move. Couldn't breathe.

The seat belt, she thought frantically. She unfastened it, then fumbled for the door.

"Wait," Quinn said. "Courtney, we have to talk."

"No, we don't. Stop talking. You'll ruin everything."

She got the door open and nearly fell out of the car. Once she'd scrambled to her feet, she turned toward the hotel and started to run. Quinn called her name again and again, but she ignored him. She kept moving, brushing away stupid tears and wondering why he had to go and spoil everything.

It took her only about five minutes to get onto the hotel property. Courtney made her way to her room, going up the back stairs to avoid running into anyone. Once she reached the fourth floor, she realized she'd left her key in Quinn's car and had no way to get into her room. Not without going back to the reception desk. She kept walking anyway and almost wasn't surprised when she saw him standing at the end of the hall.

Her bag and luggage were at his feet, but what really captured her attention was the combination of pain and anger she saw in his eyes.

As she approached, he held out her room key. She used it to let them inside. He set her luggage by the bed, then faced her. She closed the door.

"Seriously?" he asked. "You ran?"

"I'm sorry." She felt herself blushing. "I panicked."

"Ready to have an adult conversation now?"

She didn't want to. She wanted to push him into the hall and lock him out. No, what she really wanted to do was turn back time about fifteen minutes so this never happened.

"I take it you're not in love with me," he said flatly.

"I don't want to love anyone," she admitted. "And you really don't want to love me. I'm not that special."

"You're telling me how I feel?"

"No." She ducked her head. The sick feeling only grew. "Quinn, please. We're so good together the way we were. It was fun and easy. There was no pressure. I like you a lot. More than I've ever liked anyone. But the rest of it. The in-love part. I don't want to do that. I don't want to care."

She looked up and saw him staring at her.

"No, you don't want to take the chance." He shook his head. "Why didn't I see that? This isn't about me, it's about you. The risk is too great. What was it you said? Love hurts?"

"It does. I've seen it."

"If that's the lesson you've learned, it's the wrong one. I'm sorry, Courtney. I thought you were ready to be brave." One corner of his mouth twisted up. "For what it's worth, there are a lot of women who would love to know this is happening. They'd say I deserved it. They're probably right."

He turned for the door. She caught his arm. "Don't go. Can't we go back to what we had before?"

He glanced at her. "I don't want that anymore. I want something more. I want it all. With you. Or I did."

And then he was gone. He closed the door so quietly—as if he wasn't angry. As if he had gone beyond that. Courtney sank onto the floor and pulled her knees to her chest. She told herself to keep breathing in and out. That was all she had to do for now. Keep breathing. The rest of it would take care of itself.

28

THE BIGGEST PARK in Los Lobos was at the north end of town, high on a cliff, overlooking the ocean. On a clear summer's day, like today, there was no more beautiful view than this one, Rachel thought as she parked her SUV in the gravel parking lot. There might not be big shopping malls or fancy restaurants in town, but she didn't care. This was worth giving up almost everything.

While Josh unfastened his seat belt and bolted out to find his friends, she took a second to breathe in the salt air. The afternoon would be fun. She hadn't been to one of the firefighter family picnics in a couple of years. Not since before the divorce. She was looking forward to catching up with people she'd known from before. Sure, there would be questions, but she could live with that.

She pushed the button to open the rear hatch, then leaned in to grab the first of several tote bags. Her back instantly protested, especially on the right side. She breathed through the pain and admitted that maybe it was time to see her chiropractor.

"Rachel."

She saw Greg jogging toward her. He was casually dressed in jeans and a T-shirt. Both were worn and soft-looking. His

arms were muscled, his chest broad. She found herself fighting a slightly fluttery feeling in her stomach. One that made
her think how very long it had been since she'd made love
to this man.

"Hi. I brought potato salad," she told him. "And that
cucumber-pineapple salad you like."

"Thanks." He gave her a quick kiss on the mouth, then
reached for the bags. "Let me carry these. Is your back bothering you?"

She heard the words and in a second or two, when the kiss-
induced fog cleared from her brain, she would respond.

"Ah, kind of," she admitted. "It's telling me it's not happy."

"You be careful. You know what it's like when your back
goes out."

She did. It froze up and then spasmed. She was a mess for
at least three days, existing on muscle relaxers.

"I'm calling the chiropractor first thing in the morning."

"Good." He closed the hatch. "Come on. Everyone's excited that you're here."

"You told them?"

"Sure. They all like you." They walked toward the picnic
tables under the trees. "There are a few new wives and girlfriends. The guys would appreciate it if you'd talk to them.
You know, be the calm voice of reason. You're always good
at that."

"You mean be the old lady who's seen it all?" she asked,
her voice teasing.

He put his arm around her. "Never that. You're hot and
you know it."

She was? She did?

Before she could continue that intriguing line of question-
ing, they'd reached the group.

There were about twenty families along with a dozen or

so couples. Kids ran around everywhere, darting around trees and racing across the picnic area. They'd set up portable barbecues on the north end, by the fire pit. When the cooking started, several of the firefighters would stand guard, making sure no kids wandered too close.

The families with infants were clustered together. Babies lay on blankets in the shade, while toddlers explored on unsteady legs. The teenagers were huddled together as far away from the babies as they could get—no doubt discussing how hideous this all was. Josh ran with a couple other boys his age. He would be tired when they got home, she thought happily.

She'd missed this. Missed her friends. While she'd stayed in touch with several of the wives, it had been different. She was on the outside. For at least this afternoon, she was back in the circle.

"Rachel!"

A couple of the wives spotted her and hurried over. Cate and Dawn hugged her.

"You're here," Cate said. "Mike said you were coming, but I didn't believe him. You look great. How are things? How's Josh?" She lowered her voice. "Are you and Greg getting back together? It would be so cool if you did."

Dawn nodded. "It would. We miss you."

Rachel looked at her ex, who was taking her salads over to the food tables. How to answer that question? Four months ago she would have said that of course they weren't getting back together, but now she was less sure. They were hanging out more and she liked being with him. The problems they'd had before had been worked out, but she wasn't sure that meant anything more than they'd figured out how to be happily divorced. And sadly, she didn't seem to be able to directly ask what was going on or tell him what she wanted.

"We're doing right by Josh," she told her friends. "That's the most important thing."

"Too bad," Dawn said with a sigh. "Come on. Sit with us. We hardly see you anymore."

Rachel allowed herself to be led away. She was soon in the company of several of the wives, catching up with what was new with everyone. Some things hadn't changed, she thought a couple of hours later. The group always separated by sex, with the guys hanging out and the women clustered some distance away. But all that would shift when it was time to eat. Then the families would come back together. Fathers would feed babies and help out with diaper changes. Memories would be made.

Cate brought over a young woman with short dark hair. She was pretty and smiled shyly as she was introduced.

"This is Margo," Cate said. "She's dating Jeremy."

One of the new guys, Rachel remembered. Just out of his probationary period.

"Hi, Margo."

"It's nice to meet you, Mrs. Halcomb."

Rachel laughed. "Please don't call me that. I sound like my mother-in-law. Not that she's not a lovely person, but you know how it is." One of the toddlers ran by. Rachel caught her and pulled her onto her lap. Someone passed her a set of baby keys and she held them out to the little girl.

Margo sat across from her. "Jeremy said I should talk to you. About, you know, his work."

"Because you're scared?"

A blunt question, but it got to the heart of the matter. Margo picked at the grass. "I am a little," she admitted, her voice small. "I love him and we've been talking about getting married." She raised her head. Her eyes were wide. "I don't know if I can do it. Live with the worry. I'd be scared all the time. I don't want to lose him."

"Does he love his job?"

"Yes. It's what he's wanted for as long as I've known him. He's good at it, too." Her lower lip trembled. "Maybe I'm not strong enough."

Dawn came by to claim her daughter. Rachel passed her over, then returned her attention to Margo.

"We're all scared," she said calmly. "But life is scary. My father died driving home from work. It wasn't raining, it wasn't anything. He spun out, hit a tree and died. I was nine and it changed my life forever."

Margo's big eyes got bigger. "I'm sorry. I didn't know."

"How could you? My point is, people die when we least expect it. What I can tell you about the Los Lobos Fire Department is that it's one of the finest in the state. The guys train every day. They're prepared. They watch out for each other. It takes a special person to be willing to run into a burning building when everyone else is running out."

She smiled. "Yes, you get scared, but you also get to be a part of a wonderful community. You get to know that Jeremy is doing what he loves and saving people at the same time. Only you can decide if it's worth it."

"Is it to you?"

Rachel guessed no one had mentioned that she and Greg were divorced. Not that their breaking up had anything to do with his job. She'd had a few rough moments when they were first married, but she'd loved him and had known this was what he wanted to do. Not being with him hadn't been an option. So she'd made peace with his job.

"It is. I'm proud of him and so is his son."

Margo nodded. "Thank you. I have to think about this, but I'm pretty sure I understand what you're saying."

She left and Greg took her place.

"How'd it go?" he asked.

"I'm not sure. She's scared. She's going to have to figure out how to deal with that."

"You did."

"Not everyone can."

He took her hand in his. "So the captain is going to talk to you today."

"Your captain?"

She was proud of herself for sounding so normal while Greg was touching her hand.

He nodded. "He thinks it's time I started moving up the food chain. I'd have to study for the tests and then pass them."

"You should do it. You'd be great. You're so good with the younger guys and you've always been a natural leader. Now that I think about it, I'm surprised you haven't done it before."

"A few things got in the way." He studied her. "Rachel, have you forgiven me?"

The question was unexpected. "Of course," she blurted. "You were wrong to have that one-night stand, but I was wrong, too. I made so many mistakes. I was unhappy, but instead of talking about the real problems, I complained about other things. I wasn't willing to confront you or deal with us. I whined about everything except what was really going on."

"Thank you. That means a lot to me."

"Hey, Greg, let's get these burgers on."

He released her hand. "Duty calls. Save me a seat for lunch."

"Of course."

She watched him jog over to the guys at the barbecues. Her heart raced and she felt a little dizzy—just like she had in high school. She didn't want it to be true, but there was no denying reality—nearly twenty years after their first ever date, she was just as in love with Greg as she had ever been.

★ ★ ★

Courtney had spent the past five days feeling as if she had the flu. She hurt all over, she felt sick to her stomach and there was a sense of dread that followed her everywhere. Worse, she'd been forced to act like a character in a very bad farce—leaping behind doors and ducking down corridors, all in an attempt to avoid Quinn.

While she hadn't technically seen him since they'd gotten back from LA on Friday, she'd known that she could at any second. He was still living at the hotel. At some point they were going to have to deal with each other, but she wanted to put that off as long as possible—mostly because she had no idea what she was going to say.

She was more than confused—she was lost. She knew she missed him. A thousand times a day she thought of something she wanted to share with him. She wanted to see him and be held by him. At the same time, she was furious that he'd changed the rules. They were supposed to have fun together—nothing more. They were supposed to be lovers, then move on. Falling in love wasn't part of the deal.

She didn't want to love anyone. It didn't go well. Look at her mother, her sisters. Love was a disaster. Love hurt. She didn't want to be hurt. It was better to be alone. She'd decided that a long time ago, and the decision had served her well. She'd been happy. Until Quinn.

She missed him. Missed how he looked at her, how he moved. She missed his stupid Taylor Swift T-shirt and how he'd made her learn how to walk in high heels. She missed his take on the world, how he loved Pearl and Sarge and his grandmother. She missed his posse, his smile, his laugh and his unshakable confidence.

How could someone that amazing love her? To quote a movie from another generation, she wasn't worthy. But thinking she wasn't good enough pissed her off, too. She might not be as amazing as him, but she still had good qualities. She was smart and funny and ambitious. Okay, sure, there was some fear and she might have commitment issues, but no one was perfect.

She was, she had to admit, an uncomfortable combination of sad, mad and afraid. Hence the flu symptoms.

She finished her last room and returned her housekeeping cart to the linen closet on the main floor. She was doing only about a third of her normal cleaning schedule because there was a wedding this weekend, not to mention two conventions over the next week. After that was her mother's wedding, then three blissful days of almost nothing, then a wedding every weekend until the end of September.

Thinking about work made her feel marginally better. Her almost cheerful mood lasted until Kelly waved her over and said, "Joyce is looking for you. She wants you in her office right away."

Uh-oh. Her boss had found out about Quinn.

"Thanks," Courtney said, feeling her stomach drop to her toes. This was going to be bad.

She squared her shoulders and walked directly to Joyce's office behind the reception area. The door was open. She knocked once, then entered.

"Kelly said you were looking for me."

Joyce looked up from her computer and nodded. "I was. Please close the door."

Oh, God, oh, God, oh, God. Courtney did as she was told, pausing only to pat both Pearl and Sarge. The dogs were on a small, furry chaise that Joyce had bought for them. Sarge had a sock.

Courtney took the seat across from her boss and told herself that, whatever happened, she would be fine. She'd been taking care of herself for nearly a decade. She had skills, a modest savings account and the will to survive.

Joyce slipped off her reading glasses and folded her hands together on the desk. "It is completely ridiculous that you continue to act like this," she began. "You are not a maid, Courtney. You haven't been for a long time. You're managing multiple events and acting as an assistant manager. That's more valuable to me than you cleaning rooms. I want to hire three more maids and put you on as the event coordinator full-time."

Joyce's expression was stern. "I don't know what you have in your head that you have to keep cleaning rooms, but it has to stop right now. I have a business to run. I'm your boss. I'm not putting up with this anymore."

That was it? They weren't going to talk about Quinn?

"I don't know what to say," she admitted.

"I'm sorry to have to be stern, but there we are," Joyce continued. "I've been waiting for you to come to your senses, but you won't. I thought after you got your AA, you would realize that there was more for you to do here. But you're still hiding. You're still afraid. You'll do the work, but you won't take the title. Why is that?"

Even though they'd been talking about completely different things, Joyce's words reminded her of that horrible conversation with Quinn. He'd talked about fear, too. Hers. She'd always seen herself as tough—was she wrong in that?

"I appreciate your faith in me," she said slowly. "Thank you for being blunt. You're right. I should be committed to one job or the other. I love planning weddings and the other events. Thank you for the opportunity to do it. Thank you for having faith in me."

Joyce's stern expression didn't change. "Was that a yes?"

Courtney blinked. "What? Of course it's a yes. Yes, I want

to be the events planner. Full-time. I'll miss cleaning toilets, but I'll get over it."

Joyce smiled. "I'm glad to hear that because I've already hired the new maids."

"What if I'd said no?"

"I'm afraid I would have had to fire you."

Courtney was glad she was sitting down. "For real?"

"I love you, child, but every bird needs to leave the nest. You weren't flying before. Now you are. I'm proud of you, Courtney. You've accomplished a lot. Everyone's afraid at one time or another. The trick is not letting the fear control you."

Rachel put in the last bobby pin and reached for the hair spray. The updo flattered her mother's features. Maggie had decided on a short veil anchored by a comb.

"When the ceremony is over," Rachel said as she put down the can of hair spray, "I'll be able to pull the pins. The curls will stay in and you'll have a more casual look for the reception."

"I love it. Thank you, darling."

They were in Maggie's large bathroom for a practice hairstyle session. Her mother stood and walked over to her closet, then looked back over her shoulder. "Not a word to your sisters. I want them surprised."

"I promise."

Rachel was used to dealing with brides and their idiosyncrasies. She was usually one of the first nonfamily members to see the dress. Often she did a practice run on hair and makeup, and at the end the bride put on the dress to check the look. With her mother, she'd only created the hairstyle. She'd done Maggie's makeup countless times before.

"I'm afraid I'm going to need you to zip me up," her mother called.

Rachel stepped into the closet and pulled up the zipper, then quickly retreated to the bathroom so she could get the full effect.

Her mother stepped into the room.

"Oh, Mom. You're beautiful."

The dress was perfect. The lining was pale pink and strapless, but the sheer ivory lace overlay came up to her collarbones. The same overlay created long sleeves and fell to the tea-length hem. The bodice was fitted with the skirt flaring out. It swayed and moved with every step.

Her pumps were hand painted with a pink floral pattern and the date of the wedding in the design.

"My bouquet is white with hints of green, so it will show up against my dress. You girls are carrying pink flowers."

Rachel sighed. "You're stunning. It couldn't be more right for you."

Maggie's eyes filled with tears. "Thank you so much. Now help me unzip this. I don't want anything to happen to it before the wedding."

Once Maggie was back in her shorts and T-shirt, she and Rachel went out to the kitchen. They sat across from each other at the glass table. Her mother had promised lunch in exchange for the practice session.

"You've been very good to me," her mother said. "I've always been able to lean on you." Maggie poured them each a glass of iced tea from a pitcher on the table. "Maybe a little too much."

"Mom, I do hair for a living. I want to help."

Her mother looked at her. "I'm talking about when you were little and your father died. Finding out about what Courtney kept from me has gotten me to thinking. I was so desperate back then. So frightened. Phil died and then I lost the house. If Joyce hadn't taken us in, we would have been in a shelter. I had nothing and I didn't think I could hold it together. I depended on you to help me. But you were just a little girl."

"I was scared, too," Rachel admitted. "Helping you gave me something to focus on."

"I was drowning and you saved me."

"That's a little dramatic."

"Maybe, but it's true." Her mother leaned toward her. "Tell me I didn't ruin you forever. Tell me I'm not the reason you and Greg split up."

"Are you stressed about the wedding? You're acting kind of strange."

"I'm serious. Did I destroy your marriage?"

Rachel thought about all that had gone wrong. Her inability to ask for what she wanted or accept help of any kind. Greg not being mature enough to handle the responsibility. They had been in love, but love hadn't been enough.

"We were young and made a lot of mistakes," she said. "That's why we split up."

Had her mother's actions formed parts of her character that had contributed to the failure of her marriage? Maybe, but saying that wouldn't help anyone. She and Greg were responsible for what had happened—no one else.

"And now?" her mother asked.

"We're friends. We like each other again." Maybe there was more, but she wasn't sure. "I've forgiven him. That feels good. We have Josh."

"Do you want more?"

"Sometimes," she admitted. "But that scares me. I'm not sure I could handle losing him a second time."

"Why would you have to? You've learned a lot and so has he. Maybe this time it will last forever."

That was nice to think about. Being with Greg again. Giving their marriage a second chance. And while she thought they were headed in that direction, she wasn't sure. Because neither of them had actually said the words—or made the offer. She knew why she hadn't, but what about him? Which brought her to her biggest fear. That she was the only one considering trying to make it work again.

29

SIENNA POURED ANOTHER glass of wine and passed it to Courtney. Her sister cradled it in her hand. They were outside in Sienna's backyard. The night was clear and still warm. Music drifted to them from a neighbor's house.

"I just don't know," Courtney was saying. "About Quinn. He said he loved me. I can't wrap my head around that. What does it mean?"

"Not to state the obvious, but I'm guessing it means he loves you."

"What am I supposed to do with that?"

"Do you love him back?"

"I don't know. Maybe. No. I'm not sure."

Sienna held in a smile. It was nice to know she wasn't the only mentally twisted Watson sister. "Let's try an easier question. What don't you like about him?"

Courtney sipped her wine. "Nothing."

"There has to be something."

"He can be bossy, but it's always in a nice way, and I can't think of anything else. He's successful, he's kind, he loves his grandmother and her dogs, he cares about people, even though he pretends he doesn't. He's talented. I'm sure the other women in his life would be furious to know he's finally ready to settle down and I'm having a freak-out. My life could be in danger."

Sienna laughed. "Just don't tell them."

"Believe me, I won't. I'm so confused." She put her arm on the table and her head on her arm. "Tell me what to do."

"I'm the wrong person to be giving advice. I'm equally confused, but for different reasons."

Courtney straightened and looked at her. "You don't love David, do you?"

Sienna hadn't expected that. "Of course I do. Why would you say that? He's—" She closed her eyes and drew in a breath. The truth was there—it had been there for a long time. Probably from the beginning. "I don't love David."

She gulped some wine, then continued. "I tried to tell him before. I tried breaking up with him. He said it was because I was scared. That Dad's death had scarred me, but that I was the one for him. He said he'd waited for me." She drank more wine and waited for her gut to tell her what to do. "Oh, God. I have to break off the engagement."

Courtney patted her arm. "You're so brave. I admire that."

Sienna stared at her. "I can't break up with him."

"What? Why not?"

"He's out of town until Mom's wedding. Literally. He's on a business trip, then he's going to go see his family for a couple of days. He'll fly in late Friday night. I can't break up with him over the phone. That would be horrible and tacky. Plus, I have to give him back the ring."

She glanced at her hand, then pulled it from her finger and tossed the ugly ring on the table. "I want to break up with him and I have to wait over a week. I have to talk to him on the phone and I don't think I can do this."

"Breathe," Courtney instructed. "Just breathe. It says a lot that you want to face him in person. That's very mature. As for the phone, he'll be busy. You can be busy, too. Text rather than talk. That will make things easier."

"You're right. I can do this. It's fine. I'm fine." She swallowed more wine. "I'm also going to be drunk, but I'm not driving. How are you going to get home?"

"I may have to crash on your sofa."

"Of course you can. Let's do that. I'll order a pizza, we'll open another bottle of wine and deal with the disaster our love lives have become."

"That sounds like a perfect plan."

Sienna looked at her sister. "You're not happy."

"I miss Quinn."

Sienna waited.

Courtney grimaced. "I know, I know. I'm an idiot. A wonderful man loves me, and I send him away because I'm scared. It's what I did with my job. Hiding behind what was safe. Am I hiding again or being sensible?"

"You're hiding."

Courtney rolled her eyes. "You don't want to think about that before you answer?"

"Sorry, no. Look, it's always easier to see what's wrong with other people than with ourselves. You knew I didn't love David. I know you care about Quinn a lot more than you're willing to admit. So what are you going to do about it? Be brave or be stupid?"

"Ouch. Are those my only choices?"

"I'm afraid so."

Sienna had to admit she was feeling pretty damned smug. She didn't have to deal with her crisis for over a week. So it was easy to tell other people what to do.

"Do I have to decide tonight?"

"It would probably be best if you didn't."

"Then I won't."

"That's my girl."

The new recording studios were currently empty, but soon they would be filled with equipment. Soundproofing had been added to make sure that no outside noise got in, and no inside noise got out. Upstairs were offices, workrooms and a large kitchen/living room area. Writing and recording took time and energy. Sessions could go well into the night. People needed access to food and a chance to unwind.

For a couple of days, Quinn had toyed with the idea of putting in a couple of bedrooms, where artists could crash between sessions, but he'd decided against it. The sofas in the living room were enough. Access to a bedroom was only going to cause trouble with the nonmusical partners.

"It's totally rad," Peter said, his voice filled with awe. "I can't wait to record here."

"Me, too," Collins added.

"The equipment gets delivered next week," Wayne told them. "State-of-the-art. Quinn picked it all himself."

"So if you don't like it, you know who to blame." Quinn pointed to the stairs. "Be careful when you go up. It's not finished yet."

He didn't want his most successful band getting injured by falling through a wall or down stairs.

"We should be up and running by the middle of September," Wayne told him when the guys had disappeared upstairs. "Just let me know when you're ready for me to start looking for a house for you. I've heard good things about a local real estate agent. I'm going to get in touch with him." Wayne looked momentarily uncomfortable. "Should I, ah, talk to Courtney about the house?"

Quinn knew there would come a day when hearing her name wouldn't be a big deal. When he wouldn't feel the fist to the gut or a drowning sense of loss. Eventually, he would be able to be pragmatic. No big deal. They'd had a good time and then it had ended.

"What?" Wayne demanded. "What happened?"

"We're not together anymore."

His retired marine assistant actually flinched. "You didn't say anything."

"I didn't want to talk about it."

"And now?"

"Still don't."

"What happened?"

Quinn told himself not to take anything out on Wayne. Nothing was his fault. "I told her I loved her and she ran. Literally. It was impressive."

"She's scared."

That was what he thought, too. Given her past—all she'd been through—she wouldn't trust easily. Wouldn't want to take the risk. She'd been so angry at his declaration. He knew that fear lived behind the anger, but that didn't make being without her any easier.

"She'll come around," Wayne told him.

"Not so far."

"When did this happen?"

"On the way home from LA. I told her in the car." He grimaced. "Not my most romantic moment."

"She'll come around," Wayne repeated. "You two are good together. You're happy with her and she's happy with you. Don't give up."

He'd never been a big believer in hope. It generally let him down. He was more of a doer. But in this case, he wasn't sure what he should be doing. His heart said for him to go to her. His head said to give her time.

"There is irony in the fact that I finally fell in love, and the woman in question wants nothing to do with me. Maybe it's karma."

"You don't believe in karma."

"No, but it makes for a good story."

"Are we still staying in Los Lobos?"

An interesting question Quinn had asked himself. For a couple of days, he'd wrestled with going back to LA. But what would that prove? "We're staying."

"Even though you'll have to deal with her?"

"Especially because I'll have to deal with her. Better for both of us to face what happened."

"Good. The only way to get over something like that is to go through it. You're not running. That's the first step."

"Thanks."

Quinn figured if anyone knew about getting over an incredible loss, it was Wayne. He would take the other man's advice and get through it. Eventually. Because, to be honest, he couldn't imagine ever not loving Courtney. She'd fundamentally changed him and he had a bad feeling there was no going back.

Rachel told herself that this particular Monday wasn't any hotter than the other summer Mondays. That the only reason she felt uncomfortable was her back was killing her. She had an appointment with the chiropractor in the morning—something she'd foolishly been putting off. Now she was paying the price.

Of course, Heather wasn't there—as per usual. Rachel started to drag out the equipment she was responsible for, along with the water and the snacks, then stopped herself. Ask for help, she thought. It was time to start doing that.

She hobbled over to the coach. "Could you and the boys help me with the things in my car? My back's acting up."

"Sure, Rachel." He looked around. "Where's Heather?"

"I have no idea."

He blew a whistle and waved in the team. In less than a minute, her SUV was empty and the supplies were in place.

Thank goodness. Every step was a nightmare. The instant she got home, she was taking a muscle relaxer. She didn't like how they made her feel, but she didn't have much choice.

She took her seat on the uncomfortable benches and groaned. This was going to be a long, long game.

About five minutes before they were due to start, Rachel saw Heather walking toward her. Rage propelled her to her feet. All right—she'd learned how to ask for help. Now she was going to give the other woman a piece of her mind. How dare she leave Rachel with everything for the entire season?

"Hi." Heather, a brown-haired woman of average build, waved at Rachel. "You're probably surprised to see me."

"I am."

"I'm sorry about not being around this summer. I should have called." Tears filled Heather's eyes. "I just…"

Rachel felt her anger fade. She pulled the other woman to the bench and they both sat down. "What's wrong?"

"My mom had a stroke. It was pretty bad. That was hard enough, but then my dad took off. Just like that. They've been married nearly forty years and he left her. He said he didn't want to be married to a cripple."

Tears spilled down Heather's cheeks. "She's paralyzed on one side. She can't talk. I don't know how much she understands, but I feel like she keeps waiting for him to show up at the rehab facility. But I haven't heard from him in a month. Paul's been great, but he has to work and the kids are scared. I cry all the time."

"It's okay," Rachel told her, thinking this would have been good information to have weeks ago. Which she would have had if she'd bothered to ask. Instead, she'd fumed and assumed. Talk about dumb.

"I'm sorry I didn't get in touch with you sooner," Heather continued. "I should have."

"No. It's okay. You have plenty on your plate. I've been dealing. I'll ask one of the other moms to help on a permanent basis." She paused. "I won't say why unless you want me to."

"You can say my mom had a stroke," Heather told her as she wiped her face. "But maybe if you wouldn't say anything about my dad?"

"Whatever you want." Rachel hugged her. "Let me know how I can help. Oh, I know. Why don't I stop by the rehab facility? I can wash and cut your mother's hair. Maybe it would make her feel a little better about herself."

Heather began to cry again. "Thank you. That means a lot."

They sat together for the first three innings, then Heather excused herself to go check on her mother. Rachel promised to stop by the first part of next week. By then the wedding would be over and her back should be better.

Josh's team won by two. There was plenty of cheering about that. Lena asked if Josh could go to the movies with her and her son. Rachel accepted gratefully. A quiet evening was exactly what she needed.

She made her way to the restroom, then walked back to the field and found that everyone was gone. There was still equipment on the field and water bottles on the table. A cookie wrapper tumbled past in the light breeze. As she bent to pick it up, she felt the telltale jolt of fire in her hip and knew it was going to be bad.

Sure enough, as she straightened, her entire back locked. She couldn't move, couldn't breathe, as muscles tightened like a vise. Even taking a single step was excruciating. She cried out and reached for something to hang on to, but there was nothing. The benches were too far away. The pain was a wild animal. It claimed her with sharp teeth and claws, leaving her whimpering.

She thought longingly of Greg. Even when things had been

at their worst in their marriage, he'd always been there when her back went out. He'd taken care of her, once even carrying her to bed when she couldn't walk. Too bad she'd lost that in the divorce.

She pulled her phone from her pocket and dialed Courtney. The call went right to voice mail. It was the same for Sienna. With her mom, there were a half dozen rings before the voice mail picked up. A quick glance at the time told her that Lena and the boys would already be in the movie theater and that Lena would have turned off her phone.

She didn't know what to do. Finally, she dialed the fire station and asked for Greg.

"Hey, what's up?"

"I'm sorry to bother you at work," she began. She could barely speak. She was terrified she was going to start spasming any second. "I tried everyone else first. It's just..." She felt herself sinking into despair.

"Rachel, what is it? Are you hurt?"

"Josh had a game. Everyone's gone. I have things to take home and my back went out. I can't move. I'm sorry. I need help."

"Hang tight. I'll be there in five minutes."

Rachel put her phone into her pocket and started for the bleachers. She'd made it about halfway there when she saw an unfamiliar truck pull up next to her SUV. Greg jumped out, spoke to the driver for a second, then sprinted toward her.

Relief nearly made her collapse. She wanted to burst into tears and throw herself at him. Instead, she did her best to hold it together.

"Thanks for coming," she said.

"Happy to help." He studied her. "What's the best way to get you to the car?"

"Let me lean on you."

He got close and let her find the most comfortable position. She also set the pace. Once she was in the passenger seat of her SUV, he jogged back to the field and collected everything before returning to climb into the driver's seat.

"Do you have your pills?" he asked.

"Yes. And an appointment with the chiropractor. I've been putting it off. I should know better."

She thought he might tease that, yes, she should, but instead he was all business. He drove to her place and got her inside. When she was stretched out on the bed, he got her the pills and a glass of water.

"Thanks."

He hovered without sitting on the mattress. She swallowed the medication before handing him the glass.

"I have to get back to the station," he told her. "I've called Courtney. She'll be here in a little bit to check on you."

Rachel looked at the man she'd once been married to. He was saying and doing all the right things, but she had the feeling that something was wrong.

"Are you okay?" she asked.

"I'm fine."

"You seem… I don't know. Something."

He looked at her for a long time. "Nothing's changed. It's exactly as it was. Let me go see if Courtney's here."

With that he walked out of the bedroom. What on earth? But before she could try to figure out what that cryptic exchange had meant, her back spasmed and it was all she could do to keep breathing. When the muscles released, she looked at the clock and promised herself that the medication would kick in soon and then she would be fine.

"I hated those dresses," Maggie said, pointing to the pictures in the album. "My mother loved them."

Two days after Rachel's back went out and three days before the wedding, Courtney sat on her mother's sofa, looking at an old photo album. Her parents looked impossibly young and in love. The bridesmaid dresses—a hideous green with big bows in the front—were unfortunate.

"Was it the style back then?" she asked.

"No. They would have been ugly in any decade." She closed the album and smiled at her daughter. "Have I thanked you for all you're doing for me with the wedding?"

"You have."

"I want to say it again. Thank you. I'm excited about everything. You've made my day special."

"Don't say that," Courtney warned her. "No talking about how great it's going to be. I don't want to tempt fate. So far all our crises have been small and I want to keep it that way."

"Have you talked to Rachel?"

"She's feeling much better. The chiropractor did his magical thing, she's taking her pills and she's on the mend. She swears she'll be fine by Saturday."

Courtney had been through her checklist about fifteen times in the past two days. Flowers would be arriving in the morning. The food was ordered, the servers scheduled. The weather was supposed to be perfect. The tents would be put up the day after tomorrow, everyone had their dresses or tuxes and Gracie had sent pictures of the cake as it was being constructed.

"I'm hopeful," she said, crossing her fingers as she spoke, "that everything will go smoothly."

"I know it will." Her mother squeezed her hand. "I'm so glad you're the one making this happen. I'm so proud of you and your new job."

"Thanks, Mom."

"So much responsibility." Her expression fell a little. "And to think I could have lost you."

"Mom, stop. You didn't lose me."

"But I could have. You were so angry at me for so long."

Courtney really didn't want to talk about their past. "I was young and confused about a lot of things."

"You rejected me." Her mother sighed. "Perhaps a case could be made that I rejected you first."

That got Courtney's attention. "Why would you say that?"

"You were right—I didn't know what was going on in your life. By the time you were eight or nine, I was finally successful. I was terrified of losing it all again. What happened after your father's death changed me. I knew I never wanted to be dependent on anyone else again. I wanted to make my own way, no matter what."

She looked at her daughter. "I forgot about what was important. My girls should have been my priority. Somewhere along the way, that message became something else."

"I'm right here," Courtney promised.

"Thank you for that. I hope you know I'm here for you, too."

"I do."

"Then why haven't you told me about your breakup with Quinn?"

Courtney had no idea which of her sisters had tattled, but she shouldn't be surprised. "It's not that big a deal."

"Isn't it? You cared about him very much."

Not something she wanted to talk about. Courtney missed Quinn more than she would have thought possible. She hadn't realized how much he'd become a part of her life. He was the first person she thought of when she woke up and the last one before she went to sleep. She spent her days avoiding him and hoping to run into him at the same time. So far she'd seen him only from a distance.

"I almost didn't go out with Neil," her mother said. "But I said yes because... Actually, I'm not sure why I said yes. It was one of those things. By the end of the first date, I knew he was special. And then I got scared."

"What do you mean?"

"I didn't want to fall in love again. I didn't want to get my heart broken. Losing your father was hard enough, but having him not have taken care of us was equally devastating. I never wanted to be that scared again, and I knew that if I let Neil in, I was at risk."

"Neil will always take care of you."

"I know that now, but I didn't at the time. I had to believe." The smile returned. "You know what's funny? I didn't have to believe in him. I had to believe in myself. I had to know I would be strong enough to survive whatever happened. Because loving someone means giving your whole heart, and once you do that, you have no defenses. You're at their mercy." Her mother took her hand again. "I think that's what you're worried about. Being at Quinn's mercy."

"He wouldn't hurt me."

"What if he left you? What if he died? What if you loved him more? What if he changed his mind?"

All questions Courtney had been asking herself.

"Love hurts," she whispered.

Her mother hugged her. "I was afraid that was the lesson you'd learned. It's the wrong one, darling. Love doesn't hurt. Not when it's right."

"You loved Daddy and you were hurt."

"I was. But that was because I lost him. It wasn't the loving that was painful, it was the losing."

"But if you hadn't loved him, then you wouldn't have lost him."

"Perhaps, but then I wouldn't have had him, either. And that was worth everything." Her mother stroked her hair. "It's the cliché about the fact that we need rain to get a rainbow."

"I don't want to risk losing Quinn, so it's safer not to love him."

"There's a small flaw in your plan," her mother murmured. "You're already in love with him."

Courtney started to protest. She didn't love Quinn. She'd been very clear about that. She liked him. A lot. She wanted to be with him. The list of his good qualities was endless. But that wasn't love.

"I don't love him," she said firmly. "I refuse."

Maggie patted her hand. "Yes, dear. I'm sure that's going to work brilliantly."

30

BY THURSDAY, RACHEL had returned to the land of the living. Her back was better. She could move with relative ease—however, she couldn't shake the feeling of something being wrong. The problem was she didn't know what the something was.

Sienna showed up a little before noon for a trim before the wedding. The short, spiky style was easy to maintain—requiring only regular cuts and a free hand with product.

"I can't believe the wedding's in a couple of days," Sienna said as Rachel began to cut her hair. "It seemed so far away when Mom and Neil announced their engagement."

"I know. The summer's going by so fast. Josh starts school in less than a month."

"Is he going to be spending more time with his dad now?"

"What do you mean?"

Sienna winced. "Crap. I might have said something I wasn't supposed to. Do real estate agents have to keep secrets?"

"I don't know." Rachel lowered her arms to her sides. "What does that have to do with anything?"

Her sister looked guilty. "Jimmy happened to mention that Greg had asked him to start looking for a house. I guess he's tired of living with his folks. So I thought that meant Greg would spend more time with Josh. Don't say anything, okay?"

"Sure."

Rachel's response was automatic. She changed the subject to the fund-raising effort Sienna was involved with and managed to fill the rest of the appointment with casual conversation. But on the inside, she was seething.

How could he? She thought they were working toward something. She didn't know exactly what she and Greg had going on, but it wasn't supposed to end with him buying a house. She'd always thought—hoped, really—that one of the reasons he'd stayed with his folks was that he was thinking they might get back together. She'd started wondering about that, too.

But apparently, she'd been the only one showing up. Just like when they were married. She was doing all the work and he was just along for the ride. He was… He was…

She sucked in a breath as she realized she had no idea what he was doing, because she hadn't talked to him about it. She hadn't asked what Greg wanted and she sure hadn't offered any thoughts of her own. She'd gone along, she'd hoped, she'd assumed, but she'd never asked. Or been clear about her feelings. She'd never once admitted she was still in love with him and wanted them to get back together.

She finished with her sister and checked her schedule. She had nearly an hour break. If Greg had been working Monday, he would be off today. She texted him and asked him to meet her at her place in five minutes.

Rachel paid attention to the road as she drove. She knew she was in a state and didn't want to rear-end some innocent bystander. She was confused. Scared and upset and mad at both Greg and herself.

She pulled into her driveway about ten seconds before Greg

pulled up next to her. He got out of his truck and circled around to hold open her SUV door.

"What's up?"

He looked good. His T-shirt was worn with a couple of holes around the collar. He had on baggy shorts that should have been ridiculous, but weren't. He hadn't shaved in a couple of days.

She loved him and she had no idea if he loved her back. If he wanted a relationship with her or if he was just playing her. Fear swept through her—terror at losing him again. And because being afraid terrified her, she retreated to something much, much safer. Anger.

"You!" She poked him in the chest as she got out of the car and glared at him. "How dare you? Was it fun for you? Did you get a good laugh out of making me think you actually gave a damn?"

In the back of her mind a voice whispered that she might want to take this inside, but she ignored it and everything else except her unexpected and possibly inappropriate rage.

"What was with all that crap?" she demanded. "Hanging out here, acting as if you cared about me? Saying all those things about learning your lesson? It was all just lies."

For one brief second, she hoped he would pull her close and say, "Of course not, Rachel. I've loved you forever." Which didn't happen. Not even close.

He leaned toward her, his dark eyes bright with anger. "It wasn't crap. I was working the program, Rachel, even though you don't make it easy. If anyone has a beef here, it's me. You're the one who played me."

"I didn't. You started this and now you're going to twist it around? That is so like you. Well, fine. You got your wish. You hurt me. I'm hurt. Are you happy? I hope it was worth it, because know this. I will never make things easy for you again."

He took a step back and stared at her as if he'd never seen her before. "Hurt you? That's not possible. That would require you to give a shit, which you obviously don't. So no, I didn't hurt you."

What was he talking about? "You did. You're moving out of your parents' house. You're getting your own place. This summer was just a prank. You were doing everything you could to show me you still cared about me. About us. You swore you were a changed man, but you're not."

"What do you expect me to do?" he asked, his voice rising slightly. "You made your feelings very clear the other day."

"What are you talking about?"

"You called me last!" he yelled. "You hurt your back and you needed help and you called me last. You made sure you told me, too, so I would know just how unimportant I am to you."

She felt like a cartoon character—the one whose jaw drops to the ground, then stays there. "What are you talking about?"

He turned and walked away three or four steps before facing her. "Do you think I've liked living with my parents? I don't. I'm nearly thirty-six. I feel like a fool. But I did it to save money. Because I kept thinking we would find our way back to each other. I wanted to help pay off the house and have enough left over so that you could cut back on your hours and we could have another baby. *That's* what I've been doing all summer. Trying to prove myself to you. But it doesn't matter, does it? You're not interested."

Her brain had fainted or something, because she couldn't think. "You want us to get back together and have more kids?"

"I thought it was a possibility. Because I'm an idiot."

"Don't say that."

"You called me last." He glared at her as he spoke. "You were hurt and desperate and you called everyone you knew first and *then* you called me. If you cared about me, if you trusted me and needed me, you would have called me first."

"You were at work. I didn't want to bother you at the station. If you'd been home, I would have called you first. I was being nice!"

"No. Admit it. You don't care at all."

Her anger returned. "You don't get to speak for me," she told him. "You don't get to say what I want or don't want. You don't get to say what I was thinking. That's my right. That's for me. And even though it doesn't matter at all, I do care. A lot. So there."

She got back in her SUV and started the engine. She was shaking so hard, she could barely drive, but there was no way she was staying.

She made it back to the salon in plenty of time for her appointment. She drank water, took her over-the-counter anti-inflammatory and then reviewed her schedule for the rest of the day.

She'd made her point and Greg had made his. The thing was, she didn't know what either of them was going to do with the information.

Courtney didn't expect to sleep the night before her mother's wedding. She assumed she would lie in bed, going over the thousands of details she had to take care of in the morning. So she was surprised to open her eyes and find out that the sun was up and it was already after six.

She stretched and sat up. Physically she felt pretty good. Rested and determined to make this wedding the best it could be. From the pink champagne to the kazoos Neil had bought. Judging by the sunshine flowing through her window, the weather wasn't going to be a problem. Check. As soon as she was dressed, she would follow up on everything else.

But before she could duck into her tiny bathroom, someone knocked on her door. No, not knocked. Pounded.

"Courtney, get up! You have to come quickly."

She pulled open her door and saw her friend Kelly standing in the hallway. "It's six in the morning on a Saturday," she said in a low voice as she pulled her friend into the room. "You'll wake the other guests."

Kelly was pale. "Oh, I think that's the least of their problems."

"What are you talking about?"

"The bees. The ones that have been at the Anderson House? The Drunken Red-nosed Honeybees?"

"Yes, what about them?"

"They're here. I mean they're everywhere. I think maybe it's the flowers we set up for your mom's wedding. Those weird ones Joyce suggested. Or maybe the cherry blossoms. I don't know. But there are bees."

Courtney dressed in record time. She didn't bother to do more than brush her teeth and grab an elastic to hold her hair back. Then she and Kelly took the stairs to the main floor.

Before they even got to the glass doors leading outside, she could hear it. A low humming sound, like millions of tiny wings. It was a sound out of one of her mother's favorite old movies. *The Naked Jungle.* Of course, there the problem had been ants rather than bees, but the result was the same. Disaster and devastation.

Courtney hurried outside to where the staff were setting up for her mom's wedding. There were bees everywhere. On the tent, on the chairs, but mostly on the beautiful pots of flowers. Several flew by. They ignored the humans and went on their merry bee way. There were hundreds of them. No, thousands. Thousands and thousands of bees right where the wedding was supposed to be.

"We can't have the wedding out here," she breathed. "We're going to have to move it inside. In less than ten hours."

Could they do it? Fit in that many people? Dinner was a sit-down service rather than a buffet, which required more room. Plus, they'd planned on having two tents, one for the ceremony and one for the reception. But there was only one ballroom, and it couldn't hold both the ceremony and the reception. It wasn't big enough.

Her phone buzzed. She reached for it without looking at the screen.

"Hello?"

"Hi, Courtney. It's Jill Strathern-Kendrick. I'm sorry to bother you."

It took Courtney a second to put the name with the face. Or in her case, purpose.

"No," she said faintly. "No, no, no."

"I'm so sorry. My water just broke. I can't believe it. I was late last time. We're going to the hospital. I won't be able to perform the ceremony."

A man's voice in the background urged Jill to hurry.

"It's fine," Courtney said automatically. "Go have your baby. It's fine."

She hung up. Kelly stared at her. "The judge?"

"Her water broke."

"Do you have a backup person who can perform the ceremony?"

"Of course." Courtney scrolled through her contacts until she found the minister in Sacramento who'd agreed to fill in. She dialed.

"Hello?"

The voice was sleepy. Courtney winced when she realized it was still early. "I'm sorry Reverend Milton. The time. I wasn't thinking. This is Courtney Watson. I'm calling to say I'm going to need you for my mom's wedding after all."

There was a moment of silence, then the reverend cleared her throat. "Courtney. This is unexpected. When I didn't hear from you, I assumed you didn't need me. I apologize and don't know how to tell you this, but I'm in Mexico for a few days. A last-minute vacation with my husband."

"M-Mexico?" No. No! Courtney closed her eyes. "Okay. Thanks. Have a good time." She hung up and looked at her friend. "My backup minister is in Mexico."

"Oh, no," Kelly breathed. "What are you going to do?"

There was a question. What *was* she going to do?

"Ceremony and reception first, officiant later."

"Tell me what you want me to do."

Somewhere around ten, Courtney stopped to breathe and drink water. Two local bee people had carefully moved all the flowers to the far end of the property. Most of the bees had followed, although enough remained by the hotel to confirm that, yes, the wedding really did have to move inside.

She'd worked the seating chart to fit everyone in the ballroom for the reception, had come up with what she thought was a brilliant solution for where to hold the ceremony, and with a little luck, she was all done with disasters for today.

There was still the problem of who was going to perform the actual wedding, she thought, but there might be an answer to that, as well.

She finished her water, wishing it were tequila instead, then walked around to the bungalow that stood by itself. Quinn's bungalow. She'd already checked that his Bentley was in the parking lot, so she knew he was home. What she didn't know was what he was going to say.

Maybe he would tell her off. Maybe he would profess his

love again and beg her to be with him. Maybe pretend he didn't know her. Maybe he would say no.

She knocked once and waited. The door opened. Quinn stood there in all his Quinn-glory. She'd forgotten how tall he was, how good-looking. His hair was too long, his eyes were too blue. He radiated intensity and power.

Her heart cried out to grab him and hold on. Her brain added that might not be such a bad idea. But the fear—oh, how big and powerful it was. The fear made her say, "I'm sorry to bother you, but the woman who was going to perform the ceremony for my mother's wedding has gone into labor and my backup minister is on vacation in Mexico. I know you're licensed in the state. Can you fill in?"

She hated how businesslike she sounded. How impersonal. Why couldn't she be softer? Flirt or something?

"What time?" he asked.

"Five thirty."

"I'll be there."

"Thank you."

She drew in a breath and tried to think of something to say. Something that would make him smile or laugh or even invite her in. But she couldn't find any words, and before she could fake it, he closed the door in her face.

Rachel was the tiniest bit spaced out on muscle relaxers, but as she wasn't driving, she figured that was okay. Yes, she was doing hair and makeup—so there might be a small risk of things going awry. Still, she decided it was better to enjoy the wedding without having to be in pain or worry about her nicely healing back.

She'd done her own fluffing at her place. Sienna was easy—she also did her own makeup, and her short hair didn't require much. Courtney had taken a bit of time. They'd decided on a sleek, low ponytail and a smoky eye. Her baby sister was getting more beautiful by the day. Now Rachel finished up with her mother and reached for the can of hair spray.

"Are you nervous?" she asked.

Maggie covered her face with her hands as Rachel sprayed her hair. "I'm excited and fluttery, but only in a happy way. I'm so blessed. Neil's wonderful."

"He is."

Rachel finished spraying. "All right, Mom. You're gorgeous."

Someone knocked on the bride's room door. Rachel crossed to it and saw Joyce in the hallway.

"I had to come and see your mother," she said happily. "Can I come in?"

Maggie rushed to greet her friend and they embraced.

"Are you excited?" Joyce asked.

"Yes. Everything is beautiful."

"I'm so sorry about the bees."

"Don't be. They're not a problem for me and they'll be a wonderful story to tell."

Rachel left the two women talking and retreated to the bathroom to get dressed. She'd done her hair simply—half up, half down with a few curls. She pulled off her yoga pants and T-shirt and put them in her tote, then stepped into the dress.

It fit well, skimming her curves without being so tight that she needed shapewear. Today was officially her cheat day, and she planned to enjoy it.

She checked her makeup, then returned to the bride's room. Joyce was holding up Maggie's dress.

"Come on," the older woman said. "Let's get you into this."

They retreated to the bathroom. Rachel started cleaning up her supplies. There was another knock on the bride's room door.

"Busy place," she murmured as she went to open it for the second time.

She was surprised to see Greg in the hallway, looking handsome in his medium gray suit and white shirt. He was even wearing a tie. She couldn't remember the last time that had happened.

"I have to talk to you," he said, his dark gaze urgent. "Now."

He took her hand and pulled her out into the corridor, then down the hallway to a door marked *Linens*. He opened it, drew her inside and then locked the door behind them.

The room was small—maybe ten by ten, lined with shelves filled with stacks of linens. There was a maid's cart at one end and a big desk at the other.

She looked at her ex. "What's going on?"

"This."

He cupped her face in his hands and kissed her. No, that was wrong. He *claimed* her with his mouth, taking everything she had in those few seconds of contact. Heat and need and a deep emotion she was terrified was undying love swelled up inside her. Just when she was about to give in, he drew back.

"We have got to work on our communication skills," he told her. "Dammit, Rachel, I have been trying to get us back together. I thought you knew that. I thought I made it clear."

"Well, you didn't. You weren't clear at all. You were smug, but not clear."

"I was courting you."

He was? "I totally missed that."

"Apparently. When you said you called me last, I thought there wasn't any hope. I gave up. I'm sorry. That was wrong."

She thought about how she'd changed over the past few months and what she'd learned about herself. This was it— the moment to be brave.

"Then let's start over." She stared into his eyes. "Greg, I really didn't want to bother you at work. That was all. Had you not been at the station, I would have called you in a heartbeat. I swear." She pressed her lips together, offered a brief prayer for strength, then admitted, "I love you. I've been in love with you from our very first date. That hasn't changed for me. Even when we got divorced, I loved you."

One corner of his mouth turned up. "Yeah?"

"Yeah. I've been hopeful and scared and angry, all at the same time. I want things to work out between us. I want us to be good together. I don't want to lose us."

"Me, either." He cupped her face again. "Rachel, you're my world. You and Josh. But one day he's going to grow up and get his own life and then it will be us. I want that with you. I want forever. I've been trying to show you that I'm a better man now. That I'm worthy. I love you so much."

Tears filled her eyes. "You've always been worthy."

"Before," he began.

She stopped him with a kiss. "We've said all we have to say on that. It's done. We need to move on."

He gazed into her eyes. "Are you sure?"

"Yes." Because forgiveness made them both stronger.

He urged her to take a step back, then another. "You never lost me, Rachel. After the divorce, I didn't go out with anyone else. Not even once."

"Me, either."

"You're the one for me. I love you."

She bumped into the table.

Greg kissed her again. "Just to be clear, we're getting back together?"

Her heart pounded in her chest. "I'd like that."

"Me, too." He grinned. "I've been saving money for us. We can pay down the mortgage, if you want. Or cut back on work and we can have another baby. Or go to Europe. I want you to be happy, Rachel."

"Oh, Greg. Yes to whatever you want. I love you."

She flung her arms around him. He held her tightly against him.

"I swear I've learned from my mistakes," he whispered fiercely.

"I have, too. I'm going to ask for help and tell you what I need."

He kissed her again. Desire filled her, making her weak and desperate.

"Greg," she breathed, reaching for his hands and putting them on her breasts.

He groaned and rubbed his erection against her belly. "I want you, Rach. Always."

"I know. Me, too." It had been five lifetimes since they'd made love. "But the wedding."

"Screw the wedding." He chuckled. "So to speak."

She laughed, then gave a little shriek as he lifted her onto the table. "We can't!"

"Sure we can. I can make you come in less than a minute."

Well, that was true. He knew exactly what to do to her. "I can do the same with you." Then she remembered and pushed him away. "I'm not on birth control. I went off to give my body a rest. Unless you brought condoms with you."

He gave her a slow, sexy smile. "I didn't." He reached behind her and drew down the zipper of her dress. "I love you, my beautiful wife. And I want more babies with you."

"I want that, too."

"Then I would say this is our lucky day."

31

COURTNEY TOLD HERSELF that as long as she kept moving and breathing, she would be fine. It was a simple combination. Even single-celled creatures had some sort of respiration system, right? So she was fine. Perfectly fine. And later, when the wedding was over and everything had gone brilliantly well, she was getting incredibly drunk.

The reception had been moved to the ballroom. All the decorations were up, and the tables and chairs were in place. The problem of the ceremony had been solved. The photographer was already taking pictures, the guests were due to arrive within the hour and then there would be a wedding, and really, everything was going to be just fine.

Lucy, one of the maids, hurried toward her with the strangest look on her face. Courtney told herself not to panic.

"What's up?" she asked, hoping she sounded calm.

"I need your help with something."

"Okay." Courtney thought about pointing out she had a wedding to put on, but why state the obvious?

"I need to do turndown service for the bungalows," Lucy told her.

The high-end rooms were provided with evening turndown service. Courtney wasn't sure what that had to do with anything.

"And?"

"I can't get in the linen closet. The door is locked with the bolt, so my key won't work." Lucy looked away, then back at her. "One of the bellboys said that he saw your sister and brother-in-law going into the linen closet."

That was it. A couple of sentences and she stopped talking. Courtney processed the information before blurting, "Oh, my God! Are you saying Rachel and Greg are having sex in the linen closet?"

Lucy flushed. "I think so."

Courtney didn't know if she should laugh or simply curl up in a ball and surrender. "Fine," she said at last. "I'll deal with it." Even though she didn't have the faintest idea how.

David's flight had been delayed, which meant Sienna hadn't had time to speak to him yet. She'd been forced to shift her breakup plan to post-wedding. All of which was fine except she'd totally forgotten about pictures. There were going to be pictures.

There was no way David could be in them. Not when she was ending things. But as her fiancé, he would expect to be right there with the family. And everyone else would expect it, too. Which was why she was pacing at the rear of the resort, waiting for him to arrive.

Talk about tacky. She was going to break up in a hotel parking lot. It was a new low. Still, the tackiness of the moment didn't change her resolve. David had been wrong for her from the start. Although the bigger mistake had been hers. She should have told him no when he proposed. Or at least the next day. But she'd gone along. She'd been too afraid to believe her feelings, to accept the fact that, yes, she would have three broken engagements in her past. She hadn't been willing to be brave.

All that was different now, she promised herself. She was only going to do what was right. She wasn't going to care about what other people thought. Or at the very least, she wasn't going to let that caring influence her actions. She wanted to be strong and impressive—like her sisters and her mom.

So there she stood in her bridesmaid dress, waiting for her soon-to-be ex-fiancé to arrive. When she saw his car pull into the parking lot, she pressed her hand to her belly to quell any nerves, then raised her chin and walked toward him.

"Sienna!" He closed his car door and walked toward her.

She came to a stop and searched her heart—she wanted to be sure she was making the right decision. As he approached, she realized she wasn't sad. She was resigned. This was going to be difficult, but everything about it felt right.

"Hello, David." She clutched the tiny velvet bag that contained his grandmother's ring. "I'm glad I caught you."

"Sorry I'm late. There was bad weather in St. Louis." He leaned in to kiss her. She turned so his mouth brushed her cheek. He drew back and frowned. "What's up?"

She held out the bag. "I'm sorry to do this now. This way. But with you being out of town and then your flight delayed, I didn't have another choice. You're a great guy, David, but you're not for me. I'm returning your ring. We aren't right for each other. I'm not sure we ever were."

She had more she was going to say. About how she wished him the best and that she never meant to hurt him, but those words got held up by the incredible rage that drew his features into a tight mask of fury.

"Are you breaking up with me?" he yelled. "What the fuck, Sienna? My mother warned me you were a mistake, but I didn't listen. I defended you." He moved toward her. "How could you do this? What's wrong with you? Do you think you can do better? You can't. Sure, you're beautiful now, but then what? You were right about that. I can't stop thinking about what you said about your looks fading. They will. You're going to get old and fat and then what will I have?"

He grabbed the bag from her and looked inside, as if checking to see if the ring was really there. "Fuck it. I would have had to divorce you, anyway. Go to hell, Sienna. I don't need you or your ridiculous family. I'm done. You were a mistake. Stay away from me." He shook his finger at her. "I mean it. Don't think you can come crawling back and begging me to forgive you. It's not gonna happen. Bitch."

With that he turned and walked back to his car.

Sienna realized she'd been holding her breath. She exhaled and then gasped for air. Her body trembled, her mind was spinning and she had a moment where she was afraid she was actually going to faint.

Had that really happened? Had David really turned on her like that? She looked up and saw him racing out of the parking lot. He nearly hit a car driving in, then turned right and was gone.

"You're okay," she whispered as she made her way back to the hotel. "You're fine. Everything is fine." Or it would be. She would go sit in the lobby for a few minutes and calm down. Then she would spend the rest of her life being grateful she hadn't made a horrible mistake.

She'd barely walked into the main building when she spotted Courtney. Her sister crossed to her.

"Whatever you think you're doing, you're coming with me," Courtney said forcefully. "Come on."

Sienna welcomed the distraction. "What's wrong?"

"Rachel and Greg have locked themselves in the linen closet. My staff thinks they're having sex. Not only do we need them for pictures, but Lucy has to start turndown service, so she needs to get in there. I'm going to interrupt them. There's a very good chance I'll see something that will scar me for life. If I have to see it, you do, too. So you're coming with me."

Sienna pulled Courtney to a stop, then hugged her. "I love you so much. Thank you."

"For what?"

"Being exactly what I needed this second." What a great distraction. Screw David. He was out of her life and that made her happy. If Rachel and Greg were having sex in the linen closet, good for them, too.

"After we break up the sex thing, let's grab a glass of champagne," Sienna said with a laugh.

"Absolutely!"

The lobby of the grand old hotel had been transformed into a pink paradise. Pink flowers and pink bunting hung everywhere. Pink wooden chairs had been set up to create a center aisle with a pink runner of family photos. The champagne fountain flowed with pink, um, rosé, champagne.

Hotel guests were being checked in at the portico outside and then led to their rooms. Once the ceremony was over, the lobby would once again get back to what it was, but for now it was the perfect place for the ceremony.

In the ballroom, the tables were set for the dinner. There was more champagne. Pink settees made up conversation areas. The white dining chairs had been draped with pink covers. *Monogrammed* pink covers. Rose gold–colored chargers decorated the table. The DJ had embraced the spirit of the event and had shown up in a pink tux. Courtney was going to tip him extra for that.

Now she stood in back of the lobby and watched as the last of the guests were seated. Everything had come together perfectly. She should be happy and relieved. Instead, she felt… empty. The deep sense of loss had started a few days ago and only grew. Once the panic of pulling off the event had faded, she found herself feeling it acutely. It had taken her a while to figure out what was wrong, but now she knew.

Quinn.

She looked at him, at the end of the aisle, with a beaming Neil. Quinn wore all black—his tux, his shirt, his tie. Her body ached for him, but while that was interesting, it wasn't as important as the pain in her heart.

She missed him. Worse, she was starting to realize what she'd lost with him. He'd offered his heart and she bolted. Out of fear. He'd terrified her. Love—how could anyone do that? How could anyone take the chance?

Rachel moved next to her. The three of them would be walking down the aisle one by one, in order of age. Greg walked by with Josh. Greg grabbed a quick kiss from Rachel, then winked at Courtney before taking his seat.

"I don't care what you say," her sister murmured. "Yes, I had sex in the linen closet. I would do it again if I could. In fact, I may do it later. I'm in love and there's nothing you can say to make me feel guilty."

Courtney smiled. "I'm mostly happy for you. A little embarrassed and a lot grateful you weren't naked when Sienna and I found you."

Rachel grinned. "It was so hot. Seriously. You work here. I can't believe you've never done it in the linen closet. There's a table and everything."

Courtney gave her a little push. "That's your cue."

Sienna came up to her next. Her sister had already told her about the breakup.

"Still okay?" Courtney asked.

"Never better. I'm a little jealous about the hot sex, though. I won't be getting any of that for a while." They hugged. "I love you."

"Love you, too."

Sienna started walking.

Courtney squared her shoulders, clutched her pink bouquet in her hand and waited until it was her turn. She did love her family, she thought happily. They were—

She loved them. The thought repeated itself about fifteen times in her head. She loved them and it was fine. Sure, there had been tough times, but they'd gotten through them. She loved them. So was her problem romantic versus regular love?

She followed Sienna, smiling as she went, but all the while her mind was swirling and spinning as she tried to grapple with the question. Why could she love them and not love Quinn? Because if there was ever a man for her, it was him.

She reached the end of the aisle, took her place, then turned and watched her mother come into view. Everyone stood.

Maggie looked beautiful and so happy. She walked more quickly than she had at rehearsal, as if she couldn't wait to get to her man. Neil rushed to greet her halfway, and they kissed. Everyone laughed. Holding hands, they walked back to Quinn together.

He looked at them and shook his head. "I've already lost control."

There was more laughter.

Courtney wanted to join in, but she was terrified she was going to cry. Her eyes burned and her throat got tight. The truth crashed in on her. She loved Quinn, just like her mother had said. She loved him and she was scared and she'd run from him. Because she was an idiot. He was amazing. Seriously fantastic. What had she been thinking?

Okay, she hadn't been thinking. She'd been scared. Which made sense. Under the circumstances anyone would be scared. But jeez, what had she done?

She told herself she would have a meltdown later. Right now she had to get through the ceremony and the reception. Then she would figure out what to do. There had to be a way back.

Quinn held a bible in his hands, but he didn't open it. He also didn't have any notes. He simply started speaking.

"Welcome to this happy event," he began. "As many of you know, there's more to marriage than a ceremony. There is giving your best while accepting your partner as who he or she is. There's respect and empowerment. There's knowing that you are each your own person, but are also so much more when you're together. Love and commitment mean opening yourself to each other. Sharing your hopes and dreams but also your fears and the dark places inside. Love means accepting each other, acknowledging there will be both good times and bad times, but believing both are better when you're together."

Courtney felt her heart breaking. To think he'd offered all that to her and she'd run! How could she have been so wrong? So afraid?

"I've seen Maggie and Neil together," he continued. "I know they were lucky to find each other. More than that, they were brave. Willing to risk the unknown, to make the attempt to reach out, to find their way to their well-deserved happy ending. This is just the beginning. From this moment they will step out into the most wonderful, blessed journey. We can all relax in the knowledge that they are ready."

Courtney felt the tears spill from her eyes. She knew that everyone would think she was crying because her mother was getting married, and she was. But she was also crying for what she'd lost. She had no one to blame but herself. She probably would have gotten through it all if Quinn hadn't, at that exact second, looked at her.

"I'm sorry," she said before she could stop herself. Worse, she took a step toward him. Then she remembered where she was and what was happening.

Her mother turned to her. There was an expression of such love, such kindness and support, that Courtney nearly started sobbing.

"It's all right, darling. Go ahead. Say what you have to say."

"It's your wedding."

"I have the rest of my life to be married to Neil. You're my daughter and I love you. Go on, Courtney."

As if she knew, Courtney thought. Of course she did. Maybe everyone did but her.

"I'm sorry," she said again, returning her attention to Quinn. "I was afraid. Because love hurts, right? Except I've loved my family my whole life and that was fine. And it's not like there have been a lot of guys I loved. There weren't any. I don't know why. Was it me or them? I guess it doesn't matter. But then I met you and you weren't like anyone else. Being with you was fun and easy and safe and wonderful. I didn't know what I was feeling because I never thought it could be love. Then you said you loved me and I was so afraid."

She wiped her face. "I don't want to be afraid anymore. I want to be strong and brave. I want to be like my sisters and my mom. I know this isn't the right time, but I really hope you'll give me another chance. To prove myself to you. Please."

Quinn looked at her for a long time. She had no idea what he was thinking. He handed Neil the bible, walked over to her and pulled her close. "You don't have anything to prove to me, Courtney. I love you. That's not going to change."

"Good, because I love you, too."

Around them everyone sighed.

Quinn drew back and winked at her. "Later," he whispered. "I'm hearing really good things about the linen closet."

She laughed, and her whole world righted itself.

Quinn walked back to the front and took the bible from Neil. "Where were we?"

Sienna nudged Courtney and smiled at Quinn. "You were marrying them."

"That I was."

Several hours later, after the wedding and the dinner, Courtney found herself in Quinn's arms as they danced to a Tadeo song about love lasting forever.

"He'll be happy to know he's made the wedding mix," Quinn said.

"I don't know. They haven't played any Prince, and you know that's who he wants to be."

"It's a phase. He's better being himself."

She smiled at him. "I'm happy being with you."

"I'm glad. I meant what I said. I love you, Courtney."

"I love you, too. I'm sorry I freaked. I've been thinking about it. There were other guys, but no real relationship. You're actually my first boyfriend." She winced. "Can I call you that? Is it too much?"

"You still don't get it. You're the one, Courtney. There's no one else. I want to marry you." He shook his head. "That wasn't a proposal. I figure you need a little time before I go down on one knee. Let's just call it a statement of intent. So you can get used to the idea."

Marriage. Her? She thought for a second, then nodded. "I can see that. Will Wayne and the band live with us?"

"I hope not."

"But they'll probably drop by."

"Yes, so we need a big house."

"Plus, there will be babies and pets." She narrowed her gaze. "You'd better want children."

"I do. And I want you. So about that linen closet…"

She laughed. "How about we go back to your place?"

"Sounds like a plan."

Sienna sipped her champagne. Despite being dateless, she felt pretty good. Her mother was blissfully married to a wonderful man. Judging by how Rachel and Greg were making out on the dance floor, their reconciliation was going well. Josh was thrilled his parents were back together and already asking if his dad could move back tonight.

As for Courtney and Quinn, well, they had just disappeared. Sienna had the feeling they wouldn't be back anytime soon.

There was the problem of getting home, she thought, not actually worried about that. If push came to shove, she could crash in her sister's room. It wasn't likely that Courtney would be back before morning.

"Is this seat taken?"

She looked up and saw Jimmy standing by the chair next to her. She smiled. "Not at all."

He sat down. "You look especially lovely tonight."

"Thank you. So do you."

"This old thing?"

She laughed. "So no actual date?"

"I am tragically single," he told her. "I keep trying to find the right one, but so far it hasn't happened. What about you? Where's the fiancé?"

She showed him her bare left hand. "We broke up."

Jimmy raised an eyebrow. "How do we feel about that?"

"Relieved. He was a mistake. I should have recognized that fact sooner."

"Better late than never." He rose and held out his hand. "Dance with me."

"I'd love to."

She stepped into his arms and found that his embrace felt surprisingly right. They didn't speak for a long time, and when the next song came on, they stayed on the dance floor.

A server came by with yet more glasses of champagne. They each took one. She held out hers and said, "To old friends. They're the best kind."

His dark gaze lingered on her face. "To us."

The toast was a surprise, but it was nice. They'd known each other forever. Been lovers, been friends, been...

She blinked as she realized just how much Jimmy had always been in her life. It was as if, well, as if they belonged together. She touched her glass to his. "To us, Jimmy."

"Took you long enough," he said. And then he kissed her.

★ ★ ★ ★ ★

Daughters of the Bride

Book Club Discussion Questions and Menu Suggestions

Visit DaughtersoftheBride.com
for information on how to set up a phone call or
a Skype chat with Susan Mallery and your book club!

1. Perhaps the strongest theme in *Daughters of the Bride* was that of being brave. How did each of the story lines illustrate this theme? Did you recognize any other themes in the book?

2. Which character experienced the greatest transformation? What were the turning points that led to this transformation?

3. How did the sisters' relationship with each other, and with their mother, change? What events led to these changes?

4. The first time Maggie got married, she didn't get the wedding of her dreams because her mother made all the decisions. This time around, Maggie is determined to get the wedding she dreamed of when she was a teenager. What choices would you have made if you were planning the wedding of your teenage dreams?

5. Who were the point-of-view characters in this book? Why do you think Mallery chose to tell the story through those characters? Were there any other characters through whose eyes you'd like to have seen parts of the story?

6. What did you think about the way that Courtney dealt with the mean girl at Quinn's party? Have you ever had to deal with a mean girl? Or have you ever been a mean girl yourself?

7. Rachel is trying to do it all alone—like a lot of mothers. Do you find it hard to ask for help? Did asking for help make Rachel weaker or stronger? Why?

8. Why do you think Sienna accepted David's proposal in the first place?

9. Quinn didn't just accept Courtney for who she was—he desired her and admired her for it. How do you think this changed how Courtney viewed herself? And how did Courtney's view of herself impact the way her sisters and her mom saw her?

10. Rachel and Greg's happy ending took place in the linen closet at the Los Lobos Hotel. (Yes, a "happy ending" in both senses of the phrase.) Where is the most unusual place where you've made love?

Menu Suggestions

ROASTED ACORN SQUASH BISQUE
HONEY-LIME SALMON
STEAMED GREEN BEANS
DRUNKEN HONEYBEE CUPCAKES

RECIPES

In honor of the Drunken Red-nosed Honeybee that played
a pivotal role in *Daughters of the Bride*, Susan Mallery
presents three delicious recipes using honey. For
downloadable recipes including full-color photographs,
visit
DaughtersoftheBride.com.

Roasted Acorn Squash Bisque

1 acorn squash

2 tablespoons butter

½ cup diced onion

2 carrots, diced

1 stalk of celery, diced

1 clove garlic, minced

1 teaspoon fresh ginger, minced (optional)

¼ cup honey

4 cups vegetable broth or chicken broth

½ teaspoon salt

1. Preheat the oven to 425°F. Halve the acorn squash. Scoop out and set aside the seeds. Place the cut sides of the squash down in a 13x9–inch pan with about one inch of water. Roast until the skin is pierced easily with a fork, about 40 minutes. Allow to cool, then remove the skin and roughly chop the squash.

2. While the squash is roasting, rinse the seeds and get rid of the excess squashy bits. Pat dry with paper towels. Spread out on a rimmed baking sheet. Drizzle with oil and sprinkle with salt. Stir to coat all of the seeds. After you take the squash out of the oven, let the oven cool to 325°F. Roast the seeds until golden brown, stirring every 5–10 minutes. Set aside.

3. Melt the butter in a soup pot over low heat. Sauté the onion, carrots and celery for about five minutes. Add the garlic and ginger and sauté another 30 seconds. Add the honey, broth, salt and squash. Raise to a boil, then lower

the heat and simmer for 10 minutes. Blend the bisque in a blender or in the pot with an immersion blender.

4. Serve warm, sprinkled with a few of the roasted squash seeds.

Honey-Lime Salmon

1½–2 lbs center-cut salmon fillet, cut into individual portions

Juice and zest of 1 lime

1 tablespoon honey

1 tablespoon soy sauce

1 clove garlic, minced

Hot pepper sauce to taste (4 drops for a tiny kick)

1. Mix together the marinade ingredients. About an hour before you plan to eat, brush each salmon portion with marinade and return to the refrigerator. Heat the oven to 425°F. Bake salmon in an oven-safe dish until the fish flakes easily with a fork, about 15 minutes.

Drunken Red-nosed Honeybee Cupcakes with Bourbon-Honey Cream Cheese Frosting

½ cup butter, room temperature

½ cup sugar

1 egg, plus 2 yolks, room temperature

½ cup buttermilk

¾ cup honey

1 teaspoon bourbon or vanilla

1¾ cups all-purpose flour

1 teaspoon baking powder

½ teaspoon salt

1. Preheat oven to 350°F. Line 12 cupcake tins with paper liners.

2. Cream together the butter and sugar until light and fluffy. Add egg and egg yolks one at a time.

3. Mix in the buttermilk, honey and bourbon.

4. In a separate bowl, sift together the flour, baking powder and salt. Make a well in the center and add the wet ingredients. Stir by hand until there are no large lumps.

5. Divide the dough evenly among the 12 cupcake liners, about ⅔ full. Bake until golden brown, about 18 minutes,

turning the pan once. Toothpick inserted into the center of a cupcake should come out clean. Allow to cool completely before frosting.

BOURBON-HONEY CREAM CHEESE FROSTING

½ cup butter, softened

8 oz cream cheese, softened

¼ cup honey

3 tablespoons bourbon

4–5 cups powdered sugar

Yellow food coloring

1. Cream together the butter and cream cheese. Add honey and bourbon, mix well. Add the powdered sugar 1 cup at a time and food coloring 1–2 drops at a time until the frosting is bright yellow and the consistency of creamy peanut butter.

2. Put the frosting into a Ziploc freezer bag (they're sturdier than the sandwich bags) and cut off one corner in a small quarter-circle shape. Start very small, test it out and make the cut larger if necessary. Spin the cupcake to pipe the frosting in concentric circles, building up into the shape of a beehive. Top with a marzipan honeybee.

Marzipan Drunken Red-nosed Honeybees

1 box of marzipan dough (7 oz)	Yellow, black and red food coloring
1 teaspoon powdered cocoa	Sliced almonds for wings

1. For the bee bodies, knead a couple of drops of yellow food coloring into about ⅓ of the marzipan. Form two small balls and stick together.

2. For the stripes and eyes, knead the powdered cocoa and a couple of drops of black food coloring into ¼ of the marzipan. Roll small chunks into stripes and eyes and add to the bee bodies.

3. For the nose, knead red food coloring into a small amount of marzipan. Roll into noses and smoosh onto the bees. Carefully press two almond slices to form each bee's wings.

Visit DaughtersoftheBride.com to see color photographs of the Marzipan Drunken Red-nosed Honeybees.

Love what you just read?
Read on for a preview of
SECRETS OF THE TULIP SISTERS,
the engrossing new novel from Susan Mallery,
available soon!

1

KELLY MURPHY WAS willing to accept certain injustices in the world. That brownies had more calories than celery. That wearing white pants meant getting her period—regardless of where she was in her cycle. That her car would be low on gas only on days when she was running late. What she did *not* appreciate or accept was the total unfairness of Griffith Burnett not only returning to Tulpen Crossing, Washington nearly a year ago, but apparently waking up last month and deciding that stalking her was how he was going to spend his day.

The man was everywhere. Every. Where. He was the aphid swarm in the garden of her life. He was kudzu and rain at an outdoor wedding and someone blurting out the end of a movie right when you were getting to the good part, all rolled into one.

"You're putting a lot of energy into the man," Helen Sperry pointed out in a let's-humor-the-crazy-girl tone.

"This isn't about me," Kelly told her. "I'm not the one who's always there. I'm not the one lurking."

"If you keep seeing him wherever you go, a case could be made that *you're* stalking *him*."

"I'm not going to dignify that with a response," Kelly muttered as she pulled in front of the craft mall and parked her truck.

"Did you know Griffith back in high school?" Helen asked. "You're what? Three years younger? You couldn't have had the same friends."

"We didn't. I was a sophomore when he was a senior," Kelly admitted. "We didn't have any classes together."

But not having the same classes in no way meant she hadn't known who he was. Everyone had known Griffith Burnett. He'd been one of those god-like figures blessed with good looks, a brain and athletic talent. She'd been the slightly weird girl he'd never noticed...until he'd broken her delicate, young girl's heart.

"I'm sure him being everywhere you are is just one of those things," Helen said. "I'm sorry to use logic, but we live in a tiny, little town. You and I cross paths with each other all the time. I see you like five hundred times a day."

Kelly smiled. "But we're friends and I *like* seeing you."

"Back at you." Helen looked at her. "You okay or is there something going on I don't know about?"

"Nothing but Griffith," Kelly told her. "I'm sure you're right. I'm sure it's just a coincidence that I can't take two steps without seeing him." Words that sounded great but that she didn't believe for a second.

If she were anyone else, or if he weren't who he was, she might think he was interested in her...in a boy-girl kind of way. He always spoke to her when he saw her, and smiled. His gaze seemed to linger. But there was no way he wanted anything like that from her. Kelly had proof.

Thirteen years and some odd months ago, she'd turned a corner and run in to Griffith. She'd been on her way to AP English and he'd been...well, she had no idea what he'd been doing. For less than a second, as her books had gone flying, she and Griffith had been plastered together from chest to thigh. She'd never been so close to a boy before. Never been so aware...so *everything*.

Then he'd stepped back. He'd helped her pick up her books, winked when she'd stuttered an apology then had lightly, and oh so gently, squeezed her hand before she'd darted off to the safety of her class.

In those magic seconds, when his fingers had touched hers and their eyes had locked together, she'd fallen totally and completely in love with Griffith.

It had been the kind of true love born only of a pure and inexperienced heart. She'd never even been kissed. From that moment on, she dreamed only of Griffith.

Just a week later, she'd walked by him standing with his friends. One of the guys had called out something about her being "doable." A gross and disgusting comment that had made her cringe, but that had been nothing compared to Griffith's casually uttered, "I couldn't be less interested."

She'd been devastated and had immediately turned and run. She'd been so upset and hurt that she'd needed somewhere to put all that emotion. That evening she'd had a fight with her mother, the kind where things best left unsaid were spoken and lives altered forever. Kelly knew in her head that what had happened with Griffith had nothing to do with her mother walking out on their family less than twelve hours later, but for her, the two incidents were forever linked.

She shook off the memories and grabbed her copy of *Eat, Pray, Love*. Their book club was discussing it tonight—for the third time—and she vowed that from this second on, she wouldn't think about Griffith ever again. At least not for the next three hours.

She followed Helen out of the truck and into Petal Push-ers—the name du jour for the local craft mall the town hoped would be a tourist draw. There were booths where people could sell everything from handmade crafts to antiques to food. At the far end of the huge space was a big stage and reception area, along with a few community meeting rooms. All that was missing were the tourists. Vacationers loved to come to Tulpen Crossing for the tulip festival every spring, but beyond that, not so much.

Kelly wanted to say that wasn't her problem, but as a member of the tourism development committee, she did have a vested interest in getting people back to their small slice of heaven.

It was early on Tuesday night and Petal Pushers was closed. The long corridor to the meeting rooms was dimly lit and their footsteps echoed on the worn linoleum—Kelly's more than Helen's, actually. Probably because while Helen wore cute flats, Kelly hadn't bothered to change out of her work boots. Or her jeans. Or her slightly stained T-shirt.

One day, she promised herself. One day she would care about clothes and buy a push-up bra and be, if not girly, then at least vaguely feminine. She should let Helen inspire her.

Her friend was tall, with inky black hair that fell past her shoulders and startlingly blue eyes. She had plenty of curves and always managed to look sexy, no matter what she wore. Helen worried about carrying a few extra pounds, but Kelly didn't see that at all. Helen was lush while Kelly was…boring. She had brown hair she wore in a ponytail. Brown eyes. No curves, no noticeable features at all. She was plain.

She supposed she could do something to be more Helen-like but who had the time? And even if every few months she swore she was going to do something about her appearance—like wear mascara—she quickly got distracted and forgot. Until the next time.

So here she was, clumping along in boots that might or

might not have mud on them. At least book club would be fun. There was always good conversation and wine.

"Did you read it again?" Helen asked, holding up her copy of *Eat, Pray, Love*. "I didn't. I figured twice was enough."

"I read it." Not reading it hadn't been an option, Kelly thought. She always read the book and took notes. She was such a rule follower. How depressing. She needed to break out of her rut or something. Maybe it was time for her to renew the mascara vow.

They walked into the community room and greeted their friends. Paula, a pretty mother of three, had already opened the bottles of wine she brought. Someone else had set out plates of cookies and cupcakes. Kelly scanned the sign-up sheet and confirmed that she was in charge of wine next month, and that they would be reading a memoir on Eleanor Roosevelt.

She reached for a cupcake just as a few more members arrived. Sally, a fifty-something avid quilter who had the biggest booth at Petal Pushers, announced, "Ladies, we have a new member. And guess what? He's a man!"

Kelly looked at the cupcake she held. She wanted to take a big bite—or possibly run out the back exit. Or poke Helen in the arm while saying "I told you so" in a loud, taunting voice. Because she knew without turning around who she would find standing there. Like the Terminator, Griffith was back, and there was nothing she could do about it.

Griffith Burnett was used to being the center of attention—whether it was at a symposium on how micro-housing could transform the poorest regions of Africa as well as answer the needs of the homeless in the urban centers of Europe and the United States, or at a black tie fund raiser for a children's charity where he was the featured speaker. He was comfortable in front of a crowd, or so he'd thought. He found himself slightly less at ease in a room filled with nearly a dozen women, all staring at him with varying degrees of interest.

No, he thought as he scanned the faces. Nearly a dozen, less one. Kelly wasn't looking at him at all.

"Everyone, this is Griffith Burnett. You should know him. He owns that tiny house company you've all seen off the highway. He grew up here. His folks are Frank and Candy. They moved to New Mexico six months ago. Griffith here wants to join our book club."

He waited for the inevitable, "Why?" but the women only smiled and nodded. Except for Kelly, who kept her attention firmly on the cupcake she held.

"Let me introduce you to everyone," Sally said. They'd walked in together and somehow she'd assigned herself as his hostess for the evening.

She went around the room, spouting names faster than he could remember them, starting with a mother of three and ending with the reason he was here in the first place.

"This is Kelly Murphy." Sally frowned. "Didn't you two go to high school together? Or is she closer to your brother's age? I can't keep you kids straight. And what about Helen Sperry? You're the same age, aren't you?"

"I'm a year older," Helen said, offering her hand. "Hi. I think we had a social studies class together."

"I'm sure we did." He waited until Kelly had no choice but to look at him. "Hello, Kelly."

"Griffith." The word was clipped, her tone less than friendly, matching the wary expression in her big, brown eyes.

She looked good. He supposed there were some men who would be put off by the absence of frills, but he liked that about her. The sharp edges, the lack of guile. What you saw and all that. She was smart, she was determined and she wasn't going to make it easy. He'd always been the kind of guy who liked a challenge so he was looking forward to the latter.

"Why are you here?" she asked.

Beside him, Sally stiffened. "Kelly, honey, what's wrong? Griffith wants to join our book club."

"And read *Eat, Pray, Love*? I find that hard to believe."

"Is it my reading skills you doubt or my interest in the subject matter?"

The corner of her mouth twitched. He would guess annoyance rather than humor, not that he would mind seeing her smile.

"A woman's journey to emotional and spiritual fulfillment hardly seems like something you'd enjoy," she murmured.

"Do you think you know me well enough to decide that?"

Now everyone was watching and listening. He stepped closer to Kelly. Close enough that she had to tilt her head slightly to hold his gaze.

"I find everything about a woman's journey interesting. I enjoy discovering how she's different than I expected. I like the anticipation."

Someone's breath caught. Not Kelly's. Her gaze narrowed. "Next month we're reading an autobiography on Eleanor Roosevelt."

"Lucky me. I've always been an admirer."

Liar.

She didn't say the word out loud, but she sure as hell thought it. Griffith held in a grin as he watched her struggle with her temper. He suspected she was imagining smashing the cupcake she held into his face, turning on her heel and walking away. Only she wouldn't. She would restrain herself. He couldn't wait to test that restraint in every way possible.

But not tonight. Tonight was simply the next step in his plan. He wanted someone in his life—he'd decided that serial monogamy was his road to happiness and he hoped he and Kelly could come to a mutual understanding.

"Did you think the author spent too much time deconstructing her divorce in the book?" she asked. "Should we have gotten right to the journey?"

He'd thought there might be a test, but he'd hoped it would be harder. "She doesn't deconstruct her divorce. In fact there isn't much detail as to what went wrong. She does make it clear the divorce was painful."

Something he understood personally. Screwing up was never pleasant but to mess up something that fundamental sucked in a big way.

"And the part in Thailand?" Kelly asked.

"You mean Indonesia?"

She handled defeat with grace. Instead of saying something sarcastic, she flashed him an unexpected smile—one that hit him in the gut with the subtlety of a 2x4 and offered him her cupcake.

"Welcome to our book club."

"Thank you."

"Now if you'll excuse me, I need a glass of wine."

"He was nice," Helen said as Kelly drove the handful of miles between Petal Pushers and their respective houses.

No need to ask who "he" was, Kelly thought. She'd just endured the longest three hours of her life in the same room as Griffith. She'd listened to him analyze the book, make jokes and generally charm every woman within earshot. Except her, of course. But then she was the only one to have survived being rejected by Griffith, so she was special.

"Incredibly nice," Kelly murmured.

"Now you're being sarcastic."

"I can't help it. Doesn't it strike you as the least bit odd that he wanted to join our book club? There's that mystery one in La Conner. Why doesn't he join that one?"

"He's local, like us."

Griffith was many things but "like us" was not one of them. "Can you at least admit it's slightly odd that he showed up?"

Helen considered the question. "It's unexpected, yes. But it's not a bad thing."

"Not for you."

Helen angled toward Kelly. "Come on. Griffith is gorgeous. You have to admit looking at him isn't a hardship."

No, it wasn't, not that she wanted to admit anything of the kind. He'd always been one of those guys who captured the attention of every female in a three block radius. Of course he was tall, with sandy brown hair and brown eyes. But it wasn't the individual features so much as how they came together into one incredibly appealing man.

"I still wish he'd gone to the mystery book club. There are guys there. He'd feel more comfortable."

"Maybe you should tell him."

Kelly heard the amusement in her friend's voice and groaned. "You're enjoying this, aren't you?"

"A little." Helen shook her head. "Come on. Is it really so bad to have a guy like Griffith interested in you? It's been six months since you and Sven broke up. It's time to move on. Griffith is a great moving-on kind of guy."

"So speaks the woman who hasn't dated since her divorce six years ago."

"I'm very comfortable in my 'do as I say, not as I do' role in our relationship. Come on. You can't tell me you're not the tiniest bit flattered. You have to be."

"Why? Because he's staring at me? I don't know what he wants, but I doubt it's what's you're thinking."

"Why would you say that?"

Kelly turned at the corner and headed toward her friend's house. "I'm very clear on my place in the universe."

"Meaning?"

Kelly waved her hand in front of her midsection. "I'm average at best. Not beautiful, not pretty, not ugly. Just regular."

If Griffith was looking for a fancier version of a Murphy, he should check out Olivia. Kelly hadn't seen her sister in forever, but she would literally bet the farm on the fact that Olivia was still gorgeous and glamorous and wearing a designer something. Not cargo pants bought on sale from an online farm equipment supply outlet.

"It's a family thing," she continued. "I take after my dad. We're sensible people. Hardworking. Ordinary. My mom and sister are the..."

"Exotic tulips in the garden that is your life?" Helen asked drily.

"Not the analogy I was going to use, but sure. It works."

"You're selling yourself short," Helen told her. "Worse, you're saying bad stuff about my friend and I don't appreciate that. You're not ordinary. You're lovely and funny and hardworking."

"It's amazing you don't want to have sex with me right now."

"Stop. It." Helen glared. "I mean it. Kelly, you're great. Griffith finally got his head out of his ass long enough to notice you."

"I thought you liked him."

"I do. I used the phrase for effect. What did you think?"

"Well done."

"Thank you." She shifted to face Kelly. "I'm serious. You're obviously over Sven. Take a chance on a great guy."

"We don't know he's great."

"I've heard rumors."

Kelly had, too. The problem wasn't Griffith. Not totally. Nor was it her still recovering from the end of a long term relationship. She was embarrassed to admit that while Sven had surprised her when he'd said it was over, she really hadn't missed him. Or felt all that upset. Which was sad because after five years, shouldn't she have been at least a little crushed? What did it mean that she'd gone on without much more than a blink? Hadn't she been emotionally engaged at all? And if she hadn't been, what was the reason? Had he not been *the one* or was she somehow stunted?

Not a question she really wanted answered. Although Sven had pointed out that she'd never been in love with him. Which was true, if disconcerting to find out from a man.

"What's the worst that could happen?" Helen asked.

"If I slept with Griffith?" The list was really long—where was she supposed to start?

"Whoa, I was going to say if you *talked* to Griffith. I find it fascinating you jumped right in to bed with him, so to speak."

"Please don't."

"Too late now. You've subconsciously told me everything."

"I haven't and it wasn't subconscious anything. I spoke out loud." Kelly pulled into Helen's driveway.

"You're trying to distract me with facts," her friend said with a grin. "But I see you for what you are."

"I'm afraid to ask what that is."

"As you should be." Helen lowered her voice. "You're a sex-starved single woman who desperately wants to get involved with Griffith but you're afraid."

Words spoken in jest that were just a little too close to the truth. Not the sex starved part. Sex was fine, if not the amazing, earth-shattering experience the media claimed, but still. She did find Griffith intriguing and attractive and...

"He's annoying."

"Liar, liar."

"He *can* be annoying."

"Better."

"I want him to leave me alone."

Helen sighed. "At the risk of repeating myself, liar, liar."

Kelly growled in the back of her throat. "*You're* annoying."

"That is absolutely true. Just say it. You're interested. Intrigued, even. He's hot and you have no idea why he's suddenly interested, but you don't hate it."

"What I hate is being that transparent."

Helen hugged her, then opened the passenger door of the truck and slid to the ground. "Only to me, my sweet. Only to me. My advice is simple. Say yes."

"He hasn't asked me anything. In fact all he's done is stare at me and be everywhere I am."

"Then go find out why. Oh, and start keeping condoms in your purse. Just in case."

With that, Helen waved and walked into her house. Kelly waited until the living room lights came on before backing out of the driveway and heading home.

Kelly had no plans to take the condom advice, but confronting Griffith might not be such a bad idea. Maybe she could find out what he was up to. Because as nice as it would be to think he was interested in her, she knew for a fact her luck wasn't that good. Besides, he was Griffith Burnett. Even if she got him, she would have no idea what to do with him. Sad, but true.

Copyright © 2017 by Susan Mallery Inc.

Love what you've read?
SECRETS OF THE TULIP SISTERS
is on sale July 2017!